Desperate and alone

❦ ❦ ❦

Pausing from her thoughts, Sherron closed her eyes tightly. Then, as she did periodically, spontaneously, maybe just to make sure she was still alive, to hear a sound that she could control . . . in the darkness of her stinking, stagnant, living tomb . . . Sherron McKlinchey SCREAMED!!!!

The sound was a hoarse screeching plea, overflowing with hatred and hope. In the long pathetic moan she called out her children's names. She begged for her dead mother to work a miracle, to intercede on her behalf to God. She summoned the long dead, sainted, black-cloaked nuns who had taught her prayers in school. She demanded that they deliver on their promise that the good would be rewarded for their kindness.

Then exhausted, she waited. But the answer was the same each time . . . numb, barren, hateful silence.

Then aloud, in whispers, in muttered babbling, she cursed them all—her husband, her children, the police, her family, the big man, her God.

As she fell off to sleep, there was no help, no end, no answer to her prayers, no punishment for her blasphemy . . . only the steady, uncaring, endless rhythm of the waves.

Also by Ed Okonowicz
from Myst and Lace Publishers, Inc.

*S*pirits *Between the Bays Series*

DISAPPEARING DELMARVA
Portraits of the Peninsula People

POSSESSED POSSESSIONS
Haunted Antiques, Furniture and Collectibles

STAIRWAY OVER THE BRANDYWINE
A Love Story

FIRED!
A DelMarVa Murder Mystery

FIRED!

A DelMarVa Murder Mystery

Ed
Okonowicz

FIRED!

A *DelMarVa Murder Mystery*
First Edition

Copyright 1998 by Edward M. Okonowicz Jr.
All rights reserved.

ISBN 1-890690-01-5

Published by
Myst and Lace Publishers, Inc.
1386 Fair Hill Lane
Elkton, Maryland 21921

Printed in the U.S.A.
by Victor Graphics

Artwork, Typography and Design
by Kathleen Okonowicz

Dedication

To my uncle, Paul Okonowicz,
who always told me my ghost books were too short.
Here's a longer book for you to read.

Acknowledgments

I must thank those who took their precious time to
read this book in its initial and final drafts, and to those
who made excellent suggestions and provided important
historical information. In particular, I am indebted to
John Brennan, Barbara Burgoon,
Sue Moncure, Connie Okonowicz,
Mark Okonowicz, Marianna Preston,
Joe Smolka, Ted Stegura, Tom Walker and
Monica Witkowski.

Introduction

This novel is fiction.

It is an original publication of Myst and Lace Publishers Inc., and it has never appeared in any other form before. This story and all of the incidents are the products of the author's imagination, and this book is written simply for entertainment. There are no hidden messages, no secret meanings—but, I admit I certainly would love to live in a state governed by a populist governor like Henry McDevitt.

In a few instances, well-known sites and historical figures are mentioned, but those are this book's only connections to reality. There are no persons in these pages that the reader should try to match up with real people, either living or dead. All of the characters are imaginary. Any similarities to persons or actual events are strictly coincidental.

That said, we welcome you to the first novel in our new series about the DelMarVa Peninsula, a most interesting and pleasant place to linger or live.

If you are passing through, thanks for visiting with us.

If you are fortunate to be a fellow DelMarVan, we hope you enjoy recognizing some of the locations, and, just maybe, a few of the events in this story are set in your very own hometown.

—Ed Okonowicz
in Fair Hill, Maryland,
at the northern edge
of the DelMarVa Peninsula
Spring 1998

The State

of

DelMarVa

Welcome to DelMarVa

I have been a resident of the Delmarva Peninsula my entire life. I have traveled its back roads, lived in both its largest city and in the midst of its farmland. I have vacationed on its beaches and interviewed quite a few folks who live on and off the beaten track. I believe our region is one of the country's most unique, varied and exciting.

For three and a half centuries, the Delmarva Peninsula—the land area between the Chesapeake and Delaware Bays and Atlantic Ocean—has included the areas known as the State of Delaware, the nine counties of the Eastern Shore of the State of Maryland and the two Eastern Shore counties of the Commonwealth of Virginia.

Surrounded by water on three sides, the residents of its watertowns, farm villages and large cities have existed interdependently, with families, businesses and politics crossing the borders at will.

Long-time Delmarvans know each other's families and many have friends and relatives in common. Newcomers are constantly amazed that residents can't seem to go anywhere on the peninsula without running into someone they know.

Many Delmarvans believe the peninsula should have been established as one sovereign state extending from Claymont to Cape Charles, from Conowingo to Crisfield and from Cambridge to Chincoteague. In this book series, that logical event finally occurs.

Main Characters

❦   ❦   ❦

Michael Pentak
Henry McDevitt
Stephanie Litera
Charles Bettner
Randy Poplos
Anton Kulczinsky
Joe Supinski
Marty Robbins
Lydia Chase
Scott Woodyard
Carlton E. Buxton
Grace Welch
Sean Kelley
Billy Holmann
Neil Holland
Roger Dreyer
Elwood "Sugar Ray" Looney
Rev. Buck Pierce
Jose "The Snake" Andes
Fred Cox
Charlie "Dog Shit" Dizer
Horace Meeks
Sherron McKlinchey
Terry Tremble
Martin Tremble
Josette Noble
Harvey Figgs
Sue Ann Figgs
Betty Lynn Figgs Looney
Maria Quinterna

Prologue

Detective Michael Pentak was starting to doze off in the pale blue wingback chair. His slightly graying head rested against the soft material, waiting for his meeting with Philadelphia Police Commissioner Bradford Reynolds.

Pentak didn't like the man who was his ultimate boss. But the homicide detective first grade had to admit that the political appointee in charge of the city's thousands of men and women in blue had good taste when it came to his office personnel. An attractive 20ish blond, with full red lips and a captivating smile, was working busily at her desk. She was the best looking gatekeeper he had seen in a long time in the Roundhouse. That nickname had been given to the distinctive circular shaped police headquarters building when it was built, and the label had stuck permanently.

Pentak—at 46 and trim with dark brown hair lightly peppered with gray—passed the time reflecting on his 25 years on the city force. He had climbed the ranks from a rookie cop to one of the top detectives in homicide, with nearly a dozen confidential assignments sandwiched in during the last quarter century.

The Philly native had been through the FBI Academy at Quantico, worked undercover on the New York City docks with the Drug Enforcement Administration and served with a few of his buddies from IRS Criminal Investigation as a bodyguard for Presidents Ronald Reagan and George Bush when they had visited the City of Brotherly Love.

Not bad, he thought, for a Polish immigrant bartender's son from a cramped apartment above a corner rowhouse storefront in Fishtown.

They say Pentak would have gone even further, entered administration, if it wasn't for his attitude . . . and the books. It was really the writing that froze him in place and, worse yet, put his career under a microscope. He knew it was true, but if he had it to do again he wouldn't have changed a thing.

It was in 1992, when his frustration level reached the breaking point, that the writing began. A hard-nosed street cop, Pentak's investigation was being hampered because of blatant "political considerations" that intruded on three high-profile, center city murders. The first body was found at the base of the Art Museum steps. The next victim was stuffed into a hockey goalie's locker in the Spectrum and the third appeared under a stairwell, significantly close to the mayor's office, on a Sunday morning beside a private City Hall entrance.

Major contributors to the mayor's campaign war chest put up roadblocks and arranged for the "Brotherly Love Killer" investigation to be handed off to the feds, who promptly dumped it into a deep-level underground freezer. Pentak had identified a serious suspect, the son of a politically connected, mega campaign donor bigshot. Interestingly, the young man disappeared faster than a Houdini rabbit the day after Pentak was pulled off the case. It was rumored the boy had been flown by his father on a corporate jet to a Caribbean island and given a new identity. It drove Pentak crazy to see the suspect's old man on the evening news, rubbing shoulders with city officials and other smiling-faced "public servants" at city fundraisers and galas.

To vent some of his rage during the 18 months after the case's reassignment, Pentak put the story down on paper in his spare time, tossing in a few extra events and a cast of memorable streetwise characters he had met over the years. Having no idea of what to do with his virgin literary creation, he walked into an all night bookstore and found a paperback written by an ex-New York City vice cop. With the boldness of a first-time crap shooter in A.C., Pentak shipped the manually-typed manuscript and handwritten cover note to the same well-known New York City publisher. The address label was marked: "Attention: Blockbuster Cop Story Enclosed."

Five months later, in January, he was in the Big Apple, signing a contract. The following Christmas, *He Got Away with Murder* hit the newsstands, and Detective Michael Pentak was an instant local celebrity.

Although the names were changed "to protect the innocent," and the standard disclaimer was printed in the front of the book, those who knew the facts—and several who didn't—recognized the novel's similarity to the still unsolved Philly murders.

His next book, *Quota Cops in Command*, about unqualified minority and female officers appointed to authoritative/decision-making positions, generated a public outcry. In addition to a second moderately successful novel, Pentak's book caused the formation of a state investigative commission. That body eventually recommended revocation of regulations that had fostered reverse discrimination and significantly lowered rank and file morale on the Philly force.

After the effects of his second book, Pentak's job performance and off-time activities came under the watchful eye of officers from internal affairs. Their reports, and those of two private investigators, were sent regularly to staff in the mayor's and police commissioner's offices.

However—because of substantial book royalties, a contract for four more novels and appearances on TV documentaries and talk shows—city officials were reluctant to lean too hard on the ace cop. Plus, Pentak continued to work and solve cases. If there was a way to get rid of Michael Pentak, they hadn't found it . . . yet.

Pentak often laughed at the thought that he probably was still in the job mainly because his bosses didn't want him around. He had considered retiring after the first novel but, when the suits put him under a microscope, he decided to make their lives miserable.

The mahogany grandfather clock that towered over the edge of the imported oriental carpet chimed 2 o'clock. He had been waiting half an hour. Longer than most, but he knew the game. He had brought some notes to work on, and a look at the blond walking across the room every few minutes helped make the delay tolerable.

At 2:10 a buzzer sounded on the secretary's phone. She looked up at Pentak and nodded toward the inner chamber door.

Getting up from her desk, she led the detective into the commissioner's office. As Pentak entered the dimly lit room, he was struck at how Reynolds' small frame was nearly lost in the large overstuffed executive chair. The thick curtains, muted lighting and mammoth desk gave Pentak the impression that the bureaucrat was sequestered in a compound trying to figure out how to handle a job that was beyond his physical and mental capabilities.

Reynolds was a graduate of the University of Pennsylvania's Wharton School of Business and had worked for a time on the New York Stock Exchange. His Ivy League background and political connections had impressed the mayor, who appointed the "Bean Counter"—as Reynolds was called—to the police commissioner position over the protests of the police union and a large number of city council representatives.

It was apparent the mayor had calculated that he would someday use Reynolds' wide range of moneyed contacts to move up the political food chain to snag a high-paying federal appointment. So what if he sacrificed the morale and safety of an entire department, that was the way it was now in big-city politics and law enforcement.

Pentak laughed as he recalled Reynolds' first talk to the rank and file, only a week after the unqualified appointee had assumed his new position and made several uncomplimentary remarks about the force.

While speaking to a group of officers at a police union banquet hall, the question-and-answer session became a bit heated. Suddenly, the commissioner removed his jacket—

obviously, trying to show that he was one of the boys. But the macho act backfired as the audience of street cops broke up in laughter, looking at Reynolds' brand new, nickel-plated .357 magnum revolver with a 9-inch barrel.

A brown leather holster held the weapon under the commissioner's left armpit, but the tip of the extra long barrel reached to his waist. If Reynolds ever had to pull the weapon out, it would have taken so long the criminals would have walked away or drilled him into oblivion. And, if he was in a vehicle, the barrel would have knocked out a window or hit his driver in the head.

As the level of laughter fell to whispered snickers, quite a few in the audience were choking and breathing with great difficulty.

Standing, an I-don't-give-a-shit, old-time detective in the back of the room identified himself falsely as Ned Buntline—the Wild West gunsmith who had created Wyatt Earp's long-barreled handgun.

Several officers lost it at that point, and a few coughed up their beer.

Smiling to his colleagues, Detective Buntline, addressed Reynolds. "Sir! I see you have the newest handgun that, we have heard through the administrative grapevine, is going to become standard issue for members of the force in the very near future."

"Yes?" Reynolds answered, impressed that they had noticed his new gun but trying to conceal his ignorance of plans for the weapon's upcoming use by the entire force.

"Well, sir," Buntline continued, "with all due respect, sir. I'd like to know if the long-range, telescope, gyro-dead-eye, heat seeking, redline sight will be issued with the weapon as well?"

The audience murmured its agreement with Detective Buntline's query. Reynolds could see they were interested and agreed the sight was important. But, before the new commissioner could respond, another officer stood up and spoke.

"Officer Wyatt D. Holliday, sir!"

More muted laughter from the crowd.

Reynolds was sweating now, having no idea of what the officers were asking him, but the egocentric appointee was not smart enough to call upon one of his aides. "Yes?"

"Sir! I'm sure you know that the gyro-dead-eye is still approved only for federal use and it would be against ATF regulations for a city force to order them. So, I hope we don't make a mistake and order several thousand, since—at the present time and under federal regs—we would never be able to put them into use."

"Yes!" Reynolds said. "As I recall, that is correct. In response to your question, Detective Bluntline?"

"BUNTLINE! SIR!"

"Yes. Buntline. Thank you. We will not be able to place the dead-eye gyroscope, redeye . . . . " Reynolds was lost and fading into the no-man's land of small-arms weaponry.

"TRAILFINDER!" someone shouted.

"Trailfinder," Reynolds repeated, "on your .357 magnums."

"BOOOO! BOOOOOO! BOOOOO!!!" The chorus was deafening.

"I DON'T WANT ONE, THEN!" shouted someone in the back.

"ME NEITHER!" screamed another officer from across the room.

"Gentlemen. Ladies! Please. Stop. Please!"

All was lost, and the back rows began to file out of the room. The last comment Reynolds heard was someone passing near the low stage and podium, pointing to the commissioner's weapon and shouting, "Your safety is OFF!"

Responding quickly, Reynolds pulled the gun from his holster and started to examine the weapon as several officers in the front of the hall ran toward the back door.

When one of his staff members finally explained that there was no such thing as a heat-seeking, dead-eye-gyro, and that the officers were using the names of Wild West legends Wyatt Earp and Doc Holliday, Reynolds hurriedly left the building through the back door.

When he arrived at his limousine, someone already had placed a note under the windshield wipers—"Welcome to the OK Corral."

That was the beginning of his relationship with Philly's men and women in blue, and it hadn't gotten any better.

A hefty, grim-faced aide stood in the office to the commissioner's left. The man's hands were hanging in mid air, away from his sides, as if he were prepared to perform a *Gunsmoke*-style draw if Pentak made any sudden move.

Nods were exchanged all around, and Reynolds indicated for Pentak to take a seat.

It's showdown time, the detective thought. Time to tap-dance on the high wire or fall into the tiger's cage.

"Detective," Reynolds said, "I believe in being honest and getting to the point."

Pentak stared straight ahead, letting the commissioner's statement hang in the air until the non-reply was uncomfortable for everyone. It was a technique he had perfected with suspects in the box and he could see it was working equally as well on his pompous host.

"Did you hear me?" Reynolds snapped.

"Yes, sir. Loud and clear," Pentak replied, smiling. His voice was soft, muted and soothing.

"Why didn't you answer me?"

"I didn't realize you were done speaking, sir."

"I was told you were a wiseass. Obviously, my sources were correct . . . . "

"Who's that, sir?" Pentak asked softly, "Internal affairs? Mayor's rat team? State Police CID? Or maybe your overpaid Gestapo spy service?"

"Don't make this hard on both of us, detective."

"I was just asking a question to clarify your statement, commissioner."

"I'll make the statements and I'll ask the questions. This is my office and I'll run this meeting. I'm in charge of the show here, understand?"

"Yes, sir. Then, with all due respect, would you explain to me why I'm here?"

Reynolds rose from behind his desk and approached. "It's obvious you're not happy here. You like your job, but you don't like the way we have modernized the force."

"O-F-P-F, commissioner. That's how 90 percent of the working cops refer to your's and the mayor's handling of crime and safety."

"O-F-P-F?"

Pentak smiled at the question-mark expression covering both Reynolds' and his bodyguard's face, letting the silence of the pause again work its magic.

"The Officer Friendly Police Force, commissioner. Philadelphia's answer to street violence is to throw more money into a larger Police Athletic League, set up an Officer Friendly Camp in the Poconos for misunderstood convicted gangsters and have street cops teaching remedial reading in shelters when they should be on the street doing their shift. As a result, we have less cops on the job and those on the street are riding around in eight-year-old patrol cars that look like ghetto cruisers or rejects from Mayberry RFD."

"That's enough out of you, detective!"

"No, it's not enough. You're sitting on an urban riot pow-der keg every spring and summer and the only thing that you and your top-floor cronies can do is blame every street killing on the cops on the front line not doing their job.

"But when they do their job, our mighty, political phony mayor, with you trekking behind, runs to the projects and kisses up to the storefront preachers' and criminals' families. Then you pose for the cameras and promise to beat up on the accused cop, form another citizen review board and open a new playground . . . ."

"I said that's enough!"

" . . . that turns into another crack bazaar that you're afraid to shut down because being tough on crime will lose you the next election . . . and, when that happens, you'll have to try to find a real job."

"Who do you think you are, talking to me like this?"

"You invited me here, commissioner. Am I not allowed to be truthful and direct? Or are those qualities no longer respected either?"

Reynolds moved back behind his desk, looked down and took several deep breaths. Speaking softly, in measured tones, he began, pressing his palms onto his glass desktop for support.

"You're like the price of Arab oil, Pentak. When it gets too high, we have to do without it. I think your price has just gotten too high."

Pentak didn't reply. Instead, he waited and took out a Macanudo cigar. Ignoring the protests of the bodyguard, the detective lit up. Then, after a long drag, he broke the silence.

"What's your offer, commissioner? I assume that's what this is all about?"

"Very perceptive."

"I'm a detective, remember?"

"Yes. I know." Reynolds hissed as he opened a file, leafing through the officer's two-and-a-half decade history. Stopping, his finger slid to the object of his search. "You have four years and seven months to retirement, Pentak."

"And four days . . . ."

"And four days?" Reynolds repeated. "Interesting that a man who loves his job as you do would know the exact number of days to retirement."

"Wrong, commissioner. I look at them as the exact number of days I have to work extra hard under the present unrealistic job conditions to stay alive."

Slamming the folder, Reynolds snapped. "I've had enough of your shit, Pentak! Here's the deal. Full pension, 30 years. Now. Today! Forget the four years, months and days. Also, you'll retire at a grade one inspector's administrative salary. That's two steps above your current level. The offer is good until 8 a.m. tomorrow morning. Any questions?"

"Why?"

"Because we want you out and you know you want out, too. You can have it all. Take the money you earned in this job. Write your damn exposés, obviously you have plenty of material. Live the good life. Get married again if you can find someone who . . . . "

"You're close to crossing the line," Pentak snapped, and Reynolds did not continue. "Also," Pentak added, "I like my job, and I'm not quite ready to give it up."

"Then maybe I can cap off the commissioner's bag of goodies with an offer you can't refuse."

The words came from behind Pentak's chair. It belonged to someone who had been in the rear of the room the entire time, someone whose voice sounded familiar. Pentak had heard it before, somewhere.

As the figure came into the light, the detective looked up at the recognizable face of Henry McDevitt, governor of the state of Delaware and leader of the powerful Victims Rights Coalition political party.

Pentak started to stand. It was the first sign of respect he had shown toward any authority figure that day, but McDevitt waved him back into his seat.

Turning to Reynolds, McDevitt said, "We'd like a few moments alone." It was more of a command than a request, and the commissioner and his aide vacated the room, offering assistance as they closed the door.

Pentak stared at the imposing figure who smiled at the retreating commissioner. An unknown until a half dozen years ago, McDevitt had attracted national attention when he ran for governor on a platform that was basic, honest and simple: Victims first, criminals at the far end of the line.

Delaware had always had a history of voters crossing political lines. But a combination of personal charisma, captivating speech making, a hot issue and two weak major party opponents made McDevitt—a political novice and unknown—the only elected third party chief state executive in the country. Members of the Delaware legislature who had any sense quickly abandoned their traditional Liberal and Conservative party identities and joined McDevitt. With strong voter support, McDevitt was able to organize the Victims Rights Coalition that pushed a strong punitive criminal code with restrictive death sentence appeals through the Delaware legislature.

McDevitt then wooed conservative business conglomerates to provide millions of dollars for education, well-built, low-income housing and he expanded career training and jobs for the poor. It's said the reluctant corporate holdouts responded quickly when the governor threatened them with major tax assessments, burdensome additional licensing and layers of new regulations if they did not agree.

Liberals, who said McDevitt would be thrown out of office and attacked if he ever dared to visit the ghettos, were astonished when the new governor was cheered and acclaimed as a hero for closing crack houses, having deadbeat dads pay up and making delinquents clean neighborhood streets.

His opponents, who, initially, were forced to work with him, became some of his strongest allies.

Intense public pressure forced several bleeding hearts on the judiciary to resign from the bench, and McDevitt appointed young, hardball prosecutors in their place.

Developers, said to be the donors with the deepest pockets, were not immune from McDevitt's environmental crusade. He promptly denied state road access to communities that would add to congestion. No longer were farms devoured and shopping centers built beside each other. Approval of applications for new residential developments and commercial zoning were slowed down to a crawl.

"There are plenty of old houses that need to be fixed up," McDevitt told developers. "Go into the city, or the older suburban areas and make the boarded up shopping centers and abandoned houses attractive again."

Since it was their only avenue for making money, the more progressive builders followed his suggestion rather than lock horns with McDevitt, and a substantial number of blighted areas were rejuvenated.

McDevitt knew how to use the media to challenge and publicly defeat his opponents. He couldn't be classified as a liberal or conservative, because he was neither and he was both.

"Labels don't matter," McDevitt often said. "Action is what's important, but you must have a plan and priorities. My main goal is to have the state government take care of the crime victim and his or her family. Consoling the mother of a child that's been killed by a drug-crazed cretin is more important than the criminal's so-called rights to medical attention, legal assistance or hot meals. In my state, if you're stupid enough to commit a crime, you had better be prepared to pay the price, and that price is very, very high."

Of course there were numerous lawsuits, but McDevitt didn't care. He used special funding to hire the best young legal minds—many Ivy League graduates—to stall proceedings. He used the media to embarrass criminally sensitive lawyers, and he concentrated on making his state a showcase jewel that sparkled with the brilliance of a common sense approach to any issue that needed fixing.

Major news networks sent correspondents to Dover, Delaware's colonial style capital city. Politicians from other states came to confer with McDevitt. The third party governor was re-elected by a landslide along with his Victims Rights Coalition candidates, who controlled both state houses.

One California university expert on the presidency, who had been impressed with McDevitt, was quoted as saying that the Delaware governor could make a dark horse run for the White House in eight years. The brief, passing phrase was printed in a national weekly news magazine and overlooked by everyone except the Delaware press, which played it up big. But, anyone with half a brain knew a midget state with three electoral votes would never be able to field a presidential contender. Still, the idea gave the local papers something to print and made for interesting reading and cocktail party gossip.

The Delaware governor was tall, slightly over 6 feet and had pale gray eyes. A slight scar on his left cheek was the result of a tractor accident that had occurred while in his teens. At 47, he was nearly the same age as Pentak, but the governor's hair was nearly all gray. He spoke with a firm voice that betrayed more than a trace of the Sussex County, Delaware, farmland where he had been raised.

He pulled up a chair near the detective. "I'm here because I need your help, Mr. Pentak."

"Pentak's fine, sir. That's what they call me."

"Good. Hank's what my friends call me. All right?"

The detective nodded.

"We are facing major problems, Pentak. Crime, particularly drugs, is my primary concern and, despite my best efforts, it continues to be a big problem and one I want corrected.

"Those like me who want to fix it the old-fashioned way are considered bigots. The intricacies of the criminal justice system have been allowed to become too complicated. Justice is no longer served. The law, like life, is not fair. But our laws, Pentak, are way out of line. Whether a case involves family court juveniles, criminal court felons or white collar crooks who stand in the chambers of chancery, the proceedings are too long and the results, when we get convictions, are disappointingly lenient and ineffective. Plus, our state agencies are overloaded, over regulated and understaffed. We are approaching a breakdown in all of our courts, on our streets, in our social systems, in our schools, just about everywhere. Money rules the fancy lawyers who manipulate the courts, and that is the greatest crime of all."

Pentak nodded, and McDevitt continued.

"More taxes won't really solve anything, and additional services, if we could afford to buy them, are equivalent to placing a Band Aid strip on a severed artery. The meltdown in morality and denial of personal responsibility cannot be corrected by regulation, but we do not have time to teach a new generation of uneducated whiners how to clean up their homes, bodies and minds. In summary, Pentak, we are sinking in deep shit."

The detective's mind was three-quarters listening and one-quarter wondering why this governor—Hank—was giving a Philly cop a heart-to-heart in the commissioner's office in the middle of a busy Monday afternoon.

"So," McDevitt paused and offered a smile, "you're probably wondering what the hell I'm doing here talking to you in the commissioner's office in the middle of a busy Monday afternoon."

"My exact thoughts, Hank."

They both laughed.

"I need a tough, street cop. Somebody who thinks things should be done the right way, and who has a set of balls. I also want someone who is willing to break a few rules to see that true justice—not the legal system—is served. So, basically, Pentak, I want you to come and work with me."

The detective began to ask a follow-up, but McDevitt raised his hand. "Wait! Let me finish. Here's the situation and my non-negotiable offer. You take all you can get from these liberal bastards that are running this city into the ground. I have powerful support from some very unusual sources for what I am doing, and I intend to move quickly. You're my first choice, but my short list has two other very fine candidates if you refuse.

"I can offer you a home, rent free in Fenwick Island, for five years. After that time, you will have an option to buy at a very agreeable price. You will live off your pension and a law enforcement consulting grant that I will establish in your name. During this period of time you will be on call as a confidential, special assistant to me, and only me."

Pentak smiled and waited for more. *Was this Christmas Eve or what?*

"This time schedule," McDevitt continued, "which can be adjusted if I decide it becomes necessary, will allow you freedom to complete your multi-book contract. However, when those novels are done, you do not sign on for any others until you and I agree to part company. Understood?"

"So far, but what will I be doing in five years?"

"You will be with me in Washington, as head of a federal agency, or you'll be serving in my state as the chief officer of all the combined law enforcement agencies. And, I assure you, it will not be like anything you've experienced before."

Pentak's mind was filled with questions, but he knew the answers would come later. His overall grasp of the governor's offer was overwhelmingly positive, and Hank's view on crime control was a cop's version of working in the Promised Land.

"However, unlike your present employer," McDevitt added, "I am an impatient man and I need an answer a lot sooner."

"How about right now, Hank?"

"I think we're going to get along just fine, Pentak."

The two men, initially strangers, now partners, shook hands. The pact made.

Pentak took out his detective shield, gave it one last look and tossed badge #1802D on the commissioner's desk. Turning to McDevitt, the ex-Philly cop asked, "By the way, where's Fenwick Island?"

McDevitt smiled, turned away, looked out the window and pointed south. "It's about 130 miles from here, on the beautiful Atlantic coastline, smack dab in the middle of the State of DelMarVa."

1

**Five years later
March 2003**

The miniature casket was open. Fluffy white material flowed out of the inside and crept over the edges of the polished cold, gray metal. The coffin lid was open, completely covered by a display of floral sprays bearing thick, shiny ribbons.

"Granddaughter" was written in gold script against a smooth, red ribbon background.

"Love, Mommy and Daddy" showed up in white letters printed on a pale pink strip of satin.

"Sister" appeared in blue letters on a small white pillow, resting at the little girl's feet.

The wake, or viewing as they call them now, began at 7 p.m., three hours earlier. As the hands of the clock moved past 10 o'clock, most of the visitors had gone. The victim's parents were sitting in small, uncomfortable wooden folding chairs in the front row of the Martinez Funeral Home, in the Hispanic rowhouse section of Wilmington.

A few close relatives had remained in the room. They were cousins, aunts and uncles who used funerals, like weddings, to catch up on the latest news, share family gossip and recharge their childhood memories.

The combined scents of perfume, burning candles and fresh flowers could not lighten the weight of the child's death that pressed down on the spirits of the occupants.

Maria Quinterna, the dead girl, looked like a sleeping angel. She was the youngest of five children. Another was still in elementary school at St. Martin's, two were in St. Stephen's High School and one was studying nursing at Delaware Technical and Community College. Maria had been shot several times at close range. Her attacker's .38 caliber bullets had entered her heart, ribs, left leg and right shoulder, shattering bones and nerves and altering the future of each member of her family.

The last moments of her short life were spent at Manis Grocery, a small storefront on Fourth Street. Maria had just paid for a loaf of bread and two packs of gum. As she turned to leave, she faced the barrel of a black revolver that was waving at both her and the store owner.

Jose "The Snake" Andes, a drug dealer with a lengthy rap sheet had been enjoying a chemical high as he raced into the corner store. He needed money to replenish his dwindling supply and thought a quick holdup at an unguarded mom-and-pop shop would get him the cash he needed.

As the storekeeper dropped behind a stack of bread that was resting on the worn counter, The Snake fired a round into the wall. The sound scared Maria, who began to run away. Without hesitation, The Snake turned and put a slug through the 8-year-old's back, just as she was pushing open the metal and glass door.

Neighbors who had heard the gunshot screamed as the young girl's body fell forward and was caught between the weight of the closing door and its frame. Slowly, calling out twice for her mother, Maria tried to crawl outside to safety. But The Snake, who was frantically out of control, put three more slugs into the frail body. Then, he ran away with no income from a botched robbery that had turned into murder.

He was caught two hours later, hiding in his mother's rowhouse. The murder weapon was discovered in a shoe box, next to his blood-stained sneakers.

At the initial hearing, The Snake's state-paid lawyer pressed for an involuntary manslaughter charge, claiming that, since his client was high, the shooting was unpremeditated and equivalent to an unfortunate accident. He stated that his client could not be responsible for a crime he did not know he committed, even if there had been 10,000 witnesses.

There was a rumor that the state was weighing the offer, and the possibility of a deal had hit the front page of the paper on the morning of the wake. The family and certain community leaders were outraged.

A few minutes after 10, undertaker Juan Martinez escorted Gov. Henry McDevitt into the funeral parlor viewing room. He had entered through an alley entrance in the rear of the building, taking a path through the embalming room and small office. Nodding to the family, he knelt at the coffin and looked down at the sleeping painted princess. McDevitt gently touched the miniature, white-beaded rosary wrapped around Maria's tiny, doll-like hand. Silently, the governor lowered his head in prayer.

No one spoke.

The room was as quiet as a church sacristy before dawn, until the dead girl's mother began to cry. The woman's choking sobs, muffled against her sister's shoulder, filled the small room.

Roberto Quinterna, the victim's father, stood up to shake the governor's hand.

"My heart goes out to you for your loss," McDevitt said, his tone soothing and calm. His message was apologetic, an effort to share the family's pain. "Our state has let your family down and we, too, are saddened over what has happened to your poor daughter, Maria. There is no excuse."

The mother rose awkwardly. Her face was red and blotched from tears, remnants of makeup were streaming down her cheeks.

"They say he is not responsible! They say, in the papers, that he will get off, be released. They caught him. Her blood was on his face! She was trying to crawl away! The bastard walked up and shot her three more times! Like an animal! What do they need for proof? Look, over there!" She pointed at the coffin. "Have them come here and look in the box. Let them see my little angel. There is the proof. My dead baby!"

She was shouting, hysterical.

Her husband tried to calm her, but she shoved him away. Looking straight at the governor, little Maria's mother said, "I want justice. Do your understand? Can you give me justice, Mr. Governor? Or is it only words that you bring, words that sound good in front of the television cameras, words that will calm your own guilt?"

Henry McDevitt, no stranger to funerals of the innocent, looked in the eyes of the young girl's surviving family. He saw anger. . . despair. . . exhaustion. These are innocent people who are broken, their harmony destroyed, by the drug runners and users who were infesting the city like a growing cesspool of unchecked disease.

He had no quick answer. But the mother needed to hear, to know, that someone else also wanted revenge, that she wasn't alone. No safe political response was appropriate.

Gently, he touched her elbow and pulled her aside. Off by themselves, he stared into her eyes and whispered, "Mrs. Quinterna, what I say is for you, only you and you alone. Do you understand me?"

The mother bit her bottom lip and nodded. Short sobs continued.

"As governor, I cannot say in public what I am about to tell you. But, as one person to another, as one caring human being to another, I promise you the filth who did this will not escape. Do you understand what I am telling you?"

Her eyes locked on his. Her head nodded affirmatively.

"I ask you not to repeat what I am telling you. But, I swear this, on your daughter's pure and holy soul. Justice will be done—not the law, but justice. The murderer of your daughter will not live to see many more birthdays. I promise you—*muerte*. Death to the man who did this. Trust me and give me time. You have my word."

Mrs. Quinterna nodded again and hugged the governor.

As she again began to cry, her husband came over and pulled her away. "Thank you for coming, governor," he said. "We appreciate your kindness. We know you are a busy man."

Henry McDevitt took both of their hands in his and bowed his head. He then turned and nodded to the handful of relatives, shook a few more hands. Tears began to fill up his eyes, and he quickly reached the hallway that led to the rear door of the funeral home.

Turning, for one last look, he saw the dead girl's mother at the casket, leaning, whispering into the corpse's ear.

Sgt. Randy Poplos, the governor's driver, was waiting in the alley as Henry McDevitt said good-bye to the undertaker.

Mr. Martinez said it would be good if they did not have to see each other so often, but he knew McDevitt would be back. The governor had been there several times before.

During his first term, McDevitt made it a point to visit the families of victims of serious crimes. The meetings took place in homes, funeral parlors, churches, wherever and whenever he could get there, but get there he did. It was done quietly, without publicity. He severely threatened the few news people who knew about the practice, and they honored his request to keep the story out of the papers. But, Delaware is a small state and word got out.

Survivors of armed robberies and rapes were the living who received a call or visit. The dead never knew, but their families seemed to appreciate it.

At first, word-of-mouth reports of his meetings were considered rumor, a local urban legend. After all, who had ever heard of a politician caring about victims? Criminals got all the attention—state appointed counseling, medical care, psychological examinations, free education, weight training and publicly provided legal assistance, complete with all the latest delaying tactics that legal loopholes provide. A politician who cared about victims, to the extent of going to see them, was unheard of.

Randy Poplos held the passenger door open. The state police officer had been with McDevitt for more than five years and he loved his boss. Without hesitation, Poplos knew he would stop a bullet for the governor, his commitment was that strong.

As the car pulled onto Fourth Street and headed toward Route 13 south, Poplos looked at the digital clock on the dashboard, glowing 10:35 p.m., and turned toward the governor. "Are we still bound for Gumwood, sir?" he asked.

"Yes, and move it," McDevitt said. "I don't want them pulling this thing off without me."

The administrative room of the First State Correctional Center in Gumwood was filled to capacity. Camera crews from Europe, Cable News, International Broadcasting Corp., Central Broadcasting System and National Telecommunications Media were trying to push their way into the area reserved for the local press.

Print reporters from as far away as Chicago had arrived, joining colleagues from the *Washington News Herald, New York Daily Gazette* and the *Boston Common Ledger & Times.*

Delaware again had made the big time in a way that bothered some people but made a lot of other First State citizens proud. Since 2001, Delaware had been know for its reinstatement of death by hanging. On this particular evening, another convict would take a one-way walk up the gallows.

Lethal injection was one thing, but an old-fashioned necktie party was a really big show. Two years earlier, right after he had reinstated the whipping post, Delaware Gov. Henry McDevitt had proudly signed the hanging bill in front of several hundred Victims Rights Coalition supporters.

Afterwards, he took the press on a tour of the prison grounds and showed off the new execution apparatus with a smile, saying, "This gallows is a fine piece of locally made machinery. We spared no expense and had several fine Kent County carpenters build our little tower of doom. We believe that the criminals who had foolishly chosen our state in which to commit their crimes deserve to go out in style. We want them to know they will be using a genuine, American-made, hanging apparatus, just like they used in the Old West to rid the world of unwanted vermin and outlaw scum. To be honest with you, I can't wait to get the gallows going."

People thought McDevitt was crazy, and that the hanging reference was a colorful way of appealing to his fans. Hanging might be in the law, his opponents said, but it would never be used in today's "civilized" society. But, within six months the gallows was back, and Buck Pierce was the first to do the Delaware air dance.

Others followed at a steady pace, and the public and prisoners soon realized that there were two reasons that there was no need to run a direct phone line from the execution chamber to the governor's mansion. First, McDevitt announced he would never pardon a murderer, and second, the governor attended every execution.

Glancing again at the green digital clock on the car's dashboard, Poplos turned to his right and said, "We've got plenty of time. We'll make it."

"I'm not worried," McDevitt said. "But this one is special, and even more important after tonight," referring to the body of Maria Quinterna, still lying in the coffin awaiting her early morning ride to the graveyard.

It was 11:40 p.m. when the black Chevy Monte Carlo pulled up to the prison gate.

The beefy guard, who obviously was a regular at the nearby sausage house, looked inside and smiled. "How's it going, Gov'nor? Gonna send another one home tonight?"

"That's where they belong, Clarence," McDevitt said. "Got to clear them out and make room for the others who are just dying to get in here and play with you."

Clarence let out a belly laugh, hit the button that opened the gates and waved the car through.

Members of the prison's elite Correctional Emergency Response Team were patrolling the maximum security area behind the razor sharp swirling wire that topped the tall chain link fence. In the distance, a small band of less than a dozen protesters sang "Amazing Grace." It drifted through the small diamond openings in the 14-foot-high fence.

Other dark-uniformed, armed guards moved slowly through the grounds, their large German Shepherds at their sides. A Delaware State Police chopper flew overhead, it's searchlight scanning the roads, fields, prison grounds and nearby woodline.

"I figure this makes hanging number 9," Poplos said. "That's always been my lucky number. But I guess Sugar Daddy Looney doesn't feel that way."

"In less than a half hour, Mr. Looney won't feel anything," McDevitt said.

Sugar Daddy Looney, an unemployed truck driver, had been convicted of brutalizing and murdering his step-daughter, Sue Ann Figgs. The crime occurred in a secluded country graveyard while the girl's mother, Betty Lynn, was waiting tables at a truck stop diner outside Seaford.

Sugar Daddy, Betty Lynn's fourth husband, was supposed to pick up 12-year-old Sue Ann at cheerleading practice and take her home. Instead, on a crisp October evening, he turned off the four-lane highway, telling the girl he was taking a short cut through the woods.

Making sure there were no other vehicles in the area, Sugar Daddy stopped the car near Swallow Hollow Road, claiming he had a flat tire. Leaving the vehicle, he asked Sue Ann to come and hold the flashlight while he checked the back wheel.

Within seconds, Sugar Daddy grabbed the girl from behind, shoved a greasy cloth into her mouth and used an extension cord to bind her wrists behind her back.

Tossing the 4-foot, 11-inch girl over his shoulder, he carried Sue Ann's kicking body over a short stone wall and dropped her near a clump of gravestones. On the rocky ground behind a thick willow tree, he slammed the girl's back against the upright grave marker of Amos and Muriel Hammond. They were born in the late 1800s and both died in the same year—1926.

Unable to scream, Sue Ann kicked out at her stepfather. Tired of her resistance, he slapped her several times across the face, and then began beating her head with his fists. Annoyed that she wouldn't stop fighting, Sugar Daddy used both hands to smash the back of Sue Ann's skull, over and over and over, against the weathered letters that formed the Hammonds' epitaph.

With Sue Ann's moans no longer escaping through the filthy cloth, Sugar Daddy stripped off his clothes and stood over the young girl—his 5-foot, 6-inch, 220-pound, bowling-ball-shaped body was unsightly in the cool night.

Savagely, he ripped off the girl's skirt and underpants. During the fierce attack, he cursed both Sue Ann and her mother. Initially, the young girl groaned in pain, mumbling for Sugar Daddy to stop, calling weakly for help. Soon she lost consciousness and her head fell forward, the pale, smooth-skinned chin resting against her young, lifeless chest.

Exhausted from the excitement, the rapist pulled back, proudly surveyed his conquest and took several pictures of Sue Ann with an instant camera he had brought from the truck. In the night air, Sugar Daddy's chest and legs began to chill as breaths of hot air escaped from his mouth. Brief clouds of steam formed in the graveyard air.

Suddenly, a group of teenagers, carrying six packs of beer and heading for a fun night of drinking in the cemetery, turned the corner and saw the lifeless bound girl and naked older man.

Shouting, they chased after Sugar Daddy, who had grabbed up some of his clothes and run toward the woods.

The four boys followed the rapist into the brush but lost him quickly in the darkness. When they returned, they covered the girl with a blanket from the truck and tried to awaken her. She didn't respond to their efforts. One of boys cried out that Sue Ann might be dead, jumping back and pointing at the fresh blood that was seeping down the gravestone from the rear of her head.

Two boys ran to a nearby farm and called the police. A subsequent helicopter and ground manhunt produced no results. But Sugar Daddy's abandoned vehicle revealed a treasure box filled with magazines featuring child pornography, explicit photographs, assorted drugs, sex toys and videos.

A regional, all-points bulletin was released. The charges: kidnapping, child abuse, rape of a minor and murder. In downstate Delaware, and nearby Dorchester, Caroline and Talbot counties in Maryland, the search became a priority one case.

During the months following the crime, Sugar Daddy periodically sent copies of the pictures of Sue Ann's lifeless body to the girl's mother, not realizing that the postmarks might provide clues to his hideaway.

Three months later, the child killer was picked up outside an Atlantic City school yard by an alert patrolman. At the time, Sugar Daddy was leading a 10-year-old girl toward a rented van.

Delaware claimed jurisdiction, and the extradition process was swift. The trial made the national news, especially when the defense claimed they had captured the wrong man since Sugar Daddy never picked up Sue Ann. Someone had stolen his car.

When that didn't work, the defense lawyer claimed that, as an alcoholic, even if Sugar Daddy Looney did commit the crime, his addicted alcoholic state did not allow him to remember anything about the events of that day, or to be responsible for his actions.

During the trial the defense's story changed again. Sugar Daddy testified that the girl's mother had given him permission to abuse the daughter, and that, as a couple, they had participated in joint perversions with the child.

The ever-changing defense strategies did not sway the judge, jury or press. Also, residents in downstate Delaware did not take kindly to the abuse and murder of children. The five men and seven women delivered the verdict in six hours—death.

At the sentencing, Sugar Daddy announced that young Sue Ann was the best lay he ever had, even better than her mother. He also shouted that the young girl had told him that her real father had done the same thing to her.

Bedlam broke out in the courtroom when Harvey Figgs, Sue Ann's natural father, who had been present each day of the trial, dove across the railing, grabbed Sugar Daddy's skull and beat it a dozen times against the hardwood courtroom floor. The guards, not in any rush to pull away the attacker, let the father have a few extra shots and reluctantly rescued the bleeding defendant.

The only opposition to the death sentence was from the traditional anti-capital punishment groups. While their weakly-attended demonstrations and poorly-attended rallies were expected, the governor was the target of a new tactic.

McDevitt was particularly annoyed that his office was flooded with prearranged calls from paid college students, who had been hired by out-of-state religious and liberal groups to plea for Sugar Daddy's pardon.

The impressionable young minds had been convinced by several college professors that Sugar Daddy was a victim of a class system that denied him the same opportunities as others. Also, as an alcoholic, he was functionally disabled and not responsible for his actions on the evening of the murder, or for any other criminal acts during the last 20 years.

The fact that Sugar Daddy admitted he had planned the crime for weeks in advance, and that a film receipt, dated the day of the crime, was found in the vehicle, were not brought to the hired callers' attention.

Poplos, noticing his boss's silence, had a feeling that the governor seemed more interested than normal in attending Sugar Daddy's hanging. As they exited the car, very close to the warehouse that housed the Delaware gallows, Poplos and McDevitt could see the eight members of the press, chosen by lottery, standing nearby in silence.

"Get me the warden, will you Randy?"

"Sure, governor. No problem."

Two minutes later, Warden Billy Holmann, smoking a large cigar and wearing his trademark silver snakeskin cowboy boots, came into the driveway. The man McDevitt had brought up to Delaware two years before, from McCalley, Texas, approached.

The two men shook hands then huddled and spoke softly in the midnight darkness. It was getting very close to the time when Looney would be leaving the Earth. The warden nodded several times, agreeing with whatever McDevitt was saying, and then pointed with his cigar hand to a door at the rear of the warehouse.

After Billy Holmann left, McDevitt told Poplos to go in the main entrance. The governor was planning to stay with the warden and meet Poplos at the car. Afterwards, they would head over to the press conference, scheduled at about 1 a.m. at the administration building in beautiful downtown Gumwood.

As the governor disappeared, Poplos joined the media contingent. There were the three regulars, who were guaranteed a spot at each execution: Donna Blankenship of the *National Press Syndicate* Dover bureau, Mark Seznol of the *Wilmington News Chronicle* and Liz Hardy from Dover's *Diamond State Ledger.* The other five reporters were chosen during a media lottery held earlier that evening. On the night of hanging number 9, the eager representatives were from Cable International News, *Delaware Monthly News Magazine,* WNPB radio of Washington, D.C., WSAL in Salisbury, Maryland, and the *Southern Delaware Weekly News,* hometown paper of the victim and her family.

It was cold, thought Poplos, standing outside at two minutes before midnight, waiting for the school bus carrying the official witnesses to empty its load of hand-picked gawkers. The reporters watched as the 20 selected individuals—some legislators, others prison and court officials—filed through the first gate of the double-fenced perimeter that surrounded the gallows warehouse.

No name tags were worn, but a few of those passing by looked familiar.

The moon wasn't quite full, but it was a good-sized yellow plate perched in the blackish-blue sky.

A solitary guard dog, that had been walking beside its handler paused, sat down and let out a mournful howl. It was exactly 12 midnight.

"Outer gate open!" cried a gray uniformed guard, his metal badge flashing a brief bright reflection off the glare of the floodlights.

The reporters turned.

The last group to go in, it was their time to be led through the same double-locked gate that the witnesses had used moments before. The wind was gusty, toes and fingers were beginning to feel the effects of the winter night.

"Outer gate secure!" a guard shouted from behind the group.

Seconds later the call came from the front, "Inner gate open!"

They walked toward the warehouse. Another armed guard opened the wooden, barn-like door.

"Inner gate secure!" someone shouted in the distance.

It was necessary to adjust their night vision slightly, for the interior of the barn/warehouse structure was dimly lit. It was open on one side, as if a section of the building had been blown out, and the wind howled through that wide gaping hole.

The gusts made it difficult to take notes. Those with hoods had them pulled tight, other witnesses were wearing gloves and holding onto scarves that were wrapped across their faces.

About 35 people were frozen in place on the ground, standing silently, and staring up at the platform on top of the 20-foot-tall hanging machine.

It was like stepping back in time, or being on a movie set—both real but unreal.

No one spoke.

There was no sound but the gusting wind.

Warm breaths created frosty clouds when they came into contact with the cold, early morning air. It was 12:05 a.m.

The official witnesses were in the front with an unobstructed view. The reporters stood off, at some distance away by themselves. They had been forbidden to speak and could not make any contact with any witness or guard.

In a dark corner of the barn, a woman in black was sobbing. It was Sugar Daddy's sister. She was being comforted by the murderer's two, court-appointed attorneys. At the base of the gallows, with the best view of the proceedings was Betty Lynn Looney, the victim's mother, and Harvey Figgs, the girl's father. The parents were both dressed totally in white—signifying to all that the night had finally arrived for their private celebration.

They had walked in earlier, before the executioners and murderer appeared. The deceased's parents were able to get a close up of Sugar Daddy as he passed within a foot of them on his final walk to the gallows' steps.

All eyes were focused on the three figures at the top of the structure. Sugar Daddy was in the center, his hands strapped tightly to his sides by a thick dark strip of leather. His feet were bound as well. He stared down silently looking upon the witnesses.

His face was expressionless, his eyes glazed. Several of the witnesses would later say that they thought he had been drugged.

A dangling noose, waving in the strong wind, moved slowly, swaying back and forth about a foot above the trio's heads.

There were two tall, black-hooded executioners—one standing on each side of Sugar Daddy, making sure he stayed in place and didn't attempt to jump off the platform. One of the hooded assistants would throw the large wooden switch that would open the trap door and swallow up the murderer, sending him into the next world.

As in the past, the switch thrower's identity was never released. The official state killer of killers would remain a mystery.

A door opened in the distance and all eyes turned toward the sound. Warden Billy Holmann, a tall but slightly overweight man, began the long solitary walk across the warehouse floor toward the wooden gallows.

His silver and black boots clicked at each contact with the rough concrete surface.

Holmann paused at the bottom of the stairs, looked briefly at the crowd, and then began his slow walk up the 28 steps to the top. He was followed by Betty Lynn Looney and Harvey Figgs.

It was 12:10 a.m.

Holmann pulled out a single sheet of paper and moved directly in front of the killer. Despite the howling wind, every word could be heard clearly.

"Elwood Looney, according to the power vested in me by the sovereign State of Delaware, the First State in the Union, I hereby am authorized to carry out your execution. At this time, I ask: Do you have any final words before you are put to death?"

Sugar Daddy stood motionless, as if both his spirit and mind had already departed the scene. He stared from the warden, then down to the witnesses and back to Holmann. Several times, he started to open his mouth, but paused.

Suddenly, a horrible moan escaped from the bowels of the killer's stomach. Bending over and then looking up at the warden, Sugar Daddy, the former courtroom clown, grinned and snarled.

"I'll meet you all in HELLLLL!" he shouted.

The warden looked on in silence, waiting. There was nothing else to say. After six years of state-provided meals and legal delays, after a half-dozen Christmases and an equal number of frivolous appeals, Death had arrived—and it would not be leaving the gallows alone.

Catching the warden's signal, one of the hooded executioners walked swiftly behind the murderer, roughly grabbing the top of Sugar Daddy's head. He used his other hand to clench the front of Sugar Daddy's face and quickly shoved a thick piece of black rubber in the killer's mouth. The other executioner tied the two ends of a dangling leather strap behind Sugar Daddy's head, securing the mouthpiece in place.

Holmann motioned for the parents to approach. "In compliance with the sovereign State of Delaware's constitutional amendment giving power to relatives of the victims, I invite the parents of the deceased to make a statement and address the prisoner."

One of the hooded assistants led Betty Lynn to a spot on the platform approximately four feet from the killer, to insure that no physical contact was possible. The warden backed off to the side, between Looney and his dead victim's mother.

The red-eyed woman looked at Sugar Daddy, her fourth husband, and screamed, "How could you do it? How could you take my baby away?" Her sobbing was a signal that she was done. The warden directed another guard, stationed at the base of the gallows, to come up and take her away.

Harvey Figgs, a large farmer, in his early 50s, was not as emotional. He looked down on the witnesses. "I'm here to watch this scum die as horrible a death as the state will allow, but it's nothing like what he did to my family." He turned to face the gagged killer. "There's no doubt in my mind that there is a hell, and I know you'll rot there forever. And if there's any way for me to get you, you no good child killing bastard, I'll be there. My girl can't come back, but at least, tonight, your ass is dead." Then, directing his face down toward Looney's two lawyers, Harvey Figgs added, "AND IT'S ABOUT GODDAMN TIME!"

Sugar Daddy shook his head, as if trying to say something. But, at the sight of the killer trying to respond, Figgs turned and spit across the platform, his liquid missile landing on the killer's face.

No one seemed concerned. No one bothered to wipe it off.

As an assistant led Sue Ann's father away, Holmann completed his work.

"Now, by the will of the people of the sovereign State of Delaware, the First State in these United States of America, and the first state to reinstate death by hanging, I condemn you and your soul to eternity and direct the official executioner to carry out your sentence—that you be hanged by the neck until dead. May God have mercy on your soul."

As Holmann moved back, the executioners draped a

long black hood over Looney's head. The shroud was lengthy and extended well below the waist, almost covering the murderer's hands.

The executioner closest to the witnesses pulled down the noose, adjusted it so the knot was tight, pressing it up against Sugar Daddy's left ear, and stepped back.

The second executioner, who stood next to the wooden lever, went behind Sugar Daddy and checked the noose one final time. Billy Holmann had descended to the bottom of the gallows and stood beside the last step.

There was no sound in the building except the creaking of the weary boards in the aged structure. The movement of the lights, from the hanging bare-bulbed lamps that swayed in the wind, created eerie shadows against the barn's rough, wooden walls.

The final message Sugar Daddy heard was the whispered voice of one of the hooded men in black. "Just tightening this up to make sure it works right, Loonball. After all, we don't want you dangling for 15 minutes, waiting in mid air for your old neck to break. That happens sometimes, you know. Gives you a real bad sore throat when you go into the Great Beyond. Won't be able to talk right to all your killer friends."

Sugar Daddy tried to turn his head, but the hooded man placed his hand tightly across the back of the killer's neck and squeezed, forcing Looney's face forward.

"One final message, Loonball. There will be no last-minute call from the governor's office since he's not there. *I'm* here. This is Governor McDevitt, and I know you're going to fry in hell you no good bastard. By the way, I'll be holding a going away party for you when I get back to the mansion tonight. Sweet dreams, you miserable asshole."

Before Sugar Daddy could react, McDevitt, under the dark hood and unknown to everyone else at the execution except the warden, moved to his right, grabbed the handle of the three-foot lever and swiftly yanked it back.

The slam of the trap door and the sight of the body falling through the opening—then jerking and slumping abruptly—

caused several of the witnesses to jump. Looney's descent through the platform took only about three seconds.

Harvey Figgs had the best close-up view. He stared straight ahead and didn't move. Betty Lynn jumped and held her ex-husband's arm tightly. But, she, too, stared and savored the sight of Sugar Daddy's death.

The reporters' eyes were glued to the scene, trying to memorize the significant details that would create the best sound bites for their TV and radio reports. Since no cameras were allowed in the chamber, the print representatives were thinking of the most colorful words to create graphic images for their readers.

The slack rope had become stiff and straight. Looney's body, clothed in dark blue and anchored by a pair of brand new, white jogging sneakers, twirled like a rag doll. One reporter later wrote, the killer hung "like a heavy, limp puppet on a thick twirling string."

The arms, legs and head under the hood did not move. There was no sign of life. After one full minute of complete silence, of watching Looney's body spin and sway six feet above the uneven warehouse floor, Warden Billy Holmann grabbed the bottom of a long black drape.

Looking straight ahead, he walked from the gallows' steps, heading in a giant circle around the base of the structure. As he moved, the wall of black cloth, attached at the top to a metal track with rollers, followed his lead. Soon, the area directly under the trap door was covered, hiding the dangling dead body from view.

The witnesses stood still for another long, cold eight minutes. No one talked. Behind the curtain there was activity, the medical examiner checking the body, bagging it up and getting it ready for removal and disposal.

Suddenly, an anonymous voice from behind the curtain announced: "Elwood Looney is officially pronounced dead at 12:22 a.m."

Betty Sue Looney and Harvey Figgs were escorted out of the warehouse by the warden.

The official witnesses followed. Finally, an aide came for the reporters, leaving the killer's sobbing sister and his attorneys behind in the dark warehouse.

Hanging number 9 was over.

Next up, Benjamin Daniels Hatch, a homosexual, white-collar corporate communications executive, who had been convicted of intentionally giving two teenage boys an over-dose of cheap coke at a private party at his Greenville estate.

Hanging number 10 was scheduled for June—just after midnight on Friday the 13th.

rrangements for the press conference were set up at the correctional center's administrative building, located about three miles from the prison grounds. Eight chairs were arranged behind an elevated head table in the front of the room for the media representatives who had attended the hanging.

About 30 other TV, radio and print types were in the audience, waiting for information about the execution that they would run on the front page of their newspaper and use as the lead story in their on-air reports. When the first two hangings were carried out, more than 100 news outlets crammed the prison's old converted gymnasium. Now Delaware's hangings were old news and interest had leveled off. But, they still pulled in a respectable crowd by hanging standards.

Donna Blankenship, the *National Press Syndicate* reporter who had been to every recent execution, was seated in the center of the table and spoke first.

In turn, each shared their own impression of the event, each trying to get himself selected for a sound bite or quote. There were several references to Looney's final statement and more than one description of his body, twirling like a rag doll. But the last reporter to speak, Liz Hardy from Dover's *Diamond State Ledger*, mentioned that she thought the hooded executioner was speaking to Sugar Daddy as the rope was adjusted the final time.

The question was posed to the senior prison media liaison Cathlene W. Sweatley. That official—who was responsible for working with the media and who earlier had announced Looney's final meal as five scoops of butter pecan ice cream, four slices of cheese pizza, six tacos and an order of homemade french fries—declined comment.

A follow up to the same question from another reporter in the audience generated the same, "No comment," by the prison official.

When the issue was pursued a third time, Gov. Henry McDevitt, with Harvey Figgs at his side, stepped forward.

"I'll take that question," McDevitt said. All cameras and lights shifted from the press table to the governor, who was standing off near a side doorway.

"I can tell you what occurred because I was the one who operated the lever and opened the trap door. I sent Looney away."

There was a very brief pause of total silence—followed by a volcanic-style eruption of shouted questions."

"Why?"

"Is this a new policy?"

"What did it feel like, governor?"

As video cameras ran and shutters snapped, the governor waited in silence. After a full minute, when the press realized there would be no response during the confusion, the questions subsided. Then McDevitt began to talk.

"I have been to nine executions, counting Sugar Daddy Looney's justifiable and long overdue death tonight. I believe that actions speak louder than words, and that's the reason for my direct, hands-on involvement.

"I am incensed and disgusted that I have been called by organized groups of people, many young and impressionable, who have been given false information by those who recruited them. They have called my office and abused my staff for weeks preceding each legal execution, arguing for an end to the mandated death of these so-called persecuted criminals.

"Since I was elected to office by the people, on a platform to rid the state of criminal vermin, I have been very clear about my feelings, beliefs and actions regarding capital punishment. There will never, ever, be a pardon from my office—as long as I am governor—for a convicted murderer who is heading for the gallows or the lethal injection chamber.

"I will not be swayed by religious zealots or by insincere efforts that are so obviously organized and staged by certain idealistic, unrealistic and misguided bleeding heart groups. Their objective is to revert back to the days when appeals went on for decades and when the victims' families were unable to have closure on the tragedy that was inflicted upon them."

"But, Governor. . . . " the shout came from the middle of the room, from a reporter who was standing and waving his hand in the air.

"Young man," McDevitt snapped, "have you no manners? I'll take questions as I always do, when I am through speaking. And you, like all the others, will raise your hand and hope to be called upon. Understand?"

No response came from the embarrassed journalist.

McDevitt quickly added, "Where are you from, New York or Washington?"

The icy response had frozen the room into silence, but the humorous follow-up lightened the mood before McDevitt continued.

"I will tell you this—my staff has discovered organized and fraudulent telephone campaigns, by certain death penalty opposition groups—illegally using Delaware citizens' names and phone numbers—to call in inaccurate objections to what we are doing here. It will not be tolerated, and we will be taking both civil and criminal action against these organizers, organizations and the workers themselves. In some cases, we will be seeking disbarment proceedings against the members of the legal community who have been actively involved.

"My role as executioner tonight was to send a clear, final, definitive message to those who cannot understand what I have repeated to date: There will be no pardon or parole in Delaware for murderers and serious offenders. If they have discovered God in their jail cell, I am pleased they have someone to talk to who is all forgiving. I am not.

"For those who want to know if pulling the lever that finally sent Elwood Sugar Daddy Looney away affected me tonight, I will answer: Absolutely not. It was less bothersome than stepping on a cockroach in the governor's mansion kitchen.

"Will I do it again?

"Perhaps. When appropriate, yes. And I will continue to be present for every execution. Now, I will take your questions."

Two dozen hands were raised. No one shouted.

McDevitt pointed to the blond-haired woman in a bright blue suit.

"How does your cold-blooded killing of a defenseless, political prisoner, whose hands and feet are bound, make the streets any safer?"

McDevitt stared at the young woman for a moment.

"I will not answer that question because it is editorially loaded with your own sentiments, and a response will only serve your pre-designed agenda. Go back to journalism school, if you can find a good one, and learn how to present your questions in a more objective manner. Then, maybe, I'll honor you with a response.

"But, let me provide you, Miss, with a brief history lesson—since you, obviously, have arrived here without doing your research and are totally unprepared to write an objective story. Ever since 1976, when the U.S. Supreme Court lifted its ban on executions in this country, punishment by hanging, lethal injection, the electric chair and, in some cases, firing squad, has been legal. Over the last 30 years, they have occurred more than a thousand times throughout the country. Obviously, Texas and California are in the lead in total numbers, but Delaware has earned a justified reputation as a state where convicted inmates on death row will not be there long enough to decorate their cells.

"I do not care about arguments promoted by the United National Legal Defense Fund, Acquittal International, the

International Conference of Ecumenical Bishops, American Lawyers Opposed to the Death Penalty and, particularly, the opinions of members of the governments of Canada, Mexico and other *enlightened* Europeans who do not approve of what we do here. Frankly, they do not live here. They do not pay taxes here. They do not contribute anything to us except ridiculous opinions that I don't care about.

"They have not served as members of the Delaware juries that have unanimously recommended the death penalty for people like Elwood Looney. The citizens of the First State have spoken with their verdicts. It is what they want. It is their mandate that we are carrying out.

"So, if you crusading reporters want to change the way things are done here, I suggest you move into our state, get a Delaware driver's license and hope to serve on a jury so you can argue against the execution of a child killer, or mass murderer or drug dealer who distributes heroin to elementary school children."

McDevitt pointed to the opposite side of the room.

"Thomas Leonardo, WPCL-TV, Philadelphia. Do you honestly feel that all these executions are having a positive effect on crime in your state?"

"Murders have fallen 36 percent in the last two years. Armed robbery is down 41 percent. We have neighborhoods in Wilmington's inner city where, six years ago, there was a killing twice a month. Now, residents can walk down the street at night for the first time in years.

"When I was a boy, growing up in Sussex County, I used to hear my grandparents say that, in the old days, criminals would avoid setting foot in Delaware and commit their crimes elsewhere, mainly because of their fear of the whipping post. Today, with properly applied executions carried out in a timely manner for serious crimes, plus the recent reinstatement of the whipping post, we're seeing tremendous results. The number of out-of-state criminals coming into Delaware to commit crime is minimal, because they're afraid of what will happen to them when, not if, they get caught."

Another hand was selected.

"Trish Zagar, *Baltimore Bugle*. Some people might consider that attitude a bit selfish, governor, that you are pushing criminals into other states that are softer on crime. What do you say to that?

"Well, Ms. Zagar, they aren't going next door into Maryland. Your governor and my good friend Lydia Chase is doing very much what we're doing here. You've had four executions, more by lethal injection that we have, but it serves the same purpose, getting rid of the career criminal menace that has been breeding for the last 50 years, by taking advantage of misguided and unrealistic authorities who attempted to create a utopian fantasyland. But, I would like to also see Maryland use the whipping post. Then, almost the entire peninsula would be unattractive to criminals. But, we're happy with one small step at a time.

"Now, in further response to your question, I do not shed any tears or spend any time being bothered that criminals are going elsewhere. Eventually, the other states will get the message that what we're doing here is working. If they're smart, they'll follow our progressive, fair policies and get the same positive results that their citizens will appreciate. If not, they'll probably end up with more crime. Actually, the states that continue to be soft on crime are inviting criminals by their inaction and their reluctance to deal with the problem realistically and effectively, the way we are."

"Is there no mercy in your heart, governor?" The shouted question whined across the room from the woman in blue.

McDevitt stared at her, his eyes ice cold, his voice was harsh. "I save my mercy for those who deserve it. Earlier this evening I saw a 8-year-old girl in Wilmington, lying in a casket in her First Communion dress. Her parents, hard working people who observe the law, were in tears. That family is destroyed. Its entire future stolen by a low-life, unfit-to-live, drug-dealing slimeball.

"Mercy, you ask? I say that belongs with that victimized family. That's where the attention should be given. That's where you people should be searching for your stories and sharing their inconceivable grief. How many of these bleeding heart, front-pew kneeling, do-gooder singers that were outside the prison tonight visited that family after the girl's murder? How many letters or donations or prayers were sent to the victim's family members?

"You want to learn about mercy, ask that man over there, Harvey Figgs, who waited all these years for tonight to arrive. Seven years before what's left of his family could even begin to put their pain to rest.

"I believe in mercy for the victims, for the working people, for the ones who follow the law. I have no time for tear jerking, pie-in-the-sky dreamers who think murderers and drug dealers and armed robbers can be changed into functioning members of society. They had their chance, many of them have had an unlimited number of opportunities, and all they did was increase the size of their rap sheets. People read about their repeat crimes and wonder how in the world they get let back out onto the street.

"In this state, as long as I'm here, for the big crimes it's one strike and you're out. Don't call Woodburn if you're an attorney of a criminal looking for a shoulder to cry on. Tough love has arrived and it's here to stay. I have a responsibility to the honest people in this state, and they know that I mean what I say: Victims first, criminals at the end of the line and, preferably, at the end of a rope."

No one raised another hand.

McDevitt's tone and the expression on his face were not inviting.

"I expect you to print what I said accurately, and in its proper context, or you will be denied access to any further press conferences and executions while I am governor. And I'm not above calling your publisher and recommending you be fired or sent back to learn your job on the obituary beat.

"The days of editorial journalism are over, folks. Learn your job or get out of town. Also, I'll make this final statement. I am looking forward to the execution of the killer of that little girl. And, as long as I am in office, I will plan to personally drop that lowlife scumbag through the trap door.

"No further questions for me or anyone else. This press conference is over. Cathlene, clear the area and send these people back to wherever they came from."

S gt. Randy Poplos pulled the governor's Monte Carlo into the parking area behind Woodburn, the 18th-century, brick governor's mansion in the heart of Dover. Several Capitol police officers and Delaware state troopers were waiting along the driveway and on the steps heading into the rear kitchen entrance.

Word had already reached them about the governor's hands-on role in the execution. As Henry McDevitt exited the passenger door, a round of applause filled the air.

"Nice goin', Governor!" said one police corporal, shaking McDevitt's hand.

"We got our own Judge Roy Bean!" cried out another trooper.

"I'll be lookin' for you on the cover of *Weekly News*, Gov'nor!" a young cop shouted.

It was past 2 a.m. when McDevitt entered the mansion's parlor. In the room were a few department chiefs, the colonel of the state police, the governor's executive assistant Sean Kelley and, in the darkness, sitting on the steps of the main stairway that led to the living quarters, Michael Pentak, special consultant to the governor.

Several raised glasses, toasting the governor's bold action. A few shook their heads, obviously worried about the political spin-off and, more importantly, how it would affect them if McDevitt lost his next election.

Otis Camby, the chief of the Department of Social Services, spoke first. A Delaware native and a short black man, Camby had a good sense of the minority community's temperament, and his advice to McDevitt had always been right on the mark. The governor was especially interested in his reaction and comment.

"Well, fellow night owls," Camby said, "the verdict isn't in yet. After all, not everyone sits up listening to the news 'til 2 in the morning, even if there is a hanging going on. But, early reports are very positive. The governor is well liked in Hilltop, on East Side and in the projects. They believe him to be fair. I must say, to my surprise and delight, the calls to my home and office have been about three-fourths positive."

Smiles and nods circled the room.

"But," Camby added, "I'll feel better when we see the papers and, better yet, when we see the letters to the editor during the rest of the week."

Grove Passamore, head of the Department of Agriculture and well connected through family and business contacts downstate and on the Eastern Shore, addressed McDevitt. "It was a big risk tonight, Hank. No doubt about it. You got a pair of iron gonads. I know I woulda liked to have done it, probably woulda thought about it more than once. But I don't know if I coulda thrown the switch. In a real sense, we all were with you on that gallows tonight, and we'll find out soon enough if we're all gonna swing together and follow ol' Looney down the tubes."

McDevitt spoke for the first time. "But what do you think, Grove? Honestly and personally, what's your gut say?"

Patting a well endowed stomach that had seen its share of firehouse scrapple breakfasts, Passamore replied, "I think you hit a home run. I really do. I just got a feeling this is gonna be bigger than we think, in a good way."

As more murmured approval spread through the room, Sean Kelley walked toward the governor, holding a handful of messages. The phones in the communications office could be heard ringing in the background. Two police officers were covering the calls, taking messages.

"It's going crazy in there," Sean said. "Doesn't anybody sleep? Overwhelming praise. A woman whose son was shot five years ago, and the killer's still in max, wants you to take him out personally when his time comes up.

"Two or three expected protests from local amnesty groups, a civil liberties spokesperson who says he's going to institute a lawsuit because your action deprived the real prison executioner of his rightful role as a union employee. I can't believe that one," Sean shook his head. "And Rev. Peter DiMasi of the Mission of Care, Hope and Love, who is asking for an apology for calling the protesters a bunch of 'bleeding heart, front-pew kneeling, do-gooder singers.'

"We've also had calls from the four major TV networks for in-depth interviews," Sean continued. "Five other governors called to relay their congratulations, and *U.S. Weekly News* and *Pulse of the Nation* want to come down and schedule a photo shoot."

McDevitt replied softly, "My initial response is to let things simmer down a bit before we reply to any of these requests, but I'm pleased it's working to our benefit."

Turning to his guests, he added, "I also want to thank you for coming here tonight. I appreciate your presence, your support. I'm not surprised you came. I selected all of you because of your commitment to our plan, our pledge to do the best we can for the people we represent. I really think we're starting to make a real change. Let's not mess it up. There's a fine line between making giant strides and letting things move at the usual governmental snail's pace. Sometimes it takes a roll of the dice and a major action like tonight to maintain momentum. Well, gentlemen, it's late. We'll have a lot of work tomorrow. If you'll excuse me."

As the guests began to leave, filtering in ones and twos through the kitchen exit, Col. Alvin Robb, chief of the state police, and Michael Pentak were at the back of the line.

McDevitt motioned for both of them to stay and, when the room was empty, the three men sat in a small circle, each holding a drink.

Sean Kelley came in, made his excuses and said the officers would continue monitoring the phones. He would see the governor in the Georgetown office at 8 o'clock sharp.

"How you holding up, Hank?" the state's top cop asked. He was in his 60s, but still trim and in great shape. A 30-year Army retiree, the former Airborne Ranger came onto the team three years ago as a favor to McDevitt. Robb knew he was sharing the early morning session with his eventual successor—Michael Pentak.

"Pretty good, Al. Better than I thought." McDevitt paused and then continued. "You know, it felt weird standing up there, so close to that cold-blooded murderer. But I was in control, more than I thought I would be. I had considered not going through with it. But then, when I got there and saw that girl's father and mother, both dressed in white, I decided I would do if for them. If that father could have pushed that switch he would have. So, I told him before I put on the hood, I was doing it for him and his little girl and ex-wife.

"Then, you know what he did? The guy embraced me, like I was his brother or a close friend. Then his ex-wife hugged me. All three of us together were holding each other. I knew then how much they needed it done that way. And when Looney went through that hole, I just watched him, from above, swirling and turning, and I felt good it was over, that he was done, gone. And I was sure he would never get out. He would never be paroled, never escape and never hurt anyone else again, and word would get out that you can't screw up in Delaware and get away with it. I know it was the right thing to do."

"Remember Buck Pierce?" Robb asked.

The governor nodded, recalling the first inmate to do the Delaware rope dance.

"How long ago was that, Al?"

"Two years, Hank. Two years ago and it seems like it just happened, and here we are with number 9 already."

McDevitt thought back, recalling the first killer to swing. At 26, the unemployed alcoholic had killed three relatives.

Buck blew off his grandparents heads with a 12-gauge because they wouldn't give him their pension check to buy booze. Later that afternoon, he stabbed his mother 43 times with a potato peeler when she threatened to call the police if he didn't get out of her Kent County mobile home.

The cops picked up Buck hitchhiking in the northbound lane of Route 13, just south of Gumwood, a sleepy little burg of about 2,500 residents whose main employer was the prison.

His ripped bib overalls were covered with dried blood, an empty pint of cheap whiskey was in his pocket and the sticky, red coated, kitchen utensil was still in his right hand.

The jury convicted the misunderstood wino after only two hours, and he became one of Delaware's death row elders—waiting for his big day for 21 years.

As the death date approached, newspapers offered a fair number of sob stories about the "mature and caring, Very Rev. Buck Pierce," since the convicted murderer had seen the light of that old time religion during his two decades in the clink. Bayard Haywood, who was governor prior to McDevitt, was considering granting the reformed killer and model prisoner parole and a state counseling job at a half-way house in Newark.

But both Haywood's and Buck's luck ran out on election night with the arrival of Victim's Rights Coalition candidate Henry McDevitt. From the podium during his acceptance speech the new chief executive sent a message to the prisoners in the state's three correctional centers: "The party's over," McDevitt had said, "and I'll be paying you boys a little visit, bright and early tomorrow morning."

People thought McDevitt was kidding, but the governor-elect, without informing prison officials, brought along the press and toured the three facilities, pointing out changes he wanted made before he took office in January. The message was clear: Prison administrators could ignore his demands and be replaced in January, or they could make McDevitt's changes immediately and have a better chance of keeping their state jobs.

In-cell color televisions disappeared. The weight room was shut down. Telephone privileges were limited, and the prisoner's union was disbanded. A committee heavily represented by members of McDevitt's Victim's Rights Coalition was charged with reviewing prison procedures and policies and five coalition members were placed on the nine-member State Board of Parole and Pardons.

While walking through Maximum Security Wing A, McDevitt stopped by Rev. Buck Pierce's cell and went inside for a private chat. No one else was present at the meeting, but those in the hall could imagine the gist of the exchange. The press witnessed The Very Rev. Buck Pierce jumping up in the air and charging across the cell at McDevitt, who grabbed the prisoner's wrist, twisted it and held his God-fearing assailant's face against the cell floor.

As the wide-eyed guards rushed with keys to open the chamber, the reformed inmate was doubled over and snarling at McDevitt. "You no good, asshole! I'll cut your goddamn throat wide open, just like I did my Mama, when I get out of here. You hear me, Governor! You'll never finish your term, you no good bastard!"

Turning to the press, McDevitt smiled as the cameras ran. "Obviously, The Very Rev. Buck Pierce is having a bad, out-of-character, unreligious day. However, I'm fairly certain that he was not satisfied with the message I relayed to him in his cell."

"What was that?" several reporters shouted at once, thrusting microphones toward McDevitt's face.

"That parole for Buck Pierce is a fairy tale dream that will never come true. With his frivolous appeals nearing an end, the only way he will be leaving this prison is in a black rubber bag after swinging from a very stiff rope."

Ending his lapse down Memory Lane, McDevitt looked at Robb and Pentak.

No one replied, and McDevitt walked across the room and lifted an intricately cut wine decanter.

As he poured himself another glass of sherry, he said, "You know, the late Charles Terry, he was the first governor to live in this house in the 1960s, he swore that it was haunted. He said he used to come down in the morning and find the wine decanters empty. He called the intruder the 'Tippling Ghost,' because it drank all the wine. Ever heard that story?"

Robb and Pentak shook their heads.

"Well, I'm glad the old ghost, or any of the other three spirits that are supposed to live here, didn't hit the wine bottle tonight."

As McDevitt downed the rest of the glass, Pentak got up and spoke. "I don't think you realize what you did here tonight, Hank."

"Sure I do. I, Delaware Governor Henry McDevitt—at first secretly, then publicly—admitted that I put on an executioner's hood and dropped a scumbag, pervert through a trapdoor heading straight to the gates of hell. And then, for good measure, I insulted a roomful of smart ass reporters. Just another start of an early morning in Delaware, the Small Wonder."

"I think you're underestimating the significance of your action," Pentak said, as he sat down next to Colonel Robb.

"Explain," McDevitt said, his eyes focused on Pentak, interested in his comment.

"Anyone can say they want to reduce crime. It's the in thing. Hell, it's always been a safe and sure bet for every politician of every party since forever. Ever hear a politician come out and say, 'I'm all for crime' or 'I think we're a little too tough on criminals?' No way!

"It's just like anyone can say they're for the death penalty. God, 80 percent of the population is for correctly administered executions. 'Get 'em, try 'em, fry 'em.' That's the popular motto. The important thing to understand is: Why do people feel this way?"

Neither McDevitt nor Robb answered, so Pentak continued, "It's not only that Joe and Jane Average have had enough of the knee-jerk understanding routine. It's not that people are blood thirsty savages. It's not that they are mean or evil and don't care.

"The reason is simple. It's that more and more people have been victims, and if they are not, they know someone in their family who has been hurt or attacked or threatened—or, worse yet, screwed by the unequal scales of modern day justice.

"When it hits home, to you—where you live, at your work, on your street, in your car—that's when you can no longer ignore it, and that's when you want it fixed."

Colonel Robb added, "Somebody said a conservative is a liberal who was robbed the night before. Well, there's a lot of truth to that."

McDevitt started to comment, but Pentak held up his hand.

"I know you think there's nothing new to what I said, but let me finish. Here's the point I want to make, Hank. It's easy to say you want the bastard to fry or to hang or be put to sleep with a needle full of joy juice. It's quite another thing to do it. Quick! Give me the names of five—no, make it two—two other governors who would actually do what you did tonight. I bet you can't do it."

McDevitt held his glass in silence. About 15 seconds went by, and he said, "Ben Jaurez in New Mexico might. And Gov. Betty Harrison, she's a tough one, up in North Dakota, she might."

"I didn't say *might*, Hank. I said get in there and throw the switch. You put your convictions into action. You weren't alone pulling that lever, and there just wasn't poor Harvey Figgs and his ex-wife symbolically on the platform with you. You had an army of frustrated citizens, regular working schmucks—black, white, tan, yellow, all colors—who think that every politician is a sleazeball, double-talking, what's-in-it-for-me crooked asshole.

"And a lot of them expected you to be just like that, too. Hell, why should you be any different? But tonight, you moved out of the pack. And even though it wasn't your objective, you showed them that there is someone in authority, who they voted for, who will act on what he and they both believe. You've put yourself and your state under a spotlight, and I hope you're prepared to carry through—because the people, and not just the ones in your state, but all over, are going to expect a lot from you."

"What are you saying, Pentak?"

"I think," interjected Colonel Robb, "that you're right on schedule with your original timetable related to your arrival in Washington, Hank. And that our friend Pentak here had better get to work and finish his last book."

The volume of phonecalls was worse the next day. Sean Kelley had to hire four temps to keep up with the incoming overflow, and the barrage would last for three days. Nearly 80 percent were favorable and, interestingly, more than 32 percent were from out of state.

As McDevitt and Sgt. Poplos arrived in Georgetown, a crowd of more than 200 citizens had gathered in the grassy island in the center of The Circle, carrying signs. At first glance, it looked like an old-fashioned '60s protest rally. As Poplos slowed down the car, he began reading the signs aloud:

"Way to go, McDevitt!"

"Frontier Justice, Delaware Style!"

"McDevitt for President!"

"McDevitt Does It His Way and MY WAY!"

"Thanks! A Victim's Mother."

Poplos turned to his right, glancing at his boss, who was looking out on the shouting crowd. "Do you believe this, Governor? You're a freaking folk hero."

"For the moment, Randy. For the moment," he said, softly. "Tomorrow they might be calling the talk shows and making me out to be a bum."

"I don't think so, sir. I got a feeling this is for keeps."

"We'll see. Well, let's pull up and get to work."

As the Monte Carlo stopped near the front of the courthouse, across from The Circle, McDevitt tried to push open his door. Immediately, the governor was pressed upon by a mass of humanity. Pens and scraps of paper were thrust into his hand, toward his face.

Sgt. Poplos, serving as solitary escort and bodyguard was, literally, pushing and punching people out of the way. What good he would be able to do when he reached McDevitt was a question that occurred to him halfway through the crowd, but still the state cop kept trying to carve a tunnel through the circle of moving, pressing flesh.

McDevitt, trying to stand and sign his name at the same time, was being swept up with the rush. At least the flow was heading toward the direction of the front door.

Poplos had given up and made it back to the car. "This is Diamond 1," the sergeant shouted into his radio. "Back up! Back up, NOW! We're getting mobbed out here, in the Georgetown Circle! REPEAT. DIAMOND 1. BACK UP! NOW!"

Two uniformed courtroom guards rushed out the front door to help pry McDevitt from the crowd. As soon as they got him free, the crowd, almost as one, paused and fell silent. They actually seemed embarrassed that they had frightened their chief executive.

McDevitt looked at the silent gathering—all colors, old and middle aged, a few mothers with their small children—and paused. Poplos motioned for McDevitt to leave, but he held up a hand.

"Well," he said, smiling and obviously at ease, "that was some reception."

The crowd laughed nervously.

With no microphone and no script, the governor walked toward the building to the south side of the courthouse entrance and mounted the five steps. Standing at the top, looking out with a better view of the crowd, he began, "Thanks for coming out here today. It means a lot to me. Your support is important, and I'll continue to do my best so each and every one of you can live in a safe and healthy environment."

By now, three police cruisers turned the corner, their sirens blaring. As they stopped, a half-dozen tall state police officers, wearing blue-gray uniforms accented with gold, had taken up positions around the crowd and were moving toward McDevitt's side.

"Looks like my assistant thought you were upset with me and called out the cavalry," he said, laughing.

Applause and shouts came out of the audience.

"We love you, Hank!" More cheers.

"Lynch another one, Hank!" someone shouted.

"Right on! Tell 'em we can run our state fine our way!" an elderly lady called out.

McDevitt held up his hands.

"Look. I've got an appointment waiting, so I've got to run. But I promise you this. We will run our state your way. Our way. And we're not going to let any federal bigshots in Washington, or federal district judges from Philly come down here and tell us how we do things in the Diamond State."

The crowd applauded and whistled its approval.

"We've got a chance to polish our little jewel," McDevitt said, "and that's what we're going to do. All of us together. You and me. Thanks! God bless all of you."

As McDevitt headed into the building, the cheer went up, over and over, repeated in unison: "Hank! Hank! HANK! HANK!"

Louder and faster, like a football cheer, they continued until it reached a rapid, unpronounceable crescendo and the crowd burst out in applause, then cheered before dispersing.

From the side of the courthouse entrance and The Circle that has existed from Colonial days, the entire scene—from initial bedlam to final applause—was recorded by three network camera crews assigned to follow the rising star of Delaware Gov. Henry "Hank" McDevitt.

Entering his Sussex County suite, McDevitt's senior secretary, Grace Ann Welch, the stern, white-haired matron who preserved order in his Sussex County office, snapped, "You're late, Governor."

McDevitt smiled as he flew past her desk. "Good morning to you, too, Grace."

Rushing into his office, McDevitt extended his hand and apologized to his guest. Roger Dreyer, executive partner and chief financial officer of UGP Inc. of New Orleans.

"No need to apologize to me, Governor. I'm just thrilled to be in your presence. I had no idea I would be lucky enough to meet the *U.S.A. News Magazine* upcoming man of the year."

"Mr. Dreyer, I don't think . . . ."

"Please, Governor, call me Roger. I'm here to discuss a $90 million investment in your state, for starters, so I would appreciate it if we can drop the formalities. Okay?"

"Okay," McDevitt said, motioning for Sean Kelley to bring over the peninsula map and the three men began to review UGP's proposals and the five sites that McDevitt had chosen as most appropriate for the company's consideration.

McDevitt pointed out his first choice, then showed the locations for the other four, in priority order.

As Sean and Dreyer continued to discuss the advantages and drawbacks of each site, McDevitt responded to a knock and excused himself to talk with Poplos.

"I think we can send the uniforms back to their barracks now. Okay with you, Governor?"

"Sure. There's no sense in their hanging around."

"Okay," Poplos said, "but they all asked for me to get your autograph for them. Do you believe it?"

"You're kidding?"

"No way, sir. They say they won't go without them. I got their names right here. Please, sir. Keep them happy and they'll go away. I gotta work with these guys. Okay?"

Grace had six sheets of executive stationary and a pen at the ready.

McDevitt signed the papers and told Poplos to tell them not to say anything or the entire force would want to add an autograph as a condition of their next union contract.

Grace stared at McDevitt. "If you would have asked for my advice," she said, with a smile, "I would have told you to never take off the hood."

McDevitt turned, looked down and replied, "Well, I didn't ask Grace, so I guess . . . ."

". . . you'll have to put up with your growing fan club, that's what," she said. "But, I will say this, Henry," she whispered, "your grandparents would have been very proud of you. I do know that."

"Thanks Grace, I appreciate it."

"And I am, too," she added, then returned to her desk.

"Thank you. That means a lot to me," McDevitt told her.

Dreyer and Sean were standing as McDevitt returned to the room. The map was spread across the larger conference table.

"We agree," Roger said. "First in Wilmington, right downtown near the river, a 28-story tower, higher than anything you've got now. More than 800 rooms. You'll see it for miles, practically in Philly."

"What about the employment figures?" McDevitt asked.

Sean stepped forward, opening a folder. "Approximately 2,500 total jobs, 58 percent in the $26,000 range at the low end. The rest, based on performance, could extend well above that."

"Training?" McDevitt asked.

"UGP will pay for training of both skilled and unskilled help. Day care center on the premises, free for all employees. Charges for guests."

"Length of construction?"

"You give me the okay, Governor, and I'll have that sucker up and running in less than 18 months."

"And the number of jobs," McDevitt said, "does . . . ."

" . . . . does not include workers while the building is under construction," Roger said. "I figure you and I will be giving your state over 3,500 jobs, total, on this one job. Then, as soon as that's done, we start on site number two."

"Number two is in Rehoboth, north of the current boardwalk," Sean said. "Three will be in Cambridge—near the water and close to the shopping centers and recreation areas—four will be in Stanton, near the racetrack, and the final one will be about 35 miles south of Chincoteague, on the bay side of the peninsula. Just like you figured, Governor. But the other four will be slightly smaller than the Wilmington project."

"So," Roger Dreyer, rubbing his palms for the go ahead signal, asked, "when can we start?"

"When I tell you, and no sooner, and no word of this leaks or you and UGP are history. Understand?"

"Fine," Dreyer replied, "but I need to have a rough idea, a general time line."

"I'd say, if everything goes according to schedule," McDevitt said, "you're looking at ground breaking on number one in 24 to 36 months. How's that sound?"

"Well, I'd like it to happen sooner, but, we have plenty to keep us busy. Projects in Montana, Connecticut, Canada and another in the Caribbean. We can work within your time frame. How are you going to convince the governors of Maryland and Virginia to go along with this?"

"I'll handle it. Any problem with that?" McDevitt said, confidently.

"No. Fine with me. I'll leave that up to you," Dreyer said, nodding his head up and down. "But, one more question. Who else are your bringing in for bids?"

McDevitt smiled, "Roger, do you think this downstate farmer's son just fell off the peach truck? I'll let you know that after I talk to them, and then I'll be able to decide how good your deal really is. We called you in first for two reasons—you come highly recommended, and we know if we get a better deal with a smaller outfit you'll be willing to beat it. After all, we're talking five projects, not just one, and all up and running in less than eight years."

Roger shook his head, then extended his hand. "So we'll talk again?"

"Yes," said McDevitt, "but only if you don't talk. Also, as you're aware, we've had a little excitement today, so I'm going to have you leave by a different door. All right?"

Roger nodded, and Sean led him down a narrow, circular, back stairway that led into the courthouse basement.

"They used to take prisoners up and down through here," Sean said. "They also say some of the judges used to have women of the evening visit them in their chambers between cases. They'd use this as their entrance and exit to and from the building."

"So I'm being compared to a criminal and a whore. Thanks a lot," Dreyer said sarcastically.

"You said it, I didn't," replied Sean, smiling at the apt comparison.

6

The governor walked across his spacious office, sat behind his desk and began to look over his full schedule of appointments when the intercom buzzed and McDevitt lifted the receiver. "Governor Chase on Line 2, Henry."

"Thanks, Grace." McDevitt punched the button and greeted his friend from the neighboring state.

"Nice work last night, Hank."

"Thanks, Lydia. I hope you approve."

"Totally. Not that it matters. Once you go by your impulses no one can stop you."

"So what else is new?"

"Not new, NEWS!" Chase stressed. "You're all over the air. TV, radio. Talk shows. I don't think you realize how big this has become. And it looks like it's just getting started—and building rapidly."

"Well," McDevitt replied, "we had a small demonstration out here, near the courthouse, this morning."

"Protesters?"

"God, no! Fans," McDevitt replied. "I thought we'd come out okay, but I never thought it would generate such a positive response."

"Well, don't relax. The opposition still has plenty of ammunition. By next week the political cartoonists will have you on the editorial page with a smoking gun and blood dripping from your hands."

"I agree, but my aides tell me the letters to the editor underneath the cartoons will be positive."

"Let's hope," Chase said. "So," she added, changing the subject, "when can we get together? There's a lot to discuss."

"Who's to be in on the meeting?" McDevitt asked.

"You, me, plus the Eastern Shore and Delaware big names—basically, the five who want us to push this agenda along."

"Where?"

"It's your turn to be host. But the consensus is dinner in the Christina Room at the Hotel du Pont, followed by a private meeting in one of the upstairs suites. I'll plan to stay over, as will my three people from Baltimore, Easton and Annapolis."

"The Greenville connection is within driving distance and the Grand Dame from Georgetown has relatives in Montchanin. So, they'll both be fine. When do you want to meet?" McDevitt asked.

"My people are fine for Sunday night at 6 o'clock. Can you do that?"

"I'll have Grace make the calls. I know it's important we meet soon. Unless one of my group is out of the country, we'll be there."

"Everyone has to be present, Hank."

"I know. Plan that we're set. Grace will confirm. Thanks for the call and see you next week," McDevitt said.

"Fine. And Hank . . . ."

"Yes?"

"You did well. I mean it. We're all behind you on this, and I'll be proud to stand beside you."

"Thanks Lydia. I appreciate you very much. My best to Ron." The conversation was over. McDevitt set down the receiver and leaned back in his thick, dark leather chair. The tall sides wrapped around his body like a protective shield, and protection, he thought, is exactly what he was going to need.

🌱   🌱   🌱

As usual, the Brandywine Room Restaurant dinner was excellent. McDevitt and his guests were seated in the Christina Room's foyer, a private dining area set apart from the main area used by other patrons. But, on Sunday evenings the number of diners was small.

Delaware and Maryland plainclothes detectives were stationed in the Hotel du Pont lobby, and four lucky troopers—two male and two female bodyguards, disguised as separate young couples having a night out—dined at tables on either side of the foyer entrance.

Since their eyes were constantly scanning the room, they didn't have an opportunity to relax and enjoy their meal, but it was better than a Route 40 donut shop.

When dinner was over, the seven power figures were escorted to a private conference room on the sixth floor. Two guards remained in the lobby, a pair was stationed in an adjoining room of the suite and a couple stood in the hallway—between the meeting room entrance and the elevators and nearby stairwell.

McDevitt, seated at one end of the dark green tableclothed rectangle, greeted his visitors, who had taken their seats.

To his immediate left was Benjamin Bartolavich, a Baltimore real estate tycoon and owner of Bartol Development, Inc. Among his assets were eight shopping malls near Baltimore and Annapolis and three in northern Virginia, plus three luxury hotels on the Eastern Shore. He had recently been featured in the *Washington Morning Star* magazine section for his restoration of five historic inns in downtown Alexandria. At 50, he was the least vocal of the group but could be adamant and demanding.

Elyse Delmond of Easton was in the horse racing business as a hobby, into fox hunting for recreation and into playing the stock market with her deceased husband's oil and chemical fortune to expand her assets. According to the latest national business periodical her fortune was in the $195 million dollar range. A trim, attractive and outspoken woman at 62, she was known to breath fire like a dragon and drink whiskey like a sailor.

Admiral John McDonnough Jennings was retired with an estate north of Annapolis. He had seen combat duty as a pilot during Vietnam and held sea command in Desert Storm. He also was on classified duty assignments in Bosnia in the early '90s. The U.S. Naval Academy Class of '66 graduate and pilot was the most youthful looking of those assembled, even though he was older than the Baltimore developer. Jennings was a social moderate but a hawk when it came to foreign affairs and a staunch conservative when public safety issues were involved.

Maryland Governor Lydia Chase anchored the opposite end of the table. At 48, she was bright, articulate and a staunch defender of state's rights. She had reduced welfare, cut taxes and helped increase tourism throughout the state. Married to Ronald Chase, a Johns Hopkins University chaired professor of history and urban affairs, the governor had easy access to unlimited polling and demographic information that was useful in her ongoing campaign to revitalize Maryland's urban centers and remain in office. She had known McDevitt for over 10 years. They had a very close professional and personal relationship, based on trust and mutual respect.

Clayton Ward of Greenville was one of the two guests who represented the First State. A retired judge of the Third U.S. District Court in Philadelphia, he was a partner in Ward, Bennett, Wallace and Daniels, one of Delaware's oldest and most respected—and expensive—corporate law firms. Still sharp and active at 76, Ward played tennis daily. The sport was his obsession, and he had hosted several Global TennisWorld stars at his estate, complete with private clay courts and grandstands, in Delaware's secluded chateau country.

Ward could be a kindly grandfather one moment but curt and cutting the next. A faithful ally, he was recognized as a dangerous foe. A Delaware native and charter member of the elite and secretive Caesar Rodney Society, he knew where all the political skeletons were buried. It was known that he would not hesitate to strong-arm his opponents into seeing things his way.

Saundra Price, 51, known as the Grand Dame from Georgetown, was married to Delaware's chicken czar. She and her husband Peter "Poultry" Price, had turned the broiler industry into a gold mine that spread throughout the Delmarva Peninsula and beyond. From Gumwood to Seaford and from Salisbury to Cape Charles, Price Poultry signs indicated the small and large farms where chickens were raised specifically for the Price operation.

Nine processing plants on the peninsula prepared Price Poultry for delivery across the entire country and to eager markets in 37 foreign countries, from Russia and China to Ireland, Chile and South Africa.

While Peter was most at home talking to farmers in the small chicken houses and researchers in his high-tech processing plants, Saundra thrived in the board room and at high-level business, community and political meetings.

On this particular evening—in the closed door, secretive gathering—Saundra Price was in her element.

"Well Hank, ladies and gentlemen," Lydia Chase said, "shall we begin?"

Nods of affirmation came from all sides. Everyone turned toward Judge Clayton Ward, who leaned back in his chair, looked at the two governors, and began to speak.

"We're here to decide if we are going to move ahead or wait another four years. The time has arrived for us to step forward and take the lead or sit back and watch the parade pass us by. So, Henry, Lydia. I think we should hear from the two of you first. Then we'll get reaction and input from the rest of the group. All right?"

"Fine," McDevitt said, then added, "Ladies first," smiling and pointing to his Maryland colleague.

"I'll make my comments short and direct," Lydia said, looking from right to left, making eye contact with each person present. "The positive responses are still coming in from Hank's dramatic action earlier this week. It has focused national attention on his state. Delaware is in the black, financially, and its streets are safer than they have been in decades. Public opinion is astoundingly high. His opponents have no campaign platform, nothing they can get their teeth into. I say we go and make the leap. Declare as soon as possible. I'd be honored to be his running mate. I think we can do it. I say we go for it and announce immediately, within the week."

The heads shifted to the opposite end of the table, and McDevitt began to speak.

"I appreciate Lydia's comments and confidence. I have never been terribly interested in the White House. Woodburn is fine with me, but if we can accomplish what we've done here, or even match only a fraction of our success, we will have made a tremendous impact, nationally. This also will give us the opportunity to introduce our common sense approach to problems into other locales across the country. I agree we should give it a shot.

"The country needs dramatic changes. Everyone knows that, but they are afraid to try them because they aren't sure how well, or even if, they will work. By being too careful, they remain mired in their present state of stagnation and regress rather than progress. We can show that we have been successful here, and that our changes have been accepted by a wide range of the population—all classes, all races, all ages and incomes.

"It will be a lot of hard work, but I agree with Lydia. I say we go for the brass ring. And if we don't make it, we'll force the two major parties to play the game our way, address our issues and do what we want in the end. It worked for Perot. It can work for Chase and McDevitt. And, to be honest with you, I really think we can win this thing."

"Thank you, Henry," Judge Ward said. "Now," looking across the table, he said, "let's begin with our flamboyant developer. Ben?"

Bartolavich lowered his head and rested his arms on the table. He looked at the group with a painfully serious expression. "I'm all for a run for the presidency. I always have been, and I think you two can make it a real horse race. I don't know if you can pull it off, but I know I can guarantee you the financial backing of some of the largest contributors to the two major parties.

"They will want to be on your list and not be left out. They've been donating to both of the majors in the past. So, they'll just reduce their payments to them and also give to you. God knows they'll want to be recognized if you win. But you're going to have to be careful about beating on the construction trades and developers, Hank. I've seen you. When you get started on the environmental, tree-hugging soapbox, you can get the crowd to a point that they'll be ready to lynch anyone who buys a box of nails at a hardware store. We all aren't bad guys in black hats."

"You have to understand that I can't . . . ." McDevitt began, but Bartolavich continued speaking, waving McDevitt off.

"I'm not telling you what to say or how to campaign," he explained. "I'm just saying that when you get the juices flowing, it can get a bit scary to anyone who owns a backhoe. You make the run your way. My money will be behind you because I believe you can turn us around, and I believe in your approach to crime, taxation and your commitment to education and full employment. I just want to be frank and tell you exactly what I see and what I recommend."

Laughing slightly, Bartolavich pointed to the opposite end of the table. "I'll leave it to Lydia to keep you on a tight leash, or maybe we'll have her address the development and environmental issues. She can say the same thing, but she makes it sound a lot nicer. Sort of like taking castor oil and chasing it down with a shot of Jack Daniels."

Laughs and a few snickers came from the others in the group.

"Thank you, Ben," the judge said. "Who would like to go next?"

"I'll share my thoughts now, judge," said Saundra Price. "As you know, I sit on a number of boards throughout the peninsula. To a man, and I do mean 'man,' the response to what Hank has done is overwhelmingly positive."

"And with the women, Saundra?" McDevitt said, offering a thin smile.

"Not so good. Oh, don't get me wrong, I'd say it's 60 to 70 percent positive. But not as high as with the men.

They're 80 percent in your corner.

"I am all for a run for the White House. Price Poultry and every farm on the shore will proudly support one of its own. We also have verbal backing from agribusiness and research interests across the country. But when we do it, and I say when because I'm confident it will happen, I suggest you take a little of the sharpness off the point of your sword. Tone down the excitable words. Pause a little before you let the tiger out into the open. Still have him in there, ready to pounce, but bring him out only when it suits the situation. Sometimes, Hank, try to hide the fangs."

"So you want more of a double-talking, two-faced approach?" McDevitt responded. Although his tone was light and humorous, Saundra did not pick up that message and gave a sharp reply.

"No! That is not what I'm saying and you know it!" she snapped.

"I was joking, Saundra," McDevitt explained, smiling. "I understand your comment."

She returned the smile and continued, a bit more softly. "I'm not saying be different than you really are, Henry. God knows we love you, and you've gotten this far by being the real thing. I'm just saying, in the so-called age of political enlightenment, a few of the ladies need a softer, nicer, smoother candidate. That's all I want to say. But I am with Lydia and Henry one thousand percent. Count me in."

"Thank you, Saundra," the judge said. "Okay, Admiral. How do you see it."

"I say he doesn't change one damn thing. The direct approach has gotten him calls to be on the cover of nearly every weekly news magazine, and it will be sharing the solid truth of his convictions that will carry him into the Oval Office."

"Well, I'm not surprised by that comment, Admiral Jennings," Saundra said, rolling her eyes. Her response was followed by laughs from a few of the others.

"Well, I'm sure glad I didn't disappoint you, Ma'am," the Admiral said, showing his teeth from across the table. "But

I mean it. Take the hard edge, the country realism out of Hank and you've got another manipulated, false, run-of-the-mill politician. People love him because of what he says, how he says it. It's what he is.

"If Hank isn't the real thing, they'll know it. If he starts to hold back, they'll feel it, sense it. And somewhere down inside—where they have a hot fire burning for him right now, the flames will get a little smaller—they'll be disappointed. Oh, sure, they'll still vote for him. But," the admiral paused and held up his finger, "here's the key. They won't have the zeal and the drive to carry their whole family and everybody else they know along with them in the voting booth. That will be the difference, the crucial difference.

"Give them the real thing and they'll go with him to the end of the Earth. Soften him up, and you'll reduce the percentage of votes he captures by 6 to 9 percent, and in a three-way race that will be critical. But, I'm in. I say they go for it, right now, as soon as they can get an announcement together. And, if you can keep him hot, and keep his people on fire, I think he and Lydia will make it."

"I agree with the Admiral," said Elyse Delmond, cutting in immediately. "If you take the bite out of the candidate, then you take the teeth out of their campaign. I'm not going to talk long, but I say we should go for it. I'll add that I think Lydia will be Henry's greatest asset. She'll sway the undecided women. She also will carry a lot of the men because of her proven successful business approach in Maryland, because she's a good looking woman, and, primarily, because she's a strong woman who is not trying to be a man. She can play hardball, but she doesn't look like she hates every man in the process."

Laughter and a few claps greeted a smile and quick nod given by Lydia Chase.

"No way we should wait," Delmond said. "This is the year. The time is now."

"Well, it seems that I'm the last to share my thoughts on this important matter," Judge Ward said. "I'd like to preface my remarks by saying that I find it amazing that in this small state, that is almost unknown to many off the East Coast, we're sitting here discussing the future course of American regional politics and, possibly, the future of our country.

"If these proceedings were being recorded, some would think there were seven slightly unbalanced dreamers at this table. For who could imagine that the governor of the second smallest state, and the governor of our fine moderate-sized neighbor to the west, would seriously be considering a run for the White House?

"But the state of the country is such that people are so disappointed in the present situation that there is a very good opportunity for a third party to move ahead and capture the presidency. Who thought we could do it here, and we did, in Delaware. Then, no one thought it would work, and a coalition formed and it has been working quite well. There is no meaningful opposition to our Victims Rights Coalition.

"I agree that we move forward immediately. Maybe there's a bit of selfishness in my recommendation, but I want to make sure I'm around to see this happen. I can't afford to wait four more years like some of my young associates here tonight."

McDevitt and Chase exchanged glances and nodded. The others smiled as the comment caused soft laughter.

"Now," the judge continued, "I am not going to suggest a tone or philosophy for your campaign. You two will do that, just like others in the catchy slogan business will come up with a marketing theme and design.

"I want you to consider what might happen from announcement day on." His tone became more serious. His cold, gray eyes stared from McDevitt to Chase and to each face around the room. "These two people will be examined, stalked and dissected by the dirty tricks teams of the two major parties. Forget the news people. Amazingly, they actually like you two, and they've checked you out for the last several years because of your present positions.

"The major parties will be scared to death of what you have the potential to do—embarrass them into addressing issues that they have purposely ignored, coming up with common sense solutions that could have been done decades ago and, most importantly, taking away their power.

"Their control of power—the ability to dispense favors, make tradeoffs and orchestrate backroom deals, even between each other, is what they fear losing most.

"Forget their candidates, your opponents. The party leaders don't care about them. They are expendable, easily replaced in four years. But to have to exist for any time period without control, without the ability to use their power, with having to go and ask McDevitt of Delaware and Chase from Maryland for help . . . . My God! The entire concept is so foreign, so absurd, that—and I say this in all seriousness—they will not let it happen. They will not let you win. They will not let you enter the White House."

The judge paused. No one moved at the table. No one spoke in the room.

Facing McDevitt, then looking over at Chase, the judge continued. "Make the run. Lay out the issues and your solutions. Pray for a miracle, but realize that you will, at best, be providing a blueprint for others to use to solve some of our country's problems.

"Stand up and preach the best ideas you've got and they will listen. Oh, how they will listen and cheer. But also know that if your message starts to move, if your numbers start to climb, if it looks like you can win, there will be someone placed in the crowd at one of the campaign stops—and he or she will have been paid to cut you down."

"What are you saying, judge?" demanded Elyse Delmond.

"What the judge is saying," McDevitt replied calmly, "is that if it looks like we're going to win they will try to take us out, anyway they can, even if it means using a bullet."

Lydia Chase took up the conversation. "Hank and I have been aware of this for some time. We're not naive. But we've pushed that issue aside and agree that what we have to say must be shared. We're ready to win, and we have a very strong force of advisers and excellent security staff who are aware of the potential for danger. We're still going to go forward."

Judge Ward raised his hand, signaling he wanted to continue. "I'm not suggesting you decide not to run, I'm trying to lay out the worst case possibilities in front of all of us at the beginning. After all, I won't be a target, but you two will.

"But there is one more situation that may arise. I'll share that and then I'll be through. If they can't, or if they decide not to get to you by harming you physically, they will try to make a deal. And, believe me, if figures in the polls and financial support indicate you will win, the leverage you will have will be enormous. You will be able to get anything you want from them."

"Please explain the term 'anything,' judge," Lydia said.

"From personal wealth, to tangible goods, to a place on the cabinet, to your own government agency, to indefinite control and power of almost any corporation or entity that you desire. And I did not use the words 'within reason' in my explanation. Reason, at the point when they must approach you, will not exist.

"If and when that point in time comes, I must ask that you consult with us, as a group, before you give them any answer. I think that is a reasonable request. We've pledged our unconditional moral and financial support, that's all we ask in return."

"I agree," said Lydia, "but I don't see us making any deals, judge. I really don't. How do you feel, Hank?"

"I'll be willing to meet and discuss any offer that we might experience or be asked to consider. But, like Lydia, I see both of us surviving, winning and working together for the next four years on Pennsylvania Avenue. But you've got my word to come to all of you if anything like what the judge just described happens."

"Fine," said Judge Ward, rising to take the hands that were each offered by McDevitt and Chase, who walked to his sides. The others stood and applauded.

"Now," said Saundra Price, "let's make the damn announcement this week and go out and give them hell!"

October 2004

S ome consider the 2004 presidential election one of the most unusual in U.S. history. President Melvin Ellis Caurnfield, the Democratic Party winner of the presidency in 2000, resigned over irregularities involving his personal agreements with leaders of two South American drug cartels. It was proven that Caurnfield and his brother-in-law, who was serving as his cabinet secretary of drug enforcement, had allowed "a limited number" of illegal drugs to enter the country on U.S. military aircraft in return for laundered contributions to help pay off Caurnfield's massive campaign debt.

A plea bargain agreement saved the nation the embarrassment of impeachment proceedings. But, immediately after he and six White House staff associates were "assigned" to six years in a white-collar federal penitentiary—but before they were taken into custody—Caurnfield committed suicide in the Lincoln Bedroom.

With Justice Department lawyers and FBI agents frantically pursuing a very clear money trail of tainted contributions that led to more than 120 Democratic congressmen and women, the once powerful political machine disintegrated. When the smoke cleared, the liberal/socialistic wing of the party, which had been in control for seven decades, came out on top, forming the new Progressive Liberal Party (PLP).

The PLP's membership included a large number of splinter groups—primarily members of major civil rights organizations, high profile feminist groups and several big labor unions. The PLP's presidential candidate, Carlotta Benton, was a 46-year-old black woman who had served two terms as a U.S. Representative from Massachusetts.

Her vice presidential running mate was Alfonse "Big Al" Rispolli, a 65-year-old New Yorker and former president of the International Brotherhood of Laborers, Longshoremen and Skilled Trades Mechanics (I.B.L.L.S.T.M.). His enemies described him as a longtime Washington lobbyist of questionable talent and dubious character.

The media rated the pair's chances of providing charisma and excitement to the campaign as "minus 10" on a 1-to-10 scale.

Ignoring the traditional primary and convention selection process, the PLP candidates were appointed by the organization's executive board. In the closed committee meeting, diversity of representation was paramount and one's capabilities were secondary. During the proceedings, one excited board member—with a doctorate in statistics from a pedigreed, Ivy League institution of higher learning—calculated that if the new party could capture the black, female and labor votes, the PLP would win the election by more than 20 percent of the popular vote with minimal campaigning and a small amount of capital.

It took several minutes for the board members to return to the meeting's agenda, as the PLP leaders were congratulating each other on the certainty of victory in the upcoming election.

However, the new party soon found that planning on paper has little relation to the real world. Five weeks before the election, the PLP was attracting 13 percent of the popular vote . . . and there were indications that its popularity was headed in one direction—straight down into the single digits.

The Republican Party was shattered after the 2002 Congressional elections, following scandals associated with the GOP's affiliation with the religious right. Even worse, however, were illegal contributions from corporate lobbyists and kickbacks from Asian- and South American-based conglomerates to GOP party leaders in return for their staunch defense of the highly unpopular and disastrous NAFTA, GATT and APFTP treaties.

Those three agreements, signed before the end of the century, were bleeding the country's manufacturing base, but party leaders had refused to come out against the unpopular covenants and demand their repeal.

Added fundamentalist pressure from anti-abortion crusaders sapped the strength of the Republicans and their big tent, welcome-all philosophy folded like a house of cards in a monsoon.

The strongest coalition resulting from the GOP's self-inflicted implosion was the States Rights Assembly. It promoted individual, family and state responsibility, a flat 14 percent income tax and elimination of a number of entitlement programs that had been mandated by the federal government.

The torch bearers for the newly formed SRA were long-time, former GOP fixture Scott Woodyard and well-known Democrat Shirley Griffith-Tallant.

Woodyard had served as a U.S. Senator from Maine and was a Housing and Urban Development Cabinet secretary in the early 1990s. Also an ex-combat Marine, he served as a state department consultant to bureaus in the Middle East and Eastern Europe. A long history of government service, broad based experience and charismatic public speaking talents made him an attractive choice.

His running mate, Shirley Griffith-Tallant was a former U.S. District Court judge, appointed by a Democratic president. A review of her sentencings showed that her anti-crime record was not strong. As the campaign progressed, some of her public comments regarding her stand on social issues were beginning to affect the SRA ticket negatively. While she believed in state's rights, Griffith-Tallant was vocal about her belief that the public needed "to care for society's poor, homeless, uneducated victims" and that "we all"—meaning the middle class—must be willing to spend considerable money to do so, even if it meant raising taxes.

As one editorial writer put it, "Griffith-Tallant was obviously selected to complement the SRA ticket. Instead, her presence to date has only insured that its ticket—and its standard bearers—will be punched out of the ring."

With a popularity poll indicating 30 percent, and trying to maintain that level, the new party did not look like it was heading toward the top very fast.

Interestingly, the only political convention televised during the 2004 presidential campaign was the gavel-to-gavel coverage of the Victims Rights Coalition (VRC), which had already selected its candidates before the party's Baltimore convention.

Delaware Governor Henry McDevitt topped a ticket that was approved enthusiastically, and he was balanced by neighboring Maryland Governor Lydia Chase in the vice presidential slot.

Early in his presidential campaign, McDevitt proclaimed Victims Rights Day and asked every person in the country who had been a crime victim, or was related to one, to hang a black cloth—sheet, flag, blanket—from the front window of his or her home or apartment.

On the appointed morning, tens of thousands of black banners were displayed throughout the country— in cities and towns and some were even seen waving from automobile windows. Later in the day, McDevitt held a news conference and announced that those victimized people and their families—not the criminals and their misguided supporters—were his only concern.

The result was a groundswell of support that swept across the states like a tidal wave. People believed that through McDevitt and Chase the family unit and working men and women had finally gotten a voice in government. Five weeks before the election, the VRC had a lock on 29 percent of the popular vote, with interest rising.

The policies suggested by McDevitt and Chase were similar to the platform adopted by the SRA, but McDevitt and Chase appeared to be more friendly, charismatic and had a better rapport with the media than Woodyard and Griffith-Tallant.

Both the SRA and VRC advocated the death penalty, state's rights and an end to affirmative action. They wanted major inner city redevelopment, workfare and improved housing for all, plus safer schools and communities. They also stressed deportation of illegal immigrants and convicted drug dealers, a dramatic reduction in foreign imports and the rebuilding of America's faltering manufacturing power base.

McDevitt, because of his demonstrated success as Delaware's governor, however, was viewed as a friend of the environment. Woodyard, with his old GOP ties—constantly highlighted by his opponents—was hurting in the environmental area. Plus, McDevitt's polices had worked in his state. Woodyard's had potential but were unproven.

During the vice presidential debate, aired on the seven major networks, Lydia Chase buried both Griffith-Tallant and "Big Al" Rispolli, the latter who was described in a national newspaper as "a walking, breathing definition of clueless that should be placed in a laboratory for further observation and research to see if the body hosted any brain matter that lived."

During the three presidential debates the only meaningful contest was between Woodyard and McDevitt, with Benton serving as minor window dressing. However, because of the Benton-Rispolli presence, and its ability to drain diehard liberal votes, the three-way contest was shaping up to be an interesting horserace.

With two weeks to go before the election, the percentages looked like they were frozen in a block of ice.

The SRA (old GOP) held a 32 percent popular vote and close to 180 electoral votes, mainly from large states in the East, Midwest and support on the West Coast. Analysts predicted, however, that it would take a miracle for the front-running team to pull out the election with a clear-cut victory.

McDevitt and Chase's Victims Rights Coalition was attracting nearly 30 percent of the populace and more than 140 electoral votes. While popular with individuals across the country, the VRC was most likely to capture a number of smaller states in the West, South and Midwest with less electoral college power. Its power base was a conglomeration of disgruntled individuals and small state alliances. Despite a budding grass-roots-level organization and an informal national network, the VRC had done astonishingly well. But its support was broad but thin and a clear path into the White House was not to be in the cards for McDevitt and Chase in 2004.

The Benton and Rispolli experiment in liberal socialism was an embarrassing disaster, with the labor and minority coalition attracting, at best, 10 percent of the national vote and hoping for 6 electoral votes. Those figures were considered high, since experts knew that many of those polled would not bother to enter the voting booth on Election Day.

If the remaining percent of the country's undecided voters did not move in one major direction, there would be no winner on election night.

Several members of the House of Representatives were preparing for the special session that would be needed to select the next President of the United States. While some citizens thought the stalemate would be historic and exciting, those involved in operating the government were seriously worried. Nervous phone calls were being made by powerful figures from offices in such widely scattered sites as the Pentagon, the United Nations, the State Department, the Hague, the Kremlin and Wall Street.

The power brokers who ran the United States and every other country in the world from corporate board rooms, foreign estates and financial conference suites called a meeting, summoning Scott Woodyard and Henry McDevitt.

The command performance was held at 6 a.m., on Sunday morning, the week of Halloween, in an elegant row house in Philadelphia's Society Hill, not far from Independence Hall.

Ten minutes apart, separate black Cadillac limousines delivered the two major presidential candidates to the historic home originally owned by Jennifer Ross MacDowell, wife of a Colonial printer, patriot and drinking partner of Ben Franklin and John Adams. The candidates' presence was treated as a clandestine operation, with pickup and delivery arranged by contract operatives who had previously been on the payroll of the Central Intelligence Agency. Israel's Mossad and MI5 of British Intelligence.

To the rest of the world, including their respective staffs, portions of their respective Secret Service details and their families, Scott Woodyard and Henry McDevitt were still sleeping comfortably on that crisp, fall weekend morning. Neither would miss their scheduled afternoon campaign appearances—Woodyard in Camden, New Jersey, and McDevitt in Philadelphia's Logan Circle.

Five men and one woman were seated at the highly polished antique table in the Colonial-era dining room when the two men, who had been waiting in separate adjacent chambers, were invited to enter.

The historic home had been used for a variety of unique purposes over the years. At one time it housed a confidential government documents research agency. Later, it was used as a guest house for visiting foreign dignitaries. In the 1960s, it became a safe house for political defectors and, during one period in the 1970s, it was a meeting site for the staffs of both candidates before and after the Carter-Ford presidential debate, held in the nearby Walnut Street Theater.

Early on this fall morning "The Jenny," as it was called, was being used to address America's current political crisis and arrive at an important decision that would maintain the United States' uninterrupted operation as the world leader. International power brokers were there to ensure that a smooth transition of power would continue, as had occurred following every change in administration since President George Washington transferred the leadership of America's executive office to John Adams in 1797.

The gleaming dining room table was impressive and large, giving the impression the room was used for meetings more than for dining.

Henry McDevitt and Scott Woodyard shook hands, showing genuine mutual respect as they greeted each other after entering through separate doors. As the two men took their seats, the six hosts introduced themselves.

The candidates had never met any of those assembled, but their names, reputations, wealth and power were known—but rarely discussed or mentioned in the media. They included:

Joshua Kruper, executive director and chief operating officer of International Systems and Securities Affiliated—headquarters in Bern, Switzerland, and branches in 35 countries on five continents.

Malcom Mott Copeland, chief executive officer and president of InTellNet Banking and Satellite Systems Enterprises—corporate center in New York City, with offices in 59 cities around the world.

Heinrich Kamft, executive director of the World Universal Satellite Telecommunications and Photonics Research and Industries—headquarters in Berlin, with satellite bureaus around the world and regional branches in Prague, Warsaw, Sydney, London, Lima, Havana, Ho Chi Minh City, Los Angeles, Houston and New York.

Diane Berring-Goldner, majority stockholder, president and chief operating officer of Amalgamated Securities & Commodities Trading Industries, Ltd.—main office in London, with financial branches in more than 50 capital cities.

Mark K. Weinberg IV, president and world-wide production and research liaison for WorldWide Environmental Analysis and Production Inc.—corporate and research headquarters, Dallas, with offices and research complexes in 87 cities in 52 countries.

Amid Faghri Shalem, president of PetrolKey Energy Supply and Discovery, Ltd.—central office in Ryiadh, Saudi Arabia, with representatives in offices in New York, Philadelphia, Galveston, Havana, San Diego, Hong Kong, London, Montreal and Buenos Aires.

There were no smiles during the introductions and the focus immediately shifted to the purpose of the meeting.

"Good morning, gentlemen," Malcom Mott Copeland said. "We have exactly 45 minutes to resolve this crisis that your combined popularity has created."

He smiled but no one else moved. The three

valets/guards, who were obviously armed and alert, watched from the shadowed corners of the room. Two well-trained servants, who also doubled as corporate body-guards, were ready to pour coffee and tea as requested.

"This country, America," Copeland continued, "needs an elected president. It needs him smiling in front of the cameras and making an acceptance speech on election night, and it must be either of you. We . . . speaking for my colleagues at the table and a quite a few others whom we represent . . . do not want, nor will we allow, this election to be steered through the United States House of Representatives. We, and the American people, would have little control over such a media circus and the results could be disastrous for the entire world.

"Our predecessors stopped it from happening when George Wallace made his run for the White House in the late 1960s, and we pulled the rug from under Mr. Perot in 1992. Although, I admit, allowing him to come up with his own excuse was an error on our part. No one could figure out how he dreamed up that story about vigilantes interrupting his daughter's wedding, but the result was the same. In the end, he received only enough votes from a small hard-core following to make the election mildly interesting. However, our present situation, while being quite fascinating to some, is, frankly, too unpredictable for those of us who matter."

A shrill voice broke the calm. "The world's governments, economy, communications and trading markets need a predictable structure!" All heads turned toward Diane Berring-Goldner, who interrupted Copeland and thrust her comments into the mix.

"Gentlemen," she stared at the two candidates, "we cannot risk the turmoil of the international trading markets on the morning following an unresolved American presidential election. Uncertainty of this magnitude will destabilize the world economy and could even generate a spiral effect that would bring down some fragile governments. Even some seemingly well-established political systems could crumble."

"What we need," Copeland added, resuming control, "is a decision this morning. We need to know which of you will win and who will be the gracious loser. Who will pull ahead, because the other will drop out of the race within the next two days and, essentially, that will give the election away."

Woodyard and McDevitt stared at their hosts.

No one spoke.

"It is now 6:09 gentleman, and we have 36 minutes left."

The next comment came from Mark Weinberg, head of the Dallas-based environmental conglomerate.

"We are prepared to offer the loser, the sacrificial lamb, substantial compensation. The person who makes the decision to lose, to give up the quest in a prearranged fashion and walk away from this presidential race will be giving up a lot, forfeiting what is considered, by those on the outside, to be the most powerful position in the world." Weinberg smiled as he said the words and nodded to his colleagues around the table.

"We are in a position to grant that person rewards that some would think are impossible to deliver, for we have unlimited connections and our power reaches everywhere. There is nothing we cannot do."

"We are not mean spirited. We are not threatening," Copeland said, smoothly regaining control of the session again. "We are business persons who represent every aspect of commerce on this planet, from banking to food, from science to the environment. We must insure that we will continue to operate without needless interruption. We are not in the business of taking chances, and we do not like uncertainty. Unfortunately, that's were we find ourselves at this point and it is not acceptable. Are there any questions?"

Under the circumstances, with the fast approaching deadline, the brief five seconds of silence seemed like several minutes.

McDevitt spoke. "What's the procedure?"

The hosts looked at each other.

"I beg your pardon?" Amid Faghri Shalem of Saudi Arabia asked.

"Well," McDevitt said, "do we announce our decision right now? Ask for our bag of gold, or stock certificates in one of Herr Kruper's unnumbered Swiss bank accounts, or can Senator Woodyard and I have a few moments in private to talk this over? After all, I would think that we're the ones who should be given an opportunity to work things out to our mutual satisfaction."

Copeland looked at his colleagues. Nods were exchanged. "All right, Governor, Senator. You have 15 minutes to make a decision. It's 6:14."

Turning to the guards, Copeland said, "Take them to the General Wayne Suite, upstairs. Make sure it's secure, and I want two men outside the door. Have them back here at 6:30, exactly!"

"Yes, sir," the chief guard said. As one shadow led McDevitt and Woodyard out the door, the other guard followed at the rear. In the room with the world's power figures, the ornately carved cherry grandfather clock chimed four tones, announcing 6:15 a.m.

As the wooden, paneled door to the upstairs suite was closed behind them, Woodyard turned to McDevitt and said, "A fine fix you've got us into Ollie."

McDevitt laughed and raised his hand to his lips to signal that the room was probably bugged.

Woodyard nodded since he had assumed that as well.

Without speaking the two top candidates for the United States presidency walked into the spacious bathroom, turned on all the water faucets and—with one sitting on the toilet lid and the other on the edge of the bathtub—worked out a deal.

Annoyed on the first floor, Copeland scowled and shut off the audio receiver that had been placed in the center of the table. "Well," he addressed his colleagues, "it seems we've underestimated our guests. I guess we'll just have to wait until they return, in 10 minutes."

🌿   🌿   🌿

At 6:30 exactly, Woodyard and McDevitt, accompanied by two "escorts," re-entered the Jenny's dining room. As they took their seats, McDevitt produced a sealed white envelope and slid it across the polished tabletop to Malcom Copeland.

The hosts looked puzzled, and McDevitt said, "Allow me to introduce the next president of the United States, Sen. Scott Woodyard."

The hosts gave polite applause, smiled and relayed their congratulations. Before Copeland could inquire about McDevitt's letter, the Delaware Governor said, "Greetings from U.S. District Court Judge Clayton Ward, Mr. Copeland. I believe you know the judge?"

"Of course. We haven't spoken in years. How is he?"

"Good. In his 70s and still sharp as a tack, as you will see when you read my list of demands."

The room became silent as Copeland broke the gold foil seal on the heavy gray envelope.

Keeping the original, Malcom handed the one copy to the guard and told him to make enough additional copies to distribute to the others present. As he unfolded four, legal-size pages, Copeland said, "The governor certainly seems to have come prepared to our meeting."

"Obviously," sniped Diane Berring-Goldner, the group's financial market wizard.

McDevitt used the opportunity to respond. "The judge warned me that a situation like this might occur, especially if our effort had a dramatic effect on the campaign. At the time, I though he was exaggerating. But, when I received your 'invitation' earlier this week, I met with him and my senior advisers, as he had asked that I do. That document is the result of deliberations that also included vice presidential candidate Lydia Chase. I trust it all is in order and the terms will be accomplished in a timely manner. I will add that I will not accept anything less than immediate complete approval and acceptance of our demands."

"Can you summarize this for the group as they await their copies?" Copeland asked.

Woodyard, the future president, had made a verbal agreement with McDevitt about campaign issues and promises. But he had not been informed of McDevitt's demands to the committee. Therefore, the soon-to-be president was as interested in what was to be said as the committee members.

"Of course," McDevitt said. "First, let me assure you that I have the highest faith in President Woodyard's competence and honor. We have agreed on five main points that he will pursue and upon which we are in total agreement:

• A balanced budget within two years of his assuming office;

• A repeal of the NAFTA/GATT/APFTP fiascoes, but they will be replaced with an international trade policy more favorable to the U.S.;

• A 12 percent federal income tax cut this year, and institution of a flat tax of between 13 and 16 percent during his first term;

• Dramatic serious campaign financing reform; and

• A 60 percent reduction in illegal immigration, nation wide, by the end of his first term.

"If he accomplishes all of these promises, I will actively campaign for him during his re-election campaign. If he does not, I will oppose him openly, and run again. But the next time, I will not drop out of the race."

Copies of McDevitt's demands had been distributed around the table.

"That sums up my agreement with the future president. But," the governor continued, "now, from you, and to some degree, from President Woodyard, I need the following:

"My own state . . . ."

"You have your own state!" snapped Heinrich Kamft, the German solar scientist.

"Not quite," said McDevitt. "Look at the copy of the map that's provided. It shows Delaware consuming about half of the Delmarva Peninsula. I want it all. I want the nine counties of Maryland's Eastern Shore and the two counties of the Commonwealth of Virginia to become one geographical entity that will operate more efficiently. That state will become DelMarVa."

As they looked at the map, McDevitt continued. "There is no logical reason, except for arbitrary boundaries drawn hundreds of years ago, for this unique land mass to involve three state governments. The unification of this common geographical and cultural region will benefit all of the people and enable one central state authority to administer it more efficiently. Basically, it is a sensible fiscal decision."

"What reaction do you expect from the citizens of the region, governor?" Diane Berring-Goldner asked.

"According to one document we have discovered," McDevitt replied, "since 1870, and probably earlier, there has been serious interest in making the peninsula one unified state. At that time, the Eastern Shore citizens were eager, and Delawareans were, too. The First State recognized the opportunity to double its size, but there was a dispute over the new state's name and the plan died. However, with uncanny regularity, every few decades the idea resurfaced. As recently as 1998, two Eastern Shore delegates called for succession from Maryland, and even submitted a bill to begin the process. It was defeated. But in 2002, five Delaware representatives and six Maryland delegates posed for a photograph in Delmar and vowed to continue to work toward Delmarva's unification. I believe the time is right, and the people—not the state governments—will approve the idea overwhelmingly.

"Also, this consolidation will serve as a test for future mergers—such as northwestern Florida, which would be better served as part of Alabama, or the northern sliver of West Virginia, which could be joined to Pennsylvania or Ohio. The people in the Panhandle of Oklahoma might be better off as citizens of the state of Texas.

"With strained budgets, rising administrative expenses and spiraling energy costs and social service needs, regionalism is one way to maintain the character of an area but administer it more efficiently. Granted, much of the legislation to create this new state must go through Congress, and I will need President Woodyard's active backing.

"Second. I want an appointed six-year term—with an election held later for a second six-year term—for myself and vice governor Lydia Chase, who will resign as Maryland's governor to join me in serving DelMarVa.

"Third, I want legalized casino gambling in DelMarVa with no federal interference. I will use the income from five peninsula casinos to cut state income tax to zero within three years.

"Fourth, I will need substantial federal money for attractive highways—built without adverse effects upon the wetland environment on the Eastern Shore—that will lead to our cities and the new resort areas.

"Lastly, I will want federal support for a number of new economic and recreational programs. I need substantial funds for rejuvenation of the waterfowl and fisheries industries. The watermen are dying and I want high-tech research in the three DelMarVa Sea Grant Colleges to be operating at 10 times their current level in 18 months. I also will need federal assistance for large-scale urban renewal and job creation programs plus new state-initiated, anti-crime and anti-drug legislation that will be the harshest of any state in the union. This will probably necessitate building two new prisons and six boot camps within the peninsula during the next three years.

"Within six years, DelMarVa will be one of the top five tourist attractions in the country and its crime rate will be reduced to one quarter of its current level.

"These issues are non-negotiable and must be accepted before 6:45 a.m.," McDevitt smiled. "Now, according to my watch, you have 2 minutes for discussion and questions."

Stephanie Berring-Goldner leaned forward in her chair, her deep red lips moving rapidly. "Who do you think you are to come in here and make such outland . . . . ."

Copeland raised a hand and cut her off. The tension subsided.

"Very good, Governor McDevitt. Very good indeed."

"The judge is an excellent teacher," McDevitt replied. "Are we in agreement?"

"Yes. All five of your points will require federal approval, but," looking to Woodyard, Copeland continued, "I'm sure we can convince the Senate and House to approve these requests as they are tucked into several other routine bills. All right, Senator? Excuse me, I mean Mr. President, is this agreeable?"

Woodyard agreed with a nod, then added. "I'll also be glad to create a regional commission that will be charged with supporting and studying the experimental State of Del-MarVa concept and its applicability to other areas of the country. Obviously, you already have the governor of Maryland's approval, and Governor Anthony Randolph Lee in Virginia should be able to be convinced to give up two counties for the sake of the nation."

"It might be costly," McDevitt said.

Woodyard laughed, "Well, maybe we'll just have Ms. Berring-Goldner cash in a few portfolios and buy the two counties for us."

Everyone responded with laughter except the London financier.

Handshakes went around the room and the candidates were delivered back to their hotels in time for breakfast.

That afternoon, in the City of Brotherly Love, Delaware Governor Henry McDevitt, Victims Rights Coalition presidential candidate, announced he was quitting the race for pressing personal reasons and he planned to focus more on the critical needs of his home state. Following a very satisfactory meeting with representatives of the States Rights Assembly, he urged all of his followers to join with him and support Senator Scott Woodyard.

The next morning the press announced that the 2004 presidential race was essentially over.

8

January 2005-April 2007

At his inauguration on a bitterly cold January morning in 2005, President Scott Woodyard stood before the nation and said, "The United States will maintain the best of its history and pursue the brightest avenues in the future. Tradition and change—sensible, well-planned and beneficial change—will work together closely.

"There will be tough decisions in the years ahead. At first, these decisions may seem to conflict with our traditions, folkways and culture. But, the result will be a country and a world that will offer the best environment and hope and promise for all of our people."

No one knew the significance of those remarks more than Delaware Governor Henry McDevitt and Maryland Governor Lydia Chase, who had front row seats beside the new president's family.

In the months that followed, the citizens of the 14 counties in DelMarVa were informed that major changes—to be accomplished through cooperation among representatives of the three states and the federal government—were under study.

During 2006, public information sessions, open hearings and committee recommendations resolved that a new state of DelMarVa would be established on Jan. 1, 2007.

The current governor, Henry McDevitt, and his appointed vice governor, Lydia Chase, would take their oaths of office in Delmar, in the town that had always proudly proclaimed it was "Too Big for One State." Every citizen of DelMarVa was welcomed to attend the public event.

The executives' terms would enable them to lead the region for six years. Until the new capitol building was constructed on acreage already purchased between Denton and Federalsburg, DelMarVa's proceedings would be conducted in the former State of Delaware's Legislative Hall in Dover. However, the governor's mansion would remain at Woodburn.

A special election of federal representatives and senators would be held in November. Concurrently, State of DelMarVa senators and delegates would be elected, and their terms would last four years. However, any legislative district could vote a delegate out of office at any time with a 50 percent non-confidence vote. In such a case, a special election would be held.

In addition, a new appointed body of citizen representatives would be seated in the DelMarVa legislature and be in session at the same time as the state's delegates. It would include members of 50 professions on the peninsula—such as farmers, business persons, teachers, laborers, health care professionals, insurance and real estate agents, artists, watermen, engineers, police officers, firefighters, grocers, horsemen, developers, environmentalists and more. They would be able to provide input on legislation under consideration by DelMarVa's elected delegates and senators.

"In this way," McDevitt said, "the average people will have an active voice in government and be in the state's chambers watching over the actions of their elected officials."

However, all of the publicized plans were subject to approval by the general population of the 14 counties on the peninsula.

Initially, response to the decision was mixed, but Chase and McDevitt visited every community in DelMarVa as part of a public relations blitz. They promised to end income tax, to reduce crime dramatically, imprison drug dealers and to improve employment, education and housing. "DelMarVa," Chase said, "will be a jewel that the rest of the country will follow."

Major employers from Perryville to Cape Charles and from St. Michaels to Wilmington signed on. To be against DelMarVa was going against a rising enthusiastic tide.

Blue (Delaware), red (Maryland) and gray (Virginia) bumper stickers appeared, signifying the colors of the proposed new state flag. Two minor league sports teams signed on to play in the new state—the DelMarValous Demons, a basketball franchise promised to make its headquarters in Wilmington. And the DelMarVa Diamonds, a semi-professional football team, announced plans to begin construction of a new stadium east of Salisbury.

Gradually, the trend caught on and the idea, identity and ideals of DelMarVa began to grow, attracting new businesses and spreading contagious enthusiasm.

Registered voter turnout reached an astonishing 63 percent at the special election, held on July 4, 2006. The result was 83 percent in favor of establishing the new state.

Five television networks immediately established bureaus, setting up studios outside Seaford, not far from the site of the new capital.

McDevitt and Chase, along with the newest state's federal representatives, took their oaths of office in January 2007. The next day, the governor signed the five-site casino agreement with Roger Dreyer, executive assistant and assistant financial officer of United Gaming Programs (UGP) Inc. of New Orleans. Preliminary construction began immediately on the 28-floor casino hotel in downtown Wilmington, along the city's "Riverwalk Promenade."

In April 2007, a formal groundbreaking press conference was held outside at the construction site, located on the banks of the Christiana River. Standing on an elevated platform near the water's edge, within the city's landmark Victorian train station, McDevitt was asked several questions about possible increases in crime because of DelMarVa's plans to plant five state-of-the-art gambling sites across the new state. He invited Vice Governor Chase, who had recently moved from the Maryland governor's mansion in Annapolis to her home in Easton, to answer that question.

"I am aware of those concerns," Chase said. "But we will use the income we receive from the gambling profits to increase the number and quality of our police forces, and we will keep organized crime out of the peninsula."

"Tom Harrison, *Baltimore Bullet.* That sounds nice, but since police corruption is a way of life, won't the presence of casinos increase the temptation to look the other way and take kickbacks?"

Calmly, Chase responded. "For some, of course. And, to be honest, it's understandable if you're a street cop making $36,000 a year and risking your life while street hoods are driving imported cars and hauling in 10 times your annual salary in less than one month. Our plan is for DelMarVa police officers in the state, counties, cities and small towns, to be placed on the exact same pay scale and meet the same requirements. Beginning this fall, the starting salary for a DelMarVa law enforcement officer will be $60,000 a year."

Reporters shouted in a burst for clarification, and Chase responded, "Let me have DelMarVa Police Commissioner Michael Pentak answer your questions."

"Is that figure definite, commissioner?"

"No," Pentak said. "It could actually be higher. There will be bonuses for officers who initiate major crime interdiction or make significant suggestions that are beneficial to the statewide police force.

"You have to realize that the vast majority of officers never go on the take. One of the reasons that some do is because they are paid too little and the temptation is great. We are taking the inclination away from those who might even think about it.

"But, more importantly, why should a state-appointed lawyer, who is paid by the government to provide free advice to help criminals get away with crime, make more than a police officer? Day in and day out, our police risk their lives to keep our communities safe. Frankly, it's stupid not to pay them more than someone who sits in a safe office and experiences no physical risk. No longer will our police officers be insulted each time they receive their paychecks. We intend to have the best police force in the country, and we can only achieve that if we treat our officers in a first-class manner. We intend to correct this situation as quickly as we can."

"How will this affect those already on the force?"

"As you know, all active troopers in all three former state police forces have been consolidated into one DelMarVa State Police organization, with barracks assignments from Claymont to Cape Charles. For the time being, our local and county forces will remain intact and independent.

"However, all current officers—in state, county and local jurisdictions—will be given substantial pay raises, before the end of the year, to bring them up to the scale that we will offer all new law enforcement personnel. Also, immediately following this announcement, we are anticipating applications from experienced state and federal police officers from around the country. We will consider all applications, but our first priority will be to take care of our current officers. However, we will be demanding more in the way of number of arrests, advanced educational degrees and designated time spent in community information and recreation programs from all DelMarVa police personnel. We will pay the best and expect the best in return."

"What other changes do you intend to make?" asked a reporter from Philadelphia.

"Our police stations, from the largest cities to the smallest towns, will be equipped with the latest in computerized technology, expanded UltraWeb and 3-I—International Interdiction Internet—capabilities and brand new vehicles, that will be traded in every two years. No more ghetto cruisers. We will fight crime with every asset we have, and we also will be embarking on a station modernization program that will upgrade every facility and link it to every other site in the state. Also, each police headquarters and substation will have continuous communication with FBI headquarters in Washington and Interpol links as well.

"I'd like to cut off the questions on this subject now. We have other plans and will keep you informed. Thank you."

Lydia Chase returned to the podium. "This press conference is to celebrate the construction of Casino Christina. Our first entertainment complex is named after the historic queen of Sweden, and it commemorates the first settlement in Wilmington, in 1638 on the banks of the Christiana River. Today, that beautiful river winds through New Castle County, and we feel it's an appropriate way to commemorate our significant historical heritage.

"The other four sites will be named appropriately, and we are open to suggestions. We also are planning a Disney-style theme park in the southern end of the state and are talking to three amusement-oriented corporations that will be bidding for that opportunity at the present time."

"Diane Kramer, WDMV-TV. Don't you think the emphasis on gambling will adversely affect the quality of life for the people of the state?"

"No. Not at all," Chase replied. "All players must have an authorized club card to play at any machine or gaming tables in DelMarVa casinos. Each citizen of DelMarVa will be issued a computerized card, similar to a driver's license, upon request if he or she is 21 or over. Citizens of DelMarVa will not be able to play over a pre-established monetary amount in any casino in the state during a one-month period, and that will be based upon their annual income.

"Visitors from other states will be given cards, but they will be able to spend as much as they desire. This will keep the level of money coming into the state high, but it will also insure that we reduce the gambling risks to our own citizens. Mr. Dreyer of UGP assures me that Casino Christina will be open in 18 months from today. That gives us a year and a half to establish our programming in place and prepare to implement thorough and thoughtful plans.

"As Governor McDevitt has said, by the end of our first term, DelMarVa will be one of the top five tourist destinations in the country. We have a seashore, camping and gaming establishments, horse racing, a planned theme park, centuries of history, world-class museums, new minor league sports teams and a top-level entertainment complex to be built between Route 301 and Chestertown. This jewel we are polishing will continue to shine more brightly."

"What about jobs and manufacturing?"

McDevitt moved toward the microphone. "We have two auto assembly plants in New Castle County that are operating at full capacity. At the present time, we are exploring several manufacturing overtures in the Route 40 area in the northwest section of the state—near Newark, Elkton and Perryville—as well as similar activity in the corridor between Salisbury and Cambridge.

"Also, several foreign shipbuilding firms and a domestic rail car manufacturer are looking at sites in downtown Wilmington and another major foreign manufacturing operation has bought land near Cape Charles in Northampton, our southernmost county. When these agreements are signed, we will have thousands of high-paying skilled jobs for both our inner-city and rural residents.

"Two new airports, capable of handling the largest planes, are being planned—one southwest of Salisbury and the other west of Rehoboth Beach.

"We are moving, and moving quickly. If we plan and work hard together, we can improve the quality of life for every one of our citizens, and that is the primary goal of every decision we make."

"Ronald Jamal, governor! *Black People's Mid-Atlantic Monthly.* There are many who do not like the way the new state is headed. They say this DelMarVa regional governmental concept is a loose cannon without oversight and that it is more suited for the Wild West. It seems that rules are allowed to be bent at the whim of the government, which is doing whatever it wants. What do you say to that?"

The news conference had taken an abrupt turn to the left. Everyone waited for the governor to respond to the hardball that had been thrown directly at his smiling head.

"Let me ask you this, Mr. Jamal. How many street murders have there been in Wilmington this year?"

"I'm not sure of the number, but I think . . . ."

"I know, Mr. Jamal. The answer is 3. Three! I know it's

still early in the year, but compare that against the 132 shootings in this city back in 1999. Compare the newspaper headlines six years ago with today. Where there were crack houses, we've put up parks and playgrounds. Also, there has been a significant increase in the number of state- government-backed, small family businesses.

"You are right, we are bending the rules. Hell, Mr. Jamal, we aren't bending them—we are breaking the old rules in half, and then throwing them out. This state is an example of cutting edge, 21st century government— part libertarian, part socialistic, part democratic. To be honest, I don't even know what to call it, but it's working and I am committed to using whatever power, resources and imagination my staff and our state workers have to make DelMarVa safe and fiscally solid. If those people who you say are so concerned have a better way of doing things, or they have more productive ideas, tell them to come and see me.

"And if they want to selfishly hold their magic answers until the next election, fine. They can tell their plans to the voters. And we can all see who is standing here after the next election. Thanks for your question. I truly appreciate it."

December 2007

It was a week before Christmas, and Charles Bettner was laughing so hard he found it difficult to breath. Gasping for air, he held court at the large table near the street-level window in the DelMarVa Division of Revenue cafeteria. The entire building knew that was the morning gathering place for the loud, rough and rowdy group of state revenue collectors.

Bettner was retired Army. He had spent 20 years in the Military Police and retired at 38. He immediately joined the IRS as a revenue officer, the clever name the hated agency used to identify its tax collectors. After 10 years there, he moved over to the state of Delaware's income collection and enforcement division. That was three years ago.

Charles was a tall, bald, muscular man with the noticeable veins and muscles in his arms indicating a weightlifter's appearance. He was single, had no friends and lived to work. Openly admitting he never wanted the responsibilities of management, Bettner found his calling as the man who grabbed as much tribute as he could for Caesar and relished every minute of the chase.

Using his power to beat on the lowest of the low— most of whom were down-on-their-luck, hapless victims of poor business deals and bad luck—made Charles Bettner's day.

His career in collections was a continuation of his turnkey training in the military and one that the government appreciated. Whatever the reason, be it a personality defect or a need to exercise power, Charles Bettner loved his job. He often said his dream was to die on a deadbeat's doorstep, waving cheerfully to the tow truck driver as he hauled away the poor bastard's car.

"So, we're in this pathetic shack of a house, see," said Charles, sharing an old war story with six colleagues. "It's not much more than a lean-to, and the wife is a real hog and she is crying, I mean wailing. The husband is sweating. Actually, a river of liquid is pouring off this sap's bald head, and he is shaking so much I think he's going to wet his pants.

"All the neighbors are out on the street watching, because we have three tow trucks lined up to haul off his pickup, his wife's car and his kid's new jeep. Now, you've got to understand that this is in a quiet, little, run down development on a Sunday morning . . . ."

"Sunday morning!" one of the other collectors shouted, roaring as others members of the morning audience slammed their hands against the metal tabletop.

"Yes! Sunday! People are outside in their robes. They're walking their dogs, picking up the morning paper. But they won't return inside because they don't want to miss anything."

"So what happened?" somebody shouted.

"Me and Reds, my partner, tell the deadbeat that we need the money for all of the outstanding taxes, *immediately*, or we're taking all three vehicles to the yard and we're putting them up for auction. I tell you, it was a rush to see this idiot turn into a glob of jelly. He starts begging me for more time. He tells me that he can't get to the bank until Monday. Won't we give him one more day?

"Hell, I was calling him and leaving Final Notices Before Seizure taped to his front door for six weeks, and he never got back to me. So there was no room for discussion or mediation. At this level, it became personal. You understand?"

The nods from his audience indicated total agreement. "Personal, is right," said one of the others, echoing approval.

"But before I can reply, Reds, he says to the guy, 'Don't you have a bank cash card?' God, I am dying. We are talking six thousand dollars outstanding, and Reds thinks this mope can get it out of an automatic teller on Easter Sunday morning!"

The whole table let loose and the storyteller had to wait for the audience to return to listening mode level.

"The wife is calling her mother," Bettner said, "asking for a check. But I shout out to her that I need cash or a certified check. You should have seen her eyes. They looked like somebody just hit her in the butt with a cattle prod, and I'm wondering what the in-laws must be saying about the loser she married.

"So, after I have them both by the throat, I inform them I'm feeling kind. And after all, it is Easter Sunday, the Lord's Day, and all. Then I say they've got until 10 o'clock, Monday, sharp, to deliver the $6,200 to me in my office—or I'm coming back the following night. And if I do, I won't take the cars, I'll take their damn house!"

Silence.

"You could do that?" one of the younger collectors asked.

"No! Of course not," said Charles, smiling. "What do you think we are, heartless?"

Another roar from the appreciative audience.

"I was just scaring him and his old lady. But, then I explained that I have three tow trucks out on the curb. They have to be paid for, and I'm not going to cover the bill out of my pocket.

"They were quick learners, figuring they had to pay up for the tows. But dumb as they were, they knew that was better than hauling off all three cars. The bill was $186—$62 each. Oh, if you could have been there at that moment," Charles smiled, reliving the scene.

"Reds was standing beside me by this time, but he moved, very quickly, to the front window and looked out through the curtains so they won't see his face. He was busting a gut, trying to keep from laughing, as the husband and wife were running around the house, emptying wallets, cookie jars, rolls of pennies—anything that might hold a dime. Hell, I thought the husband was going to lift up the sofa cushions and look for change between the crumbs. But, here's the best part . . . ."

No one said a word. The group was waiting for the ending.

"They only came up with $174. They needed another 12 bucks. So the guy looks at me and he says, very seriously, that he's good for it. I snapped that if he had answered me when I called and didn't make me come out and mess up my Easter I might even let it go. But, in light of his poor record and previous attitude, no way. I'll send two of the trucks away, but I'm hauling off the first one in the driveway—the wife's red Honda.

"She started screaming and beating the poor bastard. He's rubbing his head. I swear, if he had hair he would have pulled it out. Then, as Reds goes out to pay off two of the trucks and tell the other driver to haul away the wife's car, the husband runs off down the hall. For a moment I thought he might be getting a gun or a knife, so I prepared myself for the worst. But he came back carrying a piggy bank. I swear to God, he stole his kid's piggy bank.

"Immediately, this small girl, about 10, comes flying in and is crying and grabbing for it. But the old man shoves her away and smashes the damn thing on the coffee table. I'm just staring at the scene, totally amazed. The guy is desperate. He's picking out quarters and dimes, pushing aside slivers of broken glass and grabbing the few single dollars scattered on the rug.

"The wife is in shock. The kid's sobbing. Now, I'm straining to hold back a gigantic roar. I'm even ready to toss in a few bucks of my own, and I don't even like the jerk. Finally, smiling pathetically, he hands me eight $1 bills and four dollars in change. I wrote him a cash receipt and dropped the money in my pocket. Reds went to the door, waved off the last tow truck and we got the hell out of there. I will never forget that day."

After a brief pause, a voice asked, "Did they come in the next day?"

"He did," Charles said. "Had a certified check to full pay every account. Thanked me for my kindness the day before. Then, as he's leaving, he tells me his wife left him and is filing for divorce. His partner skipped and he's holding the bag on the bills and he has an appointment with a real estate agent to put his house up for sale. But, at least his employment taxes are paid.

"I told him he did the right thing. God, what a loser! He was living proof that some idiots should never open a business. But," Charles said as he got up from the table, "God, that was some day. I swear I love this job."

❧   ❧   ❧

Charles' mood turned from super high to gutter low in the next half hour, following a brief but difficult conversation with Group Manger Neil Holland.

Holland, like Charles, was a career government employee. After more than 20 years with the Social Security Administration, he took a job in what was then the State of Delaware Division of Finance. Internal transfers and gradual step increases landed him in the Revenue Collection Division, in charge of a dozen deadbeat chasers.

Unlike Charles, Holland did not like the job. He didn't like his employees. He didn't like what they had to do. He didn't like dealing with the steady stream of complaints from taxpayers and, he didn't like the superior attitude that Charles Bettner displayed constantly.

It was true that Charles would forget more about collecting taxes than Holland would ever learn. But that didn't give the ace employee the right to humiliate his boss in group meetings and challenge every new idea or directive.

Holland knew he would be in his current position until he reached retirement. There was nowhere else for him to go, and he only had to last three more long, miserable years. But he didn't want to do it with Charles Bettner and his blatant antagonism and borderline insubordination. During the last six months, Holland had been seeking a way to rid himself of his Number 1 annoyance. One week ago, a memo arrived that Holland vowed he would frame. He considered the precious single-paged correspondence a gift sent to him personally from the gods.

Because of the income derived from Governor McDevitt's new economic development strategy and projections of soon-to-be bulging casino coffers, the state had been able to announce a timetable to abolish its income tax. There were definite projections that within three years the number of delinquent taxpayer accounts would dwindle and, with very few new individual deadbeats expected, the workload would continue to decline.

Effective January 1, 2008, each group manager was directed to reduce his or her force by 25 percent. Holland was ordered to lay off three employees of his choosing. There was no specific criteria to be followed. In this instance, the decision was up to the individual managers.

Those affected would be given a one-year position enhancement bonus and immediately assigned to a lateral level pay grade position in Taxpayer Service. If needed, private counseling would be available to help with any adjustment difficulties. New employment training and future job placement would be offered to anyone who was interested.

A confidential addendum to the memo suggested that this directive should be considered an opportunity to "purge the workplace of difficult employees who might reflect negatively on the division and the state by continued public contact."

Holland did not need to have a heavenly messenger with wings blow a trumpet in his ear announcing his early Christmas gift. He immediately knew the first employee he would transfer and send on his merry way.

Not surprisingly, Charles did not respond positively to Neil Holland's announcement. In fact, he didn't respond at all. The veteran collector sat frozen in the chair beside Holland's desk and looked straight ahead, motionless and silent.

Holland, thinking Charles might pull out a gun or go berserk, stepped to the right side of his office and placed his finger near the silent alarm built into the edge of his desk.

Several more seconds passed. To Holland, they seemed much longer than the actual brief time they consumed. Charles turned his head and looked at his boss with icy blue eyes. "You're happy aren't you?" His voice was soft, almost a coo.

"No," Holland replied. "It was a hard decision. Your closure rate is . . . ."

"The highest in the group!" Charles finished the sentence with a snap. "I've always been the highest. In the MPs, at the IRS, here. There never is anyone even close to me and my high production rate. That's what you want, but that's also what you don't want. Am I correct?"

There was a short, very awkward moment of silence, then Holland tried to respond. "No. . . . But, in a way. . . . "

"See," snarled Charles, "you don't even have the balls to stand up and tell me the truth. The truth is, I'm a threat to you. I'm too good at what I do. I close nearly half the group's cases combined, but you've found a way to get rid of me, to fire me because of your personal dislikes."

"You're not getting fired. It's an internal reassignment and . . . "

"I'm not an idiot!" Charles snarled. "You stand there and take away my life, my power. But I'll get it back. I've had it too long to give it up to the likes of a spineless wimp like you."

Holland was scared, but he also was angry. With his hand clutching the side of the desk, an inch from the alarm button, he stood and snapped back at Charles.

"Listen Charles, you're making out fairly well. You get a one-year bonus, keep your pay grade and still have a job in . . . ."

"TAXPAYER SERVICE!" Charles jumped up and blurted the response. "That's not a job. That's a dead end street for losers. I can't work inside, cooped up like a prisoner. I need to be out on the street, closing cases and beating on my deadbeats. Don't you dare tell me how lucky I am! You're lucky I don't jump across that desk and rip your throat out, you little pathetic twit!"

Holland tried to remain composed. Slowly, as if talking to a mental patient, he spoke in a soft voice. "I've been given an order to cut the size of this office. I have tried to be fair."

"FAIR!" shouted Charles. "You can't be serious! If you were half a man, you would have dumped those two old broads that have been here since they built the building during the Korean War!"

Holland tried to respond with equal force, but his high-pitched voice was no match for Bettner's commanding tone. "Why should I keep a troublemaker like you? You're negative. You're a loose cannon. You don't follow the rules. Sure, you close cases, but you cause more trouble than you're worth. You're a nuisance, and the time has come for me to get some relief and I'm taking it."

"So who's going to close the cases, collect the taxes, Neil?"

"Who cares, you fool!" Holland exploded. "In three years' time, there will be one-tenth of the present manpower working in collections. First, there will be no more individual taxes. That's obvious to anyone with half a brain. Thanks to McDevitt, gamblers and tourists are going to be paying most of the state's bills. Then, we'll just confiscate more of what's owed through computer agreements, direct bank levies and higher business registrations and corporate fees.

"McDevitt's utopian DelMarValous society is putting you out of a job. He's the one you should be yelling at. It's not my fault. He's your enemy. The governor has put you out on the street. You and your kind, with your barbarian tactics and public humiliation and threats, are going to the happy hunting ground, so it's good bye, Charlie."

Like a cat, Charles sprang around the desk, stopping only inches from Holland's face. The crazed employee's breath was hot on his boss' cheeks. Instinctively, Holland pressed the alarm.

"Don't ever call me that! You hear me, Neil? I hate that name. My name is Charles, and don't you ever forget it!"

Holland stared into two tiny blue spheres that were a small window to a mind filled with hate, poison and bedlam. "Sure, Charles. Fine. Sorry." The manager was praying the guards who monitor the alarm weren't on break, asleep or reading the sports page in the men's room.

"Well," Charles said, walking back to the chair, "I won't fight you, Neil. I won't leave here crying and screaming. I'll take my year's bonus pay. I deserve it and more. I'll go sit in Taxpayer Service and do squat. I'll even go to your stupid state counselor to get deprogrammed. Hell, I'll give him an earful.

"But just remember this, I don't get mad. I get even. And you know what else, Neil? I'm not going to get a lawyer and drag your ass through the court. No. I'll deal with this my own way, and, when you least expect it, I'll give you a big surprise. Oh, by the way, Neil, Merry Christmas. You've got a lot of class dropping this on me so close to the holidays."

Two uniformed security officers entered the room, interrupting the conversation. With hands on their holsters, they stared, puzzled at the calm scene.

Charles looked at them, and at the group manager. He shook his head, laughed and silently walked out of the room.

Neil waved the guards off and sat down in his chair. Some of the office staff had heard portions of the exchange through the thin prefabricated partition. No one said a word. No one moved.

Charles Bettner refused to clear out his desk.

He never came back to that office, and though he passed him regularly in the building hallways, Charles never looked at nor spoke a word to Neil Holland again.

10

February 2008

Stephanie Litera was taking another look through the papers in the manila file folder, trying to prepare for her first meeting with Charles Bettner. As senior associate state psychologist in the DelMarVa Division of Social Services and Psychological Health Care she had a variety of assignments—review of job related stress cases, coordination of in-service training for nursing staff personnel in the state's five mental health institutions and counseling employees with work-related psychological concerns.

Due to an extensive early retirement incentive program and a significant number of internal job transfers in the finance and collection divisions, her tray wasn't just full, its contents were falling onto the floor and more was being piled on the top.

Two weeks earlier, in mid January right after the Martin Luther King holiday, she had been given 46 new personnel advisement cases. In addition to her regular duties, her supervisor had sent a memo instructing Stephanie and three other colleagues to make these assignments a priority. That meant they were to meet the transferred or separated personnel within 15 days and schedule follow-up sessions, as needed, at least once a month for a six-month period.

She had wasted no time letting her immediate superior know how she felt.

"This is crap!" Stephanie snapped, waving a stack of folders in the air. "This means, if none of us takes any vacation, gets sick or dies for the next year and a half, we might be able to stick to this insane plan."

Marty Robbins, who constantly spent time acknowledging that he was named after the country western singer, had wisely remained silent, letting the 48-year-old redhead pace in front of his desk and list all the reasons why his directive couldn't be accomplished.

"That means we have to conduct, at least, two private counseling sessions EACH DAY, MARTY! That's IN ADDITION to our other *PRIORITY* duties. How the hell is that ever going to happen?"

In a brave whisper, Marty tried to answer. "Just do the best you can, Steph. I know how overworked you are. All I'm asking you to do is try."

It didn't help.

Stephanie's tone continued at a high decibel level. "And all I'm asking you to do, Marty, is try to be realistic and try to act like a manager. I want you to go and tell those idiots upstairs that this is insane, that they are degree-holding morons and that I will only make room in my schedule to give priority treatment to the mental midgets who thought up this stupid plan."

Marty wisely remained silent. He could tell she was running out of steam.

"We've got to get some more staff in here, Marty. Please?"

"I know, Steph. I know. We've got two new LPNs coming in next week to . . . ."

He cringed. The moment the words came out of his mouth he realized she would go ballistic.

"JESUS CHRIST. MARTY! Are you listening to me? Are we speaking the same language here? I'm not talking about some teeny boppers in candy stripes who are going to change sheets and clean goddamn bedpans! We need trained, Ph.-freaking-D. counselors. The state is spending all of its new found money on top cops and tourism experts.

We've got a major psychological caseload crisis, right here and right now!"

"I know, Steph. I know. I have a meeting later this week with the cabinet secretary. I'll tell her we need more help."

Stephanie was worn down from shouting and knew she had made her point. She and Marty went way back. They started out at the agency together, right out of college. He took the administrative track, she took the clinical. They were both good at what they did, although, at that particular moment, Stephanie wouldn't be ready to tout Marty's political and bureaucratic managerial abilities.

Stephanie's hand was on the doorknob. Just before leaving, she turned and said, "There are going to be nervous breakdowns and people falling through the cracks, here, Marty, and I'm not talking about the patients, I'm talking about your staff."

In the days that followed, it had been rough preparing properly for her latest barrage of clients. Thankfully, she could tell that many of them would need just a few morale building sessions. During that time they would be reassured that they were not personally inadequate and were still capable and valued employees.

Stephanie told her new clients that they, like many others, were victims of an impersonal system with a sanitary name: GRIF—governmental reduction in force. Everyone pronounced it "grief," and it lived up to its standard definition. At least, she told her new clients, the state program showed that the upper-level bureaucrats cared and were trying to address individual personnel needs.

She had only gone through about half of her cases, but she wrote Marty a memo to file, estimating that nearly half would need less than four individual sessions. There also were self-help groups to which she could refer others.

There might be a single candle glowing at the end of the tunnel. But she also had enough experience to know that as soon as she could see daylight on the other side a freight train hauling more work would be heading toward her at full speed.

It was 2:50 p.m., in early February.

Charles Bettner's three o'clock appointment was her last of the day. She planned to leave her Wilmington office by 3:45 and meet two old friends for drinks at Hartwell's Brandywine Valley Brew Pub and Steak Saloon outside Hockessin by 4:15. They were schoolmates who were considering job offers in the area and the group had planned interview and work schedules around the mini reunion.

Bettner's file didn't raise any major red flags. He had an impressive background. U.S. Army retiree. Former IRS employee. More than the standard few letters of commendation. His sick leave form was abnormal. He had not missed a day due to illness since he came to DelMarVa, and he rarely took an extended vacation. Obviously, the man loved his work.

There was one negative notation, signed by Neil Holland describing Bettner as "arrogant, troublesome and, in my opinion, at times unstable."

This, Stephanie noted, was related to a long history of petty tension and capped by the argument between the two men when Holland informed Bettner of his transfer to Taxpayer Service.

While Bettner's outburst was not appropriate behavior, it was not entirely surprising. Records indicated that he had received awards as the collector with the highest closure rate during all 12 quarters in the division. Obviously, he could not understand why his dedication and efficiency were rewarded with what he considered a demotion.

Stephanie closed the folder, checked the green numbers glowing on her desk clock: 2:59.

Mr. Bettner's case should be resolved, like many of the others, she told herself, with two or three meetings. She would listen to his concerns, reinforce his self-esteem and send him on to his new career and a long life of civil service, success and satisfaction.

As the long hand of the clock moved to 12, a knock was heard on the door.

"Come in!" Stephanie shouted, and Charles Bettner entered her office.

Rising from behind her desk, Stephanie greeted her guest and motioned for him to take a seat in one of the two comfortable, upholstered chairs at the far side of the room. Out the window of her ninth floor office, she could look down on Rodney Square, the old U.S. Post Office building and the impressive corporate structures that housed Wilmington Trust Company, MBNA America, the DuPont Company, the Playhouse and the Hotel du Pont.

At 51, Bettner's head was bald, either premature or shaved, Stephanie couldn't tell. His clothes were immaculate, as if he was wearing a civilian, security officer uniform—dark blue blazer, gray slacks, a white, heavily-starched shirt with cuff links. His black shoes were brightly glossed. The heavy soles and oversized fronts gave the impression they had steel tips. He was over 6 feet tall with a trim, athletic build.

His light blue eyes were both dull and deep, giving the impression he could be looking at you, understanding every word you said, but still be far off, planning something else.

When he spoke there was authority, security, force—the result of both following commands and giving orders for two decades in the Army. There also was the power he had learned to exercise in his IRS and Collection Division positions.

But Bettner's authority, Stephanie realized, had just been taken away.

For a moment, she thought her casefile-only assessment may have been premature. It wouldn't take her long to find out whether or not she was correct.

Following the standard drill, Stephanie began by inviting Mr. Bettner to tell her a little about himself.

"You can call me Charles, doctor," he said, stiffly.

"Thank, you, Charles. So . . . ."

"So what?"

"Speak to me about Charles Bettner."

He smiled and folded his hands on his lap. "I'm not a novice at this, doctor. I know the bottom line for this soft and smooth interrogation. It's that you and management want to know if I'm going to come in one day soon with an automatic weapon—that I probably keep in my lunchbox—and blow away my former group manager and anyone else who may happen to be drinking from the water fountain in the hall."

"No. That's not what I said, Mr. Bettner."

"Charles," he said, forcing a smile.

"Yes, of course, Charles," Stephanie said, pausing, then waiting for his response.

When he didn't speak, she added, "You don't want to be here, Charles, and, honestly, neither do I."

He stared and said nothing.

"Your case and more than 40 others were dropped on my desk, and I didn't plan to meet you or any of the other people, either. But, just like you, I got dumped on, too." She detected a slight smile of a response and continued. "My goal is to get you in and out of here as quickly as possible. Then, I can deal with the people who really need my help, those who are emotionally critical and, in some cases, physically fragile. But I have to see all of you to determine who needs to keep coming and who should be cut loose."

Bettner, who had gotten up and was looking out the window, turned slowly, looked Stephanie over from her black high heels to her short red hair and said, "So, Frau Doctor, do I get zet free or vill I be zent to ze padded cell?" His teeth gleamed, reminding her of a squeaky clean model from a toothpaste commercial.

"I don't know yet. I'll make that decision after we talk a bit."

"About what?"

"About you. Begin anywhere. Tell me what you like to do. Talk about your friends . . . ."

"I don't have any friends," Charles snapped, correcting her, then explaining without prompting. "They're nothing but trouble, sapping your energy, consuming your time, requiring more maintenance than a home or an automobile."

"So you'd describe yourself as a loner?"

"I'd prefer not to use that term. It has a negative connotation. Misguided people immediately associate loners with losers, misfits and outcasts. I consider myself a private person with unique interests that are beyond the appreciation of the masses. That is what demands my attention."

"So what are your hobbies and interests?"

Bettner eagerly mentioned how he loved serious music, collected rare coins, miniature trains and unusual beer cans from all over the world. He had traveled extensively. Stephanie was beginning to see a verbal portrait of a man whose life began at 18 when he entered the Army, blossomed during the next 30 years and, just maybe, recently ended with his demotion.

He was well-spoken and intelligent, and he probably, could have had a successful career in any field. Why tax collection of all things? she wondered.

"How do you feel about your current employment situation?" Stephanie asked.

"Do you know that there are people who break the law every day, doctor?" The statement came out of nowhere. But she didn't try to redirect his soliloquy. "I'm not talking about street robbery, date rape, child molestation or cold-blooded murder. I'm referring to simple, personal, moral transgressions that people don't think about for one split second. They commit these minor criminal acts that do not bother them at all. But the overall breakdown of society must begin somewhere and, in my mind, it starts in the workplace.

"I saw it in the Army. People would steal supplies. Tape. Pencils. Copy paper and paper clips. Not just one or two items. They would cart out cases, place them into pickup trucks and vans. They never thought they were stealing. They considered the items 'perks' of the job. Then, there were the ones who would knock off work five minutes early, and the same ones who consistently came in late. Five minutes here, three minutes there—they all add up, you know?"

Stephanie didn't respond, just took it all in. She was careful not to make any notes for fear of distracting Charles.

"Three minutes a day in the morning and three minutes more at both ends of lunch, and then another three at the end of the day, not counting morning and afternoon breaks, adds up to 12 minutes a day, 60 minutes a week, four hours a month. That's a full six days of vacation time each and every year that they are stealing from their employer.

"I would write them up in the beginning, when I was assigned to the MP unit at Fort Meade. But they laughed at me, and my superiors told me to stop reporting them. I followed my orders. Just because the decision makers didn't want to enforce regulations didn't make what was being done right. It was still wrong."

"So you think everyone should go by the rules?"

"Everyone," he said in a voice that was soft but firm. "Every single being, no matter how high or how low in the food chain. No exceptions, period."

"What about a situation where there's a Christmas party, a retirement or a birthday celebration in the office?"

"Not appropriate," Charles said. "Either do it outside of the worksite or have everyone sign for the time off."

Stephanie looked at her client. "How do you like your new job, Charles?"

"Do you want me to be honest or give you what I know you want to hear?"

She was intrigued. "First tell me what *you think* I want to hear."

"Touché, dear doctress. What I should say is: At first I was upset, hurt, confused, and yes, annoyed that they fired me and did not appreciate my fine work. Instead of acknowledging my dedication and expertise, they used my skills against me and took away my job, my life. But, as the days and weeks passed, I was able to reflect upon my new situation. Now, I view the shift of responsibility as a new opportunity, a chance to learn more, to show that I can handle rejection and adversity. By remaining on the team as an active player, I continue to work and show that I am both realistic and mature. And, maybe someday, if circumstances change, they will call me back and appreciate me again."

"Very good, Charles. But, now tell me the truth, how you honestly feel."

Charles just stared at her. Cold and motionless. She wasn't sure if he had heard her, but she waited him out. When he returned from his mental journey, he spoke. But his expression, his body, did not change in the slightest way. "That's the honest truth, dear Frau Doctor. I view this as a wonderful opportunity."

Stephanie didn't believe him, but she kept her opinion to herself.

"You don't believe me, do you?"

"No," she said firmly.

"No, you don't believe me, or No, you do believe me?"

He was playing with her, changing their roles. His eyes seemed to roam over her body. She was feeling uncomfortable. "No, I don't believe you."

"Why not? What would I have to gain by lying to you, doctor?"

Stephanie opened his folder and made a few short notes, ignoring his question.

Charles got up and pointed out the window to the street below. "Here, look out there. See them? Look!"

Stephanie moved closer to Charles to gain a better view. She looked down and asked him to be more precise.

"Pedestrians! They don't follow the traffic signals. They walk against the lights. Just because no one enforces the law doesn't make what they do appropriate. Do you understand?"

She looked at him and shook her head in agreement. "But, it would be impossible to monitor or enforce . . . ."

"I'm not talking about the absurdity of trying to enforce every ridiculous law. Do you think I'm unrealistic and stupid? Anyone with the lowest IQ knows that most laws are passed to satisfy whining special interest groups, or they are needed to legally line the pockets of a few wealthy party contributors.

"Common sense and morality are unrelated to justice," Charles added. "If they ever are in sync, it's probably the result of an accident or coincidence." His voice was harsh, but he paused quickly to laugh, perhaps at the fact that he had openly questioned his own sanity.

"I expected more from you, Frau doctor. What I'm trying to illustrate, with a readily available living example, is that all around us there is flagrant deceit and disregard for the law. In my unglamorous and unappreciated position as society's despised tax collector, I did my job. I collected every cent from every taxpayer that, unfortunately for them, fell into my personal realm, my assigned caseload. 'Render to Caesar what is Caesar's' was my code, and I followed it, lived it. You read my chart, my file. What was my closure rate, doctor?"

"94 percent."

"Very good. Despite your overburdened workload and unappreciated state, you took the time to prepare properly for my visit. I'm very impressed."

"Well, I guess you won't put me in the category of those who knock off 12 minutes early each day," she said, smiling.

"Doctor," Charles said, abruptly rising from his seat. "I think I'm going to enjoy our little visits. I'm simpatico with you. I can sense it, feel it. We're both overworked, understaffed and unappreciated. Perhaps, we may just learn to appreciate each other."

Charles looked down on her, shifting again into control. "Thanks so very much for this little introductory chat. I think we've covered enough territory today. I'll see you at, let's say, same time next week? All right?"

"All right," she said, not checking her calendar and, obviously, taken by surprise, as Charles Bettner left the room and closed the door.

Stephanie shook her head, grabbed her purse and headed for the parking lot. It was 3:40. She needed a drink. The company of old friends would distract her from thinking about a very unusual, yet quite interesting interview.

🌿 🌿 🌿

DelMarVa Police Commissioner Michael Pentak looked around the large room at the 10 regional representatives of the state's 54 state barracks police chiefs. These elected officers made up the Commanders' Council that met at 0800 hours on the first Friday of each month. With state police jurisdiction divided into 10 geographic zones, each delegate served a two-year term for five region-based barracks. The commanders of the larger barracks in Dover, Easton, Salisbury and Wilmington were permanent council members.

The initial part of each gathering was informative, with an instructional program or speaker. But the second half, after coffee and donuts, was an organized, high-level bitch session where the commander delegates of more than 1,800 state cops felt comfortable letting it all hang out.

Folders placed in front of each seat contained the meeting's agenda, up-to-date crime stats and a printout of the commissioner's tentative appointment and travel schedule.

The presentation at this particular session was a continuation of a six-part series on the importance of properly safeguarding and collecting PE—physical evidence—at the crime scene. Trooper Jerry Graves of Barracks 27 in Easton, who was working on his doctorate in agriculture, was scheduled to discuss the use of maggots and body decomposition in determining the time of death.

Those who thought there would be reduced donut consumption at this particular session were in for a surprise. Cops who could down cold coffee and stale Danish while picking through fresh guts on a hot summer highway weren't affected by full-color slides of feasting maggots.

Graves' handouts and presentation did a good job illustrating his success in using insects in case solving. This prompted Pentak to direct the trooper to deliver a proposal detailing how the basic principles of his studies could be turned into a series of workshops to be presented in each of the state's barracks.

To say initial acceptance of the idea by the chiefs was unenthusiastic was being charitable.

Pentak noticed their lack of enthusiasm, but let it pass. They were often reluctant to latch onto new ideas, but he would push them through anyway. Despite upgrading their salaries, providing the latest high-tech equipment and raising the educational level of both support personnel and troopers, some things remained the same. Cops would be cops—negative moaners who would find something to complain about if they were tossed in the Garden of Eden for a free fling with Eve and several of her naked, nymphomaniacal sisters.

After the coffee break, Pentak invited general questions and concerns.

The first comment came from Commander Willis Linton, chief of Cape Charles Barracks 54, the state's southernmost outpost.

"Commissioner, with all due respect, the boys down in my neck of the woods are a bit pre-turbed about the temp'rary duty up in Wilm'ton and Dover. These fellas been up there 'bout seven weeks now, an', to be honest, they just don' see no point in spendin' a full four months up north. I mean, no 'fense to my colleagues from the metro-poli-tain areas, but ya seen one dirty, run down, crumblin' city square, ya pretty much seen 'em all."

There was a round of laughter from most of the assembly, except the chiefs from Wilmington and Dover.

"No, I'm serious here, sir!" Linton snapped, scowling at the group. "In re-turn for sendin' my men up north, I got me a dozen city boys who can't read a road map to save their asses and they are out there, daily, in the boonies—unknowingly, I presume—antagonizin' my populace."

"Explain what you mean, Willis," Pentak said.

"Well, I'm sure it's not intentional, sir. But these boys are goin' out in the necks an' guts, down outside Parksley an' Accomac an' Wachapreague, an' they just can't understand what some of our folks are sayin'. An', for damn sure, sir, those migrants and black folk down there, plus our hard workin' old watermen, they can't understand them city cops at all. They sound an' act like college professors wearing badges. Hell, most of my people would take kindlier to talkin' to game wardens than somebody from Wilmin'ton—an' that's sayin' a lot!"

Pentak paused and leaned back. Part of his plan to incorporate the law enforcement units from the three states into a single, well-coordinated organization was creating minor difficulties. But, he still believed that cross training by area was one of several ways the single force would eventually work more efficiently.

"I know what you're saying, Willis. And," Pentak looked around the room, "I know you're not alone in your feelings. I've heard from Chiefs Barbato in Wilmington and Shields in Dover, plus Harris in Salisbury, that the municipal officers are as annoyed as you and your men. But I still feel that this transitional training is important.

"However," he added before he was hit with a prepared response, "I'm not going to ignore your concerns. How about if we cut the temporary assignments down to eight weeks? That will give them half the original time. But, I reserve the right to call them up for weekend and holiday duty in varied geographical areas throughout the year, as needed."

Willis nodded his thanks and was pleased.

"Is this official, sir?" he asked.

"Yes, Willis. So you can announce it and tell your boys they can go home after one more week."

Applause greeted the commissioner's decision.

Pentak raised his hands. "I'm not giving this idea up, it's just a modification, all right?"

The chiefs muttered, agreed.

"But, the program continues. It's the assignment adjustment time that's been reduced. I'll have my staff make up new rosters and training dates so we can complete this program sooner. You should have the details within the week. I leave it to you to alert your personnel. This will mess up some of their vacation and personal plans, but they're getting a reduction in the inconvenience of being away from home, so it will all equal out. Anything else?"

No one spoke.

"All right, then if there's nothing else, we'll . . . ."

"Sir!"

It was a voice at the far end of the table. The assembly that was just about out of their seats turned to see the source of the sound and, at the same time, let their bodies fall back into the chairs.

"Tom Brennan, Claymont Barracks Number 1, sir."

"Yes, I recognize you, chief, go ahead. You have a question?"

"Not really, sir, just a comment. But, I'll admit, this might sound a bit strange."

"We're listening. What do you want to bring up?"

"The lack of big time crime, sir."

"Lack of crime?" Pentak was surprised, but intrigued. So was everyone else.

Complete silence in the room indicated to Brennan that he had the group's attention. He also felt a bit foolish and said so. "I was with the Delaware State Police for 12 years before the reorganization of the state, sir. Saw my share of robberies, rape victims, dead bodies and even worked in vice for a time. To be honest, sir, it was exciting. Hell, it was hectic and, at times, I thought I was going to lose my mind. We were backed up with a never-ending pile of caseloads, open investigations out the kazoo, but, it was a challenge. I could get high on some of those cases. It was tough, and you knew you'd never get to the bottom of the stack, never be out of work, never solve them all. But, it was actually fun trying to battle through it."

The room was still quiet.

"My point is, that's all changed—and quite a bit. In the short time since the reorganization of the state, crime has dropped to a level that I never would have believed possible."

Pentak cut in. "We still have a serious drug problem, much of it caused from Philadelphia and Baltimore gangs trying to claim territory. And there's always going to be robbery, murder, domestic violence. None of that has gone away completely."

"I know, sir," Brennan agreed, "but the amount of criminal activity is way down. Hell, we're using top homicide investigators to direct traffic, sometimes."

"The drop was expected," Pentak said. "We've got the whipping post back, fewer death row appeals, plus there's low unemployment. People feel safer. The politicians are happy and most cops, I thought, are pleased. Are you saying they're not, Chief Brennan?"

"What I'm saying sir, is we're paying street cops 60-some grand a year. We've got guys on the force who have master's and doctorates and could be college professors. We've got FBI guys and even a few ex-CIA working here. But, there's not enough big crime to go around any more. It's overkill. I know these guys, and I can see them getting bored. And when they get bored they get sloppy—and when they get sloppy, somebody can get killed."

There were a few nods of agreement and a lot of stone cold faces.

"Sir, I'm not hoping we have a crime spree, or go back to the days when there were 169 shootings a year in Wilmington alone. What I'm saying is these highly-trained professional cops can only do glorified security duty so long. They are not going to be satisfied directing traffic at the Lewes Punkin' Chuckin' and Chincoteague Pony Swim. They are used to solving murders and bank robberies. Now they're almost ready to fight over who goes out and handles a fender bender on I-95."

A few weak laughs broke the ice.

"What I hear you saying, Chief Brennan, is we need a good ax murderer, or maybe a serial killer with a hood, a string of bank robberies or even a freeway shooter or rampaging Satanic cult to help keep us on our toes."

"No, sir. I'm just sharing what I see happening. Perhaps it's just a passing phase. I don't know. I just wanted to mention it."

"Thank you. It's been mentioned and noted. Let me get our bean counters to run through some crime numbers from last year and add in some projections. Then we'll discuss this further at another time. I'm not disregarding your concerns. To a degree, they are valid. Until next month, gentlemen and ladies. And, I suggest you feel free to call Chief Brennan if any of you have a good juicy murder in your precinct. His men, obviously, are a bit bored up there at the Pennsylvania border and ready to go up into the Keystone State and do freelance clean-up work."

Brennan waved toward Pentak and the chiefs laughed as they put on their caps.

Suddenly, Pentak stopped and raised his hands. He had one further comment. "One more thought. When I worked homicide in Philly, I recall a time when it was slow—meaning we didn't have a fresh body for about a six-hour period. It was unusual.

"I started to get antsy, and Doyle, this ruddy, old Irish beat cop—he was a bit of a barroom philosopher—told me, 'Mikey, you got to learn how to relax, me boy. Start looking for crime and it'll wait you out. Sometimes it sits, quiet and still, watchin' you from a dark hole. And, when it comes out, it'll pounce on you on all sides, to be sure, like a herd of drunken leprechauns. You don't want it that way, all at once like that when you're not ready. Best it appears a little at a time. But, that's the rub, we got no control.'

"He told me that the perps are always out there, around us all the time. It only slows down for so long. Criminals can't sit still. They've got to come out and be noticed, get their share of the limelight. That's a very important part of their game. Because, like old Doyle told me, 'That's all this is, Mikey, one big goddamn game.'

"I say we've been lucky so far. Let's hope things stay calm and our luck holds out. Maybe somebody out there, who wants to make a name for himself, is noticing how calm things are here in DelMarVa, too. I hope not. But I'm afraid when it breaks, it won't be a trickle. And when that happens, our ex-FBI suits and former CIA black operations specialists are going to earn their money."

11

Buena Vista, formerly the grand mansion of the wealthy Buck family, had played host to a number of famous visitors over the years, including President Herbert Clark Hoover during his term of office. Eventually, the stately home and land was transformed into a conference center used for official state functions. Located at the end of a deep, tree-lined driveway off Route 13 south of New Castle, it was one of the few remaining country estates able to survive in a heavily developed suburban setting.

In the impressive, open entry hall, Stephanie Litera was snapping at her boss, complaining about the wasted Thursday evening. "I tell you, I hate these things, Marty. This is your world, your responsibility, and it's unfair for you to keep dragging me along so you'll have someone to talk to."

Marty Robbins grabbed Stephanie by the elbow and steered her toward a shadowy vacant corner. A passing waiter, carrying a tray of unrecognizable appetizers, gave them a disdainful look. Stephanie glared back.

"Look," Marty said, "we both want more staff, right?" He didn't wait for her to answer. "All the directors are invited to this command performance to meet the governor and his personal aides and cabinet once a year. I figured, if I came down here, I might get a minute of his time to prod him into signing the bill that gives us twelve new counselors . . . ."

"TWELVE!" she shouted.

As Marty whispered for her to keep quiet, a half dozen nearby heads turned in their direction.

"Sorry," she said, smiling, waving weakly. "When do we get them?"

Marty rolled his eyes, "As soon as he signs the bill. I've already completed interviews, and I have letters of acceptance ready to go. In fact, I've had them ready for five weeks."

Stephanie moved closer to Marty and hissed, "You've known about this for over a month and didn't tell me?"

"If I did, you would have been camped on my doorway every morning, Steph. I just figured it would have happened by now. But, no such luck."

Stephanie fired a series of questions about the new personnel and another barrage demanding explanations for the delay. In between Marty's embarrassed explanations about missed opportunities and partisan legislative infighting, he said everyone but McDevitt finally had approved the bill. But the governor was holding it up because he wanted to sign their provision for more social service staff along with two other unrelated and still pending pieces of legislation, on the same day, in about three or four weeks.

"THREE FREAKING WEEKS!!! We have to wait a month so some clown can showboat with a capitol version of a trifecta. In the meantime, we wallow up to our necks in human mental misery."

"Look, Steph, I figured if you were here, you might be able to give me some moral support to mention the need to McDevitt, in case I get to him and get cold feet."

"Oh, don't you worry one little bit, Marty. I'll give you all the support you need, you little spineless shit." She snatched a champagne glass from a passing tray and downed the contents in one gulp. "This is insane, Marty. Do me a favor. Put old Hang 'em High McDevitt on my couch. He needs serious, one-on-one counseling."

As if it were a prearranged scene from a dark comedy, Gov. Henry McDevitt, accompanied by Vice Governor Lydia

Chase, Press Secretary Sean Kelley and Police Commissioner Michael Pentak, turned the corner.

"Did I hear someone mention my name?" McDevitt asked from his position directly behind Stephanie. A tolerant expression was on his face. Pentak and Kelley looked more uncomfortable than their boss. Chase, unlike the three men, was amused and waited to see the scene played out.

Stephanie Litera stared at the wall, and every rigid muscle convinced her that she did not want to turn around. She heard the distinctive voice of the former presidential candidate and well-loved governor. The horrified look on Marty's face and his frozen Bucky Beaver, toothpaste commercial smile reassured her that she had jumped into a very deep hole.

"So," McDevitt pressed, "who said something about me on a couch? Is this a new joke I haven't heard?"

All was lost, thought Marty.

Somehow Stephanie was able to turn around as Marty introduced her as one of the state's senior practicing psychological counselors.

"So, Marty, this is one of your top employees and she wants to have me come in for a psychological examination." Everyone waited for his reaction. Belting out a genuine laugh, McDevitt said, as he stared at her nametag. "I don't know whether to be flattered or insulted, Ms. Leteral?"

"Litera. Lee-Ter-Ra," she said slowly, still functioning on reflex action.

"I'm sorry. Well, there are a number of people who have suggested I'm crazy. Those who laughed at our White House chase, those who are upset with our casino 'empire,' as they call it, those who are enraged that I slip on the noose every now and then and, how did you say it, Ms. Litera?"

"Hang 'em High," Stephanie whispered in reply.

"Right. But what is the reason that you, in particular, would like to give me a free psycho session?"

Stephanie looked at Marty, urging him to explain.

Her boss, mute and motionless, stared back at her. The

silence during the agitated pantomime was not funny, and the governor rolled his eyes and started to move on.

Just as he took his first step away, Stephanie blurted out, "All right. What the hell!"

The top level quartet turned and waited as Stephanie announced, "I was telling Marty that I think it's a stupid and pathetic move for you to hold up the ability to hire desperately needed personnel in the social services mental health section just so you can play a grandstand number with a trifecta bill signing!"

Sean Kelley started to grab McDevitt's arm and pull him away, but he shrugged him off. "What are you talking about?"

Stephanie looked to Marty, who took a step forward, and, speaking more respectfully, explained, "We have a desperate need for more staff, governor."

"I know, Marty. I approved the additions quite a few weeks ago. Signed it and sent it on."

"No sir, you didn't. Ask Sean. They've been held up so your staff and some of the career politicians can arrange a high profile signature session in about four weeks. That's if we're lucky. It's all related to two other bills that have not yet even been passed."

"Is this right, Sean?"

The press secretary pulled McDevitt aside and started to explain that the two party leaders had "strongly recommended" holding up the social services personnel bill so there could be a big ceremony when the others were ready.

"So we have money ready to go, people waiting for jobs and other people needing treatment, and these hacks are playing old-time games?"

Sean nodded.

"Why didn't you tell me, Sean?"

"It's been hectic, sir. They said they would really be upset if they didn't get a three-bill signing ceremony. They told me they'd hold up our efforts next session if we didn't play along. I guess I made a bad call."

"That's an understatement, Sean. God, I really thought this bill was through. How long has it been ready?"

"Nearly a month, sir."

"And no one has asked about it, or told me?"

No one answered. McDevitt's face was bright red.

"Where is it?"

"In the office safe," Sean said, adding, "one copy in Wilmington and one in Federalsburg."

"Go get the damn thing."

"Now, sir?"

"NOW! It will only take you a half hour to get downtown and back. And bring a few of those new pens. I'll pass them out. We'll do it right here. Have the waiters move the punch bowl. Tell them what's going on.

"Marty," McDevitt turned to the director, "next time you have something important like this, you call me direct, understand?"

"Yes, sir."

Looking at Stephanie, whose eyes were wide in amazement, McDevitt asked, "Do you still think I need a session on your couch, Ms. Litera?"

She lowered her eyes slightly as she shook her head. McDevitt asked her and Marty to serve as witnesses. An hour later, the bill was signed and pictures taken as the two social services employees stood behind the governor. Afterwards, he gave them each a ceremonial pen.

After McDevitt walked away, Michael Pentak spent a few more moments talking to Marty. Lydia Chase approached Stephanie and they moved slowly toward an alcove, away from prying ears.

"You okay?" Chase asked.

"Sure, fine," she replied. "I just told one of the most influential men in the country he was a psycho, pushed his press secretary into a vat of boiling oil and probably created a state political battle. Other than that, it's been a quiet evening. Hell, I didn't even want to come to this damn party. Marty dragged me along."

"You got your bill signed and . . . ."

" . . . and probably lost my job, or at least got my name placed on the state big-mouth blacklist."

"Listen," Chase said, moving closer to Stephanie, "if you're going to open your mouth, be ready to stand by what comes out. Cut the weak little girl nonsense. You had a valid concern, and by bringing it up you alerted the governor to a breakdown in his staff and a major communication problem. We should have been on top of this bill and we weren't. We screwed up. You helped us out. We appreciate that. If anything, you were the only one in the room with any conviction. The governor won't forget that, and neither will I. How we handle the professional politicians is not your concern. Now, stay and enjoy the party. You deserve it."

Marty and Stephanie watched Chase move back into the crowd.

"Whoa!" said Marty, moving closer to Stephanie, "now Chase, there's a woman I wouldn't like to tangle with."

"I agree," said Stephanie, grabbing another drink. "You're driving home tonight, Marty, understand? Because I am going to get royally blitzed."

"Right, no problem, Steph. Right!" He was nodding. He didn't want to tangle with her either and agreed with anything she said.

"Damn right!" she snapped.

🌿   🌿   🌿

"This is Dr. Stephanie Litera. I'm not available at the present time. Please leave a detailed message and I will call you back as soon as possible. Thank you."

The caller did not respond to the voice mail system. Instead, she immediately called Stephanie's boss, Marty Robbins. The director recognized the caller's name and promised he would give the message to Stephanie, personally, as soon as she arrived.

Yes, he replied, she was at work, but he could not pinpoint her exact whereabouts. She was out on several field visitations and would be back around noon. Yes, he added, he knew it was 11:30 and that she must call back by 1 o'clock, otherwise it would have to wait until the next day and that would not be satisfactory.

No, Marty said, finally, his exasperation beginning to show, she did not have a mobile phone in her purse, but there was one in her car. He would call that number immediately.

Marty hung up the receiver and shouted to his secretary, asking again about Stephanie.

Yolanda, who had been with Robbins for several years, snapped. "For the sixth time this morning," she shouted, "I have not heard from Stephanie and, like I said more than a dozen times, I will inform you the moment she comes in or calls."

Marty could tell Yolanda wasn't pleased by his repeated prodding, but what was he supposed to do? He looked like an idiot, not being able to account for his staff. He knew Steph had too much to drink when she slept all the way home the previous night during the early morning return drive to Wilmington.

Stephanie's secretary already had to reschedule two appointments and she was beginning to worry. So was Marty. It was very unlike his most dependable counselor to miss work and not even call in.

He skipped lunch and waited for Stephanie in her office.

At 12:50 p.m., a slow moving, uninspiring, not quite conscious form entered the work chamber of Dr. Stephanie Litera. Sunglasses covered what were most certainly blood-shot slits that, on a normal day, would pass as eyes.

Upon seeing her boss at her desk, Stephanie slowly announced, "Don't jump all over me, Marty." Her voice croaked out the words in a hushed whisper. "I can explain. Besides, it's all your fault that I'm a walking whiskey bottle today."

"Who gives a damn about you being drunk, or even being five hours late for work and not calling in, or having to cancel your morning schedule? Not me," he said, sarcastically. "I'm just royally bent out of shape because just over an hour ago I got the third degree about where you are from Grace Welch. And, that, my dear drinking friend Stephanie, I do not need."

"Who the hell is Grace Welch?" Stephanie asked, moving slowly and shielding her eyes with her hand to avoid the sunlight streaking in through her side window.

"Executive administrative assistant to Henry McDevitt, you boozed up bimbo!" he snapped.

"So, what could she want with me?" she asked as she lowered the blinds to keep out all natural midday light.

"How would I know? And I wasn't about to ask. Besides, I didn't even know where you were. Do you think I was going to let the governor's staff know that I am clueless about what my people are doing? Look, forget it! Just call this number, and do it now! You have to get back to her before one."

"Why?"

"Don't ask me. I'm just your messenger boy. Maybe they want to put you on their staff—but they'll have to realize you only work half days after party nights." Rolling his eyes, he added, "You must have made a great impression last night."

"Do you think they're going to fire me?"

"Hell, no! If that was the case, they'd just tell me to do it. I don't know what the hell they want."

Stephanie asked Marty to stay as she dialed the number. A woman answered, recognized Stephanie's name and immediately put the psychologist on hold.

She waited a full minute and was ready to hang up when she heard a man's voice.

It was the governor.

"Ms. Litera?"

"Yes?" She was scared to death, and she tried to sit upright, but it still was painful to move.

"I've been trying to get to you all morning. Marty said you were out doing some field work."

"Yes?" There was a question mark at the end of her reply.

"Look, I've got to be at a meeting in Baltimore, and we're leaving in about five minutes . . . ."

"Yes?" Stephanie's mind was still affected by the remnants of floating alcohol-saturated brain cells, and the prior night's embarrassment added to her confusion.

"You're probably wondering why I'm calling."

"Well, yes. Look, I want to apologize. I didn't mean to insult you last night."

He cut her off. "No. You've got this all wrong. I'm running late, and I'm sorry this has to be so abrupt, but . . . will you have dinner with me tonight?"

The question slammed against her forehead like a mud-pack hitting a wall. "Tonight?"

"I know it's short notice, but I'll be back by five, six at the latest. I can get up there by seven. How about seven o'clock at the Hotel? All right?"

"I don't know . . . I think . . . ."

"You're booked? I mean busy?" he asked. "It is a Friday night. I understand. Well, maybe another time. I'm sorry to have . . . ."

"No!"

"No what?" he asked. "Not another time, either?"

"No," she snapped, her foggy brain could not keep up with the rapid conversation, and her voice telegraphed her aggravation. "I'll do it. Okay. I'll be there!"

There was no answer. Apparently, she thought, the governor noticed that she was annoyed.

"Hello?" she called. Then repeated, "Hello?"

"Sorry." McDevitt was back to her. "That was Grace, telling me I have to hang up, the car's here. So you'll be there, then? Thank you. Great! I'll see you tonight, at seven."

Marty's eyes had grown to a size that consumed his face. Gradually, he got up from the chair in the corner of the room and moved toward Stephanie's desk. "Did I understand that conversation correctly? Are you going out with McDevitt? Steph? Please, tell me."

She stared at Marty and replaced the phone gently, to avoid making any unnecessary noise. Rubbing her forehead, she said, "My head is breaking. My stomach is twisted in knots. My vision is a blur, and the governor is taking me out to dinner."

"Where?"

"The hotel."

"Du Pont?"

Stephanie snapped, "Damn it, Marty, where do you think, the old Terminal Hotel on Front Street? I guess he meant the Hotel du Pont. He just said, 'hotel.' Hell, in this town that's what it means. Are you dense, or what?"

"Hey! Easy. Don't get upset with me. You didn't have to say yes if you didn't want to."

"Right!" she replied. "I should have said, 'No thank you, governor. I've already made plans.' Or, maybe I should have asked him, 'If I say no, will I lose my job?' "

Marty laughed and started reminding her that she was single and available and so was McDevitt. He had never married, was relatively attractive, financially well off. Plus, Marty added, if Stephanie and the governor hit it off, she could put in the word for Marty and the office from time to time.

"Why did I agree?" she asked, aloud, ignoring her boss's scheming and holding her forehead in both hands.

"Because you were flattered, intrigued and . . . ."

" . . . in a weakened state. God, I must be freaking nuts. But," she turned to her boss, "not a word of this to anyone. Understand?"

He nodded as he crossed his heart.

"I mean it, Marty."

"Only," he said, "if you tell me all the dirty little details tomorrow morning. All right?"

"Fine," she agreed, "but I can promise you, there won't be anything to tell."

"We'll see. We'll see," he cooed. Standing by the door, he added, "And to think it was me, taking you to the party, who played a major role in bringing you two together."

"Thanks a lot," she said, shooting him an obscene gesture as he hurriedly left the room.

12

At 10 minutes before seven on an unseasonably mild winter evening in February, Stephanie entered the lobby of the Hotel du Pont, a stately, five-star hotel in the center of Wilmington. Built in 1912, the historic structure radiated Old World elegance and charm. Presidents, actors, statesmen, corporate tycoons and du Pont millionaires had stayed in its rooms and closed multi-million-dollar agreements under its roof.

Other hotels associated with both national and international chains had moved into the city as a result of the urban renewal and casino development acts. But the "Hotel," as it was called, still remained the pinnacle, and it had never seriously been challenged for its coveted position.

Dressed in a long, sleek black dress, matching heels and a single white strand of pearls, Stephanie felt reasonably comfortable with her appearance. A hot shower and several pain killers had helped her prepare for her encounter. Most of the lingering headache pain was gone.

She still had doubts about her decision to agree to meet with McDevitt, but there was nothing she could do about it now. Realistically, she planned to suffer through the meal as quickly as possible, head home early and try to forget everything that had happened during the last two days.

It was 7:05 when the black Monte Carlo pulled up to the entrance and the governor was greeted smartly by the regally uniformed doorman. McDevitt jumped out and moved rapidly toward the revolving door, pushed through the metal circular frame and scanned the lobby.

He smiled when he recognized Stephanie. As he approached her, an elderly woman stopped him and said a few words. The governor shook her hand and engaged her in a soft, personal conversation.

By the time he freed himself from his fan, Sgt. Randy Poplos had arrived. McDevitt and his bodyguard came forward together, and the governor made introductions.

"This is Ms. Litera, Randy. She's the one who suggested that I needed some psychological testing."

Smiling, the plainclothes officer offered his hand. "A pleasure, ma'am. All the people in the office asked me to send their regards and tell you they agree with your professional assessment."

Stephanie blushed and forced a smile, thinking she must be the laughing stock of the executive wing.

"I'll be in the lounge, sir. If you need me, just push the beeper."

"Fine, Randy. We'll be fine. Check on us about 9:30."

As Poplos walked down the hall toward the Green Room Bar, the newly reacquainted couple entered one of the region's finest restaurants.

A tuxedo-clad host led McDevitt and Stephanie into the formal atmosphere of the Christina Room and seated them at a corner table next to the large fireplace. Hanging directly above them was "White House," by Jamie Wyeth. Eleven other originals by members of the Wyeth family were displayed under muted lighting throughout the large dining room.

Adjacent tables were kept empty, giving the governor and his guest a degree of privacy.

Dark, ornately-carved wood covered the walls. Pale white, Classic Rose German china, polished silver and sparkling crystal added to the formality of the setting. However, McDevitt was anything but stuffy. By the time the main course began, Stephanie was actually beginning to enjoy herself—in spite of her efforts to the contrary.

They shared their backgrounds. She was from an Irish-Italian Catholic family that had settled in Wilmington in the early years of the 20th century. The governor grew up in the heartland of Sussex County and he never really knew his parents. They had died in a car accident when he was quite young, and he was raised by his grandparents.

At 57, McDevitt was nine years older than Stephanie, but his appearance was younger than his years.

At the University of Delaware, she had been active on *The Review,* the campus student newspaper, and she also was affiliated with student theater and environmental groups.

The governor had been president of his senior class in both high school and at Salisbury State University, where he earned a pre-law degree. He graduated from Widener University School of Law and, eventually, worked as a state prosecutor in Sussex County. He was conservative in his approach to the criminal justice system and spending tax-payer money on government programs. But, he was quite liberal regarding economic policies, social attitudes and personal freedom.

After completing a master's in psychology at UD, Stephanie earned her doctorate at Penn and returned to the First State—then Delaware—to help mend damaged minds. She considered herself a liberal, but said she was more real-istic than most. She assured McDevitt that she was by no means a card-carrying member of the ACLU.

Stephanie found that the governor had a good sense of humor, but she also could tell that the real person was hid-den behind a protective shield.

She was honest and direct when responding to his ques-tions, and he found that refreshing. Only three members of his staff consistently gave him their honest opinions—Michael Pentak, Marty Poplos and Grace Welch.

They both liked the Eagles, had no interest in baseball and occasionally ate scrapple for breakfast.

It was a little after 8 o'clock, during dessert, that the con-versation began to wind down. He was having black coffee, she was drinking tea.

"I'm glad you agreed to come tonight," he said. "To be honest, I thought you would decline."

"To be honest, I nearly did," she admitted.

"But you didn't."

She shook her head, agreeing with him.

"Why not?"

"I don't know. I do know that I almost called back and canceled, but I'm glad I didn't. I did have a nice time."

"Well, the next obvious question is, can we do this again?"

Stephanie paused.

"Well?" he pressed for an answer.

"I don't know . . . ."

Her mind, which had been relaxed all evening, started to move into warp speed, tossing out concerns like an exploding volcano showering the scene with stress-filled lava.

She didn't even know what to call him. She had consciously phrased her sentences so she wouldn't have to use a name. But, at this point it was getting awkward.

"Hank," he said in reply. "My friends call me Hank. I'd like you to do that, too."

"Okay. . . Hank."

"So, how about next Saturday? Can I see you for dinner? I'm having a small party at Woodburn, entertaining a few foreign visitors. I'd like you to be there. I can have Randy pick you up."

She felt awkward. "I don't know. I just don't feel right about this."

"Why not?" he asked.

"Because you're the governor. I never wanted to go out with anyone who was in such a high profile position. I'm a city girl from a rowhouse. My parents were blue collar. I'm simple. I have a simple life. My work keeps me busy, I have no personal complications. I don't know if I'm ready to get involved."

McDevitt smiled. "Do you know what it's like for me, trying to find someone to go out with, a real person to talk to? Sure, I can find a knockout airhead who wants to get me into bed so she can say she scored with Governor McDevitt. I don't want that, never did.

"I have a hectic, pressure-filled life. I enjoy speaking to someone like yourself, someone who is not part of the plotting, agenda-oriented world in which I must exist and where I always have to be on guard."

She didn't reply, so he continued.

"I was impressed by your honesty last night. I'm impressed by your wit and conversation and, frankly, I find you very attractive. I don't know where this will go. All I know is that I have just had a wonderful evening. The time flew by. We weren't interrupted, happily. I consider that a miracle and a good omen. So, I'd say if you also had a good time, let's do it again and see what happens."

As Stephanie pulled on her napkin and began to answer, she saw McDevitt's chin lift abruptly. Together, the two diners watched as Sgt. Poplos raced through the restaurant and headed straight for their table.

The soft voice and warm eyes of a few minutes ago were gone. McDevitt had shifted into business mode and he braced for the news—troubling news—that he knew Randy was carrying.

"Sir. Sorry to interrupt," his eyes darted to Stephanie and came back to his boss. "Mike Pentak's on the line and this one's a doozy."

McDevitt grabbed the miniature phone, put his eyes down and listened.

As Stephanie waited quietly, Police Commissioner Pentak explained to McDevitt that a Russian diplomat, on a night out in Rehoboth, drove his car through a redlight a little after 7:30. The driver killed a 7-year-old girl who was walking with her family, crossing Rehoboth Avenue and First. The mother, who also was hit, was taken to the Sussex Emergency Trauma Center in Lewes. The father was with them. The car missed him. Physically, he was all right.

Normally, the entire town would have been empty, but the week-long warm spell in the middle of winter had brought out an unusually large number of beach visitors. Many were enjoying the spring-like weather and celebrating the start of President's Weekend at the beach.

The police, who were immediately on the scene, could see that the driver had been drinking. He was so drunk he was uninjured and couldn't even stand up. A crowd of people who had been walking along the boardwalk in 50-degree weather, saw the entire accident. It was a small mob scene, people trying to get at the driver. It was a miracle the driver didn't run down anyone else.

"He was going about 60 miles an hour. The victims were from Baltimore," Pentak added. "Father's a contractor, mother's a school teacher. The boys in Barracks 35 have the drunk in a cell, but they're afraid to give him a breathalyzer test."

"Why?" asked McDevitt.

"Hank, there's a major problem," Pentak said. "The guy's shouting he's got diplomatic immunity. His comrades have a condo in Ocean City. Their number was in the guy's wallet. They were called and are on their way up to get him out. We're expecting a call from the State Department any minute. To top it off, the guy's acting like he doesn't speak any English. Just keeps shouting 'dip-lo-mat!' and 'im-mu-ni-ty!' To me it sounds like he's been through this before. We're at a standstill until we get some direction here. What do you want to do? The book says we've got to release him."

"The girl's dead?"

"Yeah. Only 7 damn years old." Pentak's voice was weak, but bitter. "She went under the car, and he dragged the kid about 200 feet. There's a long trail of blood and bone on the street. Ripped her entire back right off. What was left of her ended up in the middle of the street, halfway down the block. Then he crashed his Lexus into the edge of the boardwalk. Hell, if it wasn't for the benches between Dolle's and the Candy Kitchen, we'd be fishing him out of the surf."

"What do you want to do, Mike?" McDevitt asked.

Calmly, the commissioner said, "I say we keep him in a cell, tell his Ruskie buddies to go screw themselves and send him up to Wilmington's Central Prison Facility. He'd never make it out alive. But you and I know we can't do that."

"Why not?"

"Because he's goddamn untouchable."

"What would we do if it was somebody else, from New York or Chicago, or even a foreigner from another country?"

"Just what I said, Hank. Keep him and have a few of the old timers work him over in private for a statement, tell his people to get screwed and drop the bastard in an unlocked cell in CPF. With luck, he'd probably never make it out and at the worst we'd get sued."

There was silence on the phone.

"So, Hank. What do I tell the chief?"

"Where are you now, Mike?"

"On Route 1, north of Lewes. I'll be there in 10 minutes."

McDevitt said, "Tell Chief Buxton that nobody talks to the killer until you get there. Can you get an interpreter down there tonight?"

"Sure. I know a guy in Wilmington, works for the courts when they need him. I'll give him a call."

"Fine. I want a complete signed confession from this asshole. I want it in Russian and in English, and I don't care how you get it. But first, get him out of Rehoboth tonight. I want him under maximum security—get a few of our ex-CIA guys and have them show us what they can do. Is that safe house available on Slaughter Island?"

"Yes," replied Pentak. "Not in use now. I'll have him out of Rehoboth within the hour and I'll stay with him on Slaughter until you get there."

"Fine. Make sure you've got a heavy escort. You don't release him for any reason, and absolutely no one talks to the press. Total blackout. As far as you know he's been lost in the system."

"Are you crazy, Hank. This is federal stuff. They're going to squeeze you on this one."

"I've been squeezed before. I'll be at the hospital, visiting the parents. Also, call the police in Baltimore. Get the names of their closest relatives and send a car up there and bring them to the hospital. Then get them rooms at the Boardwalk Victorian Regency. And, Mike, keep everyone quiet about this entire crime with the press. Anyone talks, even says hello to a reporter, they're out of a job. No leaks. Nothing."

"Right. What do we do with the comrades when they arrive?"

"Buxton's a good chief, the best we've had down at the beaches in a long time. Fill him in. He can tell any diplomats that give him trouble that I'll get to them when I'm good and ready. No one—not the feds, Russian consul, ACLU, or the goddamn U.N. ambassador or U.S. troops—I mean nobody, sees this guy except our people. Understand?"

"Right," Pentak agreed.

"I'm on my way," said McDevitt and he passed the phone to Poplos.

Getting up from the dinner table, McDevitt said, "Sorry. I've got to run. We'll call an officer to drive you home. Think seriously about next Saturday. I'll call you."

McDevitt gently shook Stephanie's hand and turned from the room, racing beside his bodyguard who was leading the way through the exit doors.

                    ⚜   ⚜   ⚜

As Poplos and the governor approached the New Castle County Airport, a DelMarVa Army National Guard helicopter was waiting. Enroute, McDevitt phoned Lydia Chase at her home in Easton. She had been alerted by Pentak and was expecting the call.

The governor asked her to call up the legal team they used for critical situations. It included three DelMarVa prosecutors and an equal number of private counsels on indefinite retainer. McDevitt directed Chase to have them all review the DelMarVa Incorporation Agreement involving arrangements among the three former states and the U.S. government, particularly as they related to diplomatic immunity. McDevitt said he wanted the answers to several obvious questions by 5 o'clock the following morning. A press conference would be held later in the day and he needed information before he was hit with reporters' questions.

Chase knew that McDevitt needed to know the limits of the state's ability to ignore federal diplomatic immunity statutes, particularly when the circumstances related to a major crime involving injury or death. It also would be important to know the extent to which the governor could be held personally liable if he ignored international law.

As soon as he hung up, the car phone rang. Poplos looked to his right as the governor picked it up. They had just arrived on the runway and two uniformed DelMarVa National Guard airmen waved vanity tag DMV-1 forward.

The helicopter blades were beating through the wind and the sound was entering the vehicle.

Pentak was on the line. "We've got the bastard and we're on our way out of town."

"Is Buxton with you?"

"Yes, here he is."

Carlton E. Buxton was the youngest barracks chief in the state. A business degree graduate, he joined the Maryland State Police right out of college and moved up the ranks rapidly. His family roots were in North Carolina, so he adjusted well to the rural area he initially patrolled near Cambridge and Crisfield. By the time he was 30, he was promoted to sergeant. After solving three long-open homicide investigations involving illegal drugs entering the peninsula through a migrant worker network, he was promoted to lieutenant.

Pentak appointed Buxton chief of the resort areas extending from Lewes to Fenwick Island because of his ability to relate to the younger, fun-seeking vacationers and still meet the needs of the year-round permanent residents, which included a large number of retirees.

Buxton would allow both tourists and residents a liberal degree of latitude, but when they crossed the line he knew how far to react and did so in appropriate stages.

"Buxton here, governor."

"Hi Carlton. What do you have for me?"

"Things are going as well as can be expected, sir. Anton Kulczinsky, that's the name he's given us, is presently in the company of me and the commissioner. He's in the back seat between troopers Harvey Potts and Leon Daisey, two good old farmboys from down near Exmore. And, by the way, sir, they're both parents themselves and they aren't happy about the little girl and her family's loss."

"Good. I'm ready to board the chopper. Be in Lewes, at the hospital, in about 30. We should get out to Deep Creek Refuge and onto the island in less than two hours."

Buxton shared some interesting information with the governor. According to a search of motor vehicle records and the M & MCI (major and minor crimes index), the name of Anton Kulczinsky, Anthony Kilclineski and Anton Kilczensky appeared 26 times in the last five years. Seventeen of the entries were parking fines, totaling more than $1,600 that were still outstanding.

Four were for operating a vehicle under the influence, all within the last three years. In one case, Anton drove the vehicle into a liquor store window. The follow-up file showed that the store owner was unable to collect any damages. "Diplomatic Immunity" was stamped on the folder.

Two other stops were after high speed chases down Highway 1, through Dewey and into the center of Ocean City. Anton was run off the road after damaging three police cars.

The notations: "Diplomatic Immunity. Case Closed."

The last three incidents involved minor moving violations.

"But," Buxton added, "our diplomat apparently knows how to speak English when he needs to. The female officer in one of the minor violations noted in her report that she was 'verbally abused in very good English, even though the subject acted like he didn't understand me when I pulled him over.' "

McDevitt thanked Buxton and began talking to Pentak, who had grabbed the phone. "How long before your Russian interpreter friend arrives?" the governor wanted to know.

"They're picking him up and flying him down to the island. He should be there about the time we arrive."

"Don't wait for me, Mike. When you get there, have the two officers start the process and squeeze this bastard good. I want both confessions—in Russian and English—handwritten and signed by tomorrow morning. Then I want our boy Anton under heavy guard in a solitary room."

Pentak replied, "We've got two CIA alumni waiting at the safe house and a team of others posing as electrical work crews on Route 16, stopping traffic and sealing off the island. So how much pressure can we apply to this scumbag?"

"Do anything you have to do, just don't leave any marks. How's the press situation?"

"They were camped outside the precinct house, but we went through Carlton's sub-level tunnel that goes out from the basement, under the sand dunes and through the old World War II communications bunkers. No problem at all. But the news hounds continued snooping around."

"What about Anton's buddies? Have they arrived from Ocean City?"

"Sure. We told them to stand outside with the press like everybody else. They didn't like it. Obviously they are used to the royal treatment. But Carlton told them there wasn't enough room inside. We got three calls from the State Department, but somehow they got cut off during transfer from the dispatcher. You know it's hectic down here. Sometimes high technology and human error combine to let you down."

"Seems like you have things under control. I meant what I said. Anybody talks and they're history."

"I passed the word, sir. We're clear on that. Everybody's on the same page. We all want this guy to swing. See you soon."

"Right. Thanks, Mike."

❧ ❧ ❧

McDevitt was tired of going to funerals, visiting hospitals and talking to victims' relatives. Things had slowed down for a time, but he knew it would never end.

The dead girl's mother was in a private room. Her shoulder was broken and her face cut, but she would be okay—after plastic surgery on her body and years of therapy on her mind. The father, a big man who looked like a sharecropper with large hands and no neck, only had a few cuts and bruises. His daughter had been a few feet behind him, walking to the side of his wife, when the speeding car ate them alive.

"I was telling them to hurry up, that we'd be late for our dinner reservations," he said, sitting in a chair with his hands pressed against his head. "I wasn't yelling, you know, just trying to have them keep up with me. That's when the car came over. I froze. I just FROZE!"

He was crying, upset that he couldn't save his daughter and protect his wife. "I didn't do anything. It was too big, coming too fast. I should have been holding her hand. Then it would have got me and not them. I was in such a rush."

McDevitt walked forward and put his hand on the man's back. The father grabbed the governor's wrist and squeezed. Then, slowly, eventually, he let go.

"They say the drunk who killed my Katika is some kind of foreign diplomat. I heard somebody say that you won't be able to do anything with him. That he's going to be able to go back to his country."

Randy Poplos, who was standing near the door, looked at McDevitt. The governor grabbed the man's shoulders and stared into the father's eyes. "I'm leaving two state police officers with you and your wife. Understand?"

The father nodded.

"They're outside the door. No one will bother you. My staff members will be here in the morning and we're bringing some of your family down to be with you. Get some sleep."

"I want to see Katika. Where's my little girl?"

"You'll deal with that tomorrow. The nurses will give you something to help you sleep. This hall of the hospital is off limits. No reporters will bother you. We'll keep you informed of what's going on. Trust me. The man who killed your daughter will not get away with this."

"I heard the nurses talking, off to themselves. I heard one of them say he was untouchable."

McDevitt whispered to the crying man, "Believe me, no one who does something like this is untouchable."

13

Joe Supinski jumped off the helicopter and ran across the lawn at Liberty Manor, the name of the safe house hidden on Slaughter Island at Deep Creek Refuge. Anton Kulczinsky was inside under heavy guard.

Commissioner Pentak met his friend at the front door and ushered him inside the Victorian-era hunting lodge. Like a hotel, the entry hall extended three stories above their heads. It was decorated with lifeless trophy heads of animals that, in happier days, flew, swam and ran.

Supinski had grown up in Philly and attended South Catholic High School with Pentak. After getting out of the service, Supinski moved to Wilmington, bought a rowhouse in the Browntown section and got a job at the post office. He worked the night shift in the New Castle mail distribution center at Hare's Corner and was disturbed about being pulled off the job and flown 120 miles in the middle of the night with no explanation.

"Damn, Mike, what's going on? Three of your unsmiling, bald-headed goons come in, flash badges and grab me out of work. Hell, my boss hates me as it is for all the time I take off, volunteering at the port and in court. Now, you come along and hammer a few more nails in my coffin. This better be good."

"It is," Pentak said, as he explained the situation and told Joe he needed him to verify the wording of Anton's confession and, more importantly, play a major role in the interrogation. They were seated in a gaming parlor that displayed several more animal heads in a frozen state of staring. The furniture was the same color as the walls, brown or some other shade of dark wood.

The two men were alone. A few guards could be heard pacing on the polished hardwood outside the door in the main hall.

"Can you help us out?" Pentak asked.

"Sure. If it gets too involved, if I can't understand something, I'll let you know. But it should be fine. I've done this before."

Pentak paused. He was putting a lot of faith in his high school friend. He also had never asked Joe Supinski to work on such a serious case before.

"Joe, I've got to ask you something."

"What?" the mailman said, still twisting his neck to peer into the corners of the room, slightly distracted by the hunting souvenirs, trophies and impressive Western landscapes.

"How do you feel about the death penalty?"

"Huh?"

"The death penalty, Joe. What's your gut feeling?"

The interpreter stared back, thought a moment, and said, "Mike. I trust you. You can trust me. I may be a post office flunky, but that's because it's a mindless job that allows me to do what I want in my spare time. I spent four years in the Air Force Command Satellite Intercept Station, located in a West Berlin intel center. You should know that from my file.

"That was in the days of the Wall. I listened in on Warsaw Pact communications. Sometimes it was Ruskie, Polish and Czech at the same time, and I handled it. I was very good at my job, had a Code 7A clearance, that's well above Top Secret. And, if you read my file carefully, you know I was involved in more than a few interrogations of captured agents, both as a translator and interrogator. I'm not a dummy, Mike. My parents came from Poland because they didn't like it there. Thank God they did, or I wouldn't be here with you now."

Pentak was about to speak, to clarify his concern, but Supinski continued in an angry tone.

"Don't insult me, Mike, by asking my views on the death penalty. You either trust me or you don't. And if you don't, I wouldn't be here. But I'll answer you this way: Like most people, I believe in justice but not the law. They aren't the same thing. Sometimes, you have to break man's imperfect laws to do the right thing, to attain justice, and in my book that's fine. There is nothing you can do here, in your fancy hideaway, that I haven't see happen in Berlin. Satisfied? Now, are you going to fill me in on our situation or do you want to put me on a chopper heading for home?"

Pentak smiled and gave the translator a summary of the killing in Rehoboth and said that DelMarVa police had snatched the diplomat.

Supinski nodded, obviously impressed with the cops' initial response to the situation.

"As I see it," he said, "you probably are sweating bullets because this diplomat asshole is telling you he's got immunity and that his people are calling every assistant secretary at the State Department who they ever shared a shot of vodka with. Plus, they're probably sending some bigshots to find him and take him back home, all under Washington's and the U.N.'s protection.

"But, since you've got him here, in the middle of nowhere as far as I can tell, I surmise that you and McDevitt are going to get him to sing. God, Mike, if McDevitt snuffs home-grown American products who deserve it, common sense tells me Anton is probably swinging from a rafter downstairs already and you'll want me to forge his signature."

Pentak smiled. "Thanks," he said. "This is going to be a hairy situation and we're all a bit tense."

"Hell, Mike, relax. I used to be in on these several times a month, but it's been a while." Supinski rose and said, "Let's go and see what our boy has to say."

A concealed elevator, hidden behind a massive hall closet, transported the two men down four levels into a subterranean basement. Pentak explained that the lower floors were added during World War II as a center to monitor sea traffic in the Chesapeake Bay. Radar and surveillance technology at that time were concerned with German submarine infiltration, which could cripple domestic and military shipping.

Although never publicized, the "Eastern Shore Underground Network," with several similar complexes on both sides of the Chesapeake Bay shoreline, was responsible for identifying and directing Coast Guard sub chasers to more than 68 unpublicized Nazi "kills."

By the mid '50s, the secret sites were abandoned and turned over to the state. Most were sealed up and a few were used for storage of munitions and disaster relief equipment. The one on Slaughter Island became Maryland's Emergency Communications Control Center, renovated to operate as the state government's headquarters during a natural or military disaster—primarily in the event Annapolis, Maryland's capital city, had to be evacuated.

Supinski watched as the twin silver metal doors parted, revealing a very wide hallway that extended more than 100 feet straight ahead.

"This was remodeled a little over a year ago, for special guests like Anton. On this floor we have six interrogation chambers and six observation rooms, three pairs on each side. Each with recording and video capabilities."

Supinski turned slowly and followed Pentak as they were allowed entry into Control Station A, through a door of the left side of the hall. Each observation room resembled a fully equipped television production studio, with state-of-the-art electronics, a half-dozen color video monitors and black-faced communications equipment with glowing red and green digital displays. Integrated touch panel systems, resting in front of each shift commander, enabled operators manipulation over every human sense except taste. This was done using touch-sensitive graphic screens indicating icons that controlled video, audio, lighting and temperature modification.

"Use this place often?" Supinski asked.

"No. As a matter of fact, he's our first real guest. We've had test runs, but you could say Anton is our virgin."

"And I get to help break him in?" Supinski said with a sly grin.

"Right."

The two men moved to the side of the room that was occupied by four police officers and two civilians. They were looking through a two-way glass window and moved aside to allow the commissioner and his guest a better view. Through the glass, Supinski could see Anton, inside the adjacent room and seated at a table. There were three chairs, one for the prisoner, bolted to the floor, and two on the opposite side for his interrogators.

Anton's hands were cuffed and attached to the tabletop. The loops of the restraints, which were a soft composite plastic that left no marks, were fastened somewhere below the table surface, dramatically restricting the prisoner's arm movement.

Anton wore no shoes and was dressed only in boxer shorts and socks. A digital monitor displayed on the observation room wall indicated the temperature in the interrogation room. While observers were working their digital wizardry in 72-degree comfort, the prisoner—and his guards—were locked in a chilly 28-degree icebox.

A change of clothes was waiting for the translator. Pentak had estimated the postal worker's size, explaining that they thought it would be best if Supinski played the role of a sympathetic Russian Embassy official.

The expensive tailored suit fit very well. It resembled those worn by New York U.N. diplomats. Russian flag cufflinks capped off the outfit.

"We're relieving the guards every 30 minutes," one of the technicians explained. "The prisoner isn't as lucky, but we are varying the temperature on him. Our physicians suggested that the best way to disorient him is to jump from 28 to 88 degrees every 20 minutes. We'll be shifting to the high temperature range in exactly four minutes."

Supinski noticed a CD player that was useful to drive a victim mad, with high decibels of all types of objectionable music and piercing sounds. He had seen the technique work well in Berlin.

The in-house technician and shift commander pointed at the prisoner and explained that Anton had not eaten for several hours, but was being given very small sips of water. He had no bathroom privileges and the desired effects of steady pressure and stress were beginning to show.

The shift commander handed Pentak and Supinski duplicate files. Inside was the prisoner's local criminal history and much more, including education, military service and covert experience and current assignments. His case officer's name was Stanik, who directed Kilczensky in his real job in Washington—an industrial spy who specialized in securing research data on telecommunications prototypes. His latest target was a microfiber research complex in Timonium called XZP Ltd.

Over the speakers, Anton was repeating "Voda . . . . Pozhaluista. Voda. . . . Voda . . . ."

"What's he saying?" Pentak asked.

"He's repeating the word 'Water.' He wants water," said Joe.

Pentak signaled for them to head for the hall. As the two guards left the room, Pentak, Supinski, in his new suit, and two other shirtless officers entered. The temperature was moving up quickly.

Anton opened his eyes.

"Kak dela?" Supinski said.

The prisoner responded immediately and enthusiastically, obviously thrilled that he had someone to whom he could talk. A long litany of Slavic gibberish filled the interrogation room and flew through speakers in the observation center. Voice activated tape recorders captured every sound and video cameras rolled continuously, recording every moment of action in the adjoining room.

The look of excitement on Anton's face indicated that he

thought the embassy had sent his savior to take him home.

Pentak, seeking some idea of the prisoner's comments, looked at Supinski, but the embassy impostor stared ahead and said nothing.

Sitting down at the table opposite the now sweating captive, Joe noticed that Anton's lips were raw and he was still shaking with chills despite the oppressive heat.

The visiting interpreter began speaking in a whisper. Although the level was soft, a laser microphone, situated directly above the stationary table picked up every word very clearly.

Supinski told Anton, in refined Russian, that the embassy would be coming to pick him up soon. A deal had been made, but he must sign the confession and admit to everything.

The prisoner shook his head, violently, back and forth. Beads of sweat flew across the room leaving droplet stains on the floor. As Anton's uncontrolled head motion continued, Supinski drew back his right hand and slapped Anton hard, across the side of his face.

"You stupid fool," Supinski said, continuing in Russian, "The girl is dead, the American blacks are rioting. My name is Janek. The embassy general consul from New York was in Washington. He and the ambassador both agreed that you should explain yourself to these country idiots. It doesn't matter what you say, you have immunity and will be released and on Aeroflot for Leningrad tonight!"

"But they hit me, kicked me," Anton said, lowering his voice. "I want to kill these black bastards. I swear I will!"

"Quiet! Fool! I can get you out of here. They sent me from New York, flew me down here. Let's get this over with and get out of here. Go get some vodka, find some American whores."

"I don't know. I can't think. I need water. I can't talk, can't think."

"Let me talk to them." Supinski got up and walked over to Pentak, who had moved with the two guards to a far corner. Within minutes a glass of cool water was brought into the room. The guard also dropped a pen and a pad of paper on the table.

Randy Poplos and the governor had just entered the observation room.

As Supinski returned to his seat, he began talking. "These goddamn Americans are stupid," he whispered. "You will be a millionaire when you're free from this place. You will sell your story to the news programs these idiots love to watch. The consul and ambassador were distressed over your detainment, but they said we will obtain major trade concessions because of what they did to you illegally."

Anton had not yet bought it all. The water was gone. He stared at Supinski and asked, "Who sent you?"

The postal worker leaned forward, whispered in Anton's ear, "Stanik. And she wants you back to complete your assignment with XZP."

Satisfied that Supinski was genuine, Anton's parched lips let out a smile. "I have held out a long time, yes?"

"True," Supinski said, nodding.

"You will put that in your report? That I never said a word of English to these pigs in uniforms?"

"Of course. You did well."

"More water and then I will write."

"Fine. You write it in Russian. Then, I will make a copy in English and you will sign both. Do you understand?"

"Yes, but when can we leave?"

"I have a diplomatic car outside. The minute we hand the pigs your statement they will have one of their people review it. If acceptable, we will be free to go. But," Supinski stressed, "there were scores of witnesses. They are not as stupid as they look. Be sure to put everything down, exactly as it happened. Exactly, or we'll be here all night."

"I don't remember it all. I was drunk. Speeding. I saw the girl. I was laughing and directed the car toward her. I hit her, did I not? I hate all these American bastards. I ran her down? Yes? And her ugly mother, too?"

"Yes," Supinski said, his throat holding down the disgust, "you hit them both. But," he paused and said, "don't put in your thoughts. They don't need that. Just what you did, the actions. There is no sense in giving them more reason to hurt you."

"They can't hurt me any more," Anton said, laughing. "You are here with me. To hell with them! I will tell them why I did it. Why I hate them. I'm a diplomat. Untouchable. Then, Janek, you can take me home. Yes?"

"Yes," Supinski said, smiling, patting the prisoner on the forearms. "You are right, Anton, to hell with them all. Write down what you think of them, the stupid American police pigs. Yes. Do it! Tell them the truth about themselves."

As the exhausted and delirious prisoner wrote three full pages, Joe "Janek" Supinski paced the length of the cell. Back and forth he walked, pausing only to respond to any questions or requests from Anton. To increase his credibility, Joe cursed the Americans and talked about their stupidity. He pointed at Pentak and made insulting remarks about him in Russian. Anton laughed. Then, the fake diplomat ordered clothes, shoes and more water brought in for his new friend.

When he was finished, Joe looked over the document, asked a few questions and took it into another room. Within 10 minutes, he had translated it into English, had the papers reviewed by a DelMarVa attorney and was given the okay to take both documents back in for Anton's signature.

Entering the room, Joe shouted at the biggest black cop in English. "You ugly, fat pig. Release my comrade, and do it now!"

Anton, now dressed in his clothes, the handcuffs removed, smiled at the officer and his eyes twinkled at his new embassy friend.

Immediately, Anton rubbed his wrists, picked up the pen and wrote his signature at the bottom of each document.

Joe Supinski walked to the table, picked up the pen and checked over the papers. As Anton began to stand up, the interpreter moved toward the prisoner, grabbed him by the neck and shouted, in English, "Not so fast, asshole!"

Anton froze in mid stance. The realization of what had happened reached his mind about the same time the huge black officer punched him in the back and tossed him like a rag doll across the room. The cuffs were back on and Anton knew that this time his crime against America was not being overlooked.

"Pig!" the prisoner spat. "You stupid American! I should have known it was a trick with your gutter Russian. Your mother was a pig of a whore who screwed her way to America!"

Suddenly, Anton shifted to English. "I will kill you, you American asshole!" he shouted. The switch proved timely; since, at that moment, McDevitt, Poplos and Buxton entered the interrogation room.

McDevitt walked over to the table and looked down on the prisoner. "You're never going back to your homeland, comrade. You're never leaving DelMarVa, and we've got a nice cell waiting for you on death row with a lot of deranged American bastards—bigger, meaner and uglier than Officer Potts over there."

The 230-pound state trooper flashed his ivories at Anton.

The prisoner was screaming, cursing, foaming at the mouth in Russian, English, whatever words he could spit out.

Grabbing the papers from the interpreter, McDevitt said, "Nice job, Mr. Supinski. We are indebted to you." Then as the governor exited the room, he shouted towards the control room window, "Drop it down to 20 degrees for about a half hour and see if that will chill him out."

❧   ❧   ❧

There was a call from Lydia Chase waiting for McDevitt when he, Pentak and company exited the elevator and returned to the main floor hall.

The conversation was relatively long and McDevitt made some notes. After returning to the table in the Liberty Manor parlor, he shared the news with the others.

"Apparently," he said, "we've had a large stroke of luck. At the time the laws creating DelMarVa were being drafted, an energetic law school intern remarked that there was an unusually large number of vacationers from Washington, D.C., who regularly visited Ocean City and Rehoboth Beach. Knowing our strong stand on law and order—and the public's negative view of foreign diplomats getting away with crimes—the promising student suggested that the new state might want to insert a provision that foreigners who committed capital crimes in DelMarVa automatically waived their right to hide behind the international shield—more commonly known as diplomatic immunity.

"At the time, everyone thought it was a frivolous but interesting inclusion. Apparently, some thought it could become a test case for later use throughout the country. No one thought such a loophole would ever pass Congressional scrutiny, but somehow it did. It was a legal fluke. When the federal negotiators found out, they were so embarrassed they made sure the unique provision received no publicity and was buried down deep in extra fine print. Nevertheless, our legal staff and the federal boys agree that it's a valid clause. Despite all our efforts to keep him here illegally, Anton is ours, legally, and was all along."

"Plus," added Pentak, nodding at Joe Supinski, "we have one, I mean two, signed confessions."

McDevitt suggested the other men get something to drink. He walked to a bedroom on the second floor, closed the door and picked up the phone.

He knew the private number and dialed.

It only rang once. "This is Governor Henry McDevitt. I need to speak to the President."

He listened a second and then interrupted the speaker.

"I know it's 4 o'clock in the morning. Don't you think I'd be sleeping and not dare consider calling him if this wasn't important?"

Within two minutes Scott Woodyard was on the line.

Quickly, DelMarVa's governor explained his side of the situation, stressing the girl's death and the signed confession, adding the growing national public intolerance over the misuse of diplomatic immunity.

The President began to protest McDevitt's desire to keep

the drunken Russian diplomat. But, the President was speechless when he realized that McDevitt's renegade state had a legal way to disregard diplomatic immunity in capital cases. McDevitt stressed that, if necessary, he would be willing to share the law and how it was enacted with every state and municipality that might be interested.

The President, in a very short time, agreed to call the Russian president and resolve the situation to everyone's satisfaction, except Anton's—thereby minimizing publicity about DelMarVa's unique law.

As he returned to the group waiting on the first floor, McDevitt poured himself a glass of scotch and predicted that the morning newscasts would feature a statement from a representative of the Russian president surrendering the Slavic diplomat to the authorities in DelMarVa and voluntarily revoking Anton's diplomatic immunity.

When he finished his drink, McDevitt suggested that Mr. Supinski keep the suit and stay the night, although it was nearly sunrise. The governor asked Pentak to contact Grace Welch and reschedule his morning appointments. McDevitt planned to get a few hours rest before his noon press conference and, since it was almost sunrise, he didn't think it was proper to call Stephanie Litera.

14

February 2008

Stephanie Litera stared at her client. At the beginning of Charles Bettner's second counseling session, the psychologist had invited him to talk about himself and, after a few quiet moments, that was his first comment.

"Do you know what it's like to have power, doctor?"

"Yes. To a degree, everyone has some type of power, whether it's over themselves or over someone else."

"True. Quite correct," Charles said. "But I'm talking about absolute control—to look at a man or a woman, and to see, Frau Doctor, by the look in their eyes, that they know that you are in charge. Nothing spoken, you understand, only the mental, silent transfer of that harsh, unpleasant realization. It's quite a sensation, and one that few experience—and those who do never forget it."

"Did you have that experience, Charles?"

"Yes," he said, softly. "I've lived with power, many times. But, I don't want to talk about that."

"Fine. What do you want to talk about?"

"Anything else."

Stephanie leafed through the folder. "I'm wondering, was it the control, the freedom, the decision-making ability, the independence—or a combination of them all—that attracted you to collection work?"

"All that and more," he said, smiling. "You have just

scratched the surface, Frau Doctor. I found having the independence and authority to make on-the-scene decisions, that affected others who were filled with fear, quite satisfying."

"So you enjoyed your work?"

Charles seemed amused at the lameness of her question. "Enjoyed is not correct. *Loved* is a more appropriate description. I *loved* to come in every day. *Loved* to close the hardest cases. *Loved* to excel where others failed."

"But," she picked up the conversation, "what you really are saying is that you loved breaking your subjects down, making them cry, watching their whole lives crumble, seeing their dreams destroyed, at your hands, am I right?"

"I won't deny it. Honesty is the best policy. Right?"

"What did your father do, Charles?"

His head snapped around so quickly that if it wasn't connected to his body it would have landed in Stephanie's lap. "What did you say?"

"Your father. I want to know what he . . . ."

"No comment."

"That won't do, Charles. I want to know about your family."

"I repeat. No comment." His voice was almost a hiss this time.

"Why the reluctance? Why the hesitation? Didn't you like your family, Charles?"

He remained quiet, walked to the window, ignoring her. Then, after a few awkward moments, he answered, but he did not look in her direction. He seemed to be talking to his own reflection in the glass. "I would wager that you know the answer. Don't you? It's probably in my personnel file, which, I assume from your question, is in your control. Correct?"

"Yes."

"So," Charles turned and said, "it's all there. Charles Doe, no family, no last name, abandoned at birth in St. Angela's Charity Hospital in Richmond, Virginia. A single note, attached to a tattered blanket, said, 'Please take care of my son, Charles. Thank you, a sorrowful mother.' "

Charles recited the message from an implant deep in his brain. Continuing, he said, "Between the ages of 1 and 15, the homeless boy was tossed and transferred 11 times to various foster homes. I bet the reports say the little tyke was an intelligent lad who also excelled in sports. But, and here's the best part, doctor, the boy was a loner with an introverted personality—which could be taken by some as a superiority complex because of his elevated IQ."

"Did you write this file, Charles?"

"No, but I know it quite well."

"Let's get back to the question about your father, or should I say fathers?"

"What do you want to know? How many I had? Too many. Were they good with me? No. Were they abusive? Most certainly. Did they strike me? Yes, but often with a belt and, in one case, with a metal bar.

"But, then, why did they hit the pathetic boy, you want to know. Probably," Charles continued, "because most of my foster mothers liked me too much, and the big, brave, macho bastards were jealous and took it out on me. It was no sweet suburban existence for little Charles. No indeed."

Bettner's eyes had glazed over. He was back, decades earlier, seeing a mind-generated movie of a horrifying scene from his adolescence. The young teenager of 15 screamed, but the older, stronger, larger man ignored the cry and hit the boy again and again and again. Then, with Charles' foster mother looking on, the big man shoved the skinny boy's face into the rusted, scum-stained bathtub from which the animals drank, located behind the barn.

Thick flakes of sludge—green and brown and yellow—floated on the surface. Some hunks of slime moved aside as the angry farmer shoved Charles' face deep below the surface. The thick hand grasped the back of Charles neck until the boy was almost unconscious. Blackness was approaching. Water was entering his lungs.

Suddenly, surprisingly, the hand let loose and the boy's head exploded above the surface. Shaking off the water and slime, Charles rubbed his face with his shirtsleeve. Looking around, he saw the big man, beating his wife, Charles' step-mother, with a gnarled tree branch. She was being punished for pulling her husband off the boy. In a rage, the drunken farmer struck her huddled body three, four, five times. The wood of the branch striking through the skin and contact-ing the woman's leg bones.

Charles, weak from nearly being drowned but realizing the woman had saved his life, instinctively grabbed the wooden handle of a rusted pitchfork. As the man raised the club to hit the screaming woman again, the wet and disori-ented boy charged at the man from behind. Running, with-out thinking, without hesitating, Charles drove the dark brown iron pokers into the center of the farmer's back.

In midstride, the man dropped the hickory stick. As the hefty neck twisted slowly to the rear, the farmer's wide eyes saw Charles, shoving and twisting the pitchfork prongs deeper into the older man's body.

The woman, suffering from pain and fear, turned away and cried. To make sure his stepfather was going to die, Charles shook the handle of his makeshift weapon, ripping nerves and arteries, inflicting the maximum amount of inter-nal damage. Blood, bright red streams of it, began to flow from the four openings in the dead man's back. Through his stained tee shirt, down his green, soil-covered work pants, over his brown, dung-coated boots and onto the ground below.

Charles smiled as he left the oozing corpse that had flopped against the barnyard dirt.

Carefully, the boy carried the new widow into the house. After placing her in bed, he went out and buried the still warm body beneath the darkest corner stall in the milk barn. There were few visitors to the Bettner farm, located 18 miles outside of town. He didn't worry that anyone would ask about the dead man's whereabouts. Not for a while anyway.

Accidents happened in the hills of Virginia. People didn't ask questions, kept to themselves. Men went hunting and didn't return home. Old timers worked on their moonshine stills and disappeared. What may have seemed strange to city people was normal, hazardous, everyday living in the hills.

Charles Bettner was back in the present, smiling for a moment as he recalled that time, years ago, when he thought he was going to have a home.

"So, Charles?" Stephanie said, loudly to get him to respond. "So, you did not get along with your male foster parents?"

"Actually, that's not entirely correct. I had problems with most of them, all, in fact, except the last. Dear Mr. Bettner. I liked him so much, I took his name. He was my last foster father."

"What happened to him?"

"He disappeared when I was in my teens. No one knows where he went, disappeared on the river while fishing. They never found his body. A few say he ran off, since he owed a lot of people money. I stayed on and helped my mother work the farm."

Stephanie jotted a final note to end the session. She felt they had covered enough ground. While most of her recently assigned clients were only slightly disturbed and hardly interesting, Charles Bettner was different.

She would talk to Marty before the next meeting and explain that she was intrigued with this particular client. She felt there was more below the surface and a few extra meetings might be necessary.

Charles' comments about power trips and his hesitancy regarding his childhood experiences, sent up a few red flags. Besides, she found him fascinating in a bizarre sort of way, and meeting with him would probably break up a series of routine conversations with her other clients. Charles Bettner was no normal abnormal, she told herself. He was among the more intriguing of her maladjusteds.

"Until we meet again, doctor."

"Yes," Stephanie replied. "How about next week? Same time."

"Of course," he said, flashing a smile. "As a troubled and recently demoted employee, my time is your time."

🌿　　🌿　　🌿

The end of February turned abnormally cold. Charles shoved the heater to high and waited in the underground garage for his Blazer to get warm. He smiled, pleased that he had enjoyed another appointment with Stephanie.

She was stylish, intelligent, and, he thought, could probably become attracted to him as their meetings continued. After all, why did she plan to see him each week when others were given a one-shot interview and sent on their way or directed into group counseling.

It was obvious he didn't need any extra help. He was as sane, no, more sane and more intelligent, that 98 percent of the people who worked in the state. NO! That's not true, make that 98 percent of the people alive.

If things went according to plan, he would ask her out to dinner soon. If she didn't accept he'd still have their weekly meetings to look forward to, and those encounters would allow him to continue to work his charm—eventually she would come around.

She could tell he was intelligent, a hard worker, a war veteran, a dedicated employee who had gotten the shaft. That all would work to his benefit. Women like to nurture those in distress, he thought. He'd have to work on that fine line between anger about being demoted and playing the lost puppy who needs a hug, a caress, some female understanding and attention.

That was next week's plan.

But first was his weekend trip to Wicomico County. He had been looking forward to that for a long time—his first chance to meet a member of his new family.

🌿　　🌿　　🌿

It was the fourth Sunday in February and—come rain, sleet, snow or blazing cold winter sunshine—the place to be was the volunteer fire hall in Shepherd, Maryland, home of the 42nd annual muskrat and scrapple festival.

Close to a thousand dinners were dished up—mostly eat-in, family style—during the six-hour event. The Shepherd Fire Hall Ladies Auxiliary had been cooking freshly caught marsh rabbit (a more tender name for muskrat) for three days prior to the arrival of the crowd.

The 4-pound aquatic rodents that live in the peninsula wetlands and feed on cattails and farm crops are legal for trapping from December through early March. During that time, thousands of the rodents' pelts are sold by area trappers to buyers who travel down to DelMarVa from the big cities up north.

A famous urban legend surrounds the lowly muskrat. According to the story that has been handed down for generations, a well-known, Eastern Shore of Maryland restaurant owner discovered that he was running out of muskrat and couldn't get any more for a big winter tourist weekend. To solve his dilemma, the proprietor paid several area boys to catch cats from nearby towns. He then cooked up the cat meat—which he considered an acceptable secret substitute—and served it to his customers to get through his temporary 'rat shortage.

Some still claim they know some of the people who ate there that weekend. But, when the tasteless facts were made public, the restaurant owner was nearly tarred and feathered, and his building was burned to the ground, twice.

Since the carcasses of both animals are very similar, today, cooks at the few remaining restaurants that serve up 'rat on a regular basis demand that their suppliers leave the animal's head or webbed foot on the freshly skinned meats when they are delivered for cooking.

But, on the annual festival weekend in Shepherd, the eager eaters knew they were getting the real thing. An array of 'rat sandwiches, 'rat stew, 'rat burgers and even a few experimental 'rat fritters were complemented by crisp rectangular slabs of sizzling scrapple. A hundred 10-pound packages of that distinctive DelMarVa delicacy had been picked up on Friday afternoon from four plants in nearby Sussex County.

Charles left his black Blazer at the edge of the extended parking lot in a leveled cornfield. He headed toward the entrance of the old, white, concrete block fire hall. It was 1:30 in the afternoon. Rat dinners had started hitting the smacking lips of farmers, trappers and tourists promptly at noon.

About three dozen travel trailers with out-of-state plates were parked close to the bright red side door. They had arrived on Friday afternoon; many of the occupants of these mobile homes turned their annual excursion to Shepherd into a long weekend getaway.

Charles' bald head was covered with a green John Deere baseball cap. Its beak and back were stained with grease, giving it a broken-in look. He wore dark sunglasses and was smoking an inexpensive, thin cigar. An expensive fake black mustache covered his top lip. A large, dark blue coat, red and black checked shirt and standard blue jeans rounded out Charles' down home appearance.

With over a thousand visitors in the village, strangers didn't stand out this weekend in Shepherd, unless they arrived in a coat and tie. That had been done on occasion, usually by politicians during campaign years.

During the last few years, interest in muskrat had been dying out and only a few restaurants still offered the distinctive peninsula dish on a regular a basis. Therefore, serious rat eaters flocked to Shepherd each February to share tales of the glory days of the marsh rabbit.

For most of its history, the small-town festival had been a moderate success, but more recently it had grown into a big tourist money maker. The dramatic upturn came in 1999, soon after a Washington, D.C., reporter stumbled on the event and ran a feature write up that was carried in papers across the country. Now, even the locals had to get in line for a seat. But much needed tourist money was left behind, so complaints from the regulars were few. After all, they only had to be nice to the visitors one weekend a year, then they could go back to their charming clannish attitude and ignore anybody who took a wrong turn and found the village by accident.

After paying his $12 at the door, Charles saw an empty metal chair at the end of a folding banquet table. Tipping his hat, he took the vacant seat and settled in.

Friendly introductions were tossed across the disposable yellow plates and white paper tablecloth. Ricky was from Trappe; Elwood and Erma had come over from Millsboro; and Delbert and Ned had "drove up from Wachapreague."

A lot of the farmers wore shit-kicker boots underneath clean jeans and flannel shirts. Caps were in style, but none were worn backwards.

Three tables of black watermen and farmers sat together at the far end of the room. Self-segregated, they were having as good a time as everyone else. A steady stream of eaters continued to flow through the front door. More people were coming in than going out, but the hall only held about 250. It would handle the crowd, but Charles could see it would get crowded during the peak time, around 3 o'clock.

"Dig into this 'rat, boy!" shouted Ricky. "We ain't gonna eat it all!"

"Yeah!" Delbert called out above the noise, "it's soft and smooth when it's hot. Look at them juices," he added, lifting a spoonful out of the ceramic bowl. "Them ladies'll be here with more. So dive on in. No sense lettin' it get stiff and cold on ya."

Charles smiled, reached across the table and started making himself a platter, starting with a spoon of soft home-made mashed potatoes, adding a fresh baked roll and a helping of stewed tomatoes.

Ned tossed a piece of gray scrapple on his plate and shouted, "This scrapple's just right! As I always say, there's only two things I want my wife to do good. One's cook me up a perfect square a scrapple and the other's . . . ."

The table paused, quiet and waiting.

" . . . . cook me up some good 'rat stew!"

Everybody exploded in laughter and Elwood whispered something into Erma's ear, causing her to smile and nod.

A local, four-piece bluegrass band was on the stage, playing country and western standards. A few folks were on the floor, not dancing, but rather swaying to the music as they moved from table to table, hailing friends and renewing old times. That plus eating were the main events.

The afternoon moved along quickly. Charles didn't eat much, just took a few small samples of the delicacies. Many in the room were serious consumers of regional cuisine. Heavy pot bellies were in abundance, but women eaters were sparse. That was to be expected, since most of the local ladies were working in the kitchen.

Not too many females, even country women, got excited over a plate of food that consisted of ground up pig brains, lips and heart or the flesh of an animal that had spent its life swimming in the tidal marsh.

It took about an hour, while he politely engaged his partners of the afternoon in nonsensical chatter, for Charles to spot him. He was tall, beefy, obviously a farmer. He appeared to know a few other people, but it was obvious he had come alone. A wide, brass buckle in the shape of a horseshoe held his belt to the sagging jeans. Tall-heeled and pointy-toed cowboy boots anchored his body to the concrete floor.

His hands were large, like the paws of someone who used them daily in his work. If he wasn't a farmer, then he would probably be a mechanic or blacksmith. One of the three, thought Charles. But any of them would do.

Charles waited patiently. His eyes constantly darting from the lips and faces of his friends for a day—Delbert, Elwood, Erma, Ricky and Ned.

God, these people are idiots! Charles thought, silently speaking to himself through a fake smile. *I wish I had them all in the back of an enclosed truck. I would connect a hose from the exhaust pipe to the inside and drive them around until they were fumigated to death.*

The next move was up to fate, and she was on Charles' side that cold Sunday afternoon.

Across the hall, the targeted farmer rose from his chair and tugged on his belt, moving his jeans up snug and comfortable. Zipping his red down-filled coat, the high-heeled boots headed for the back door.

Charles moved quickly, nodding at his friends and smoothly stepping across the hall's dance floor. By the time the farmer was at the rear exit, Charles was one step behind, grabbing the door before it closed.

Practically walking together, the two men headed for a row of white portable toilets that stood in a row by the edge of the cornfield.

"Cold as hell!" shouted Charles, as he moved beside the red coated man.

"Damn right!" agreed the stranger, lighting up a small, cheap cigar, its pungent odor surrounded the pair.

The gods were good, thought Charles, for they were the only two souls in the lot. Sunlight was fading in the west. It was nearly 5 o'clock. The food fest would be winding down soon. He knew he would only get one chance. Charles would have to make his move soon.

"You from 'round here?" Charles asked.

"Yeah! Over in Welsley, only five mile up the road. Why?"

They continued to walk as they talked.

" 'cause I want some directions to get back over to the Bay Bridge quick like. Can ya help me out?"

"Sure," said the smoker. "Ya head outta town offa this road here, then ya . . . ."

"Wait," said Charles, "I gotta take a leak bad. How 'bout if I meet ya out here and ya show me on a map I got in my veehicle?"

"No problem. I gotta go, too. Be out in a sec'."

The two men hit separate toilets and Charles was delighted. *Simple as shooting rat in a marsh,* he thought. *Just a little more luck and I'll bag my first trophy.*

Charles was waiting as the farmer came out. They walked about 50 feet, to the back of Charles' Blazer.

"Damn cold out here!" Charles said. "Go on an' hop inside. I'll turn on the heater while I get us the map."

"Good idea. No sense freezin' my ass off. Like my momma always said, 'Only a damn fool'll turn down a good thing.' "

Charles laughed. Once inside, he shoved the heater onto high. It would take a few minutes for the warmth to start blowing. Leaning over, in front of his passenger, he opened the glove box. After tossing the map on the stranger's lap, Charles reached under the front seat and pulled out a small whiskey bottle.

"How 'bout a quick one?" Charles asked, holding the brown glass container in his right hand. The bottle was wrapped in a thick white rag.

"I don't think so, man," said the passenger, still opening the map. "I gotta drive, an' I can't afford to get no more points. Damn cops don't give ya no slack nomore, nohow. Hey!" he said, suddenly, "this map ain't good for shit! It's Jersey!"

"Hell!" replied Charles, sounding annoyed. "Reach in there and see if ya can find a DelMarVa map, or an old Maryland one, will ya?"

As the farmer leaned forward, Charles uncapped the bottle and tilted it, pouring a heavy dose of chloroform into a white rag. He moved, quickly, like an animal pouncing. His hand tapped the stranger's left arm. As the farmer turned, Charles shoved the cloth, hard, up against his face—so hard in fact that the back of the man's head hit the Blazer's side window.

It took less than five seconds for the powerful drug to work. Careful to open his window and let in fresh, cold air, Charles allowed the stranger's body to slump forward as he closed the bottle cap tightly. Quickly, he placed the cloth and the glass container into a plastic bag, sealed it tightly and lowered the heat.

Now, thought Charles, was the most dangerous part of the day's work—leaving unnoticed. Up to now, fate, luck—no, not luck, there was no such thing, destiny— had been on his side. Two more minutes and he would be on his way south, out of the area and heading toward home.

With no one in sight, Charles let the farmer's body slump backwards, as far as he could, so the unconscious body was upright and its face was turned away from the side window. He reached across and affixed the seatbelt as best as he could, but Charles knew if a cop stopped him the "sleeping man" in the front seat could be a problem. But, he'd have to risk it until he got away from Shepherd's Main Street. Unfortunately, there was only one entrance/exit from the lot.

Slowly, he pulled the black Blazer out of its slot and aimed toward the street. A few stragglers were stumbling out of the hall. No one he recognized, thankfully. Three cars in front of him were waiting to get out. The lead vehicle was stopped, the driver talking to a local about some non-sense. If he had been in the city, Charles would have laid on his horn, but not today. Not this special night of nights.

Patience.

Patience, he told himself. *Remember, all good things come to those who wait . . . and*, he added, *those who go after them.*

The first car pulled out. Two to go and he was on his way. Charles needed to turn left, away from the fire hall.

Two, three people walked in front of his Blazer. They waved. He smiled, nodded slightly, keeping his head down.

One car left and then he'd be gone.

But it stalled. Tried to start.

No luck.

He could tell the engine was flooding.

Then, from the right, three people came out the side exit. They had to pass near him to reach the parking lot, to his left. The trio was approaching from the right. He recognized them.

Ricky from Trappe.

Delbert and Ned from Wachapreague.

The rat-eating threesome moved slowly, stumbling from the heavy helpings of homemade chow, the pitchers of cheap beer, the heat of the crowded hall. *Maybe they wouldn't look up.*

They were directly in front of his grill.

The rusty, yellow Citation in front of Charles tried to start again. It chugged. A few weak gasps of excitement escaped from under the hood. Four blue puffs of smoke belched from the tailpipe . . . then it died.

"DAMN!" the owner shouted. Charles could hear him cursing, see the man punching the dash.

Hell! Charles thought, beads of sweat were forming on his upper mustached lip.

Ignoring Charles, who was perched in his driver's seat, Delbert walked toward the dead car and talked to the driver. Ned and Ricky had passed and were heading into the lot. Charles felt slightly relieved but kept his eyes down. He couldn't maneuver the Blazer around the Citation.

Delbert shouted to his companions. Slowly they responded and walked back toward the exit. A line of trucks and cars was forming in the rear. Somebody honked. A half-dozen impatient drivers were waiting to leave. None wanted to escape the town of Shepherd more than Charles.

Ricky was looking under the Citation's hood.

"Push the damn crate outta da way!" somebody shouted.

"Screw you!" Ricky yelled back, waving his arms, tossing an obscene gesture. "HIT THE GAS!" Ricky screamed at the driver.

A few more chugs, lots of smoke and then, finally, clear engine contact was made.

Delbert, Ned and Ricky cheered, jumping in the air like they had scored a touchdown, hitting high fives and laughing.

The embarrassed driver waved his thanks and drove off, slowly this time, not wanting to flood the engine and stall again.

The line of cars began to move.

Charles eased forward, cursing silently and, at the same time, willing the annoying trio of Good Samaritans to turn and leave. Two of them did. But, as he smoothly passed through the exit, Charles could feel Delbert, standing within three feet of his window and staring at the driver's side of the Blazer.

But Charles didn't slow down, didn't turn, didn't acknowledge that he saw anyone or anything.

Within 30 seconds, he was out of the town limits of Shepherd, never to return.

Next stop, he whispered, *home. I have to take Father home.*

15

Stephanie's Saturday afternoon was a snapshot of chaos. Her car broke down in her hairdresser's parking lot, and she had spent two hours carefully avoiding the mention of anything that could give any hint that she was having a second dinner with the governor. Even on the ride home, provided by her sister, Stephanie kept the secret, saying she was scheduled to speak at a conference in Philadelphia that evening.

God! she thought, as she was trying to get dressed, *How long will I be able to keep this thing quiet?*

At that moment, her phone rang. Randy Poplos was on the line, announcing his arrival at her home in 15 minutes.

Stephanie decided that under such bizarre circumstances her relationship with his governorship would never have a chance to ignite and move to a higher level of intensity. She was going to make sure it ended before it began. She would tell Hank that the tension was too much for her to handle.

Sgt. Poplos pulled up at precisely 5:30 in DMV 2, a black Cadillac limousine with shaded windows used for transporting visiting dignitaries. He held the rear door open for Stephanie as she raced toward the curb. Thank God none of her neighbors was out. But, that didn't matter. Nobody who lived in the rowhouses of Trolley Square and Forty Acres went about his or her personal business unnoticed.

Little old Irish ladies sat in rocking chairs beside the front windows in parlors and in second-floor bedrooms, watching the comings and goings of everyone on the block. Some even used binoculars. Stephanie would bet her paycheck that sweet old Mrs. McMrudy was, at that very moment, directing her wrinkled fingers through the rings on her old-fashioned, black rotary phone.

On the other end of the neighborhood gossip's line would be Mack McMrudy, desk sergeant in Wilmington's Barracks 3, who looked up all the license plates for his lonely mother. It was against police policy, but that didn't matter. Besides, if he didn't do what she wanted he'd be written out of the will, hassled by the whole family and, worst of all, not invited over for her Sunday family dinners. It was easier to risk his job and pension, so the sergeant gave his mother the information and got her off his back.

Stephanie cringed. Hopefully, she thought, Mack would think dear old mom had been hitting the sauce when she called in the latest tag number. But, after tonight, all that would be over because Stephanie knew this was going to be her last date with the governor.

"You okay, Miss?" It was Poplos' voice from the front seat. Their eyes made contact for a brief second by way of the car's rearview mirror.

"Yes. Yes," Stephanie said. "Thanks."

They continued the drive without speaking until they reached the I-95 connection with Route 1 South, near the Christiana Mall. "Can I ask you a question?" Stephanie said, breaking the quiet.

"Shoot!"

"How long have you been working with the governor?"

"Five years, Miss."

"Call me Steph, please."

"Okay, Steph. Five years."

There was another period of silence. The longer it continued the more awkward it seemed, probably since the earlier brief conversation ended so abruptly.

"You're the first one, Steph," said Poplos.

She responded in a startled tone. "What?"

"The first lady I've ever been asked to escort to the governor. What I mean is, he doesn't do this every week, or year, or ever. We're all very happy he likes you and that you seem to be nice. So, I just figured you might be wondering and thought I should say something. Hope you don't think I was out of line?"

"No," Stephanie smiled back. "Thank you. It was nice of you to tell me. It's natural that I was wondering. . . ." A few seconds passed and Stephanie asked, "What's he like?"

"How do you mean?" Poplos asked.

"Earlier this week, when we were having dinner. You came in with information and he changed dramatically—from a smooth conversationalist to a . . . a hard-edged . . . . He was immediately different. That's the way it appeared to me."

"Look, if I give you an opinion, it's biased. I love the governor. I would take a bullet for him, and so would 90 percent of the other guys on the force. Governor McDevitt has given the guys and women in law enforcement more respect, higher pay, better equipment than anybody before, and he's made our job safer. But he really cares about the people and his state. You thought you saw something odd the other night. Hell, last year, soon after the new state was formed, President Woodyard and his wife were visiting the governor. They all had plans to sit together at the running of the Delaware Handicap.

"The governor had given the President a tour of the new capital building construction in Federalsburg that morning. On the drive up to Delaware Park, we heard a broadcast that a general store owner had been gunned down near Seaford. The governor stopped the car, called Vice Governor Chase and asked her to fill in as escort to the President.

"We pulled off the side of the road and waited for her in a McDonald's. It was close to the Easton State Police Barracks. We were in a presidential limo, so the governor requested that a trooper from Easton bring over a cruiser for us to use to get to Seaford.

"We didn't have to wait long, but I'll never forget what happened. Here's the scene. The governor, and the President and his wife, who's a real bitch, excuse my language, and me, are sitting in a McDonald's parking lot. And Governor McDevitt sends a Secret Service agent, from one of the three so-called unmarked cars that were trailing us, inside to get all of us burgers and fries.

"It was a thrill for me to watch this thing happen. Then, when our trooper arrives, the governor asks him if he wants something to eat and then sends the agent in a second time. You should have seen this bigshot fed. He was red as a beet. But the best part is, the governor didn't have any money and was asking the President and his wife for 15 bucks to cover the cost. And here's the President of the United States going through his pockets and complaining that it was going to cut him short on his betting money later that afternoon."

Stephanie joined in laughing with Poplos, who added that the news crews that were following along with the President recorded the whole thing and it made the evening news.

"But," Stephanie asked, "why did the governor go to the crime scene. What could he do? Weren't the police taking care of it?"

"Yeah," said Poplos, "they were. But it happened that the governor used to work in the country store that got robbed. The person who was beaten and shot was the former owner's son and a high school classmate of the governor's. He was real upset. It was a rough day for him."

"Did they catch the robbers?"

"Yeah. Two days later in a crack house in Baltimore. They both admitted to the robbery and shooting. Their lawyer told them if they 'fessed up they'ed be out in about three to five."

"I guess they've already been hung," Stephanie added, with a hint of sarcasm.

"No. They didn't go to trial."

"Why not?"

"Seems like sometimes the Good Lord works in wonderful ways. Our guys picked them up in Charm City and were bringing them back to the jail in Georgetown. No one can still figure out how it happened, but while the troopers were gassing up their vehicle, the two killers got out of the police car, got their cuffs off and took off running. The police called out several times, verbal warnings then shots in the air, but they just wouldn't stop. They were shot dead trying to escape."

🌾   🌾   🌾

It was just before 6:30 p.m. when Randy Poplos opened the front door of Woodburn and escorted Stephanie inside. The spacious, first-floor foyer was lit by dim lights, a burning fireplace and a half-dozen candles. Before she could look around the antique-filled room, Governor Henry McDevitt descended the wide stairway that filled the far end of the building.

Sgt. Poplos excused himself and said he would be in the officers' security room, off the rear of the mansion's kitchen.

Both Stephanie and the governor nodded.

"You look beautiful," he said.

"Thanks," she said. Then, looking around at the empty building, she asked, "Where are the party guests?"

"I lied," McDevitt said, with an embarrassed smile.

"I beg your pardon?" Stephanie didn't understand.

"There's no party."

She stared at him. Silent.

He continued explaining. "I figured if I asked you to come out to dinner with me alone again so soon after the other night you would probably refuse. I thought I'd have a better chance if you believed there would be other people here. Are you upset?"

"Yes!" Stephanie said, her tone and appearance reflecting annoyance. "But," she added, softening her tone, "I'm absolutely starved, so I hope you at least planned for us to dine."

McDevitt's face reflected honest relief. "Yes. I made it myself. I hope you like chicken."

"Chicken's fine," she said, adding, "let me help."

Together, they went into the mansion kitchen. He had already set the dining room table. This time Stephanie wasn't surprised when she had a wonderful dinner.

She shared more about her work, her family, her hobbies and interests.

He gave her a history of the building, relating some of the history as he walked her through the first-floor rooms and he showed her the wooden door in the basement that was a tunnel entrance to the St. Jones River that was part of the Underground Railroad.

After the dishes were cleaned, they had coffee beside a comfortable fire.

She had another wonderful evening. So enjoyable that any thought of never seeing Henry McDevitt again was the farthest thing from her mind. They each were seated in wingback chairs at opposite ends of the fire. He had removed his tie, but was still wearing his jacket.

She had removed her scarf. Her black beaded top revealed the smooth round tops of her breasts. The candles continued to flicker. Music—Sinatra, singing "What's New?"— was coming from somewhere. It didn't matter.

"You didn't have to lie to get me to see you again," Stephanie said.

"I was hoping, but I wasn't sure. I thought the party idea would help."

"Well, it didn't hurt, but do me a favor. If you ever ask me out again, tell me the truth. Okay?"

"All right."

"You have to understand, a lady likes to know where she's really going so she can plan what to wear and how to prepare. This bait-and-switch routine can get old and annoying very quickly."

"I understand. Well," McDevitt said, walking toward her chair and taking her hand, "it's getting late and I haven't shown you the upper floors of our haunted mansion. Are you interested?"

"In what?" Stephanie said.

"In a private tour."

"That would be nice," Stephanie said as she stood up, her hand holding McDevitt's, their bodies brushing gently. She did not pull away. He pulled her closer.

With candles flickering and the ghosts of governors past watching, the two lovers kissed on the stairway landing. Soft and light, then harder.

As their lips parted, Stephanie said, "What about that tour?"

"It's a big house," said McDevitt. "It could take all night."

"That's fine," she said. "I guess Randy can blow out the candles."

McDevitt laughed and, that night, he started to fall deeply in love with a woman who, just hours earlier, had vowed to never see him again.

🌿   🌿   🌿

McDevitt was an early riser and went down to make coffee, allowing Stephanie to sleep a bit longer. He realized she might feel a bit awkward, appearing downstairs after their first evening together with police officers only a few rooms away.

Returning to the bedroom, he woke her gently and offered her one of his robes. During their private breakfast in the master suite they talked and laughed, relaxing at a small table near the window that overlooked Woodburn's gardens.

He pointed out to where the ghostly hanging tree had stood, before it was cut down in 1997 during the Carper administration. According to legend, Patty Cannon's slave-stealing gang attacked the home, trying to snatch some fugitives, who were hiding in Woodburn's cellar.

When the authorities arrived, the gang ran off.

"Unfortunately, one poor kidnapper hid in the old

poplar tree," McDevitt said. "But he was up there so long, he got tired, slipped and fell, causing his neck to get caught between two branches. He strangled to death. They say his moans and cries can still be heard, along with the rattling of the chains he had clutched in his hand as he died. Even into the early part of this century, school children and adults would not walk on the sidewalks of Woodburn at night. They'd cross the street and sometimes break out in a run to avoid the hanging ghost."

Stephanie, who enjoyed a good story, smiled at McDevitt, who she noticed seemed to be proud of the legend.

He saw her interest and explained that he enjoyed having someone with whom he could share the tale.

"There are several hundred stories associated with the house," he said, seriously. "I'd be glad to tell you another each time you stay over."

She didn't catch his humor immediately, then let out an unexpected laugh along with dribbles of warm coffee that had gotten stuck in her throat.

As she coughed, he passed her a napkin and apologized for the bad timing of his delivery.

McDevitt explained that he had a relatively light schedule that Sunday. Only an evening speech at the Historical Society of Accomac County, at the Chincoteague Fire Hall.

When Stephanie asked about the rest of his week, the governor grabbed his book and read off three luncheons and four dinner speeches, plus nine events during the upcoming weekend.

"How do you do it?" Stephanie asked. "You must go crazy."

McDevitt waited a moment, then said, "Yes. That's true and, yes, I have gone crazy."

Picking up his calendar, Stephanie was amazed that McDevitt's staff had him booked through the end of the year and into the next, even making commitments during Christmas Eve. On some weekends in the summer, the governor was making a dozen stops a weekend—from Friday night through Sunday.

"It's like a campaign tour," she said, with amazement in her voice.

"Political life is one, continuous campaign, Steph. It never stops. Never ends. But you get to meet a lot of interesting people, good people, and go to a lot of nice places."

"Sure, I can see a few of them listed right here: the International Goose Callers Contest, the Crab Derby Race, the World's Largest and Greatest Ever Steam Show in some guy's backyard, the Scrapple Tasters Tournament and the World's Fastest Chicken Plucker Championship. Are these for real?"

"Sure are," McDevitt said, "but you left out the annual Muskrat Skinnin' Gathering, the Town of Oyster's Official Oyster Shuckin' Festival and the Ramblin' Raccoon Catchers Dinner. Now, that last one is for men only and definitely, strictly by invitation."

"I guess you're telling me that now, in case getting a ticket to that grand event was the only reason I was coming on to you. At least I know early in the relationship how far my charms will get me, so I can decide to disappear."

"Yes," he said, smiling. "I want everything up front and out in the open. I don't want any arguments when I head out with Randy this fall to the Coon Hunters Lodge alone."

She shook her head as she replaced his book on the nearby table. "Why do you go to all these things?"

"To be honest, it has to be done, and most of the time it's enjoyable. The people expect it. But the problem is that 10, even five years ago, it was still possible to attend all of the big events throughout the year—because there weren't as many.

"You'd hit the oyster festivals in the winter, the major holiday parades in the spring and the boating and decoy festivals in the summer. Fall would come and there would be a few football games, and you'd try to never miss the Punkin' Chuckin' in November, plus the Thanksgiving and Christmas open house candlelight tours at the county historical societies. Then, all of the sudden, it's New Year's Day and you'd start all over again.

"But, today, every town, every development, every ethnic and special interest group, every arts league and social society has an event—and some have more than one a year. If you go to one group's affair, then the others expect it. You can't blame them for wanting their governor to be accessible and to show he has interest in the people, especially in this new state of ours."

"But you must get worn down and, I bet, even confused."

McDevitt smiled, showing he appreciated her understanding. And, at that moment, he hoped her consideration and intelligence would be applied to their relationship when the tough times came.

"Sometimes," he looked at her with a smile, "I've stared out at the audience, or at the people dining, just before I'm about to be introduced and, honestly, I've had no idea of where I was." Then laughing, he added, "But, a little concentration and a few well-written notes help deliver me back to the correct scene and it goes off well. It's a problem shared by all people on the talk circuit. You just keep going, keep scheduling and, at times, make sure you carve out windows of opportunity to regroup, relax or get away. Up to now, I haven't had a good reason to slow things down a notch or two. But I could be persuaded."

"Well," Stephanie looked across the table and smiled, "do you want me to be persuasive?"

McDevitt laughed, "I'd say you already have been."

She added her own laughter to his comment. Then they started to plan the remaining hours of their day.

They headed out, alone, on a private trip to Rehoboth, where she ran into the outlets and bought some casual clothing, then they walked on the sand at Cape Henlopen. They both loved the beach in winter, especially when there were no crowds and traffic.

They had a late lunch in Snow Hill, at a quaint bed and breakfast inn that was owned by one of McDevitt's college friends. Their table overlooked the Pocomoke River and, afterwards, the couple took a walk through the town. In travel brochures, the small Worcester County village boasted about the large number of restored Victorian homes within its boundaries. McDevitt remarked that strolling the historic streets in any season was like being inside a turn-of-the-century painting. When they returned to Woodburn in early evening, their mood was bright, invigorated by the enjoyable day and the brisk chill in the air.

As they walked through the mansion's kitchen door, Randy Poplos pulled into the driveway in an unmarked car. He had been following them at a discreet distance all day, and he waited outside to drive Stephanie back to Wilmington.

In the master bedroom, as they gathered her things, McDevitt pulled her towards him. They held each other tightly and kissed, at first softly, then passionately. As they began to walk toward the stairway, she stopped him and asked, "How do you want to handle this?"

"What do you mean?"

"This won't be a secret for long. Soon people will know that we're seeing each other. Delaware, I mean DelMarVa's, a small state. What they say is true: 'Everywhere you go, there's somebody that you know.' Plus, people see things. People talk. People love gossip and rumor and . . . ."

"And a story about the governor going out with a beautiful psychologist is bound to be the talk of the town."

"Unfortunately, yes, and I appreciate your compliment. But, on the serious matter, can I tell anyone? Should I tell anybody? How do you feel?"

"It sounds to me like you're not running away from this?"

"No. I'm willing, no, make that eager, to give us a try. I want to know what you think about this. You've been in the spotlight and should have a better understanding of these matters."

"How do *you* want to handle things?" he asked.

"I'd like to make it as normal as possible, and that means I don't want to sneak around. While I don't want to broadcast it, I'd like to be able to tell my sister, my parents, whomever I'm comfortable with. When it gets out, I imagine it will be in the news for a while and then blow over, right?"

"Right," he said. "So I suggest we both respond that we are dating and having a wonderful time. Is that agreeable?"

She kissed him on the lips, then pulled away slowly and smiled.

McDevitt walked her to the car. Instead of getting in the back door, she grabbed the front passenger door handle. "I think I'd like to ride up front. That way we can compare notes about you. All right?"

Sgt. Poplos smiled at McDevitt, who laughed and gave her a final hug.

"Drive safely, Randy." Then, through the closed window, McDevitt shouted out to Stephanie, "I'll call you tomorrow!"

❧ **16** ❧

March 2008

Charles Bettner watched from Stephanie's office window as three city workers painted a bright green stripe down the center of King Street, getting ready for Wilmington's annual St. Patrick's Day Parade. The marching show was the last winter event, alerting those who were still hibernating from the cold that spring was only days away.

Stephanie sat in her usual spot, pen in hand, waiting for Charles to make a comment that she would consider important enough to add to the blank paper resting on the top of his folder.

As he turned away from the window, he stared at his counselor. More than once, in the privacy of his bedroom and study, Charles had imagined that Stephanie Litera was attracted to him. As much as he wanted that to be the case, he laughed at the absurdity of the thought, especially after hearing rumors about her and the governor whom he hated.

"So, Charles. What do we want to discuss this week?"

Obviously, Bettner had come prepared. Without hesitation, he replied, "Confidentiality."

"What?" Stephanie asked, quite surprised at his comment.

"I want to be assured that, even though the state is paying for my 'treatment,' anything I share with you is confidential, under the client, representative arrangement."

She didn't answer immediately.

"Well?" pressed Charles.

"Is it important to you?"

"Yes."

"Why?" she asked.

"Because I trust you, and because there are things that I believe you can help me with. But I can't be entirely candid, unless I feel sure that my comments will not leave this room and," he added with a tight smile, "that no one will see the notes you are taking."

"I have no problem with that," she said. "I'm here to improve your overall health through psychological assistance. If it will help you be more comfortable, truthful and increase the speed of your improvement, I will do all I can to assist you. Actually, everything is confidential. However, if I were pressed to release information it would only be those facts directly related to your work habits and your actions and attitudes involving your employment."

"Explain, please."

"If you tell me about life threatening procedures or criminal activity on the job, abuses, theft, use of illegal drugs or a dangerous situation during working hours—even favoritism, nepotism—it's a long but non-specific list of actions—those I would have the responsibility to report. Hazardous situations.

"But, I am not to share your personal beliefs, actions, activities, past pressures, or even behavioral attitudes and issues related to your character or personality. Therefore, as an extreme example, if you want to tell me you committed a murder when you were 12 years old, that's no one's business and it is not to be included in any report or to be shared with anyone. That's where I take my job and responsibility seriously, and I am confidential to the strict letter of the law. If anything, I go out of the way to shield my clients from intrusion because I believe the level of trust I, we, have established is more important than anything or anyone else."

"I have your word on this preservation of non-work related confidentiality?"

Stephanie nodded, "My word."

Relaxed and reassured, Charles opened the conversation with comments about his mother, his last and most loving foster mother.

He spoke fondly of how her bright red hair, green eyes and slim figure made her attractive to every man in the county, and several were especially eager to pursue her after her husband's disappearance. But, Charles said proudly, "I kept her safe from them, driving off several who I decided were unworthy of her."

His tone was happy when he recalled the pleasant memories of their time together, but he shared his anger when she announced she was moving away, to live with her sister in Chicago—and that he would be left behind.

Stephanie tried to coax him to speak, but he closed his eyes and shook his head, fighting the urge to tell more, obviously hesitant and careful of what he might say.

Abruptly, Charles said he did not feel well, excused himself and ended the meeting.

In the privacy of the parking garage, protected in his vehicle, he stared at the pitted concrete wall. He could see Mrs. Bettner, years ago in the farmhouse kitchen, patting his hand, telling him everything would be fine, that they'd find him a new family, one with a new brother or sister his own age. She said she had to go, but that she cared for him.

Then, like an explosion in his brain, he saw his fist, his balled powerful fist, punch her across the face. She fell back, but he didn't stop. Charles was on her, beating her, punishing her for deserting him. For several minutes he sat watching the mental video and saw the blood appear on her face. The black bruises. The screams were there again, so real he could almost hear them inside the Blazer.

Exhausted, he recalled how he rose off her body and cursed her for destroying his family, their small happy family. He walked out of the home and never went back. Never saw her again. Years later, after a string of odd jobs, he enlisted in the Army.

When the memories faded, he took out his handkerchief

and dabbed the tears that had streaked his cheeks, took a few deep breaths and drove toward home.

❧ ❧ ❧

The tall man with the brown beard, red cap and dark glasses was standing on the corner of Fourth and Walnut streets in Wilmington. It was 9 o'clock, one hour before the step off of the annual St. Patrick's Day Parade.

His puffy, dark blue ski jacket held back the chill from the windy March morning. A Kelly green plastic vest indicated he was an official of some type, involved with directing traffic and assisting parade participants. The Daughter's of Erin Cultural Society's Junior Hibernian Dancers Club was forming for the march. Proud parents were dropping off pixie-like performers who would show off the best of the Old Sod's dance steps along the parade route.

Charles had arrived earlier that morning in a van stolen the night before from a car leasing agency compound outside New Castle. The gray Dodge was parked a few blocks away. He would use it to leave town and then transfer his human cargo into his black Blazer.

It was 9:10 when he saw her, walking two young girls across the street. They passed within a few yards of his vantage spot. Her hair was red, like his mother's; her skin was milky white; and the figure was trim and athletic. A pair of jeans covered her legs, legs that Charles knew would be slim and tapered and soft to the touch.

Casually, he moved a few steps closer, just in time to hear the conversation between the mother and a club chaperone.

"Hi, I'm Sherron McKlinchey, just dropping off Colleen and Kathleen," she said.

"Thank you, ma'am," the older man said. He was big and burly and reminded Charles of a pub bouncer you would expect to see in any bar in Dublin or working class saloon in Boston. "You can pick them up at the end of the parade route, at Twelfth and Market."

"Oh, my sister will do that. I've got to run right after I see them perform. But they know she'll be there. I just wanted to let you know."

The man nodded as the girls kissed their mother and waved good-bye.

Charles walked a half block up the street, memorizing the children's names and thinking about how easy it had been to pick up the vest and badge at the temporary parade headquarters. As he surveyed the surroundings, Sherron McKlinchey paced swiftly by. Allowing her a 15-foot lead, Charles pulled the cap down further on his forehead, stared at her through wraparound sunglasses, and followed at a respectable distance.

Fifteen minutes later, he took up position at the corner of Eighth and Market, a block from the reviewing stand, keeping his prey in sight. The victim's head bobbed up and down, making sure she would have a good view of the marchers when they arrived. As the excited mom checked her camera—at 9:50, just 10 minutes before the parade was to start—a concerned but helpful parade official Charles Bettner made his move.

Beginning to talk as he approached his mark from behind, he called out, "Excuse me, ma'am, but are you Mrs. McKlinchey?"

Startled, she turned quickly, looked up at the tall man with sunglasses and cap, and started to respond. But Charles ignored her and continued talking. "Your daughters—Colleen and Kathleen—they said I'd find you here. There's been a slight accident, and I need to escort you . . . ."

"Oh, my God!" she exclaimed, thinking the worst. Her hand instinctively rose to her lips. A few people turned.

Smiling, Charles quickly interjected, "No! Nothing to fear. A costume problem is all. One of the girls needs your help with a snap or a something or other, I don't know." His smile helped calm her and she shifted to a relaxed state.

What a naive, trusting soul, he thought. *This will be so easy.*

She started to walk back the way she had come, south on Market, but Charles stopped her. "Please, come with me," he said, pointing to a side street. "It's close to parade time and we have to rush. We can use the city van. It's parked a block from here."

She followed him as he walked, keeping up a brisk, official pace. Charles heard her steps to his rear, moving away from the crowd and the eyes of any curious spectators. The van was parked on Shipley Street, at a corner that did not get much traffic.

As they stopped, she thanked him for his help and mentioned her surprise that a city official would be concerned with such a trivial problem.

Reaching the van, he opened the passenger door and replied. "No problem! I'm just doing my job and helping a citizen in distress. You get in first."

Slamming her door, he looked in and admired her smile. It was just like his mother's—soft and sparkling, innocent and trusting. Mrs. McKlinchey had no idea that after entering the van her prior world of bliss and minor family emergencies would become only a memory.

Once behind the wheel, Charles called out, "Seatbelts!" and used the automatic switch to lock the doors. Pressing softly on the pedal, he pulled out and headed south, gaining speed as he quickly passed Fourth Street where the dancers had assembled. He was putting precious distance away from the parade area.

His captive started to question, even protest. Suddenly, the scent of fear filled the van for the young mother realized what might be happening. As she opened her mouth, the "click" of a switchblade knife cut off her inclination to scream. The gleaming, silver metal tip was under her left breast, pressing into her coat, the gleaming blade cutting through the material, advancing through layers of fabric and getting closer to her skin as Charles slowly applied pressure.

"I don't want to hurt you, Mother," Charles said, his eyes on fire, "but you must listen to every word I say. Understand?"

She nodded, her mouth still open.

Following his orders, Sherron didn't speak again, and they drove in silence, south of the city. Somewhere between New Castle and Delaware City, Charles turned into a deserted factory parking lot. The area was decorated in 21st century urban decay—junked cars filled with trash, vacant buildings with broken windows and pieces of paper and litter trapped in the gaps of rusted chainlink fencing.

As soon as the van stopped, Charles slapped his captive's face, hard enough to leave a mark but not draw blood. Sherron McKlinchey sat frozen as Charles bound her wrists and covered her mouth with gray duct tape. She made no effort to resist. Shock had consumed her senses and immobilized her mind and body. She responded like a ragdoll to his orders. Easily, he directed her into the rear section of his Blazer, which had been parked on an asphalt surface behind a burned out warehouse, awaiting the transfer of stolen human freight.

As he tossed a blanket over her huddled body, Charles warned her, "I'll be taking you home to Father soon. But, if you try to resist or get away, I will go back and get your two little girls, and you don't want them to come with us, do you?"

Unable to speak, Sherron shook her head, trying to show him that she would agree with whatever he said.

Charles smiled, reached down and attached the open end of a pair of handcuffs to the young woman's left ankle. It ripped into the leather of her expensive black boot. The other silver ring was locked to a bar of metal on the underside of the rear seat.

"I'm going to go back to the van for a moment," he said, offering a grin. "Don't want you to wander off, now. You could get hurt out here, you know."

Her efforts to figure out what was happening and how she might get away were useless.

Charles, wearing black leather riding gloves, emptied the contents of a red plastic gasoline container throughout the stolen van. Soaking a pile of rags, he tossed a match into the open rear double doors and watched for a few seconds to be sure the upholstery and carpeting caught fire.

Casually, he walked back to his Blazer, pressed on the radio and drove away. As the flames roared and consumed more of the interior of the kidnapping van, any clues about who may have been inside were eradicated.

"It's a long drive, Mother," Charles shouted from the front seat. "You may as well get some sleep. I'll be sure to wake you when we get home."

🌿   🌿   🌿

It took two days for the Wilmington morning newspaper to run her picture, and even then it was on Page B-3, buried in the bottom corner of the local section.

Charles was in his ranch home, in a quiet, nondescript, cookie cutter suburban community close to U.S. Route 40 between Newark and Elkton. Seated at the light maple desk in his basement study, he smiled at the photographs he had taken of Father and Mother in their site of captivity. The images were tacked on the bulletin board that faced him from the wall directly behind his overstuffed chair.

He looked down at the smiling face in the two-week-old newspaper. It displayed calmness and security, the expression was confident. At that moment when the family picture was taken—probably at a party or during a vacation—Sherron McKlinchey believed she would live forever, have it all, raise her children and see them married. She would be at the christenings of her grandchildren, most probably outlive her husband and die at a ripe old age.

Then, because of a chance weekend encounter—of being in a certain place at a certain time—her game plan of life had been rewritten, all within the space of a two-minute conversation with a stranger.

But, Charles thought, the impact hasn't dawned on *them*, just as it hadn't yet completely reached the confused and terrified brain of Sherron McKlinchey. But she was safely tucked away and would have plenty of time to guess about her uncertain future.

He laughed to himself—just like Father at the muskrat party in Shepherd—Mother never had a clue about what was happening, why she was chosen, what it was all about. But

she was always smarter than Father, always had been. If anyone will be able to figure it out, Mother will be the one.

Hell, he thought, nobody else in DelMarVa has realized
what was happening. Horace Meeks' disappearance in February hardly got any news play, only a tiny inside-page,
three-paragraph note in the Crisfield and Salisbury papers.
They didn't even print a picture of the poor bastard.

In the article, his family said Horace had a history of
going off on his own for months at a time, then reappear-
ing unexpectedly. But Charles knew the days of Meeks' res-
urrection routines were over. Father had reached the point
of no return and was permanently settled in the new family home.

Maybe it was time to give the rest of them a wake-up
call, Charles thought.

It was the governor he was after, that bastard McDevitt
who had gotten Charles fired from his job. Plus, now he
was moving in on his woman, Stephanie. Charles wouldn't
tolerate that. McDevitt wasn't good enough for her.

Charles had given the style of his revenge a lot of
thought and decided to hit the chief executive where he
was vulnerable, in his new state's tourism industry. He had
begun snatching the members of his new family, once a
month, from events that occurred across the new state.

Looking up at the empty slots on his family tree bulletin
board, there were several framed outlines awaiting more
photographs. Like the first two, as soon as they were settled
in, he would take a picture with his instant camera and
place the image against the pale background of his cork trophy board.

Unfortunately, two weeks had passed since the parade
and Charles was the only one who knew the plan. Part of
him wanted to share the plan, and the other part of him—
the stronger, patient, dominant Charles—wanted to see how
long it would take them to realize what he was doing. *They
were so pathetically stupid.*

Putting on a pair of white surgical gloves, he ripped
open a sealed ream of blank copy paper, pulling out a few

blank sheets from the center of the stack. Next to them he placed two plain white #10 envelopes.

While whistling a happy tune, he typed out a message on his computer, placing it within the lines of a rectangular box. When it came out of the printer, he placed $40—two $20-dollar bills—inside the folded paper and sealed the fresh envelope with tape. He would not leave any traces of evidence or clues by licking the envelope. Slowly, he repeated the process, but the second message was addressed to a different location.

Later that day, in Baltimore's Inner Harbor, still wearing gloves, he tossed the two sealed envelopes into a blue mailbox. Then the kidnapper walked off and took a tour of the floating museum, the *U.S.S. Constellation*.

That night, back at his basement control center, Charles stared at the pair of stars in his picture gallery. Rejuvenated, he picked up the State of DelMarVa Tourist Bureau's Booklet of Events, the free official guide listing hundreds of state activities from which he would make his April selection. It was in that month when he would find a young fat boy who would become the first of Charles' siblings.

🌿　　🌿　　🌿

Michael Pentak had called the emergency meeting of the Commanders' Council for 7 in the morning on the fourth of April. Everyone was on time and seated. No one had to be told the session was for serious work.

A folder bearing the state seal rested in front of each of the 14 regional barracks representatives. The packets were filled with biographical information about two missing persons, one who disappeared in February, the other in March.

The most important item was the duplication of the newspaper notice that had appeared three days earlier in the *Salisbury Sentinel*. A similar announcement had been sent to the *Wilmington News Chronicle*, but its unusual content raised a question and police officers were alerted.

Most of the chiefs were aware of the item, those who weren't read it in silence.

The new DelMarVa family
is pleased to announce the recent marriage of
Horace Meeks,
formerly of Shepherd, Maryland,
and
Sherron McKlinchey,
formerly of Wilmington, Delaware.
The new couple plans to have a large family,
with many children in the near future.
At present, they both are very happy in their new home.
Best wishes to all involved.

The officers rested the papers and raised their eyes toward Pentak, who already was speaking.

"This appeared in the paper downstate on April Fools' Day. Thankfully, the *Wilmington News Chronicle* didn't run it. That would have been a disaster." He paused and looked at the chief from the southern DelMarVa outpost. "Okay, Dean, tell us what happened at your office down there."

Dean Lively, a tall trooper with a southern drawl, looked around the room as he spoke.

"I had Horace Meeks' daughter, his common-law wife and his mother. They were all in the barracks screamin' at the desk sergeant. I tell ya, there was more activity than fleas on a hot griddle in there. They were wavin' the paper, wantin' to know what we were gonna do about this here practical joke. They were shoutin', askin' if we caught up on things and found their Daddy yet. We tried to calm 'em down, but they went clean down to the papers before I could get up with 'em. Then, the Baltimore and Annapolis news picked it all up. After that, I had all kinda calls comin' in, nonstop.

"Horace Meeks is still missin'. Last thing they knew, he was headin' to the muskat dinner in Shepherd. Since he's really from down over near Pocomoke, I guess that's what the reference is in the ad, to him disappearin' while in Shepherd. A few friends remember him bein' there, but nothin' more. Hell, they got a thousand people eatin' and drinkin' there that day alone. Sell tickets at the door, so there's no way we're gonna find out anything, unless we hit a stroke of luck.

"But we had a few men over there doin' some initial canvassing, and, to be straight with ya, we got not one damn clue in hell about where he's at. Then, we got some joker puttin' this kinda crap in the paper. I like to died when that come out. But, we may be going through the rubs now, but we're hittin' at it right well. Keep in mind that this fella's run off before, and I sure hope that's the case now. If it is, this whole show is a sick joke and we'll come up with Horace soon."

"Thanks, Dean," Pentak interrupted, trying to cut off the commander and regain control and focus. He redirected his remarks to the gathering,

"The connection between Meeks and McKlinchey is something we've been looking at for the last 48 hours, since we were alerted to the Salisbury paper's announcement and the one that didn't run upstate. The latest report, as of an hour ago, is there is nothing obvious, no prior contact, no relationship, no similar interests—absolutely nothing what-soever that connects these two people. This is based on ini-tial computer cross referencing and our first on-site inter-views with relatives and friends."

"Except," said Carlton Buxton of Rehoboth, "that they both appear united or connected on April Fool's Day in a wedding announcement . . . ."

"However," said Pentak, ignoring the interruption, "we don't know the validity of this information or the identity of the sender. And these two citizens are both missing. Com-ments? Questions?"

No one was eager to speak.

Pentak filled the dead space, instructing each of the chiefs to review the personal material on the victims in the folders. Any and every shred of input—no matter how insignificant or farfetched—was to be directed to the new task force, to be headed by Pentak. It would grow, if nec-essary. Currently, it included investigators who had been detailed in from barracks in the geographical areas where the two disappearances had occurred.

The lab reports had not yet been returned, but it appears there were no distinguishable fingerprints. The paper, envelope and laser printer were common and available at any chain store or mail order house. The envelopes were mailed to the newspapers from downtown Baltimore. The notice had been sent directly to the classified advertising departments, with instructions and cash, more than enough to pay the bill.

No return address, no name or signature.

"We either have a very clever prankster, who is causing us—and the families—a lot of embarrassment and trouble, or," he paused, "we have a very serious problem. If that's the case, the information in this message is telling us there are going to be more disappearances in the very near future."

Each chief hoped for the best, but most already knew they were probably at the earliest stage of a rapidly escalating crisis.

Pentak gave the commanders of the Downtown Wilmington and Salisbury barracks orders to provide an update on their respective missing persons investigations in four hours. They also were to revisit the disappearance scenes, re-interview witnesses and look for new ones. Within 24 hours, all of the files and the newly formed task force personnel would operate out of facilities in Dover's Crisis Command Center.

"I want to know everything about these two people, down to their favorite ice cream flavors. Interview their families, co-workers, best friends, neighbors, priests or rabbis. Meeks' trail is already cold. As you know, if this is a serial situation, being the first victim, he would have been our best source of leads. But, let's move on the woman. She disappeared from the parade. Someone must have seen something. Find them and get all the facts and fast.

"As usual, no one is to talk to the press," Pentak said. "We don't want the public to think this is anything more than a schoolboy game, and we intend to fully prosecute the youths when they are caught. That's the line I will give to the media, and that's your response, but only if you are backed into a corner and have to say anything at all. Best to keep your mouth shut and bite your tongue.

"Now, I have to face the cameras and you all have lots to do. I want to have a handle on this real soon, and I do mean real soon. I want those two people found. The words 'at present' in this message gives me the impression that these people are still alive, but we don't know for how long.

"The governor is looking at us to solve these cases, and I don't want to see another announcement in the papers about anything even slightly similar to this. Understand?"

Gail Reshnick, chief of Barracks 9 in North East, said, "How do we keep a lid on the press if we have to talk to the classified departments and tell them we need to be told about any other announcements like this one? Plus, we're asking them not to print it."

"Good question. The governor is meeting with the publishers of all of the region's newspapers—including out of state—plus TV and radio representatives, this afternoon in Federalsburg. He'll be asking them to give us some lead time for the investigation to get in high gear before they start muckraking and trying to scoop each other with sensationalized exclusives. I think that will buy us a few days, *maybe*, but only a few days. After that, there's no way to stop the news, and it will be open season on us. The only way to keep the shit from hitting the fan is to find those two people, and the idiot that sent out the announcements."

🦋   🦋   🦋

As Michael Pentak stood on the steps of the DelMarVa State Police Headquarters building in Dover, avoiding more media questions than he answered, Sherron McKlinchey stared across the table, at the slowly decomposing body of what used to be Horace Meeks.

She could hear the sound of the sea in the background. The waves were hitting a beach in a regular pattern, invading the shore over and over again, like the morning ticking of an old-fashioned clock breaking past the barrier of a pillow.

The room was gray dark, not inky black but approaching it. She also could tell the prison chamber was partially submerged into the ground. The thin, narrow windows, which were located near the ceiling, had long ago been painted black to keep out the sunlight and eyes of any passing intruders. Irregular scratches allowed slits of light to enter when the sun reached that side of the building—apparently west, since it seemed to peek through just before sundown.

There were only two doors. The one to the outside, through which she had arrived, was locked from the outside with more than one device. Sherron knew, for she listened to every sound, especially when her captor left her behind.

The other door, to her right, over in the darkness, was at the top of four wooden steps and apparently went into the main house.

She figured she had been a captive about two weeks. So far, he had only visited on weekends. He must have a job. *God,* she thought, *if his coworkers only knew what he did in his spare time.*

He left a small, bare, 40-watt bulb dangling from the ceiling to illuminate the center of the damp, stuffy room. The glow never reached the corners. Sherron didn't want to think what might be lurking, living, waiting there. She could hear the rustling at times.

Mice? Rats? Something bigger?

She wasn't sure. What kind of fat furry creatures lived in a wooden shack in the middle of nowhere near the water? She forced herself to keep her head and eyes focused on the outside door, keeping herself from giving in to the temptation to turn toward the direction of the noises.

Looking to her left was not pleasant either. Her roommate, Horace, had been there since she arrived. But only briefly, for about an hour, had she seen him alive.

The two captives had spoken only a few words of greeting, exchanged first names, before the big man killed her permanently seated companion.

Sherron noticed that when the big man came, he rarely spoke. And when he did he called her "Mother." Mother this and Mother that.

She replied with nods and grunts, offering little conversation. She was careful not to set him off, especially after seeing what he did to Horace.

Sherron's hands were free, but one foot was manacled to the chair, which was bolted to a large wooden log nearly 20 feet long that was set flush and flat in the dirt floor in the damp cellar. There was enough chain to allow her to reach the nearby metal bucket to relieve herself. A roll of toilet paper was nearby, and she used a separate white, dented metal basin on the floor for washing. But, since it was only changed once a week when he came back to visit, the water did not remain clean enough for use past the second or third day.

There was no soap, deodorant or toothpaste.

At least the two-gallon container on the table contained clean water, and, on the positive side, Sherron had it all to herself.

Horace Meeks was stiff, stale and stinking in a lifeless state of grotesque gray-green, his skin already rotting. The exposed portions of the body were pitted from the effects of bites by airborne pests that had landed for nibbles. There were other gaps on his skin, indicating areas where crawling insects had stopped and feasted.

Sherron hated the crawlers as much as the stench.

She watched them inch their way up the wooden table legs and creep, ever so slowly, across the distressed, splintered surface. Others climbed up the chair legs to reach Meeks' rotting body.

When she was awake, Sherron spent much of the day brushing roaming crawlers, scouts she named them, away from her area of the table. The ones that she couldn't reach advanced from the far side of the room and marched in single file straight toward her former "husband."

Whenever he came, the big man left her food in packages—mostly cereal and crackers. When fruit was tossed in the wooden bowl, she grabbed it quickly and held it close, so the bugs couldn't get to it. There was just enough food to keep her alive, but it wasn't adequate to provide even basic energy. Her captor's forced diet was only a few degrees above starvation, an abstinence-from-food health plan to ensure that his captives would stay weak and be unable to offer any trouble, even if they dared consider it.

Apparently, things hadn't worked as planned with Horace Meeks. Even after a few weeks alone in the room the first prisoner had saved enough stubborn strength to make his move. It occurred almost immediately after Sherron was delivered to her new home.

Over and over she recalled her first moments in the filthy room that had become her cell.

The big man pushed her into a chair, chained her leg, took off her blindfold and announced, "Mother, meet Father!"

She could still see the smiling jailer, standing between her and Horace, when, suddenly, like a rabid animal in a rage, Horace latched onto the big man's left arm and sunk his teeth into the captor's skin. Sherron saw teeth breaking through the surface causing blood to flow. The growing stream of red liquid was seeping out of the edges of Horace's lips and teeth, which were clamped, chomping down hard into the big man's forearm.

Sherron had closed her eyes and turned away to block out the big man's screaming, the pounding noise and fight on the tabletop. She didn't want to believe any of it—the damp smell, the terrifying reality of where she was and the horror that was happening.

For the first time in her life she wished she was blind and deaf. But she prayed that Horace would win.

Then, after an indefinite amount of time—less than a minute, several seconds, who knows—there was a wounded, deathlike howl and then silence. The fight obviously over. Slowly, she opened her eyes in time to see the big man twisting the silver blade of a black-handled hunting knife in small circles in the center of Horace Meeks' chest.

More blood flowed, but it was not the big man's this time. It was Horace's. Blackish red liquid dripped down the front of the dead man's clothing and onto the lumpy dirt floor, soaking into the dry earth. Initially, it made a flowing sound, then slow trickles and drips continued to form a pool in the darkness under the table.

"Welcome to the family!" the man said, smiling as he wrapped soiled rags around his damaged arm. Then, obviously angry and upset, he left. Sherron heard him latch several locks from the outside and an engine revved up and he drove away.

Now, thinking back, she wished she had taken a more active role in the fight and helped Horace. But that single opportunity was long gone.

It happened in the first moments of her first day. Now it was Day 17. Maybe 15, or even 20? Day 14? She wasn't sure. The exact count didn't matter. At least she was alive.

She had not bathed or brushed her teeth or run a comb through her hair. Her clothes were soiled and stuck to her skin. She had not walked farther than a few hobbled steps and her body ached from lack of movement and exercise. When conscious, her mind flipped between moments of thoughtfulness and terror. She was afraid to think about the present or dare to hope about the future.

The big man had emptied the soiled chamber pot once a week, during his visits. The stench in the room was ungodly, repugnant—like being trapped in a phone booth with the smell of rotten eggs mixed with sour milk and body gases. That alone made her want to die. But she had two daughters and a fine husband. Surely they were looking for her. They had to be, and the police were, too. They wouldn't give up, and neither would she.

She vowed to see them again. They would be a family again, but first she would see the big man dead. Next to living, she had already decided, killing the tall stranger was the most important thing in her life.

She glanced at Horace Meeks' corpse. There was no more dripping blood—that had stopped a long time ago. There was no more life, just rot and gray matter where a real person once had been. He was horrifying and pathetic.

She knew him for only minutes, now for weeks she had been forced to sit as a partner, to keep vigil over his cadaver. A few times she prayed for him. But then she stopped and prayed for herself. She needed help more than Horace.

The real Horace was safe, in a better place. She wondered how long before she would look and smell and stink just like him.

She wondered when the big man would take the dead body away, but she wouldn't ask, knew better than to speak. She had tried to talk to him only twice. The first time he ignored her, the second time he came over, silently stared at her, then grabbed her hair, slapped her hard across the face and walked away.

Pausing from her thoughts, Sherron closed her eyes tightly. Then, as she did periodically, spontaneously, maybe just to make sure she was still alive, to hear a sound that she could control . . . in the darkness of her stinking, stagnant, living tomb . . . Sherron McKlinchey SCREAMED!!!!

The sound was a hoarse screeching plea, overflowing with hatred and hope. In the long pathetic moan she called out her children's names. She begged for her dead mother to work a miracle, to intercede on her behalf to God. She summoned the long dead, sainted, black-cloaked nuns who had taught her prayers in school. She demanded that they deliver on their promise that the good would be rewarded for their kindness.

Then exhausted she waited. But the answer was the same each time . . . numb, barren, hateful silence.

Then aloud, in silent whispers, in muttered babbling, she cursed them all—her husband, her children, the police, her family, the big man, her God.

As she fell off to sleep, there was no help, no end, no answer to her prayers, no punishment for her blasphemy . . . only the steady, uncaring, endless rhythm of the waves.

17

It was warm. Spring had arrived. Charles was nearly finished with the session. He had been talking about his boyhood friends, playing baseball, Army and Cowboys and Indians. Only in passing did he mention his very fat, very mean foster brothers.

She pressed him to share his thoughts, but he changed his focus, modified his tone.

As in past sessions, he didn't tell her the bad parts about the early years when his bigger, stronger foster brothers sat on his back and held him down while the other neighborhood kids rubbed mud in his face, made him eat the liquid dirt.

He didn't share his memories of the classmates who laughed at him when he wore his clothes inside out, or the ones who snickered when he didn't know his last name. He didn't speak about the PTA family nights that he could never attend.

No. He just told Stephanie what he had wanted it to be like. Everything that wasn't.

As they were ending the conversation, Charles asked, "Do you believe in God, doctor?"

Pausing briefly, Stephanie said, "Yes."

"Why?" he asked.

"Because I was taught to believe and because I have faith."

"Faith in what?" Charles asked.

"I'd rather not discuss this, Charles." She tried to change the subject. But he persisted, in a smooth, non-threatening, mannerly fashion, and she eventually replied. "Faith that He is there for me if I need Him. Faith in the fact that there will be a better life in another world, at another time. Faith in the goodness of people. That most of them truly care for one another. That He helps the weakest of us through other people on Earth. Faith in a lot of things. Why?"

Charles didn't reply. Then, after a few seconds, he asked, "Then why does God let evil exist? Why does he allow even helpless little children to be hurt by those who are bigger, stronger and meaner? Why are sisters and brothers cruel? Why do they fight? Why are they jealous? Why do they hit and abuse one another? Why doesn't he put a stop to the small, important things? I'm not talking about major problems— like ending war and mental illness and world famine and concerns on that level. If He's supposed to be so good and caring, and if He knows everything, why does He even let little children suffer? Why can't He fix that, if He's so damn great?"

Stephanie stared. Charles had been very calm, never once raising his voice. Continuing, he mentioned the gruesome murders on the front page of the morning paper.

"How can a God, who is all good, allow those two teenage boys in Georgia to hack their own mother and father to death, burn their body parts in the family woodstove, take their Lincoln Towncar and drive to DisneyWorld for a weekend with their parents' credit cards? Don't you think that proves that the Great Almighty is not caring or not all knowing, or probably not even there at all?"

Stephanie had no quick reply. Charles was seeking answers no one could give, but they were valid questions that millions of others had thought about at some point in time.

Softly, she said, "I'm a psychologist, not a theologian. I have no easy or understandable answer. Life and people aren't fair. That's all I can say. I guess that's why faith is so very important."

Smiling, Charles nodded, then turned at the door and said, "Keep the faith."

It was totally dark.

The single bulb dangling above the room had burned out sometime in the midst of the night before. Sherron sat chained to her seat at the family table beside the remnants of the rotting Horace Meeks mannequin.

No sliver of moonlight crept through the slits of the darkened windows. It was pitch black and, unfortunately, she was awake.

Periodically, the terrorized captive turned her head in the direction of scampering animal footsteps, scurrying in the corners and across the open stretches of the uneven dirt floor. It was a reflex. She couldn't see anything, but her head reacted and her eyes tried to focus in vain through the ink-like blackness.

Exact time had become an unknown, and the solitary breathing member of Charles' new family tried to keep track of the passing of day and night by the alternating pattern of sunlight and darkness. According to the tiny lines she had pressed into the tabletop with her fingernails, and later a sliver of wood she had pulled off the underside of the table, it was probably a Thursday or Friday night, but she wasn't sure.

She had passed her captivity trying to memorize the lay of the room, straining to see into the corners and determine what might be hanging on the walls. She was hoping for anything that could someday be used as a weapon—in the event she could free herself from the foot shackle, or be released temporarily by her captor.

But fear arrived along with the big man whenever he visited. When he was gone, hate and revenge stopped by to tarry. She realized they were the only two emotions that might keep her alive. Physically, she could feel herself beginning to weaken. The food was inadequate, and the filth and stench were making her ill.

The realization of her own stupidity, in allowing herself to be tricked, to be kidnapped, was humiliating. Those three minutes—from the time she met the big man to the moment she was locked into the van—changed her life.

There wasn't an hour that went by of every waking moment since she arrived that she prayed she was trapped in a slow moving nightmare, that she would awaken and be shaking in her clean, comfortable bed—that her two girls would be running into the room or shouting at each other in the hall, that her husband would be holding her in his arms.

But those were dreams and reality was a nightmare.

Sherron knew she had to stop dreaming and develop a plan. That would keep her going longer than he might expect. As she sat chained in silence, she memorized every self-defense move she had ever learned at the YWCA. She thought of where on his body she would sink her teeth if he ever got close enough—his nose, his neck, his hand, his cheek.

She imagined him screaming in pain and his blood dripping down her throat. She wanted to consume his life like he had taken hers. Sherron could see herself ripping into him with her teeth as she smashed her white enamel chamber pot against his balls. She prayed she would have the strength when the chance arrived.

Suddenly, she heard movement outside. A vehicle stopped and footsteps approached the door. She prayed it was a hunter or fisherman who had stumbled across the long vacant hideaway. She would have embraced a burglar, teenagers out drinking or escapees from a DelMarVa chain gang—anyone who might release her from her stinking hell.

But, as she heard the keys placed in the exterior locks, she knew it must the big man.

When the door opened, no light entered. It was night—Friday night. She was right.

Immediately, he noticed the dead bulb.

"Oh, Mother, I'm so sorry," he said. The voice actually sounded concerned. "How long has your light been out?"

"On- only a d-day . . . I think," Sherron whispered, afraid to annoy him, but careful not to be difficult.

Heading into a dark corner, she heard him pull a bulb from its paper container, then twisting sounds as he removed the small dead globe and replaced it with a new one.

Her head and eyes turned to her rear, and she saw Charles as he lowered his arms from the new dangling bulb. He was tall enough to reach the socket without a chair. The ever-present Buck knife was flat against his hip, the sheath attached to his wide black leather belt.

"I'll leave the door open for a few minutes, Mother," he said. "The smell in here is ghastly. How do you stand it?"

Sherron did not respond.

For the next half hour, he delivered more food and supplies, dumped her chamber pot, set a fresh jug of water on the table and made himself a place at the head of the table—to her far right—opposite the insect-eaten, putrid gray flesh of Horace Meeks.

Totally ignoring the corpse, Charles placed a fresh red apple plus a chocolate milkshake, fast food cheeseburger and greasy fries in front of Sherron. Since it was warm, Sherron figured there must be some civilization nearby.

As she grabbed for the much appreciated food, Charles shouted. "NO! First, we give thanks to our Lord!"

She folded her shaking hands and followed his lead as Charles bowed his head and began to speak. "Lord most wonderful, we thank Thee for this food and for the many favorable blessings Thou hast bestowed upon our holy family. We pray that Thou wilst continue to protect us as we do Thy work, and that Thou wilst allow us to grow as a loving unit—one that wilst follow Thy teachings and make Thee proud—unlike so many others in the world today. We especially pray for our deceased Father, who remains at Thy altar with us in body, but who stayed only for a short time in our keeping before he had to depart. We know his spirit is with Thee in heaven. For all this and more to come, we thank Thee with all our hearts."

Sherron was starving and in pain. It was torturous, waiting for Charles to stop so she could devour the fresh food.

"We also pray for Mother, who is most good and who stays home and cares for our needs, as all good mothers should. We ask Thy blessings, protection and love for all of us, and even for those who may wrong us. Amen."

Charles looked up at Sherron and smiled.

"Amen," she whispered, weakly.

They ate in silence, Sherron finishing her meal well in advance of Charles. Without comment, he picked up the wrappers, bagged the trash and took it outside. When he returned to his seat, he looked at his captive.

"Mother, you do look a bit dirty and tired."

Sherron stammered, searching her slow-moving brain for the right response. "No-o-o. I'm f-f-fine. . . ."

"I have a surprise for you," he said, smiling as he left the table and walked up four steps that led to the main house. A few minutes passed and she could hear a strange sound in the background, but it was indistinguishable. Sherron couldn't connect it to an image.

A half hour passed and Charles, now clothed in a heavy, light gray, terrycloth robe walked toward her with a ring of keys. A large "V" of separated material exposed his naked chest.

Fear and confusion raged in her mind as he leaned over her body and placed a thick, ragged rope over her head. The coarse noose fit loosely but still scratched her dry skin. Gently, he tightened it around her neck. Then, reaching down, he unlocked her thick, crude ankle bracelet.

At first she feared he was going to hang her from one of the beams in the roof. When that didn't happen, she still had no other idea what he was planning. Whatever it was, she was powerless to resist. Her fear was mixed with hate and revenge, but she wasn't ready to attack. Her plan wasn't finished. Slowly, she followed as he motioned her to rise. Her steps were weak and short as he held the dangling straight end of the brown rope and led her toward the steps in the dark corner of the room.

"Careful, Mother," he said, as they got to the top step and entered the cobwebbed and littered narrow hallway of the home. Rows of candles lit the alcove and Sherron held tightly onto her guide's arm. She hadn't walked in weeks and her muscles were trying to regroup and recall what to do.

"That's it, Mother. Let little Charles help you along."

A sharp right turn through an open doorway delivered Sherron into an old bathroom. A white, ball and claw foot bathtub was half filled with dark water.

He responded to her look of concern.

"Don't worry Mother, the water may be dark and not fit to drink, but you can bathe in it . . . and I will help you."

Dread took over as her eyes scanned the room lighted by what seemed to be a thousand candles—glowing white, red, green, blue, black. They were flickering from perches on the broken shelves, in windowsills, on the floor in corners and along the walls. Others were lined up on the sink outlining the basin.

Everywhere.

The room was warm and smelled like perfume from the burning scents. A wooden chair stood at the base of the bathtub. Charles' seat she surmised.

He was going to be there as she bathed. Watching, maybe touching. The idea of being violated made her body frigid and stiff. As she stood in the middle of the room, he approached, told her to get undressed and settle inside the tub. Then he left the room.

In a robotic state, Sherron removed her clothing and walked toward the sludge covered liquid. She closed her eyes as she stepped slowly through the ice-cold water—wondering what foreign matter and slime might be coating her skin.

When she was seated, her tar-stained leash floated on the surface, stretching out in front of her face. Charles returned and handed her a glass of dark liquid. It smelled like wine, but it was impossible to identify for sure.

"Drink, Mother," he ordered

Sherron was in no position to protest. In two fast gulps, attempting to get the ordeal over quickly, she downed the liquid then coughed, reacting to its bitter taste.

"Very good," Charles said, stroking her tangled hair with his hand. Walking away he lit a cigar and settled in the chair, front row center, the best seat in the house. During the entire time it took him to slowly smoke the long, large Churchill, he stared at her and said nothing.

Nearly a half hour passed. Sherron focused on the red glow of the tip of the burning tube that faced her, its aromatic smell mixing with the burning candles. In and out . . . . In and out . . . . . His breathing was rhythmic, a muted, slow-paced metronome.

She could faintly see his face, sporting a glowing, proud smile that appeared and departed behind the pulsing red light. Not knowing what to do or expect, Sherron sat still for some time then grabbed the pitted bar of soap and washed herself as best she could—trying to conceal her naked body beneath the dark water. Then, the room began to spin. Dizzy from whatever Charles had mixed in her drink, she closed her eyes and fell asleep.

Smiling, he stood, crushed out the stub of his smoke in the sink basin and left the room without speaking.

Early the next morning she awoke chained to her table, dry and naked under a light gray terrycloth robe. Charles was seated nearby, smiling.

Before she could recall the details of the hours of bathroom horror, he spoke, soothingly.

"You were very bad last night, Mother, doing what you did to me. But, I'll forgive you this time. Just don't let it happen again. It's not right for you to abuse me like you did. It's a good thing Father is gone, or he would be very upset. But we'll keep it our little secret."

As Charles got up and walked toward the exit door, Sherron's gut wrenched. The inside of her stomach twisted and stretched. She pressed one hand against the center of her chest and shoved the other tightly between her legs.

Could he have drugged me with the wine, taken me, raped me? she wondered.

"NO!" she screamed. The spittle shooting from her mouth flew across the room. "YOU BASTARD!! YOU NO

GOOD BASTARD!!!" she shouted at Charles, the words escaping before she realized her mistake. Her balled fists hit the top of the table, causing the water jug to jump and two precious pieces of fresh fruit to roll onto the dirt floor, unfortunately beyond her reach.

Almost out the door, Charles turned, raced back and stood by Sherron's side and grabbed her hair with one paw. Savagely, he yanked her head back until she was looking straight up at his face, her neck extended to its limit.

"You unappreciative WHORE! I said I wouldn't tell Father, and you don't even show me the slightest appreciation. If you were a decent Christian woman, you would have fought me off. But you let me have what I wanted, because it's what you wanted. So, NEVER! EVER! talk back to me again!"

Sherron shook her head as Charles released his grip. She thought that the pain was over, but Charles gripped her hair again. This time he smashed her face—two, three, four times—against the rough, splintered wooden tabletop. With the last contact, Sherron blacked out, never knowing that Charles' final act was a loving kiss on her forehead—where the bruises and bumps were already beginning to form.

❧ **18** ❧

April 2008

H ardly nothing much ever happened in Hardley. For forever the site was a mere crossroads, an acciden- tal stop sign location, and for 51 weeks of the year it remained a never-would-be-anything-more-than-a-noth- ing spot on a DelMarVa road map.

But from Thursday night through Sunday afternoon on the last weekend of April, the tiny white dot—located east of Cambridge, north of Bestpitch, west of Reids Grove and south of Linkwood—becomes a bustling, hot-time-in-the- old-town-tonight place to be. Because that's when the Civil War re-enactors came to call.

No one recalls who thought up the idea, or how the national extravaganza started. According to local lore, in celebration of the Civil War Centennial in 1962, a group of Confederate States of America, gray-clad rebel re-enactors pitched three tents and camped out for the weekend. The next year, Yankee-clad troops set up a half-dozen canvas shelters across the road.

The early participants engaged in water balloon battles, fireworks artillery clashes and BB gun firefights.

Within four years, there were 200 participants and, by 1971, mock battles were taking place in the corn and soy- bean fields and Maryland state police had to send out extra troopers to direct traffic.

In 1998, 3,000 re-enactors, from as far off as Texas and Illinois were represented. Spending the long weekend at "Hardley: The Best Civil War Battlefield Spectacular" was listed in the *National Civil War Re-enactors Tabloid Guide* as "the country's extravaganza re-enactment, a place to be, to see and to be seen."

Camp women in long, wide-flowing dresses cooked chicken, steak and ribs over open campfires. Weekend warriors in wool uniforms shouldered muskets, and scores of iron cannons were trucked in to belch smoke and an occasional shot at the enemy. Money prizes were awarded for authenticity, but the gathering's highlight was Sunday's "Hardley a Battle," which began at sunrise and lasted until noon.

Keeping with strict policy, no modern conveniences were allowed anywhere near the battlefield, except for cellular telephones that were carried only by medics in the event of a serious accident. Unless it was a genuine critical wound, no dedicated re-enactor would allow him or herself to be called off the battlefield. It was all part of the game, why they were there, what made these people tick.

Following orders without question—as was the practice a century and a half before during the War Between the States—was accepted and expected. As the gray coated Johnny Rebs lined up to rush across the field at first light and break through the Union lines, Charles Bettner viewed the battleground through his antique telescope from the shade of a thick-trunked, spready oak.

Surveying the Southern lines, he spotted the drummer boys, two of them standing beside the 16th Richmond Volunteer Irregular Infantry. Charles knew the routine. He had attended many re-enactments in his time. The boys would be ordered to reinforce the voice commands for attack that would be shouted by Major General L. B. Sharpless, seated nearby atop his white charger.

It was almost time.

The young lads would stand back as hundreds of attacking zealots let out the famous "Rebel Yell." Then the drumming would continue at rapid-fire speed as the wild-eyed Confederates passed, heading toward enemy lines to meet death, claim victory or be driven back in defeat.

Leaving his tree, Charles moved forward.

The general had raised his sword. Charles was 50 feet away.

The leader gave the command. Charles was within 30 feet of the boys.

The general's horse lunged ahead, leading a mass of sweating humanity, uncomfortable and irritated in heavy gray wool. Waving vintage wood and metal weapons, the weekend warriors passed by at full run.

The drummers beat harder, the men's wild screams pierced the flat farmland. Drumsticks bounced rapidly off the flat, tight, cowhide heads.

Boots and hooves sank in the earth and thick wet clumps of mud rose up. Small clouds of dust rose from the dry sections of hard ground. The young boys closed their eyes. They didn't need to see what they were doing. Their hands quivered in rapid succession, the tips of their sticks causing the staccato noise.

Charles stood behind the smallest, fattest boy, dressed in a miniature version of a Johnny Reb uniform.

When the drums ceased, the boys began to relax. They laughed and smiled at each other, proud of a job done well. Their part was over, they thought.

"ATTEN—SHUNN!"

The young drumming duet froze, responding to the voice that came from behind.

"ABOUTTT FACEEE!"

They spun around and stared into the flat stomach of the tall, black-clad figure, complete with thick, red-colored, mutton-chop sideburns. Charles wore wrap-around, non-issue sunglasses to hide his eyes. His black, full-length frock coat covered his body from his neck to his knees. A bright white shirt and black string tie completed his costume. White gloves masked his hands, black shinny boots covered his feet. Rather than a soldier, Charles looked like an old-fashioned undertaker, waiting to follow the flow of the battle and pick the bodies clean of jewelry, watches and gold teeth.

Charles' lips were the only part of his body that was exposed. As they moved, he delivered a false, but well-perfected, Southern accent.

"You, son," he pointed to the fat one. "What's your name, troop?"

"Terry Tremble. . . ." the boy responded.

"TERRY TREMBLE, WHAT, TROOP?"

"Terry Tremble, SIR!"

"That's better, son," Charles, drawled. "And you?"

"Martin Tremble, SIR!"

"At ease, men," he said.

He watched as they relaxed and smiled. In order to minimize his time with them, he quickly determined that they were to move to the Yankee lines at the end of the battle, which was taking place about a football-field distance away. The older brother, Martin, did most of the talking. Charles could tell the boy was a little leery of the conversation and he identified Martin as a possible problem. But that didn't matter. The smaller, fatter one was to be the day's prize.

As the spectators' eyes focused on the organized bedlam of the battle, Charles identified himself as Colonel Horatio Cannon, a Union spy and said, "You two boys are under arrest!"

While fat Terry smiled, Martin, at 12 and three years older than his bother, began to ask questions, but he was silenced when Charles said they were to be taken to the Union camp and interrogated about General Sharpless. Slinging their drums over their shoulders, the boys were led toward a grove of trees at the far edge of the parking area.

With the battle in full force, the lot was empty of potential witnesses. Halfway through the metal maze, about 100 feet from Charles' Blazer, the older boy stopped.

"I quit!" he whined. "This is stupid! I'm going back!"

The fat boy watched in silence as Charles bent over, grabbed the older brother by the collar, lifted him several inches off the ground and snarled into his face. "You little no good bastard. I'll snap your goddamn neck right here if you don't keep your shitty little mouth shut and keep moving, understand?"

The boy started to protest, but Charles, with his left hand still holding Terry, tightened his grip on the older, dangling boy's throat. Gasping for air, the boy's eyes began to widen and he tried to nod, but his chin could not move.

Satisfied he would have no further trouble, Charles lowered the boy to the ground and, holding them both by the collars, headed toward the grove.

He tossed them both into the back of the Blazer. With their backs pressed up against the metal cage-like barrier that separated the back seat from the storage section, terrified eyes stared at Charles, who was standing near the open rear hatch.

Comfortable there were no lingering spectators, Charles was annoyed that he had bagged one over his limit. He didn't want, didn't need them both—just fatso Terry.

Holding a roll of gray tape, Charles ordered the older boy to put out his hands. Scared, but still stubborn, he shook his head and shoved his hands behind him.

Charles leaned in and moved close, very close, pushing them both into a corner so Martin's back was practically covering Terry. "You may pull this shit with your parents, you little asshole, but when I tell you something you had better listen and move fast, understand? Or," he pulled out his hunting knife, "I'll carve off your fingers. Then your drumming days will be over. You won't be able to write you name and you'll spend the rest of your life eating through a straw."

Slowly, the older boy, with hands shaking, offered his wrists, which Charles bound quickly. His smaller brother put out his hands immediately. After they were both bound and gagged, Charles tossed the drums beside them, covered his living booty with a gray tarp, closed up the back and drove off.

Extra dark tinted glass ensured that no one could see who was inside the swiftly moving vehicle. Unfortunately, the older boy had throw him off schedule. Instead of heading home immediately, Charles was forced to drive northwest, toward the Chesapeake Bay. He would have to dump the wiseass brother off before he took Terry—who years ago had sat on Charles and made him eat mud—home to take his place beside Father and Mother.

❦   ❦   ❦

Gov. Henry McDevitt looked up from his Georgetown office desk and didn't like the expressions on the faces of the men who had just entered the room.

Michael Pentak and Carlton Buxton moved swiftly. Even before he came to a complete stop, Pentak placed a single piece of paper into the governor's hand.

"We've got a major problem, sir," Pentak said.

McDevitt raised his hand, signaling for the commissioner's patience as he read in silence.

> *The growing DelMarVa family*
> *is pleased to announce*
> *the addition of the first of many children.*
> *Master Terry Tremble,*
> *son of Horace Meeks and Sherron McKlinchey,*
> *born in Hardley, DelMarVa,*
> *April 27th, 2008.*
> *The growing family, especially Mother and Son,*
> *are very happy in their new home.*
> *Love to all.*
> *Keep the faith.*

"I assume this is one of the missing boys from the event last weekend?"

Buxton and Pentak nodded.

"The date of birth on the announcement coincides with the date he disappeared," said Pentak.

"Where did this announcement surface?"

"Wilmington. This one anyway, sir," said Buxton. "We have task force members checking with the other media now. If it follows the pattern, they'll probably discover another one in Salisbury, Cambridge, Ocean City maybe. But, who knows? The postmark on this notice was from Atlantic City. Not Baltimore like before. I actually doubt that our man will use the same newspapers."

"But it only names one of the brothers," McDevitt said, obviously worried.

"Right," said Pentak. "My guess is that he only wanted one and is going to get rid of the other one, somewhere other than this new home he refers to."

"So you're out searching?"

"Yes, sir, we are," Pentak replied unenthusiastically. "There are 200 police looking for one kid, or two kids, or dead bodies. Like I said, it's not good."

"Anything else?" McDevitt asked.

Pentak pointed toward the announcement. "There's a reference we don't like. Look where it says, 'The growing family, especially Mother and son, are very happy.' That seems to indicate that Meeks, the first one kidnapped, may be dead. We're not sure. No way we can be, but that's what some of the task force and the shrinks who have read this think."

"What about the media. Have they reacted yet?"

"That's worse, sir," Pentak said. "They're aware of the latest notice. They've already dubbed this guy—or whoever it is—the 'Snatcher.' They're going with the story that the three disappearances are related. Some of the articles are warning that he's going to hit another festival every month. Actually, that was one of our scenarios, but we never went public with it. It was just a matter of time before the press latched onto it.

"Unfortunately, we couldn't be sure of its validity until it happened again. Now, with the boys' disappearance, he's established a general pattern and we know we were right. But we hoped we wouldn't be."

"Any witnesses at all?" said the governor.

"Again, nothing," said Pentak. "This guy must be invisible or leading a charmed life."

"Two task force interrogators, they both were formerly with the FBI, are going to visit the parents again," said Buxton. "That's where we're hoping to get something, anything. They were at the event. Mother was a cook. Father was a Rebel infantryman. The boys must have been grabbed during the battle charge. Everyone was focused on the action so no one cared about anything else that was happening."

"No one saw them go off? Drive away? What did they do, just disappear?" McDevitt asked Pentak.

"The police estimate there were close to 7,000 re-enactors, spectators and vendors out there last weekend, in a country crossroads. It was organized bedlam with everyone in costume. Hell, even if someone saw something, our guy could have been President Lincoln or Robert E. Lee, so we would still have nothing other than a guess at height, weight and sex—if we're lucky. But our guys are asking questions, looking for anything, hoping to get lucky."

McDevitt stared for a moment, then hit the intercom. "Grace, tell Randy to get the car ready—I've got to head out. And, please, cancel my appointments."

Before McDevitt left, he arranged to meet that evening with Pentak at the governor's mansion. That afternoon he had to go to Princess Anne and share a few moments with the parents of Terry and Martin Tremble.

❧ ❧ ❧

Pentak, Sean Kelley, Grace Welch and Stephanie Litera were waiting for McDevitt as he entered Woodburn's dining room. AP wire service printouts were spread across the table. The story would appear in newspapers across the country the next morning. In addition, Snatcher stories based on on-the-scene interviews would be sure to make *The New York Times*, *Washington Post* and Philadelphia and Baltimore dailies.

McDevitt and Poplos had heard features on every local hourly newscast and the Snatcher's work at Hardley, Wilmington and Shepherd was on the evening national TV and cable broadcasts. It had not been a good day.

"How'd it go with the family?" Pentak said, as he rose and pulled out a chair for McDevitt.

Nodding to Kelley and smiling at Stephanie, he lowered himself into the seat and offered a response as weary as he looked. "It was difficult. They wanted me to bring good news, that their children are fine. How do I tell them I have no idea of where their kids are, or who took them, and that I doubt that we'll be able to bring them back home?

"I never thought," McDevitt continued, "that there would be anything harder than going to funerals. At least then there's some sense of closure, for me and for the family. These disappearances and the uncertainty are going to extend the grief for everyone involved. I played the role and tried to give them hope. That's about all I could do. Now," he looked up at Pentak, "tell me that we have more than that. Tell me something good."

No one spoke and Grace Welch, the usually stern and steady taskmaster, excused herself to make a fresh pot of coffee.

"That bad?" McDevitt said.

"That bad," Pentak repeated. Pulling out some notes, he began to bring McDevitt up to date.

Like the other announcements from the kidnapper, the latest communication yielded nothing more than the educated guesses they had discussed earlier in McDevitt's office. Again, there was no physical evidence on the document and not enough text to gain any details or texture of the perpetrator's personality or characteristics. Also, Pentak said, two other announcements had surfaced, one at a radio station in Ocean City and another at a television station in Philadelphia. Apparently, the perp was beginning to send his announcements to a wider audience. That indicated he was getting bolder and might be raising the stakes in the game.

"Does that mean he would be grabbing more than one a month?" McDevitt asked.

"We don't know," Pentak replied. "We don't know much."

Sean spoke up, saying that an editorial on a regional

NPR station said if the disappearances didn't stop DelMar-Va's growing tourist industry would see the effects of the Snatcher in the coming months.

"People aren't going to risk going out if they think they aren't coming back, that they'll just disappear off the face of the Earth," Sean said.

McDevitt looked at his commissioner. "Do you think there's anything to that, Mike?"

"I think it would take several more disappearances for the state to take a big hit," Pentak replied. "But that's not my area. Let me tell you where we are with the task force. We met this afternoon and added two former FBI agents who are now with us. They both have spent time in the bureau's Child Abduction and Serial Killer units. Their input may give us another perspective, and they're to report by tomorrow. We've still got next to nothing in leads, and the trails are getting colder even as we sit here. But we've got some smart people with us.

"From another standpoint, we've tried to look at the situation sequentially and from every possible angle. Do we have a loose cannon, or is someone out there playing a calculated, mathematically-based game with some strange agenda? Are there any connections with the three events— the types of places where the abductions occurred and, most importantly, is there any possible connection among the people who have disappeared? We've looked at it geographically, by date. Hell, Hank, we've even gone as far as analyzing it astrologically, using the times of the kidnappings, and even looked at the victims' birthdays.

"Since there's been no hits yet, we've got three computer geeks at the University of Delaware in Newark doing a numerical breakdown according to moon phases, mileage distances between the crime scenes and sea tide schedules. I don't know what they hope to get but . . . ."

"But we're reaching that far." McDevitt finished the sentence.

Pentak continued, shifting the conversation to what they did know. "Only one crime has occurred each month. If the perpetrator is building a family, then a mother, father and two children are already accounted for. But, with only one of the boys mentioned in the note, I'm afraid that we may be getting a very bad signal from the kidnapper."

"What do you mean?" McDevitt asked.

"He might not include the other kid in his collection. And, if he doesn't, he probably already disposed of him. We're also trying to predict what he'll do next," Pentak said, waiting for McDevitt to give him the go ahead to continue.

Seeing a nod, the commissioner went on. "He, and I'm assuming it's a man, has got a father and mother, apparently that was Horace and the McKlinchey woman. The first child is a boy, but I suspect a few more children as the next immediate targets."

"How many?" McDevitt asked, looking up as he leaned back and rubbed his palms against his cheeks.

"I'm guessing," said Pentak, "but if I was writing this as a novel, I'd expect two or three more kids, of varying ages—and I'd watch for all ages from infant up to 18. Maybe even toss in a grandparent to throw the cops off even more."

No one spoke immediately. Pentak waited a minute, then continued.

"Probably, the next strike will be somewhere during May, and this presents us with our most serious concern yet. We compiled the number of more significant events in the 14 counties based on the past five years—everything from fire hall pancake breakfasts to major tourist attractions—and we came up with 218 potentials for May.

"These include biggies such as Old Dover Days, St. Michaels Mid-Atlantic Maritime Festival, the Chestertown Tea Party and Chincoteague's Migratory Bird Celebration, major re-enactments at Fort Delaware and the Easton Jazz and Artworks Festival."

"Then," added Sean Kelley, "there are other freelance events that we don't know about—church bazaars, flea markets, senior center programs, yard sales, Boy Scout camping trips and school band concerts, amateur plays and day care open houses."

McDevitt looked across the table at Stephanie. "You're a psychologist. What do you think?"

Eyes turned toward the governor's special friend. She had been brought down by Pentak at McDevitt's request. They waited for her response.

"You've got at least two FBI psycho shrink profilers working on this," Stephanie said. "They're experts who have been trained in this field. There's hardly anything I can add to your database. I can't help you solve this . . . ."

"I'm not looking for a solution," McDevitt explained. "Our two profilers are in Wilmington, but they're not from here. They're new to the peninsula. The others, from the bureau, are down in Washington. They come up when we have an incident, then they go back and do whatever analysis and deep thinking they get paid for. God knows. Mike gets periodic reports and that's about it. Maybe the two recent additions to the task force will help. We don't know. In my opinion, they're all guessing as much as we are. If we had an answer or solid lead from them, we wouldn't be here.

"If you want to know the truth, I believe the feds aren't losing any sleep to help us solve these cases. They like seeing DelMarVa cops embarrassed because our troopers make more than an FBI agent. But, that's my opinion. Come on, Steph. We're just brainstorming, bouncing around ideas. Who, what kind of a person are we looking for? What should we expect? Where should we focus? Where would you go next to embarrass us, to drive us crazy?"

Annoyed at being put on the spot, Stephanie said, a bit impatiently, "I'm just a state-appointed counselor, someone who deals with troubled employees, with people who have minor work-related problems."

"Good," said Pentak, growing a bit irritated and speaking from across the table. "Tell us about this troubled soul, this messed-up person with a problem. If you were to guess, to imagine, based on what's happened already and what's been said tonight, what do you think might happen next and what kind of person should we be looking for?"

Stephanie took a moment to organize her thoughts. Then, as if she were sharing information with one of the many association gatherings she'd addressed over the years, she began, "Without full details of the case, I'd say you have a very angry and clever adversary. He, and, without hesitation, I'm sure it is a man . . . ."

"Why?" McDevitt asked.

"Because of the clues," she replied. "It's blatant taunting. The ads in the newspapers—the public events where he chooses to perform his crime and no one sees him—all of this is a public challenge to the authority and professionalism of the law enforcement agencies in the state. I'd say that is, traditionally, a male approach, similar to an old-fashioned, out-in-the-open duel.

"Already, his objectives are producing results. Because of the obvious inadequacy of the law's response, there's been a decline in tourism reported, plus national bad press for the state. I also would imagine that all of this will progress to a higher level of dissatisfaction that will include negative media editorials and personal political attacks. They will be directed at you both, in your roles as governor and as police commissioner. Then, they will zero in on the ineffectiveness of the entire police force. When it reaches that level, public impatience will grow quickly and exponentially."

Sean, who was in charge of the public relations arena, said, "So we should expect negative letters to the editor, rough handling by a few talk show hosts and some editorial flack."

"Yes," Stephanie said, "but your worst fear is that the victims' families will start to question the ability of the best paid state police force in the nation to solve these crimes and stop others from happening."

There was a pause. No one spoke for a few seconds, then McDevitt resumed his questioning. "Back to our subject—this kidnapper or killer. Any specifics on this nut? Is he crazy, an oddball, would he stand out in a crowd, look different from the average person?"

Stephanie shook her head. "You are not dealing with an idiot, Hank. Nor is this a poor retarded person or someone of low or marginal intelligence. You are not looking for someone with a limp or hunchback or speech impediment or a third eye, for God's sake! If that is where you've been concentrating, you are way off base. This person is calculating and slick. He probably is a power junkie and in total control of himself and his surroundings all week long at work. He is an honored, recognized employee that you could sit next to, have a conversation with about the Ravens or the Eagles or the status of the stock market.

"But, I doubt if he has a family. I would bet he's a loner, with few if any friends. He's someone who goes to work, returns home and stays there. He has no out-of-work social interaction with individuals or groups. If he goes to church, he goes alone. If he goes to a baseball game, he always buys a single ticket. But, there are a lot of people out there like that, and that's why finding him is so difficult."

No one spoke.

"What you have to understand," she continued, "is that he could be anybody who appears to be totally sane. Hell, Hank, he could be someone on your cabinet, or a smiling face you met at last week's Sons and Daughters of the American Colonists banquet.

"Just because he is doing things that you or I would never consider—things that would make a great Hollywood movie theme—does not mean he is crazy. He could be a genius who simply gets his kicks out of running your entire state police force around in circles.

"But, the fact that he is playing with human beings, manipulating real people to send his message, is the reason I think you should worry. Obviously, he considers his captives expendable. Then there's the sexual issue. . . ."

"What's that?" Sean snapped, obviously surprised.

"Many well-known criminologists and criminal psychologists theorize that most serial kidnappers or multiple murderers are driven by sexual motives, in addition to any other objectives on their agenda."

"Meaning?" Pentak asked.

"Meaning," Stephanie replied, "that our victims will probably suffer some level of sexual abuse at the hands of their captor. But, not even the most experienced psycho cop can tell you with any accuracy the level or the intensity of the abuse. It could range from voyeurism and photography to domination and degradation of unspeakable degrees. But, unfortunately, we won't know how bad it is until he's caught or his victims are found."

McDevitt's face did not move, but the atmosphere in the room was anything but positive. After an uncomfortable silence, he asked, "If you had to make an intelligent guess, what type of background does our man have? Who would you focus on if you were in charge?"

"I'd concentrate on someone very intelligent, and someone without a serious police record. Someone who had a difficult childhood and who, himself, may have been abused. I believe his actions were triggered by an unexpected event that he could not control. And that is the key. I have a feeling he has a grudge against someone—a boss or someone important. The kidnappings and publicity are how he's getting noticed and getting even as well," Stephanie said.

"It's my bet that he's got military or police force experience," added Pentak. "Carlton and I agree on this, and we've ordered a list of current and former armed forces and law enforcement personnel who still live in the state."

"Great!" remarked Sean, sarcastically. "That will give us six million names from the Dover Air Force Base alone. Then, what happens if it turns out to be one of our own, a top cop? God, we'll be done then. That would make a great final story to close up shop on."

"Thanks for your positive attitude and faith in our police force, Sean," Pentak said. "We all appreciate it." The commissioner's voice was white ice cold. The governor's aide mumbled an apology and lowered his eyes, mentioning frustration and overwork as he rubbed his forehead.

Perhaps not selecting the perfect moment, Stephanie asked aloud, "What will you do when you catch him?"

Pentak, McDevitt and Kelley all stared at the woman on the sofa.

"What do you mean, specifically, Stephanie?" Pentak asked, breaking another uncomfortable silence.

"Well," she paused as she looked at the three men, "will you let him make it to trial or will he meet up with an unfortunate DelMarVa 'accident'?"

McDevitt stared at the other two men, then looked at Stephanie and answered in a very controlled voice. "We will bring him in . . . if we can, if he cooperates. But," he said after a brief pause, "we all have agreed that we will make very sure he never hurts anyone again. Does our direct approach to this problem disturb you?"

Stephanie was ill at ease, but responded with nervous conviction. "No matter what he's done, he's still entitled to a fair trial. I believe in that. Don't you?"

"I believe he's entitled to justice," McDevitt replied. "Unfortunately, in this day and age, in many people's minds, the law should bend too far to make sure the criminal has rights. But, at the same time, justice remains rigid when it comes to the needs of the victims and the ultimate good of society. In that way, law and justice were not always the same thing, at least they weren't until now."

"So you're the one who makes sure they are?"

No one spoke for almost 10 seconds. Pentak got up and answered. "Yes. We make sure justice and the law work together in this state. Frankly, that means we make damn certain a criminal that has seriously hurt innocent citizens will never do it again. And especially this asshole."

Stephanie locked on the police commissioner's eyes. "No matter what?"

It was McDevitt's turn to reply. "No matter what."

The cold mood was awkward. McDevitt stared at Stephanie, waiting for a comment. When none came, he pressed her. "You don't agree, do you?"

"No," she said, looking directly at the governor. "No matter what anyone does, he or she deserves to be treated with respect and fairly."

"Even if it's a cold-blooded murderer who kills for enjoyment? Even if he destroys innocent lives? What if the victim is someone you love? If this animal out there right now—with a man and a woman and young boy now part of his private, sick, human body collection—added one of your relatives to his growing family, would you still be so compassionate and caring?"

"Yes." Stephanie's answer was quick, there was no hesitation. "I may not approve of what the criminal has done, but two wrongs do not make something right. We have to raise ourselves above the level of evil. We have to show by example; we must demonstrate what is proper and right. We must be honorable so they will learn. Otherwise, we're no better than they are."

McDevitt, who had just spent an hour talking to another family of victims, was in no mood to turn the other cheek or listen to idealistic chatter, especially from the woman he loved. He was annoyed, frustrated and deeply disappointed.

"Well, let me say this, Stephanie. I'd bet my next term that if you were kidnapped by this animalistic bastard you'd be singing a different tune."

"Then you'd lose," she said. Her voice was firm, her face a stiff statue of defiance.

No one else in the room spoke. McDevitt suggested that they pack it in for the night.

The session wrapped up quickly. Stephanie, seeing the governor's annoyance, decided to head back to Wilmington. It was obvious that he was consumed by the disappearances and mentally exhausted. After the tense exchange, she was not in a good frame of mind either.

They hugged awkwardly and agreed to call each other in a few days.

While riding up Route 13, past Ronny's Market and the Gumwood Rest Stop, a portion of Stephanie's mind was bothered, uneasy. She had experienced her first mini-argument with her lover and she didn't like it. But, everyone was under unusual, intense pressure. Things would be better if they allowed some time to pass.

She didn't believe in vigilante justice and she had made her feelings known. It may not have been a wise thing to do, but at least she felt she should get some credit for being honest.

As the car passed slower moving traffic, she realized that there was something else, a more serious, hazy concern that couldn't be pulled into focus. As hard as she tried, Stephanie couldn't drag a clear image from the back edge of her mind and fine-tune it properly. Rather than disappearing completely, the mysterious, annoying message continued to gnaw in the dark corner of her brain.

It could be one of a hundred things—what she needed at the store, her concern over Hank, worries about their relationship, uneasiness with being asked for input about a case that seemed unsolvable and, finally, her embarrassment for questioning Hank and Mike's methods.

Eventually, she knew, the issues would find their way through the mental labyrinth and arrive at the place where they could be identified and evaluated. Until that time, they would continue to nag at her from a distance.

🌿   🌿   🌿

McDevitt was alone in Woodburn, the governor's mansion he had called home for several satisfying years.

He poured himself a scotch on the rocks and walked to the French doors that overlooked the grounds rolling away from the first floor of the building. The old-fashioned street lamps sent a soft glow onto the irregular brick pavements and mature shrubbery. Carriages used to roll down these streets, and men in top hats and women in flowing gowns had passed by the mansion, talked and laughed in the building, stood in the very spot he was standing at that moment.

McDevitt smiled, recalling his first visit. He was 10 years old, on a school tour that included stories of the ghosts that haunted the building and grounds.

He and his friends were in awe of the round-topped,

wooden door leading to the basement tunnel that had been used by runaway slaves from the St. Jones River. But it was Patty Cannon and her kidnappers that had intrigued him the most. In the early 19th century, the murdering innkeeper claimed scores of victims at her home and traveler's stop at Reliance, west of Seaford.

The small structure still stood on the portion of the Mason-Dixon Line that ran north and south. Until the formation of DelMarVa, that line had divided the old states of Delaware and Maryland.

Patty made much of her fortune kidnapping free blacks and selling them back into slavery. At the time, the slavenapper was described as "a most vicious, degenerate criminal as ever walked the earth." Some scholars who specialize in DelMarVa history consider Patty the peninsula's first and worst serial killer.

Until now, McDevitt thought.

He found it both troubling and interesting that such a horrifying historical character had fascinated him in his youth. He had been drawn to her because of her string of bloody crimes. Now, nearly 200 years later, another crazed criminal was roaming the region. But this one, McDevitt realized, was having a larger impact on the state and its citizens. Apparently, history was repeating itself.

But Patty Cannon poisoned herself before she could be executed for her crimes. McDevitt did not intend for the modern-day kidnapper to escape the full force of DelMarVa justice.

19

May 2008

Carlton Buxton and Michael Pentak arrived at the edge of the dock in time to join a half-dozen members of the State Police Evidence Response Team and the three task force investigators who were talking to 72-year-old Nevitte Teague. The short, wiry and opinionated Eastern Shore waterman had hauled in the body. Six passengers, who also had been cruising on the 80-year-old skipjack *Molly Deal*, were giving statements to other officers. The day tourists were huddled in the parking lot, near their bright-colored sport utility vehicles. In appearance and attitude, they were as removed from Teague as a gourmet cappuccino was from a cup of stale cafeteria Joe.

While Buxton spoke to the crime scene coordinator, Pentak glanced at the mound of dark green resting on the front end of the narrow wooden deck.

Buxton caught up with his boss as they walked toward the body.

"Bad luck, Mike," Buxton said, frowning. "The crime boys say the water's washed away any PE that might have been on the victim and clothes. If we found the kid on the ground, they might have been able to lift some fibres, trace some footprints or cast some vehicle tracks. But, with floaters it's real tough to get much of anything. They'll scrape under the kid's nails and hope, but that's about the best we can wish for."

Pentak nodded. He had already suspected what Buxton had reported.

Stopping at the mound, the commissioner knelt down and placed one knee on the wooden deck. Gently, he pulled back the wet green blanket that had been used to cover the bloated corpse of a 12-year-old boy. Carlton shook his head and looked way. The youngster had been in the water over a week, and his face and limbs had been more than a few satisfying meals for families of crabs and hungry fish. Chunks of milky skin were missing, but the soaking gray Confederate uniform left little doubt that the remains belonged to one of the missing boys, most probably young Martin Tremble. The parents would have to be called for the official ID.

Several fingers were missing off the hands, which were still bound by gray masking tape at the wrists. The piece that had been placed across the boy's mouth as a gag was loose, half off. It probably began to separate in the water. Two ceremonial drums—their flat, cowskin heads busted, their bright paint bearing the letters CSA—were tied by thick rope to the boy's ankles.

A deep slash across the boy's throat indicated that he was probably dead before he was tossed into the water. Apparently, it was the floating drums that caught the boat's attention.

"Sick bastard," Pentak hissed, staring at the body. "I want this asshole, Carlton. I swear, and I wouldn't be upset if he didn't make it to trial. You hear me?"

"I hear you, Mike. Loud and clear."

Dropping the green cover, Pentak stepped off the boat and walked with Buxton toward the area of the interrogation. Neither was going to interfere. The on-site officers were in charge, but the two men arrived in time to hear the fisherman complain that he was being questioned about the same thing for the fourth time.

Cap'n Nevitte Teague did not like police of any type. But, he admitted, at least they weren't game wardens. He spit on the ground as soon as he mentioned those words.

Reluctantly, he explained again that he had been taking a private party for a scenic look around the bay.

"We set outta Rock Hall and went up past Tolchester. We was gonna head back down towards Queensto'n and was gonna come back up to finish up our little cruise," he explained. "Over near Eastern Neck, one of the passengers, he says he's spotted somethin' a floatin' offa the port side. I turned the wheel an' took 'er in closer, tossed out a hook line and set to draggin' it aboard.

"I had no idea what the hell it was," he said, pausing to spit another chaw of Red Man tobacco on the ground, this time directly in between the interrogator's shoes. "We start t' haulin' her up on deck. An', all at once, the ladies, they start screamin' to hell. This one big fella, he drops my grap'lin' hook. Then he gets hisself sick as two dogs an' goes aft to start heavin' his brekfist offta side.

"Me and Little Nev, that be my boy, we hauled the barrels on board an', hell, then I seed what the commotion is about. There's a floater tied right tight to 'em. I got on the horn and called up the Coast Guard. I don't want no trouble over this. Hell, now I gotta give the money back to them foreigners. Lost a whole day out here. I woulda been better off to go drudgin', but took out this party last minute. As a favor. Ya know? If I knowed what was right, I shoulda left them friggin' tourists on the dock and never drugged them damn barrels outta the bay."

❦   ❦   ❦

SNATCHER STRIKES AGAIN!
—*Diamond State Ledger*

**SNATCHER SLASHES ONE VICTIM,
THREE STILL MISSING!**
—*Donna Blankenship,
National Press Syndicate*

POLICE MAKE NO HEADWAY IN SNATCHER SLAYING!
—*Southern DelMarVa Weekly News*

MAY MAY NOT BE A MERRY MONTH
—*Wilmington News Chronicle*

The headlines were not kind. But the sick humor making the rounds was worse. One story said Pentak's task force was as dead in the water as little Martin Tremble.

Discovery of the dead drummer provided no clues to the killer's identity, his motive or where or when he would strike next. Everyone believed another victim would disappear in May.

Several minor fairs and outings rescheduled their events to the fall, hoping that the snatchings would be over before then. Others hired additional security guards.

On May 1, Charles Bettner appeared in Stephanie Litera's office for his scheduled appointment. The conversation focused on his new position and how he had adjusted. During the session, he even mentioned that he was beginning to like his job.

As their time drew to a close, he mentioned an older foster sister, with whom he had been madly in love.

"She was one of the most beautiful, most kind, most caring people I have ever known," Charles said. "She protected me from the world, when it was cruel. I left that home abruptly, and I never saw her again. I sometimes wish I could talk to her, just one more time. I hope she's doing well."

"Why did you leave, Charles?"

"Oh, the family was transferred away, and I wasn't able to relocate out of the area."

"What a shame," Stephanie said. "How old were you then?"

"In my first year of high school, I think."

"What did you like most about her, Charles?"

"Her genuine kindness toward me, and I remember that she had long blond hair. It was so perfect, it fell like fine, smooth, yellow gold resting on her shoulders. I used to love to run my fingers through it. Sometimes she would let me brush it, as she sat in front of the mirror."

Recently, Charles had given a lot of thought to his former foster sister. Initially, the time with her was wonderful. At the age of 13, he was madly attracted to his foster sister, who was four years older. At first he wanted her as his friend, but eventually his interest became romantic.

He was awkward at the time. As a foster brother, he looked up to her as being caring and smarter, someone with whom he could talk, share his concerns and his deepest thoughts. And she responded.

He recalled the summer day she was in her room. They were alone in the house and he worked up the courage to ask her for a kiss.

She smiled at him and gently touched her lips to his forehead. Excited, he decided to go into her bedroom later that night, after everyone was asleep. Unfortunately for young Charles, she did not share his romantic interests. The moment she awoke, she let out a horrifying scream.

Charles begged her to be quiet, but she wouldn't stop. He tried to put his hand over her mouth, but she bit him and continued screaming louder. As Charles turned to run, the girl's father was standing in the doorway.

She cried that Charles had attacked her, had tried to rape her and then showed her father her torn nightgown. Charles tried to explain, but was unable to talk as the large man's fists beat against his face and stomach.

The next day he was sent back to the state home to await assignment to another foster family.

Recalling the memories of that incident took only a few seconds during the session, and Charles was quickly back in control.

As Stephanie finished marking her notes, he looked up and said, "I've decided that I won't be coming to see you any more."

Stephanie wasn't surprised. "I expected that, Charles," she said, smiling.

"You've done a lot for me, helped me modify my perspective, appreciate change and learn a lot about myself. I'm quite grateful."

She smiled. "Well, I'll really miss our time together," she said. It was an innocent comment she had made hundreds of times. She said it to all departing clients, but Charles believed there was more to her message than she intended.

"You don't have to," he said, staring at her intently.

Stephanie looked up, confused. "I beg your pardon?"

"Now that we're no longer involved in a professional relationship, I'd like to take you out to dinner, and I think we should get to know each other better."

Freezing a surprised smile on her face, Stephanie answered slowly, "I don't think that would be a good idea, Charles." Closing the folder, she got up and walked behind her desk.

Charles followed and moved closer. "Please, give me a chance," he said. "I think we should meet away from here, share our interests. Eventually, we might become more than just friends."

As he advanced, she backed farther away. But he closed in as he spoke. His voice was smooth, not excited, but steady. He was ignoring her comments, her signals, her obvious lack of interest.

"I think you should at least give me a chance. Everyone deserves a chance. Don't you agree?"

Raising her voice slightly, Stephanie said, "I'm sure you're a very nice man, Charles, but I can't handle a new personal relationship now. I'm involved with someone, and it wouldn't be fair to you or me. So, please, I'm flattered, but it's not appropriate. It's simply not a good time."

Standing silently and facing her with a glacial stare, Charles snapped, "It's McDevitt, isn't it?"

"That is none of your business!" Stephanie replied. She was done being polite and her voice was harsh. "You were a client and nothing more. Now that relationship is over and my personal life is none of your business. It's time for you to leave. Now!"

Without saying a word, Charles went out the door, and Stephanie picked up her phone. When Marty answered, she told him she wanted to meet after work for a few stiff drinks.

℣   ℣   ℣

Old Dover Days, the annual Covered Bridge Plant Sale, the Hymn Sing Camp Meeting and Ocean City's Springfest were all successful and uneventful. When no snatchings occurred anywhere else during the first week of May in Del-MarVa, the police and the public were relieved. Of course, the presence of additional paid security personnel working overtime throughout the state was apparent at each public event.

During the second weekend, the Mother's Day Tea Party and the Birth Defects Gala Ball in Wilmington occurred without incident, as did the Bay Bridge Walk, the Chincoteague Main Street Folk Festival and the Nanticoke River Cleanup and Oxford Boat Building Festival.

By the latter half of May, the tourists were returning and the police were keeping their fingers crossed, for the Snatcher had not reappeared.

When the third weekend passed—and such events as Polkas in the Park, the Great Choptank Canoe Race and A Day in Olde New Castle occurred without incident—some believed the worst was over. But Pentak ordered his troopers to continue at full overtime strength through the next two months. Memorial Day Weekend was approaching and the commissioner didn't want to reduce his concern or the heavy police presence until he had the kidnapper in a cell. Unfortunately, it appeared that the Snatcher was going to have to be caught in the act.

While sentries on the last weekend of the month were protecting race fans at the Delaware Handicap, guarding those attending dozens of Memorial Day veteran observances and keeping surveillance at scores of other festivals, Charles Bettner sat calmly in the outdoor bleachers, watching the commencement exercises for the 78 graduates at Villa Theresa High School for Girls. The attractive campus was located on the grounds of a former shipping millionaire's mansion on the banks of the Tuckahoe Creek.

Dressed in a black suit and a stiffly starched white

priest's collar, Father Charles blended in with the smiling audience. His fake newspaper press pass and large complicated looking camera added to his clerical credentials. Identifying himself as an associate editor for Baltimore's *John Carroll Catholic Chronicle*, he explained that Villa Theresa's commencement and its graduates had been selected to be featured in the well-known religious weekly. Upon arrival, he talked with the senior class faculty adviser and school principal. Both were more than eager to help arrange a private interview after the ceremonies between Father Charles and three selected students.

Since parents had been instructed to wait in the stands and parking lot and were not allowed to enter the school after the graduation, the principal told Charles he could have a few moments alone with the three top graduates.

The late May afternoon was bright and the breeze cool as Charles used his zoom lens to focus in on the seniors he would meet. During the ceremony, he placed them in preference order.

His first choice was Kathleen Pietlock, a blond-headed beauty who was president of the National Honor Society and class valedictorian. She would begin pre-med classes at Villanova University in the fall.

Josette Noble was next in line. Another blond, she had earned a vocal scholarship to Catholic University in Washington, D.C., and had opened the ceremonies by singing the National Anthem.

His last choice was sports star Carrie O'Neil, who was heading to either Notre Dame in Baltimore or Georgetown University on a basketball and swimming scholarship. She was tall, attractive, but had dark brown hair. That was the only drawback.

Charles decided he would feel proud adding any of them to his family.

As the graduates marched in single file from the stage, heading toward the school gymnasium doorway, the principal directed the three women into an empty classroom. Father Charles said he needed about 10 minutes alone with each girl.

He asked them all the same questions, about their upcoming summer, career plans and family situation, name and address. As he finished each interview, he took a photograph for the regional weekly and questioned them casually about their plans for the rest of the day.

Unfortunately for her, Josette Noble was the winner. She told the friendly priest that she commuted each day to school from her family's home on Kent Island. Her parents had left immediately after the ceremony, and she was to meet them for her graduation party, scheduled to begin at 6 o'clock. She had three hours to get there, but first had to stop on the way at her boyfriend's home outside St. Michaels.

Father Charles mentioned that he had another assignment, but it was on Tilghman Island and he had never been there. Since they would be going in the same direction, Josette suggested that the priest follow her, and he agreed eagerly.

Less than an hour after the graduation ceremonies had concluded, Charles Bettner, in a rented brown Toyota sedan, was following Josette Noble down Route 50.

As they made several turns, passed by the busy roads and drove three miles further into the country on Route 33, Father Charles began tooting his horn and waving out the window for Josette to pull off the road. She looked in her mirror and responded to his gestures, stopping in a vacant lot that had once served as a small produce stand and flea market parking lot.

Charles ran out, raced to the back of the car, handed her his black jacket and quickly crawled under the trunk of her car.

"What's wrong?" Josette shouted, her voice expressing confusion and concern.

"It's horrible!" he shouted from below. "Your whole back end was smoking like it was going to catch on fire. Didn't you see it?"

"No!" she said, searching for some evidence of the problem. "I don't see anything."

"It must have stopped when you shut off the engine, but I wouldn't drive it anymore. How far are we from your friend's?" he asked.

"Only about 10 minutes," she said, still confused, but now also worried about her car.

"Well, I can take you there right now," Charles the cleric said, looking at his watch. Reaching through her open window, he took her keys but was careful not to touch any other part of her vehicle. "Get in and I'll drop you off. I'll probably be late for my interview, but I can't leave you out here. It wouldn't be safe."

It was obvious he was in control and the girl, unable to gather her thoughts, sat down in the passenger seat. She kept staring at her vehicle and was confused. "I don't think there's anything really wrong," she started to say. "Why don't I just try to drive it a little more and . . . ."

"And have it explode and kill you on your graduation day? That can happen, you know. Look, I'd feel responsible. We'll be at your friend's in a few minutes and he can call for a tow. Okay?"

Feeling better about the decision, she nodded. "Thanks," she said. *He is a priest, and he does seem interested in helping . . . and he looks very concerned.*

"No problem," Charles replied, as he pulled out onto the highway and headed west. Josette directed him to turn left. She needed to get him in the direction of the road to the Oxford-Bellevue Ferry. Instead, her driver made a U-turn and headed back the way they had come.

As the girl protested, Father Charles pressed harder on the gas pedal and the Toyota moved even more quickly, passing her abandoned car and meshing easily into the heavy spring traffic flow.

Too scared to jump out and too stunned to scream, Josette looked at the driver, who glared back and said, "Make one move, or make one little sound, and I'll beat you senseless, you understand?"

She shook her head as fear started to wrap its hot arms around her young body. Worry was closing in and she was fighting the desire to faint.

Smiling, Charles addressed his passenger. "You little fool," he snarled. "All anyone has to do is put on a collar and any Catholic responds like a programmed animal. I could probably go into a bank and rob it with this collar on and half the tellers would ask me to give them a blessing."

Josette did not reply. She was too busy thinking about her stupidity and was trying to work up the nerve to jump out of the moving car.

"You touch that door handle and I'll crush your throat with my fist. Do you understand?"

She nodded slowly.

"Good," Charles said. "I don't want you to do anything stupid. I won't hurt you. Just be patient and when I stop I'll explain everything."

The girl nodded and remained silent as they drove together for about 45 minutes, taking back roads that Josette never knew existed. In the forested scrublands between Ellendale and Harbeson, Charles slammed on the brakes and turned into an overgrown field of tall brush. Still terrified, angry and confused, Josette couldn't move. Her arms were wrapped around her body, physically holding herself together.

In a clearing, 200 feet off the road, behind tall swamp reeds he stopped the Toyota, grabbed the girl, led her away from the car and tossed her into the back section of his Blazer.

"You said you'd tell me what's going on!" Josette snapped at Charles, who had removed his collar and tossed it beside her.

Laughing, he leaned forward and handcuffed her ankle to the bottom of the seat. As she moved away from his approach, he shoved a saturated rag of chloroform against her face. Within seconds she was asleep. As he had done before, a five-gallon container of gasoline did the job on the rented car and, as the black plume stained the clear spring air, he pulled out onto DelMarVa's back roads.

Charles headed southeast and aimed in the direction of Bishop. He'd change the Blazer's tires tomorrow. Even if they found the burned out Toyota and started to put the pieces together, there'd be no way they could track him down. As always, he had thought of everything.

He looked at his watch. It was a little before 6, about the time her family would be looking out the window for little Josette Noble to appear. Charles turned on the radio to an oldies station. "Special Angel" was just finishing. A good sign he said, smiling to himself, looking to the rear at his special, sleeping angel, driving toward home under the protection of Father Charles. He finally had the blond-headed, loving sister he had always wanted.

🥀　　🥀　　🥀

The sound of the motor and tires moving over a parking lot made of gravel and oyster shells caused Sherron and Terry to lift their heads. It was late and the slim slivers of light had long since passed away from the thin entry cracks of the blackened windows.

The captives' eyes met across the table, and Sherron motioned for the boy to remain calm as the sound of latches being released carried through the wooden door.

Her gray robe was stained, filthy from weeks of unwashed wear. Terry's clothing was soiled as well. He had not yet been treated to a bath, and Sherron could not bring herself to warn him what one might be like, especially since she was unsure of what might happen to the boy.

The big man entered, pulling along a young girl clothed in the white dress she had worn under her graduation gown.

As he swung her to the ground, she fell inches from the boots of Horace, who was now several months beyond the point of no return.

She began to let out a scream, but stopped as soon as the big man raised his hand.

Apparently, thought veteran captive Sherron, the new girl was smart enough to keep her horror inside. *Trading physical brutality for silent mental torture was the Golden Rule of captives*, Sherron thought.

With a hard swing of his right leg, Charles kicked the new arrival's ribs, directing her toward the empty seat next to Terry. Like a spider trying to avoid being crushed by an advancing boot, Josette crawled into the chair and sat motionless as she was chained to the metal loop sticking up from the sunken log.

From across the table, Sherron motioned with her fingers for Josette to be calm, to keep quiet. So did the young boy, who was seated at her right.

No one dared speak as the big man roamed the room. He picked up the boy's and woman's chamber pots, went outside and returned with a third one for the new arrival. Three two-gallon containers filled with fresh water were placed on the table along with some fruit, cereal boxes and crackers.

But on this night, for the first time in weeks, the big man sat down at the table, opposite long-dead Horace, and spoke.

"My name is Charles, and I'm head of this family."

No one spoke, but Josette bit her bottom lip. Sherron and Terry tried to remain focused and awake, for the lack of food and the stench of the room was making them weak and sick.

"I have more who would like to join us," he said. "More children, of course, and soon, if all goes well, my wife will arrive to meet you."

Then, he got up, looked at them for what seemed a long time, and went out and shut the door.

As the locks were put back into place, Josette started to scream and beat her hands against the table. But neither Terry nor Sherron paid the recent graduate any attention. The two old-timers were grabbing for the fruit and cereal, hoarding their share that would have to get them through the week until he arrived again, hopefully, with more supplies.

20

June 2008

*The growing DelMarVa family is pleased to announce
the addition of its first daughter.
Miss Josette Noble,
daughter of Horace Meeks and Sherron McKlinchey,
and sister to Master Terry Tremble,
born in Stevensville, DelMarVa, May 30th, 2008.
The family is planning several more additions.
Love to all.
Keep the faith.*

Michael Pentak sat in the living room in the Kent Island home of Mr. and Mrs. Francis Noble. The Annapolis corporate attorney, who also served as a Villa Theresa trustee, was not much better off than his heavily sedated wife.

The announcement had been delivered to the Noble home by a regional courier service only three hours earlier. The unsuspecting driver had been picked up for questioning, and personnel at the company's Washington, D.C., office, where the parcel had originated, were being interviewed as well.

Pentak's task force was confused. By making a broad daylight graduation grab and changing his method of notification, the Snatcher had outwitted them again. Some psychological experts believed that sending the bad news directly to the victim's family displayed a higher level of cruelty. By doing so, he raised the stakes. Whatever the motive, the authorities were scurrying for clues in several directions. However, to the media and public, DelMarVa's finest looked even more inept.

Since the girl had been missing following her graduation the previous Saturday, police authorities feared her disappearance might be related to the series of unsolved kidnappings. Unfortunately, no one had thought to include graduation exercises among the events placed under heavy surveillance.

The newspapers covering the coffee table in the Noble home were not kind. The headlines had linked the graduate's disappearance with the string of kidnappings even before the family had received the courier's announcement.

GIRL GRADUATE: GOING, GOING, GONE!
—Baltimore Bullet

SNATCHER, 5 — COPS, ZERO!
—Wilmington News Chronicle

PENTAK'S TOP COPS AT THE BOTTOM OF CLASS
—DelMarVa Monthly News Magazine

TOURISTS CANCELING JUNE RESERVATIONS
—Southern DelMarVa Weekly News

SHORE EVENTS POSTPONED 'TIL FALL
—Diamond State Ledger

DELMARVA: A CLUELESS STATE
—Washington News Herald

A shaded sidebar at the bottom of Dover's *Diamond State Ledger* reported an unfortunate, but still newsworthy incident.

FATHER BEATEN BY WELL MEANING MOB
—by Liz Hardy

Little Creek—A Philadelphia man was hospitalized after being attacked by a number of unidentified vigilantes Saturday afternoon outside Little Creek. Craig Cohen, an accountant returning home from a day trip in Ocean City with his son, Bobby, stopped at a community yard sale in Little Creek, a picturesque fishing village off Route 9 east of Dover.

At some point, the boy started to cry and began shouting, "LEAVE ME ALONE! I WANT MY MOMMY! I WANT MY MOMMY! I WANNA GO HOME!"

The father, commenting with some difficulty through a bandaged face from his bed in the Kent County Emergency Physicians Hospital, said he "was just trying to stop my kid from screaming."

"When Bobby resisted," Cohen added, "I grabbed him firmly by his wrist and started leading him toward our car. He began shouting for help and screaming. But I continued dragging him along, trying to get him inside the vehicle, so I could calm him down."

Unfortunately, Cohen never made it to his car. A group of motorcycle enthusiasts, passing slowly through the small watertown, noticed the disturbance. One of the riders—who some witnesses say "had appeared to be drinking"—shouted that it must be "The Snatcher! Let's git 'im, boys!"

"I swear I never even saw them coming," Cohen said. "All I know is that my kid is screaming one minute, and the next, I'm at the bottom of a pile of black leather with six beefy guys using me for a punching bag."

By the time authorities arrived, the Good Samaritans had departed. Cohen was found on the roadside and taken by Kent County Emergency Medical Team personnel to the nearby hospital. He is listed in stable condition with three broken ribs, a concussion, sprained right wrist and fractured left leg.

"I swear I'm never coming back here again!" Cohen said. "Not until your kidnapper is found. God, you people are really uptight. A parent can't even pull on his kid's arm without being afraid that he's going to get stomped to death."

Josette Noble's parents looked up at Pentak.

"So what are our chances, commissioner, of seeing our girl again?" the father asked.

"We've got more than 200 men, investigating this case full time, and for the first time . . . ."

"I didn't ask you for a grocery list of what you're trying to do!" the man snapped. "I asked: Are you going to find my girl and bring her back alive or not?"

Pentak looked directly at the frustrated father and said, "Honestly, I don't know. You asked for the truth, and that's what I'm telling you."

The mother began to sob.

"I'm sorry. If I could trade places with your daughter, I would," Pentak said softly. "But I can't make any promises. For the first time, though, we have eyewitnesses who saw the suspect. We've created a composite likeness that's based on their interviews, and we're circulating this throughout the region."

He passed a copy across the coffee table toward the parents, who looked down at a face that was similar to Charles Bettner, except for the additions of a priest's collar and dark sunglasses. "If this is our man, someone will see him and we'll nab him."

"Before or after our little girl is dead?"

There was nothing more to be gained by continuing the conversation with the grieving parents. "Hopefully, before," Pentak said, rising to leave. "We'll continue to do our best and keep you informed. Good-bye. And, I am sorry."

❧   ❧   ❧

Sean Kelley raced quickly into the governor's office, balancing a letter that had just been opened by a correspondence secretary and placed carefully in a wire basket.

"Look at this, Hank, but don't touch it!"

Reading the message placed on the top of his desk, McDevitt's face reddened:

> **You cost me my job.**
> **So I'll lose you your state.**
> **Your month will be June,**
> **Early, middle or late.**

"Mike Pentak's on his way in. He's coming back from a meeting with the missing girl's parents," Sean said.

McDevitt nodded, taking a few minutes to walk around the office and gather his thoughts. So the motive was out, someone was trying to get even with him for some apparent job loss. *But,* McDevitt wondered, *how was I responsible? What's the connection, and how can we use this to catch this sick bastard?*

By the time Pentak arrived, McDevitt had a list of questions and ideas to share. Together they decided to maintain increased security at events and add two more troopers to McDevitt's personal staff in each of his offices.

"I don't really like this, but if you think it's necessary . . . ."

"I do," replied Pentak. "This guy has been out to get you all along. He just decided to do it through innocent victims. Now, he's getting more blatant, showing himself at the graduation, sending you a personal threat. I think this is heading toward a showdown, and I don't want you on the losing end of this thing. Understand?"

McDevitt nodded. "But he can still strike anywhere in June, take more people, even two or three. This could be his way of making us dance, throwing us off."

"Yes," Pentak agreed, "or he's so sure he can get to you that he's giving us a challenge. We can ignore it, but if he goes for you and we're not ready, we'll kick ourselves. We can respond by being prepared, but he still may go elsewhere. We're in a no win situation, but I'd feel better if we beefed up the bodyguards. All right?"

"Hell," McDevitt said, "you'll do what you want anyway, so fine. Just tell them to give me a little breathing room every now and then. But, Mike, I want you to find this guy, and when you do, I want to see him before you bring him in. Understand?"

"Yes."

After Pentak made the call assigning more staff to the governor's security detail, he told McDevitt that the FBI and CIA were running the composite sketch through their computers, matching physical characteristics and all available eyewitness information with those who were ex-military, GS employees and state workers.

"Add recently fired as well," McDevitt said, "anyone who got the boot over the last year."

Pentak nodded, adding that the suspect's photo would be released to the media the following day, June 2.

"How's morale, Mike?"

The commissioner shook his head. "Low. At least we've got a composite sketch from the principal and teachers from Villa Theresa's. But we're not even close. All we're doing is responding to this nut's clues."

"Any luck with the car fire?"

"Not really. There was a similar torching the same day that Sherron McKlinchey disappeared. But, if it is our man, he did a real job on it. Burned out to a pile of ashes and a fried metal frame. Nothing left. Hell, they could have nothing to do with what we're after. So far, I think he's been sending us out into left field, but we've got to run with it. It's not good, but we've got no other choice. What we need is a break, and real soon."

"I see we're getting hit pretty hard in the press, too," McDevitt said.

"It's not just the traditional media," Pentak said. "Now the vulture culture junkies are into the game. That's what they consider this, you know, just a big damn entertaining game. It's sick."

"What are you talking about?"

"It's all over the Ultra Web. There are a dozen surf sites where you can make bets on where and when the next victim is going to get snatched. Hell, Hank, any school kid can pull up a list of potential events in the coming months that these idiots think the Snatcher may hit. If he wants, the bastard can see where the majority of people think he'll strike next. There's even one Ultra page where they are actually giving this bastard suggestions. It's a sick world out there, Hank. Like we don't have enough to worry about. But I've had to detail two of our people to monitor the ghoul sites. Who knows, we might get a decent lead. At the pathetic state we're in, we can't afford to overlook anything."

"Tell me some of the theories about what he's done with them," McDevitt said. "Where do we think they are?"

"Hell," Pentak got up and walked to the window, "we've gotten leads for over 320 sightings of the missing people, and 120 on e-mail alone. One was as far away as New Mexico. Within the region, we have 45 officers doing nothing but tracking down leads and interviewing those who have called or sent in information—no matter how absurd."

"Give me the absurd," McDevitt said.

Pentak rolled his eyes. "Alien abductions."

"What?" McDevitt snapped.

"Right!" Pentak said, nodding weakly. "Nearly a dozen leads are related to UFOs. One person claims to have seen all of the missing persons being beamed down through a roof into a vacant hunting lodge in the marshes northeast of Smith Island."

"And you followed it up?"

Pentak nodded, frowning. "Look, Hank, just suppose the poor bastards were really in that hunting shack and we didn't look. So we did, and they weren't there, of course. But it was a lead. We're that desperate. Hell, I'm almost to the point of putting their pictures on milk cartons."

"How far behind are you with the tips?"

"As of this morning, we have checked out about 180 leads, with no positive results—other than rousting some homeless people in abandoned factories and closing down a few migrant cockfighting games. That leaves us more than 140 yet to do, and new ones with more potential are put at the top of the list. Hell, we haven't gotten to the report about moaning spirits in a coastal ghost town or the dead Nanticokes and Susquehannoks who have come back to get even with the white men who took their land."

"Add more men," McDevitt said.

"Hell, Hank, I said I've got 45 men on this. We've got to have some available for daily law enforcement and crime fighting. How many do you want?"

"Double it!"

"I can't!"

For the next few minutes, the two friends shouted and argued, venting pent up frustrations. Finally, they sat down and agreed to assign all state police to 12 hour shifts and to make initial contact on the backlog of leads within 72 hours.

Before he left, Pentak suggested McDevitt cancel his appearances for the next two weeks, to give his security men time to work. When that didn't fly, he requested a copy of McDevitt's personal and public schedule for the rest of the month.

"Call Grace in Georgetown," he said. "She can give you the schedule and provide any last minute details you need."

"Fine, and where will you be tonight?"

"Woodburn. Randy is bringing Steph down about eight. We're going to try to put things back on an even keel, have a quiet dinner and stay in and watch a video. Tomorrow, a newspaper reporter is coming here about 11, then I plan to complete my annual end-of-the-legislature budget request. They want it early so they can rip it apart for an entire month, and that's it. I won't be leaving or going anywhere, until I attend the state college graduation on Sunday. That's right here in town. Lydia is speaking, and I intend to be there with her."

"Fine. See you sometime tomorrow," Pentak said, as he left the office and headed back to work.

🍃   🍃   🍃

Charles Bettner, wearing a pair of tight fitting, black riding gloves, was waiting comfortably in the living room of Stephanie Litera's home. His shoes were wrapped in plastic bags, his one-piece, tan jumpsuit was new. Bought that morning at Sears, it had no traces of his home or the farmhouse hideout. Charles had been in Stephanie's residence since 2 o'clock, having entered through the cellar door. For two hours he wandered casually through the three-story, corner rowhouse on Delaware Avenue, examining her clothing, inspecting her furniture, the contents of her refrigerator and medicine cabinet and reading her mail.

He spent almost an hour in Stephanie's bedroom, resting in her bed and fantasizing about how nice it would be to take her there. But he was patient. He was saving their first time for another, more special, place.

Through his surveillance during the last two months he knew her routine. On Fridays she arrived home quickly and prepared for McDevitt's driver, who usually picked her up by 7 o'clock. That gave him plenty of time to take care of business and get her out of the area.

As he closed his eyes and waited for her arrival, he pressed the switch on his small, black micro-cassette recorder. Stephanie's voice filled the room, her bedroom. But the conversation was awkward and irregular--the disjointed result of spliced comments that Charles had connected from clandestine recordings he had made during counseling sessions in her office.

"I . . . love you. Yes," Stephanie's voice said, erratically. "Yes, Charles. . . . Yes. I will . . . like to . . . see you again."

He smiled as he listened to her unreal comments. He recalled the way she looked, how she smelled, her walk and smile.

As he rested, he also knew that the police were closing in, but only because he had helped them by providing a half-dozen eyewitnesses at the girl's high school. If it wasn't for that gift, he could have continued his snatching spree indefinitely. But he was getting bored, and his objective had changed from revenge to pleasure. With Stephanie as his new bride, he realized he could have both—by depriving McDevitt of his lover and making his personal psychologist a permanent part of his family.

Charles recognized the idea as the natural flowering of his superior intellect. It had come to him only a few days before, as he was emptying out his Bear home and moving his belongings to the family refuge.

Of course, he had left a few souvenirs behind for them to find, but they'd have to do the rest on their own. He wasn't going to deliver the police any more clues.

Charles' Blazer was parked on Scott Street, only two blocks away. He had no concern that his plan wouldn't work. He had gone over it in his mind dozens of times. That was his method, to plan and replan, to plan and review. Chance and luck helped, but, as he learned from Uncle Sam, nothing beat good, old-fashioned reconnaissance and preparation.

Time passed quickly that Friday. He rose to the window as her teal green Firebird pulled up to the curb. Quietly, he hid in the kitchen, behind the wooden pantry door. He knew Stephanie entered through the back doorway.

He heard her footsteps approaching on the walkway, the even clipped pace of his woman. As she came closer and stopped, he recognized her slim figure and attractive face through the kitchen door's lace curtains.

Stephanie took two steps into the room and casually tossed her purse on the butcher block counter.

Charles struck quickly, grabbing her from behind and squeezing her neck with his forearm. He smiled as he smelled her body, felt it next to his.

"Don't move! Don't scream, or I will snap your neck and your life will be over. Nod if you understand me!"

As instructed, Stephanie moved her head as best she could.

"Good. Now walk back with me toward the chair, and don't try anything that would upset me."

Unaware of her assailant's identity, Stephanie stumbled along, slowly scanning the room, praying for a weapon of some kind to appear. As he pushed her into the wooden seat, Charles raced around and faced her. At that moment she started to scream his name, but he stopped her outburst with a punch to her face that had just enough force to knock her out.

Gently, he placed her body on the kitchen floor, took out a needle and inserted the tip into Stephanie's left arm. Charles smiled as the point broke the smooth skin. The chemicals would keep her sedated for several hours. He secured her ankles and hands with a white extension cord, carried her into the living room, placed her on the floor and rolled her body inside an oriental carpet. He had noticed the useful prop during an earlier uninvited visit.

Locking the kitchen door, he exited through the rear of the house, ran down the alley. A few minutes later, he returned to her side fence entrance. Two white metallic signs attached to each door panel of his Blazer advertised: "Cherry's Custom Carpet Cleaning."

It took him only five minutes to haul the rug from the home and load his reluctant bride into the vehicle and drive away. But before he did, he left a photograph of himself—without a collar, mustache or hat—on Stephanie's kitchen counter. With a felt tipped pen, he wrote across the bottom "Best Regards, C.B." Laughing to himself, Charles Bettner locked the back door of Stephanie Litera's home.

🌿   🌿   🌿

When she awoke Charles was just passing the old Virginia state line. Prior to the formation of DelMarVa, the signs at the border truckstops and highway souvenir shops proclaimed: "The South Begins Here!" and "Welcome to Dixie!" Now the boundary markers were fading from prominence.

Still disoriented, Stephanie tried to raise her tied wrists. With difficulty, she looked at her watch—8:15. She was to have been picked up by Randy at 7. At least they would know something was wrong.

Immediately, she started to wonder about her larger problem: Why Charles had taken her and where they were going.

"Ah, sweet Doctor Stephanie, finally awake I see," Bettner said, hearing the movement in the back of the Blazer.

"Where are you taking me?" she asked. Her voice did not sound like her own. She was curled in the rear of the vehicle, rolling to the left as it took a hard curve.

"Home to meet the rest of the family, my dear. Soon, you will take your place as my bride. Excited, Stephanie?"

"Please, don't do this, Charles," she said, trying to lift her head to get a view of him.

"Don't disappoint me more than you have already, Dear Doctor. I thought you would realize it was me. I gave you enough clues in our sessions. But, you had no idea. How incompetent and sad."

Stephanie felt his harsh words slap at her. But he was correct. Charles exhibited all of the signs. No family. No friends. A self-centered and intolerant personality. He had recently lost his job. What a fool she had been.

As if reading her mind, he said, "You ought to be embarrassed, no make that infuriated and humiliated, with yourself. Professionally, you blew it big time, Stephanie. I can see the headlines: 'Former patient of governor's lover identified as the Snatcher!' Your incompetence is an embarrassment. I can only assume your brain was more interested in what was between your legs during our little encounters."

Stephanie did not reply.

Charles continued, enjoying the opportunity to sermonize to a captive congregation of one, "I knew right from the start that you were one of those pathetic idealists who believes there is untapped 'good' in all of God's lovely creatures. You and your kind think there is no such thing as 'evil,' that we all live in an 'everybody-loves-somebody' world. But, now you've come face to face with reality—not 'be happy' psychology. How does it feel to be a public failure?"

Humiliated, Stephanie closed her eyes and began to pray. It wasn't until 15 minutes later that she realized the seriousness of her situation.

As the Blazer stopped, Stephanie heard screams coming from somewhere, but she couldn't imagine their origin. Her high heels made it difficult to stand. She leaned against the old wooden building while Charles used three different keys to unlock the thick silver padlocks.

As he pulled the door open, the wave of dank stench made her gag, but he grabbed her by the hair and shoved her into the dark, dirt-floored room. Something scurried past, right in front of her left hand. It was small and covered with fur. She immediately yanked her hands off the ground and tried to stand.

But Charles kicked her back and her chest landed hard against the ground. "Don't move!" he shouted.

Lifting her eyes as far as she dared, she saw the group chained to the table. The missing people.

At that moment, Stephanie witnessed the abominable results of her inability to treat DelMarVa's deranged kidnapper. The horrifying realization that she had been alone with the killer for so many weeks made her retch. Steadying her body with one hand and holding her neck with the other, she kneeled and opened her mouth, throwing up the bile contents of her stomach onto the dirt floor.

The three captives began to howl like animals, shouting and demanding food and water from their keeper.

After locking the door behind him, Charles walked toward the table and demanded quiet. "I've come back with my bride," he said, proudly pointing to the huddled form at his feet.

The prisoners sat silent, their minds only on food and drink, but fearful of upsetting the master. They didn't dare talk or move.

"Good," he said, smiling. "I think you should get to know each other." Abruptly, he pulled Stephanie up by the hair, tossed her toward the table and chained her to the floorboard. She sat directly opposite what was left of

Horace Meeks. After three long months, some sections of bone were wearing through his flesh.

"Stephanie," Charles said loudly and pointing around the table, "that is Father. Over here is Mother."

The wretched, filthy form of Sherron McKlinchey made a nervous nod. The pathetic woman's eyes were bulging from their sockets. Her lips were puffed and parched, and her exposed skin was covered with scabs and sores. She had existed there the longest, since mid March, nearly three horrifying months.

"And here is our fat little brother." Terry Tremble was sniffling, but trying not to cry. After six weeks chained in the room, he had lost all of his fat and was nervously tapping his fingertips on the tabletop.

"Lastly, we have big sister." Josette Noble's blond hair was no longer soft and fine. Traveling through the stiff straw were tiny sand fleas and a few other black crawling insects. But they didn't seem to bother her. Her blue eyes were like ice, staring straight at Charles. Her body was rigid, her attitude defiant. She had only been there a week, so she appeared to be the healthiest member of the family.

Stephanie recognized them all from the pictures in the paper. She knew their names but dared not use them for fear of setting Charles off into a rage.

"My bride will stay with us, and I've now moved everything here. So, I will be with all of you from now on, in the adjacent end of the farmhouse. Any questions?"

Sherron raised a blistered finger of her right hand.

"Yes, Mother?"

"Wa-Waa-Wa-t—t—ter. P-p-pleas-e," she whispered, her voice hoarse and dry.

"Oh, yes. How thoughtless of me. I left it in the car. Let me get your food and water. I was so excited to introduce my Stephanie that I forgot."

Before leaving, Charles gathered up the chamber pots and then headed outside. Since his family was secured, he left the door open and a welcome fresh sea breeze blew in, cleansing some of the stench.

"Grab all the food you can as soon as he puts it on the table," Josette whispered to Stephanie. "These two will take it all, and they won't give you a single thing to eat. Believe me, your water ration goes faster than you think, so don't drink too much."

Sherron and Terry glared at the new arrival, not eager to share their weekly rations. But Josette looked upon the newcomer as a good sign—at least Stephanie could provide an update on what was going on in the real world.

After he distributed the food, Charles made a farewell speech and promised he'd return soon. No one knew what that meant, but Stephanie noted that they all seemed very happy he was leaving. With arms holding pieces of fresh fruit and full jugs of fresh water nearby, they smiled as he left them alone.

❧   ❧   ❧

When Stephanie did not answer her door, Randy Poplos rang her phone from his car, but there was no answer. He called McDevitt, who suggested a call to Marty at home

Her boss confirmed that she had left the office soon after five and was heading directly home. Randy told him her car was parked outside and asked if Marty had a key. The answer was no, but her boss lived only two blocks away and he said he would head right over.

As soon as Marty arrived, McDevitt gave them permission to break into the house. After a quick search, Randy called McDevitt back.

"She's not at home, sir. But I think we've got a more serious problem. Her purse is in here, plus her briefcase, and there's a photograph with writing across the bottom, saying: 'Best Regards, C.B.' "

"Charles Bettner," added Marty, who was standing beside Poplos. "He was one of her recent clients. He was transferred a few months ago into a lower level job because of a cutback in the finance division. Stephanie was counseling him."

As soon as Randy relayed the information to McDevitt, the governor shouted back, "Jesus Christ, Randy! He's our man and he's got her. It wasn't me he was after in June, it was her!"

"I don't understand, sir!"

"I'll explain later. Put Marty on the phone."

Within minutes, 20 state troopers were sealing off four square blocks and knocking on doors seeking witnesses. Another police car was rushing Marty to Stephanie's office to secure Bettner's casefile.

While one team of officers combed Stephanie's home for clues, others were heading to Bettner's last known residence.

Pentak was on his way up from state police headquarters in Dover with a signed search warrant, and troopers from Barracks 9 in North East, Barracks 7 in Elkton and Barracks 6 in Newark had sealed down the suspect's development off Route 40.

Officers broke in the front and back doors of the small rancher and searched every room. But the entire house was vacant—except for the den in the basement. Hanging on one wall was a large tan, cork, bulletin board. Pinned to the chart were pictures of all his victims.

At the top of the list were Horace Meeks—labeled "Father" and Sherron McKlinchey—"Mother."

The pictures showed the farmer's decomposed, blood-stained body seated at a wooden table. The background of the room was dark.

Sherron McKlinchey did not look much better, except she was still alive, barely.

One picture showed the older Tremble brother, before he had been tossed in the bay. He was lying on the ground, blood oozing into a pool from the wide gash across his neck.

"Little Brother" Terry Tremble had lost considerable weight, and sat stiffly at the family dinner table. The picture of "Sister" Josette Noble's face displayed hate and anger.

The last row of more than a dozen pictures were labeled "Stephanie Litera—Wife." Apparently they were taken over a period of time, while she was at work, walking near her home, entering the governor's car at Woodburn, shopping in the mall, leaving work and entering her car. Stephanie obviously had no idea she was being photographed for some time by Charles Bettner, who had been recording her comings and goings.

A half-hour after the forced entry, McDevitt arrived at the suspect's home. Dozens of news reporters with tape recorders and video cameras were shouting for a statement.

Ignoring them, the governor entered the building. Downstairs, he stood with Pentak in front of the photo board. An army of technicians was going over every inch of the residence, taking away microscopic materials that would be examined and analyzed in the state and FBI laboratories. They were looking for clues as to where Bettner had been and possibly now had gone. Photographic experts were waiting to take away the board and examine the pictures for any background details that could provide information about the kidnapper's lair.

"So it wasn't me, Mike," McDevitt said. "It was her. He planned to get to me through her."

"It looks that way."

"What's our next move?"

"We're getting statements from his coworkers, neighbors, people in the Trolley Square area near Stephanie's home. So far, nobody in the neighborhood ever talked to the guy for more than the time it took to say hello. The people from his work are telling us that he was just plain scary. Hell, he threatened his manager when he was demoted. It's a classic nutcase and, to top it off . . . ."

"Right . . . she was his counselor. God! What a mess!"

"Look, Hank, at least we know who we're looking for. Now we can concentrate on this guy and no one else."

"What do you expect next? Ransom? Some kind of contact?"

"Actually," Pentak said, "I don't expect him to do anything, not for a week or two. I wouldn't be surprised if he pulled another snatch just to throw us off. We have to keep at it and wait and pray. But we know we're looking for a black '99 Blazer. That's what he drove. Unless he's dumped it already. We're also down to our last backlog of leads. Maybe something will click there. I know you don't believe this, but I think we're getting close."

McDevitt pulled Pentak aside and whispered harshly, "Listen, Mike, I'm trying not to lose it. But the reality is that this asshole has the woman I love locked up somewhere and he might just kill her. Right?"

Pentak nodded.

"So don't tell me we're getting close. I want him found. And, unless I'm mistaken, since he's taken her for his wife it might mean that he will dispose of her last, or is that just wishful thinking on my part? Tell me."

Pausing before answering, Pentak took a breath and said, "I think you're right. If she was his last and selected for his most honored position on the board, I do think she'll be safe longer than the others. How safe? Who's to know. To be honest, God only knows what this sick bastard is doing to these poor souls. I really fear for all of them and we need to find them fast."

McDevitt patted his friend's shoulder and they both walked toward the front door. Pentak stood before the microphones and announced that the suspect was former state tax collector Charles Bettner, that he is believed to be the serial kidnapper, and that he had claimed another victim—state psychologist Dr. Stephanie Litera of Wilmington.

❧ 21 ❧

July 2008

Three weeks had passed since Stephanie's abduction with no word from the kidnapper. The police had placed phone taps at her parents' home, in her empty office and home and on McDevitt's private line.

No one else had been abducted. The police were still checking out leads and working overtime at weekend festivals that had not been canceled.

The grandfather clock near the wide governor's mansion stairway chimed 10 times on the hour, distracting Michael Pentak, who was leaning back against the couch, tired from another long day that had gone straight to nowhere. McDevitt, dressed in jeans and a short-sleeved knit shirt was coming in from the kitchen, where he had just dropped off Italian subs to the officers on duty in the communications room.

The two men were alone—McDevitt in a chair he had pulled up beside the sofa where Pentak was lounging.

They passed the time talking, trying to keep from thinking about the frustrations caused by the Snatcher, who had taken control of a portion of the recreational life on the peninsula by making it his personal hunting ground.

Eventually, the two men began sharing memories from days when life and living were less complicated and not as stressful.

"When I was a kid," Pentak said, "my father was a workaholic. No one used that term in those days. All of us just figured it was a natural way to act. It's what you had to do to survive. In our house, if you weren't sleeping you had to be working."

McDevitt agreed, saying there was no leisure time on the farm either, lots to do from sunup to dark.

Pentak laughed, thinking how today's youth would respond to some of the things he and his sisters had to do. "Every damn Sunday morning," the commissioner recalled, "when every other kid was sleeping in until 9 to get ready to go to 10 o'clock Mass, my father had us up and working. We were cleaning the bar—washing glasses, mopping the floor, filling beer cases, collecting trash. We started at 6 in the morning! Hell, it was the one day a week we were closed. Nobody was coming in, but it had to be done by 7. I only asked my father 'why' one time."

"What did he say," McDevitt inquired.

"He said, 'Because I told you to,' and that was enough for me."

McDevitt nodded, signaling he also had lived a similar scene.

"On my grandparent's place, we had cows to milk, chickens and horses to feed, fields to take care of, plus the house and outbuildings to keep up. If there was a slow day, which was rare, we were out there chopping wood for winter. We did a lot of that after dinner or when it rained.

"We went to church every Sunday. On that one day, we were able to rest. No stores were opened, because of the Blue Laws back then. Mostly, we would visit relatives, or they'd come to our place and have a big supper. Us kids would play while the parents sat and talked or played horseshoes. It was a good life. But I have to admit that I liked payday the best."

"You got paid!" Pentak was surprised.

Laughing, McDevitt said his grandfather would call him into the kitchen every Saturday night. The two of them would sit at the metal table, and the young boy who would be governor was asked if he thought he had put in a good week and deserved to be paid.

"Of course," McDevitt said to Pentak, "I always said 'yes.' Then, my grandfather would set down his pipe and reach deep into the side pocket of his faded overalls and pull out 250 shells—five boxes of 50 rounds each.

"They were for my rifle. On Christmas when I was 8, he gave me a .22 rifle. He told me I would have to learn to shoot, but he also taught me to respect it and to always be safe. Then, he looked at me very seriously and said if I ever did anything wrong with that .22, he would cut off the stock and toss it on the woodpile. Then he would bend the barrel in the vise—and I'd have to wait until I was 21 to buy my own gun.

"I was very careful and never had a problem, and I became an expert shot. Every free chance I had—at nights, before school, on Sundays—I'd set up a target. Usually it was a hand drawn bullseye on a sheet of paper or a penny balanced between two nails. I would step off the distance until you could hardly see the target. Then I'd drill it good, and each week I would go back for another 250 rounds. I practiced so much that I got rid of all those bullets every week. I never had any left over. When it was time for me to go hunting, I never came home empty handed. I could hit a moving target that most people couldn't even see."

During a long pause, the two men agreed that waiting for something to happen was tough to handle. But, Pentak explained, learning to be patient was a skill that career cops learned over time.

"What made you go into law enforcement?" McDevitt asked.

"My uncle was a cop, and I thought it would be neat to carry a gun."

McDevitt smiled. "Have you ever shot anyone?"

"No," Pentak said. "In over 30 years, I've never fired a shot, other than on the range. But I've busted quite a few heads in my time," he added, smiling.

"Do you ever think about your wife?"

Pentak looked up, then lowered his eyes and grabbed the glass of beer from the nearby table.

"I'm sorry," McDevitt said, knowing it was a sensitive area. Pentak's wife of 17 years had died after a long, painful fight against cancer more than 15 years ago.

"No. It's okay, Hank. Sure. Not a day goes by that I don't recall her, even after all these years. Sometimes it may only be for a few seconds, but, yes, I remember her. When I saw how happy you and Stephanie were, it reminded me of my time with Charlene. God, they were good years. Being a cop, we couldn't spend the time together that we should have, but she understood. I just did my best, but fate wouldn't let her be around long enough. Death took her too soon. But," he looked up and forced a smile, "you learn to go on. We all do. What about you?"

McDevitt looked up, surprised. "I've never been married."

"Right," said Pentak, "but there was someone at some-time, right?"

The governor nodded, looked up and spoke. "Yes, there was, and I lost her, too."

Pentak waited, then McDevitt continued, slowly at first.

"She was beautiful, wonderful, and her name was Laura. God, I loved her. We were both 21, talked about getting married. She was from a family farm on the other side of town. It was summer, and my brother, Georgie, loved her, too. But he was only 13. I was so crazy in love that I stupidly used to get jealous when she paid attention to him.

"Anyway, we never set a date or anything. It was just understood. I was out working at my grandparents' place one summer day, and she and her family had this fruit and vegetable stand at their place. The stand was about 100 yards back off the road. Georgie was with her, helping out, and I was to go over and have lunch . . . ."

McDevitt got up and walked to the window, then continued. "The two Scroggins boys, brothers from a shanty-town about five miles away, were out joy riding. They were older, in their 30s and built like bulls. They worked in the fields, baling hay. I remember how they used to lift cows at the fair, they were that strong."

It was getting harder for McDevitt to continue and Pentak waited quietly.

"They drove up the lane, and they must have been drinking pretty heavily, because they took out two fence posts. As best as anyone can determine, the two of them raped Laura, did it on the top of the open wagon that held the corn and straw. Her parents weren't home. After the brothers each took her, they beat her badly to keep her from talking. But before they were through, my brother, Georgie, must have come out from behind the barn. He ran at them and tried to help Laura.

"Oh, God, they just beat him into a bloody pulp . . . . When we found him, we couldn't recognize the poor kid's face. They killed him out there in the dirt driveway.

"I guess when they realized what they had done, they lost control. Laura was found crawling toward the house, probably trying to get help. The back of her skull was crushed from blows delivered by the flat end of a shovel."

The two men's eyes met. Silence joined them for a short time.

"The cops picked the killers up that night at a ginmill called the Road House, dead drunk. Read them their rights. They were charged and convicted of second degree murder. Three years later, Sammy Scroggins, the older one, walked away from work release and killed a little girl in Boston. He served another 10 years in a jail up there and was knifed in a prison fight. No loss. His brother, Archie, got out in five years. The result of overcrowding plus good behavior—a model prisoner, they said."

Pentak noticed that McDevitt's tone had changed. The governor's voice was almost robotic, unfeeling.

"Archie came back to Seaford to live at his parents' place. I ran into him a few times. He'd just smile and laugh, like it was all a big joke that he was back in town and free."

"Damn!" Pentak said. "That must have been hard as hell to take."

"Yes, it was. That's when I decided to study law. I thought I could make up for what happened to Georgie and Laura by becoming a prosecutor and taking others like the Scroggins brothers off the streets. To this day, I couldn't even scrape up sympathy for killers and pushers if I tried. I'll never let one go, even if it means an innocent hostage has to die. Better one good life be sacrificed to get rid of a killer who will just do it again and again. A lot of people don't agree, but that's what I believe—and I've been there, in the victim's shoes."

"It must have taken a while to get over it," Pentak said.

"Quite a while," McDevitt said, "but it was worse on my grandparents. They raised us, brought us up when our folks died. After Georgie was killed, I saw the life drain right out of them. I buried them both within 18 months. Lost my whole family just like that."

McDevitt paused, then continued. "You see it in the movies and it's entertaining. You can't comprehend what it's like until it happens to you. That's when you really meet crime. That's when you can smell its stench, when it rips out your guts and it makes you gag and won't let you sleep. And it doesn't end when when the criminal act is over. The effects continue. No one is immune, and when it does occur to someone you love, I tell you, it hurts like hell for a long, long time."

Pentak asked one more question. "What happened to Archie?"

McDevitt stared at the commissioner and spoke slowly and softly, "Oh, he died during that first year after his release. Strange, though," the governor said, looking straight into Pentak's eyes, "He was killed from a wild shot in the woods. It was only a .22, but, unfortunately for Archie, it caught him in the temple—a freak hunting accident on the first day of deer season."

❧   ❧   ❧

Trooper Fred Cox had been tracking his prey for nearly two weeks. The trail started in Chincoteague, led him to Saxis, sent him up to Hooper Island and landed him down at the Craneville dock. He had spent two days in the fast-asleep, half-a-horse hamlet, but had come up empty. The tall state trooper was nursing a soda and planning to give up and head toward home when a boatload of boisterous watermen burst through the doors of the Floating Dock Country Cafe.

The dingy saloon was built on a surplus U.S. Coast Guard dock that the owner had purchased for a song. One night, a few of his drinking buddies decided to nail a portable, six-foot-long bar onto the deck. Later, they added a wall or two, then a roof—next came a few room dividers, old arcade machines and, finally, a small kitchen. After they erected a roof, the resulting Floating Dock Country Cafe was a one-of-a-kind hangout that was tied to a pier on the Wicomico, not far from where the river meets Monie Bay.

Its clientele were grizzled watermen and local inhabitants of the hideaway region. Every now and then a few lost, preppy tourists would appear, but they would usually exit quickly, deciding it was better not to even place an order.

"Friends in Low Places," an old Garth Brooks song, was playing in the background. Perfect pick, Cox thought to himself, as he looked up at the framed handwritten sign hanging on the wall beside the end of the bar. He totally agreed with its message:

> **There ain't no other place,**
> **Anywhere near this here place,**
> **So as far as you and I can tell,**
> **This here must be the place.**

The floor tile was a mixture of overstock rejects. Hundreds of multicolored squares formed an indistinct, erratic pattern that could give you a headache if you tried to focus on the floor as the floating platform swayed with the tide.

A tattered and sagging Confederate flag dominated one wall, while assorted stuffed waterfowl and glass-eyed fish were displayed in a scattered pattern on the other three walls. A continuous wooden shelf, jutting out about a foot below the ceiling, framed the entire room, displaying old fishing tools and traps plus an occasional donated trophy and antique.

Cox was drinking soda out of the can. He was careful not to ask for a glass. No sense taking a chance with his health. If cleanliness was next to godliness, he thought, the Floating Dock was not knocking on Heaven's door.

From his perch behind the bar, Cap'n Nate looked over at Cox. He had quickly gathered from a rather direct, no-nonsense conversation, that the trooper was waiting for Dog Shit Charlie, and the captain pointed the old timer out as soon as the seaman grabbed a seat. Cap'n Nate, the establishment's owner, cook, custodian and bartender, didn't want any trouble with the law. Besides, having the state boys hanging around always hurt business. So the Cap'n figured he would give up Dog Shit and that would send the trooper on his way.

Usually, a stranger seeking out a local would first have to answer a few dozen questions and suffer a good dose of abuse from the regulars, but Cox's 6-foot, 3-inch stature and his angry mood warded off any attempts at interference.

With a hand the size of a bear's paw, the plainclothes trooper grabbed Dog Shit's shoulder and easily dragged him to a corner table in the swaying saloon. The weather was getting nasty and that had a direct effect on the bar's movement and Cox's deteriorating temper.

Dog Shit was not an old man, but at 58 he looked closer to 72 from a hard life on the water. He was in sad physical shape, so hunched over that his clothing hung from his body as he walked. To Cox, the waterman looked like a slow moving pile of dirty rags. Luckily, Cox had caught up with Dog Shit before he started in on the sauce, but the remnants of cheap brew consumed on the workboat was still flowing through the sailor's bloodstream.

After quick introductions, Cox had his subject's undivided attention, especially when he told Dog Shit that he could talk now or spend the rest of his brief life on a state prison farm filled with queers, perverts and psychos.

"I don't know nothin' about nothin', I tell ya," whinnied Dog Shit.

"Tell me about the screaming ghosts," Cox whispered, almost embarrassed for allowing the words to escape his lips.

Totally surprised, Dog Shit paused, his jagged, black rotted teeth formed a pathetic, irregular smile, and his body suddenly shook with quiet laughter.

"So, somebody heard 'bout what I saw and they sent ya, huh?"

"Yeah," Cox said, "they called in the story and someone said it started with you. So, they sent me. Now get on with it and tell me what you know. Now!"

"I think I could use a bit of liquid replenishment," said Dog Shit, knowing from years of experience when to push and how far.

Cox signaled the bartender for a shot and beer, and Dog Shit perked up like a monkey anticipating his morning banana.

"Talk!" Cox snapped as the bartender delivered the drinks and turned away from the table.

"Ever heard o' Madison City?"

Cox shook his head.

"You from 'round here, boy?"

"Rehobeth. Not the beach, the town over near Crisfield."

"Damn!" snapped Dog Shit, "I knows it well. Been all over 'round there—Hopewell, Marion Station, Byrdtown. Hunted, fished, crabbed. Yeah. I know them parts real good. So you don't know about Madison City?"

Cox gave a second negative reaction.

"How old would you be, boy?"

"Old enough. What is this 20 goddamn questions? Look, I'm here to check you off my list. I've been after you for two weeks, and now that I've got you you're gonna answer my questions. I'm not here to answer yours. Understand?"

Dog Shit nodded, picked up his shot glass, opened his mouth wide and tossed the contents down his throat. Cox thought that the old man's taste buds didn't get much of a workout, since the whiskey flowed straight down, heading for his gut where it would give him a warm glow and loosen his tongue.

"Madison City's a ghost town."

"Where?"

"Not too far from here, in Virginia," said Dog Shit. "Everybody thinks they only got ghost towns out in the Wild West, like Tombstone and Silver City, or whatever they're called. But we got 'em here, too. No fish left, no town left. Simple as that. Everybody goes off and nobody comes back. I know. I been to 'em lots of times, too. Heard and saw them ghosts, too."

"When was the last time?"

"That'd have to be 'bout four, five weeks ago. I been out on the bay, workin' pretty steady at the time. By myself, doin' a little huntin', too."

"Where's this ghost town exactly?" Cox interrupted.

"On the coast. On the ocean, not the bay side."

As Dog Shit sipped on his free beer, he explained that years back there was no way out onto Chincoteague and Assateague Island except by sail or steamboat. Before they built the present road and causeways, linking the island to the mainland and Route 13, everything—furniture, food, mail, animals, carriages, building supplies and even funeral caskets—was shipped out of Madison City's dock.

It was a small but thriving town on the ocean. But for the last 50 years, after the roads took away all the business, it had no reason to exist. Now, there's nothing, only a few empty buildings, stone foundations, tall swamp grass and spooky stories—about the forgotten coastal ghost town.

"Now," said Dog Shit, smiling and waving the empty soldier he had just polished off, "I'd sure think better with another beer."

"Maybe you'd get a cold case to go if you tell me everything you know, and if it's useful."

That was just enough incentive to get Dog Shit down to serious business. He eagerly explained that he did a little market huntin', which involved some illegal duckin' plus some trappin' out of season. In February, it was cold as hell out there one night. He was near Madison City checking his traps, and it was pitch dark. Dog Shit noticed a Jeep driving with its lights low, into the tall grass, back towards a deserted farmhouse and barn close to the water.

Since he didn't have anything to do, and nowhere to stay, he holed up in another one of the farm's vacant outbuildings overnight. Nobody ever came there anymore, so he figured it was real strange to see a vehicle in the area.

"A bit later, in the middle of the night," Dog Shit said, "I heard these blood chillin' screams. Like death itself, ya know? God, I packed up and got the hell outta there and didn't come back for a week or more. Scared the hell outta me, I tell ya."

Cox became a bit more interested with the mention of the vehicle. He pressed Dog Shit for more information. Did he see the driver? Did he hear or see anything else?

"He was a big man. Tall and strong, bald, too, far as I could guess. I watched one night later, when I went back. He was lockin' and unlockin' the door to the summer kitchen. Half buried in the ground, ya know what I mean?"

Cox nodded and Dog Shit continued.

"I guess I seen him three, four times in all. I got close enough one time, I think it was 'bout six weeks ago, to hear the voices comin' from inside. They were moanin' and sounded to me like they were fightin' in there. I gotta say, I'm superstitious an', like my Momma, I believe in this spirited stuff. I know that place, whole town, is haunted. I even seen the ghosts in the kitchen, havin' a meetin' at the table. That's when I ran off and never went back."

"Tell me everything you saw, and get it right," Cox ordered as thin beads of sweat started to trickle down his neck. He was so intense, hanging on the drunk's every word, that he didn't even notice that the barge was rocking like a buckin' bronco.

"I sneaked on over this one night, when that Jeep wasn't home," he said. "The waves was beatin' up the beach real good, makin' a lot of noise to cover my steps and the rustlin'. I crawled up to that low window, 'cause the door, it was all locked up with bolts an' locks an' all. But the window was all painted black, so somebody comin' by couldn't see in, I guess. But ya could see some bits o' light shinin' on out. I crawled over and put my eye and face right up there, 'gainst it real tight. They was only little slits to look in, but I could see them all havin' a meeting.

"God, they looked scary, all dirty and old, like a bunch of witches in a convent. I think that's what they call it when those old girls meet together like that to make their plans. There was this one that looked to me like he was dead, sittin' at the table, not movin'. But they're all talkin' an' screamin' at each other."

"How many were there?" Cox asked.

"Four. I think 'twas four. Maybe three. I didn't stay too long. I was scared. They say the heebies can latch themselves onto a person an' follow 'im home. I wouldn't want them a comin' home with me, if I had me a home, which I don't. Still, I didn't like it there. There was a lot of moanin' and cryin', reminded me of, like they was all dead souls seekin' their rest. It was like they wanted t' die and nobody would let 'em. But, hell. What do I know. I'm just an old drunk who likes to talk to anybody that'll listen."

Cox leaned close to Dog Shit and said, "Are you telling me this is all a game, old man?"

"No!" replied Dog Shit, obviously worried that the trooper was upset. "All of it happened. It's just that when I told it to anybody else, they said I was nuts. An' they was gonna get me put away. So I stopped tellin'. Does it make any sense to you?"

Cox shook his head. "Maybe."

"Well, I don't wanna go to no nut house for tellin' the truth, understand?"

Cox smiled. "No way, Dog Shit. You're not going anywhere. But this is serious and those people in there might be the missing persons we're looking for."

"Oh, my," Dog Shit said, rubbing his unshaven chin and giving Cox the eye. "If they ain't ghosts and they's the one's you're seekin', does it mean I get me some kinda ree-ward?"

"I don't know," said Cox, rising from the chair. "But you're coming with me," he added, grabbing Dog Shit's coat collar and pulling him along toward the bar. Cox paid Cap'n Nate for a cold case of Natty Bo and told him to hold it for Dog Shit until he returned.

"You're going to take me to this place and show me exactly where it is," Cox said.

At 2 in the morning, the trooper was at the wheel, listening to Dog Shit Charlie, who was directing the DelMar-Va cruiser due east on a seldom used back road that paralleled the old Maryland-Virginia state line.

More than once, Cox considered reporting his destination and the status of his investigation to dispatch central. But he decided against it. If this was another wild ghost chase, and he had been on many, he would be the laughing stock of the entire force. He had already imagined his partners calling him Ghostbuster and taping pictures of Casper on his locker.

If Dog Shit's lead was real, Cox would be on the horn and have the place surrounded in less than an hour. To him, at that instant, the gamble to keep quiet a short time longer was worth it.

♨   ♨   ♨

Stephanie quickly discovered that family life in Charles Bettner's commune was nothing like a summer vacation with the Cleavers. Even though the residents of the summer kitchen all were prisoners, each captive had a different level of hate and tolerance for the mysterious keeper—and fellow members of the new family.

Little Terry stared at the ceiling and was terrified of the man. But, to get extra favors, the boy tried to be a friend and agreed with everything Charles said. Josette loathed the master and didn't hide her feelings. Sherron, sat with her hands folded under the table, nervously rubbing them back and forth, and never moved her upper body. Stephanie figured the woman grabbed at the Irish parade was approaching the end. She was wearing nothing under the gray robe. She would do anything to keep Charles happy, thinking she might gain his confidence and he might let her return to her family.

Both Sherron and Terry were leery of Stephanie, openly questioning her connection to Charles. They were quite interested in her "bride" status, and Stephanie figured that they probably considered her a spy. They also watched to see if she would get special privileges, since she obviously was the favorite of the big man.

On the fifth day of her captivity, when she had had enough of their whispered remarks and accusations, Stephanie snapped, "Look, you filthy idiots! I'm chained here just like you are, or are you blind and can't see that? I'm not having a great time. I don't have any extra privileges. I'm stuck here waiting for him to return and toss me some food and water, and I'm sick and tired of listening to your shit and crap!"

Sherron and Terry drew back, but Josette let out a laugh and clapped, showing her approval.

"What we have to do," Stephanie said, making sure her eyes glanced at all of them, "is work together to get out of here."

"Wh-wh-whooo d-d-died and made you b-b-boss?" asked Sherron, her stutter delivered in a tiny, hoarse-like whisper filled with malice.

"I'm not being a boss," Stephanie said. "I'm just trying to figure a way to get us out of here."

When no one responded, she looked toward Josette and the two of them began to discuss ways of getting loose and, if they had to, killing their captor.

22

Cox slowed the cruiser to less than 15 miles per hour and hesitantly followed Dog Shit's verbal directions, pulling off the highway onto a narrow gravel road and moving cautiously through tall marsh grass.

It was nearly 3 in the morning and visibility was low. A layer of fog and a light mist had settled over the wetlands, making driving difficult and dangerous.

After parking the car, Dog Shit explained that it was a half-mile to the hostage barn and the waterman led the way, picking his steps quickly but carefully through the marsh, motioning for Cox who was close behind.

When the trooper questioned Dog Shit's path-finding ability, the older man snapped, "You don't trust me none, then turn 'round 'n' git the hell outta here. I'll go it alone. An' if ya git your foot caught in a trap, don't go callin' to me fer help then."

Since he could only see two feet ahead, Cox decided reluctantly to put his faith in Dog Shit and follow his trail guide to who knew where.

When they had walked about 15 minutes, Dog Shit signaled to stop. "The house is up ahead, only 'bout 100 feet."

"How the hell would you know?" Cox snarled.

" 'Cause I's standin' next t' one of my very own traps," Dog Shit said, grinning and causing the trooper to offer a silent apology.

Moving closer, the outline of the heavily damaged remnants of a once functioning farmhouse came into view. The mist was less thick near the shore. Leaning behind a tree, Cox was able to make out a crumbling front porch roof, broken steps and a number of smashed windows. Attached to the three-story main house—which was held together with black and brown weatherworn wooden planks—the half-sunken summer kitchen rose weakly above the brush-covered landscape.

A sliver of light shot through a low single window, and Dog Shit pointed in that direction. "There she is. That's where I seen 'em and I betcha they's still down in there."

"Wait here!" Cox ordered, and the trooper crept slowly across the high grass of the front yard. His heart was pounding, not knowing if the kidnapper was anywhere nearby. A small mound of dirt lead to the low window. Cox crawled the last 10 feet and cupped his hands over his eyes to try to look into the room.

It did not take him more than a few seconds to realize that Dog Shit Charlie had delivered big time. The trooper recognized Stephanie Litera, whose face he could see. Josette's back was to the window, but Cox decided she and Terry Tremble were the ones seated on the same side of the table.

Sherron McKlinchey, her face pockmarked and her hands out of view was next to Horace Meeks.

Cox took a few more precious seconds to memorize the physical layout of what he could see in the room and he reviewed his options for a rescue. They would want to know everything he saw when he reported the scene to headquarters. As he turned to leave, he noticed two vehicles parked near the bolted entrance to the kitchen—a black Blazer and a light gray or white Ford panel van.

Dog Shit was waiting behind the tree when Cox returned. After a brief conversation, they agreed that Dog Shit would head back to the cruiser and call in the report. There was no way that Cox could find his way back alone, and he decided to stay at the scene. He didn't want the hostages moved or murdered when he was so close to getting them free.

Cox would wait 35 minutes for Dog Shit to get to the cruiser, report the location and return. If he didn't make it by that time, Cox would activate Priority 9 and make his move alone.

Dog Shit shook Cox's hand and mumbled something about a case or two of the good stuff that he'd be due. Then the rag-clad trapper disappeared into the fog. Within seconds, Cox could hear nothing but the sound of the ocean waves meeting the nearby beach. He checked his watch, 2:48 a.m. He would give Dog Shit until 3:30. Then he'd rip open the wooden door and hope for the best.

Dog Shit had worked the guts and wetlands of the area for nearly 50 years. He had no problem retracing his steps, but he also knew when he was being followed . . . and he was.

Not stopping to listen or give any indication he was spooked, Dog Shit unlatched the snap on the leather case of his hunting knife. It had skinned a good number of 'coons and 'rats in his day. He figured it could do a good job on who or whatever was stupid enough to move in too close for comfort.

The killer was clothed totally in black. Like a dark shroud pursuing his target, Charles moved along the thick, white fog, just out of Dog Shit's range of vision. A half cape waved in the wind as he danced above the marsh, his bald head glowing occasionally in the darkness.

Cox's car was just on the other edge of the newly planted cornfield. The crop had not yet started to take root, and Dog Shit moved easily through the flat earth. Seeing the cruiser, he broke out in a high-speed run. Upon reaching the front door, he smiled, congratulating himself on a job well done.

"Damn, I still got what it takes," he said aloud to himself, holding his knife at the ready.

As he grabbed the driver's door handle, reviewing Cox's instructions on operating the radio, a thud came from the rear of the car. Dog Shit looked up just in time to see a tall, black-clad figure race across the trunk, onto the roof and land its feet in the waterman's face.

Falling to the ground, Dog Shit quickly rolled to his left, avoiding the attacker, who had aimed to pounce onto his victim.

As Dog Shit rose and turned, grabbing for his knife, there was no one in sight. Only the empty car and nothing else. Slowly he began to turn to his right, to look behind, when a pain sprang up from his thigh. Looking down, Dog Shit saw the bald man's hand, twisting a knife, back and forth, in the old trapper's thigh. The blade was buried deep doing maximum damage, only the hilt was visible in the killer's hand.

"AAAHHHH!" The scream, a howl of pain, pierced the air and traveled in all directions, to the road, into the corn-field and out toward the sea.

Cox heard the cry—realized his guide was gone and knew there was nothing he could do to help. Cox also figured the killer was not in the house and now was his best time to move. Without hesitation the trooper ran for the front door and began working on the locks.

He imagined time moving quickly, but he tried to avoid that distraction. Adrenaline was pumping, and Cox focused on getting inside the room and getting the hostages out.

He began to panic when he beat on the door and realized it was not made of wood, but metal. The brown and black paint was made to look like planks. He had no tools, no explosives, no equipment. Everything was in the trunk of the cruiser.

The killer would be there any minute. Standing back three feet, Cox aimed and shot at the first lock, but the bullet ricocheted dangerously off to his left. A second shot hit its mark and one of the three locks was open.

Before he could make a decision about his next move, flashing red and blue lights came flying across the driveway from the field. As the cruiser screeched to a stop only three feet from Cox, he saw Dog Shit Charlie's dead body, lying like a deer trophy across the hood. Streams of blood were pouring down the vehicle from a hole in the waterman's leg and a wide gaping slash across his neck.

A tall man in black approached, pointing the barrel of a state-issued scattergun at Cox's chest. The trooper slowly dropped his gun, and, before raising his hands, touched a button on the top of his holster. He then waved his open, empty hands in the air above his head.

"Very good, officer," said Charles, his back and Cox's front illuminated by the car's headlights. There was a sign of satisfaction on Charles' face but there was annoyance in his tone. "You are not as stupid as your friend here. It's a wise man who knows when to fight and when to back down."

Cox stood motionless.

"Not a talker, obviously," Charles said, moving closer until the shotgun barrel was pressed firmly against the trooper's chest. "If this were a scene from the movies," Charles continued, grinning at his captive, "I would ask you if you called in your location, and you would shake your head, indicating 'Yes.' Then you would say help is on the way and I should give up and you would make me a deal. But, you see, this is real-life horror, and we both know about that, don't we?

"If you had called your superiors, you would not have sent the old fisherman back to your car. And, they would be flying overhead in choppers and closing off my beach. So, I am safe to assume that you are here alone and that no help is coming . . . ."

"Don't be so sure about . . . ."

Officer Fred Cox's mouth was still moving as the blast of the shotgun ripped through his chest and pellets exited through his back, displacing every body organ and human cell in between. The blast scattered a thousand minute pieces of blood and matter onto the ground.

In the two seconds that it took the shower of blood to land upon the weeds, the officer's brain finally realized that his body was dead, and "about" was the last word he would deliver in this lifetime.

Charles tossed the gun onto Cox's oozing chest and headed for the door to check on the family.

🌾   🌾   🌾

"We've got a Priority 9!" shouted Dispatch Central Supervisor Karen Brooks. Activity on any shift could go from lounge level calmness to life-threatening uncontrollable within seconds, and a Priority 9 designation always sent activity off the charts.

The clock read 0315—3:15 a.m.—and she entered the code that would identify the name of the initiator, his or her rank, current assignment and last identified location.

Priority 9 was the brainchild of commissioner Pentak. By activating a microchip button placed in each officer's on-duty holster, the signal would provide the sender's location and alert Dispatch Central duty personnel to an emergency situation. Since the tracer was to be used only in the most serious circumstances—mainly when an officer was incapacitated, anticipating being taken hostage or under fire—the response by other units, carefully controlled through headquarters, was usually overwhelming and immediate.

With the DelMarVa hostage crisis in its fifth month, those officers assigned to the task force were instructed to signal when a positive ID was made. As soon as the computer screens displayed Cox's current assignment, the dispatch staff believed there was a high probability that a hostage sighting had been confirmed.

As her staff reviewed Cox's chart, Brooks placed a call to commissioner Michael Pentak, who was located at Woodburn only a few blocks away from the Dover Communications Center.

The green letters on the black screen read:

Name: Cox, Fred
Age: 37
Years on force: 11
Current detail: Operation Discover/Snatcher Task Force
Current assignment: Citizen leads
Current case folder: Charles "Dog Shit" Dizer
Last known location: Craneville, Dmv.
Time of last contact: 11:45 p.m.

Other personal and career information was listed on subsequent screens, but Brown and her unit were primarily interested in pinpointing Cox's current signal location before the commissioner arrived.

An electronic map of the state of DelMarVa appeared, filling up a screen that consumed an entire 15-foot-high wall. It extended from the ceiling and ended three feet from the floor. The tracer was blinking at the ocean shoreline. Only a few years ago the location was on the dividing line between Maryland and Virginia. Today, according to the wall map, it was the site of no town, no historic site, no recreational area. But it would soon be well known to the task force that had been running into dead ends for the last several months.

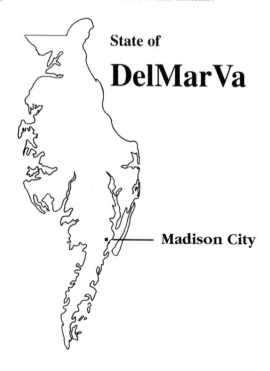

State of

DelMarVa

Madison City

Heads turned when Pentak and McDevitt arrived. Both were informally attired. Their expressions were intense and they listened to every word that Karen Brown spoke.

Only 15 minutes had elapsed since the signal had been activated, and a number of nervous cops were awaiting instructions. Pentak had planned for this moment and gave orders quickly. An embargo was placed on the release of any related information to the press, and the blackout included contact with every member of the media.

Chief Mike McCabe in Newark was ordered to create an emergency hostage diversion at the vacant fibermill factory off Paper Mill Road. Three ambulances from local volunteer fire companies were dispatched to that scene, as well as a SWAT team from Wilmington and K-9 units from the Elkton, Hockessin and Middletown barracks.

The manufactured crisis would be sent over open broadcast channels and attract the attention of the media, who had been following the Snatcher case relentlessly.

At the same time, six military ambulances were ordered to leave—at three-minute intervals using different gates and without sirens—from a DelMarVa equipment warehouse located on the Wallops Island National Aeronautics and Space Administration federal facility outside Chincoteague.

Members of the Blackhawk Strike Team (BST) from Stone Orchard in Northampton County would be choppered into Wallops and driven in civilian vehicles to positions a half-mile from the site pinpointed by Cox's tracer.

DelMarVa Coast Patrol units were moving eight high-speed patrol craft from Ocean City and Chincoteague with orders to cover the shoreline and stop all boats in the area. Nothing was to leave the mainland for a 10-mile stretch north and south of Cox's signal.

Chief Ronald Hands of Barracks 27 in Chincoteague would meet the BST and be in charge of land operations until Pentak and McDevitt arrived. They would board a State Police helicopter that was fueled and waiting behind headquarters.

By 0430 every piece of Operation Discover should be in place and the perimeter would be sealed.

W   W   W

Calm and unaffected by his recent kill, Charles entered the family room, smiling to his adopted clan.

They had all heard the gunshots and hoped their salvation would be coming through the door. Unfortunately, God again had turned down their prayers.

Sherron, wringing her folded hands on her lap, kept her head and eyes glued to the table. Terry looked straight ahead, looking at the darkness in the distance. Josette and Stephanie turned and faced Charles, watching his approach.

Stephanie froze and closed her eyes as he kissed her forehead and said, "My sweet. I've missed you today."

She shuddered, noticing the flecks of fresh blood that were splattered on his shirt.

Gently, he placed his hand on Josette's shoulder. "And dear sister, how are you this wonderful morning?"

"Get bent!" the young girl snapped.

Charles' reaction was swift and Stephanie cringed as he slammed his right elbow into the side of her skull, below her ear.

As the young girl groaned, Charles grabbed her cheek with his left fist and hissed, "You will never learn, will you, my big sister? You will never change. You are still the same wise-mouthed slut you've always been." Raising his knife, he put the blade near her hair, brushing it with the silver tip. "Perhaps I should decorate your pretty face with a nice homemade tattoo?"

Josette said nothing, her eyes wide with fear and rage, a trickle of blood running down her earlobe.

Trying to distract him, Stephanie called out, "Please, Charles, come here. Help me with my water jug. It's empty. Leave her be. Please. I need your help."

Turning away, he looked at the psychologist and her filthy, stained body at the end of the table.

"You are so considerate, my Stephanie. But when will you learn not to interrupt me when I am busy?" Moving closer, like a cat pouncing on a bird, he hit her across the face with the back of his hand. "A good wife knows when to speak and when to be silent. But," he said, laughing, "you will learn. YOU ALL WILL LEARN!" he screamed.

As the captives glanced at each other, Charles went outside. In only a few moments he returned, dragging in two legs. One was attached to what was left of Cox's destroyed body. The other was Dog Shit Charlie's corpse. With a grin of pride, he deposited the dead duo in the room directly behind Terry and Josette.

"COMPANY!" he shouted.

When no one spoke, he filled in the void with his own comments. "Look! It's been nearly five months and this is the best they could do—a dead cop and a dead drunken fisherman! You are no closer to leaving, but at least you have two more companions to talk to. Keep in mind, though," he laughed, "all they're good for is listening."

As he laughed at his own joke, he walked over and stroked Sherron's dry, bug-infested hair. She kept her face down, her eyes closed. Her hands were rubbing against each other nervously on her lap as Charles continued preaching.

"You all hate me. I know. All except for Mother, here." He knelt down and touched Sherron's grimy face. "Look at me, Mother. Aren't you, at least, proud of me?" he asked.

In an apparent state of shock, Sherron McKlinchey shook her head and whispered a hoarse, "Y-Y-eeess."

Charles smiled. "Maybe you would like to have another bath, Mother? Yes?"

"Th-th-that wou-ld-d b-b-be nice," Sherron said, nodding.

Josette and Stephanie were amazed. The woman had told them about the bathroom experience, and they were both waiting for Charles to appear with a noose in his hands for them.

Smiling, he said, "Good, Mother. Maybe we could take my bride and sister with us. But, we'll talk of that later. Now, with these two enemies out of the way, I am in very good spirits today. So, I want to show you a little toy, a surprise; something I've planned for all of us ever since the beginning. This is what will happen if anyone ever comes here and tries to separate us, tries to break up our wonderful little family—like those two fools who tried today."

From his shirt breast pocket, Charles produced a miniature, gray remote control box. It had yellow and red stripes and was about half the size of a pack of cigarettes. Holding it up, he flicked a button and, above the hostages' heads, six amber lights came on in the ceiling of the dark summer kitchen.

"Yes," he said, "look up there, my children. Because above those lights, in the roof, sits 400 gallons of high octane gasoline and six very reliable detonators. If I press this red button, everything above our heads will ignite within 30 seconds, and the entire barn, house—everything now standing in the area—will be gone. This little gizmo has a range of two miles and I can be on my way and gone from here . . . and you all will be gone, too, but in a different sense," he said, laughing at his own cleverness.

"So," he said, shutting off the activation switch and replacing the box in his pocket, "don't ever think you will leave me, for I am with you, watching over you, even when I'm not here."

As he turned to leave, Sherron, her voice hardly able to reach across the table, called out to him. "C-C-Charl-l-les, my s-s-son."

Everyone looked at her, wondering what she wanted, if she had lost it totally.

Returning to her, Charles knelt at her side.

"I . . . I am-m pr-pr-proud of you," Sherron said, her voice only a weak whisper.

Startled, Charles looked down into her eyes and she pulled her right hand out from under the table and began to embrace him.

Josette and Stephanie glanced at each other, thinking the oldest surviving hostage had finally flipped. As they watched Charles put both arms around "Mother," they saw Sherron's left hand reach as high into the sky as her wretched, bony arm would allow. Then, with all of her strength, all of her rage saved up for months and weeks and endless hours in the stench-filled hovel, she shouted as she plunged the thick, black, sharpened stick deep into his back. "I HAAAATTEE YOOUUUUU!"

As the blade reached its mark, Charles reacted by clenching her tightly and then screamed the screech of a shocked and betrayed madman. Bolting up, he twisted and squirmed, trying to reach the homemade knife—the crude weapon that Sherron had been crafting, working on in silence for months, waiting for the right moment to strike.

Knowing he had to remove the splintered blade, Charles thrashed and groped, but the weapon was just out of the reach of his fingers. As his nerves and internal organs began to shut down, he started to stagger—first away from his captives, then forward. Dizzy, disoriented, his feet gave way and his body landed face down across the family kitchen table.

Four sets of terrified eyes focused on the big man.

Was he dead?

No one was sure.

No one wanted to touch the body for fear of awakening the madman and suffering his vengeance.

Stephanie, realizing they had to get the remote control device, stood up and reached toward the body, but the foot chain limited her mobility and reach.

Stretching, she was able to get to the wooden knife. With two hands, Stephanie grabbed the blade and twisted it in circles to inflict maximum damage. Then she pulled it out and held the weapon tightly.

Josette, who was further down the table, rolled the body over. Scared, she moved a step back when she saw Charles' eyes staring straight up at her.

"Reach into the pocket and get the remote!" Stephanie ordered, shouting as loud as she could.

But Josette was frozen in place.

"NOW!" Stephanie shouted. "For Christ sake, Josette, get it! NOW!"

Carefully, the teenager moved toward Charles' body. Suddenly, he reached up with his left hand, grabbed her throat, and held on tightly.

"Bitch!" he hissed. "No good, lying, stealing, filthy bitch!"

Stephanie was too far away to help and shouted to Sherron, "Get the control, hurry. NOW!"

As Josette's air passage was being crushed, Sherron stretched her hands as far as possible, got to the pocket and pulled and out the remote. But, as she moved away, Charles kicked his leg against her arms and the small box landed on the dirt floor, out of reach of any of the chained hostages.

Suddenly, little Terry Tremble jumped onto Charles. In a rage, the boy began biting the big man's left arm, trying to help Josette. Blood from the back wound was still dripping onto the table, and Josette was using both of her hands and all her strength to keep Charles from crushing her throat.

He can't hold out much longer, thought Stephanie, the wooden blade still in her hands.

As he tried to fight off the two children, Charles pulled back, moving closer to Stephanie's end of the table. Supporting himself with his right hand, he rested it flat on the planks, his back to his hand-picked bride.

The fat paw seemed to be just within her reach. With all her strength she raised Sherron's homemade weapon, holding it in both hands high above her head, and aimed.

She knew she had only one chance.

As the wood made contact and pierced his flesh, Charles howled and the room fell silent. Her aim was perfect, but providence helped. As the point swept through the top of Charles' hand, the blade kept moving and imbedded itself into a portion of the table wood that accepted the weapon and would not respond to the killer's efforts to pull it out.

His right hand was useless, and the loss of blood oozing out the back wound had sapped his strength. Finally, his left hand fell from Josette's throat and dropped by his side.

Exhausted and out of strength, Charles fell back onto the table, wounded and defeated. Smiling, he said in a weak voice, "The keys are in my right pants pocket, Little Brother Terry. Take them out and unlock the shackles."

Still scared, the boy did not move, but Stephanie told him to get the keys. She knew Charles was no longer a threat, and the sooner she controlled the remote device the better.

Stephanie unlocked the family, secured the firebomb control and directed Josette and Terry to use all of their chains to lock up Charles. Laughing, he watched helplessly as they covered his chest with the rusted links that had held all of them immobile for weeks.

"I'm not going anywhere, and I certainly won't die here." His right hand was still attached to the table by the wooden knife. "Go call the police from the car outside. Be sure to tell them to send an ambulance, and do it now!" he hissed.

Stephanie led the group out of the room. They exited slowly. They were weak and terrified.

The child killer and kidnapper was on the table, a barely living display chained to the site where his captives had been humiliated and had waited for the help that never came. Stephanie was the last one in the room. She looked back at the monster and wondered what else he had planned for them, what brutality they would have suffered.

Quietly, Josette, Sherron and Terry returned to the room and gathered at the table to give him one last look.

"Get away! You idiots, or I'll kill you all," he said, but his voice was weak, his ability to create fear was gone. Without power he had no control.

"I'll get out and find every one of you, you know that I can and I will. You'll never hide from me. Never, you no good bastards. I'll be back." His last three words escaped through clenched teeth.

Without responding, the former hostages walked away. Stephanie and Josette grabbed the legs of Trooper Cox and dragged what was left of him outside. Terry and Sherron each took one of Dog Shit Charlie's legs and did the same. Then, someone locked the door.

"LET ME OOOOUUUTTTT! LET ME OOOOUUUTTTT!" Charles shouted. But he was only heard by the four hapless souls who were leaving, and they didn't care what he wanted.

It was shortly before 5 o'clock in the morning. The sun was peeking up from the edge of the ocean, and the sky was beginning to turn light blue in places. Stephanie was driving Cox's cruiser, following the ruts in the swamp grass that it had created when it arrived only a few hours ago. Josette was riding shotgun. In the backseat, Sherron cradled Terry in her arms.

They could see a roadblock ahead. Guns were pointing at them.

Stephanie flashed her high beams three times and stopped the car. She got out slowly, raised her hands above her head and started walking toward the spotlights.

Pentak and McDevitt, who had been talking to Barracks Chief Hands and preparing to move in, ran out from behind the barricade and headed for Cox's car.

As the local chief directed EMT personnel to the hostages, McDevitt and Stephanie embraced and cried. Pentak joined them quickly, pulling Stephanie and the governor into his dark green command vehicle to get an update on the situation.

Quickly, she gave them a summary, explaining that Charles was still alive and chained to the table. As she sipped on fresh water and waved off immediate medical attention, she described the gasoline booby trap, the location of Cox and Dog Shit's bodies and handed the small gray box to Pentak.

The three of them were alone in the van. Pentak looked at McDevitt, who was staring at the woman he loved, holding onto her hands. The two men could only imagine the hell Charles Bettner had inflicted upon the victims and their families.

"It's up to you, Mike," McDevitt said, looking at the remote control that was resting on the table. A series of video pictures, from cameras mounted on helicopters, showed the site of the farmhouse and additional views of the target from each of the locations of the four assault units. "No one is within range and the perimeter is secure," the governor added.

The room was silent for a moment. Carefully, Pentak picked up the remote control, looked at the governor and Stephanie and said, "I'd know what I'd like to do, but I don't think I can make that call."

"I can," said Stephanie, snatching the small box from Pentak's hand and flicking on the activation switch. "And I say we fire him."

It was less than 30 seconds from the time she pressed the red button to the time that the explosion occurred, enough time for McDevitt, Pentak and Stephanie to leave the van and head toward the ambulance that would transport her to the Southern DelMarVa Medical Center.

Epilog

"This is WDMV-TV reporter Diane Kramer, reporting live from the outskirts of Chincoteague, Del-MarVa, where Police Commissioner Michael Pentak has released a report that four of the five hostages were rescued today in a daring raid by members of the Operation Discover Special Task Force.

"In the operation, coordinated by Chief Ronald Hands, Trooper Fred Cox, of Rehoboth, Mr. Charles Dizer, of Saxis, who provided valuable information, and Mr. Horace Meeks, a hostage from Shepherd, were killed.

"Before he was able to be captured, suspect Charles Bettner committed suicide by igniting a firebomb that he had placed in the vacant farmhouse where he had kept the hostages, some for several months.

"The action took place at the former site of Madison City, a deserted coastal town that, at one time, had been a busy port on the Atlantic Ocean side of the peninsula.

"The relatives of the hostages are being flown to the Southern DelMarVa Medial Center, where they will be reunited with their families.

"In other news:

"Jose "The Snake" Andes, has lost his last appeal for the slaying, five years ago, in a Wilmington grocery store, of 8-year-old Maria Quinterna. The killer will be given the death penalty. Judge Marcus Servantanos denied the killer's final appeal and the hanging is to be carried out in Gumboro within two weeks.

"Earlier this evening, former Russian diplomat Anton Kulczinsky was found dead from unknown causes in his Wilmington Central Prison Facility jail cell. He was convicted of killing a young girl in Rehoboth Beach while driving under the influence of alcohol. Authorities are investigating the cause of his death. He was serving a life sentence without parole.

"It is expected that, in the morning, DelMarVa Gov. Henry McDevitt will announce his engagement to Dr. Stephanie Litera, one of the recently freed hostages.

"This is Diane Kramer, of WDMV-TV, reporting for *Your Eye on DelMarVa*."

❦   ❦   ❦

Following the death of former tax collector Charles Bettner, life in the State of DelMarVa returned to normal. But evil never rests. It appears from time to time, to remind the good that there is another, darker side of life.

In **Halloween House**, a new sinister shadow of crime stalks a small peninsula watertown and threatens the calm of the ideal, showcase state . . . and beyond.

(Release date—Fall 1999)

Excerpt on page 299.

❦   ❦   ❦

Halloween House

(an excerpt)

Ol' Mose could hear the sounds of traffic, coming over the meadows. The source was about four miles in the distance as the geese fly. The night was black and crisp, but the glow from several rotating searchlights flared across the sky. It was the end of October and, like clockwork, Craig Dire had opened up his three-story tobacco barn to anyone and everyone who wanted to come up and see the horrifying sights.

Crazy people, Mose thought, as he shook his head and relit his well worn pipe, sitting in a cane rocker on the wooden porch of his small home in Blacktown. Only crazy people would stand in line for up to three hours to see them creatures in wild costumes screamin' and carryin' on and actin' like they was being tortured to death.

Tall, black iron gates with spear-like tips closed off the 800-foot paved lane leading to the main entrance of Dire's Mill Mansion. Two of Craig Dire's full-time security guards were assigned to keep unauthorized vehicles from entering that private section of the estate. If the main gates weren't locked, some of the overflow crowd would have tried to head up the driveway and cut across the open fields to get to the front of the line.

For the past eight years during the last two weekends of October, Craig and Melinda Dire had turned a portion of their property into a Halloween lover's extravaganza. The inside of their barn was a state-of-the-art chamber of horrors, with moving mechanical and human figures of vampires rising from coffins, zombies climbing out of open graves, devils appearing behind clouds of red smoke and, the highlight of the show—three young witches trying to break through their glass enclosure and attack the passing crowds.

As more than 400 people waited in the steadily moving line, puppeteers, musicians, jugglers and mimes walked through the crowd, entertaining those who were awaiting their turn to enter Halloween House.

Smiling and leading four members of the press on a tour, Craig Dire stopped on the edge of a hill, about 30 feet from the winding line, and pointed with pride.

"Here you are," he said, "the long and winding road of satisfied citizens enjoying good clean fun during the height of the Halloween season, compliments of Craig and Melinda Dire!"

"Where's your wife, Mr. Dire?" asked Diane Kramer, on-camera reporter from WDMV-TV, *Your Eye of DelMarVa*.

"Ah, good question, Miss Kramer. You'll see shortly. All I'll say right now is that Melinda likes to take an active role in our little production."

The reporters jotted down a few notes and then looked up, waiting for more. And Craig Dire wasn't one to disappoint the members of the press.

"This successful enterprise was my brainchild, a healthy, entertaining family event where all of DelMarVa could come—for free I stress—and enjoy a horrifying evening of blood-curdling fun. Of course, we have an age limit—no one below the age of 8 is allowed to experience Halloween House. That's because we don't want our little ones up all night screaming and crying from the frightful scenes."

"Could you tell us how expensive this is?" asked Tom Harrison of the *Baltimore Bullet*.

"No problem. I'd estimate that with the scenery— which is different each year, the security patrols, extra police for traffic control and, most importantly, the professional actors from New York City that we hire each year, we spend in excess of $60,000. But, what better way to show the community how much we care than to throw a party and invite everyone to come?"

"I've heard that since you were born on Halloween, this is something like your own private birthday party. Is that right?" The question came from Liz Hardy, the reporter from the *Diamond State Ledger*.

"I won't deny that I enjoy Halloween more than the Yuletide season. The amount of decorating we do at Christmastime is far less than the effort we expend on Halloween, as you can imagine. So, in a way, I will admit that this is a fun event. We use real coffins delivered from a casket company. We buy the hogs heads, freshly butchered from the slaughter house, so those rotting eyes and bristly snouts you pass on stumps of logs are as real as can be." Smiling with pride, he added, "You should see the reaction when someone touches them and the dead slime gets all over their hands and clothing. It's absolutely delightful."

The reporters took more notes and jotted down the verbal pearls that Dire knew he was dispensing.

Seeing his comments were having the desired effect, he continued, "Everything is as close to the real world of horror as we can legally make it. When Baron Zomdee, our zombie, crawls out of his grave and heads for the passing line of gawkers, they are truly glad there is a wire mesh screen keeping him contained. And those who get too close can smell the stench from his rotting flesh. It's much like a mixture of rotten eggs and dead crabs left in the August sun.

"When my gray-haired werewolf swings over the crowd on a rope hanging from the rafters of the barn, the men actually clutch their women for protection. I recall the night we had a fraternity group from Salisbury. They came with their dates. We heard the jocks boasting as they approached the barn doors. They were complaining that this was a weak show, a lame attempt at horror. Essentially, they came with an attitude."

Craig paused, laughing aloud as he recalled the night.

"I instructed my werewolf to drop into the crowd and, literally, pick up the biggest athlete he could find. That year, Wolfman, who was quite a huge specimen standing well over six feet in height and built like an Olympian, fell from the rope and all of the fraternity men grabbed their women and hid behind them. As instructed, Wolfman moved directly toward the group, latched onto the biggest jock and carried the young man out the door. Unfortunately, the student was so scared he began shouting, 'Let me down! Put me down!' It was pathetic and the crowed roared with laughter. When he was released, the boy was so embarrassed that he walked back to his car and waited for his friends to finish the tour. We have it all on film. I forgot to mention that there are 18 security cameras in the barn and we file the tapes every year."

"In light of that incident," Diane Kramer said, "I'm a bit surprised about your age limit. Do you think it's really appropriate to allow children as young as eight into your private chamber of horrors?"

It was obvious Craig was stung by the comment. "I beg to differ with your terminology, Ms. Kramer," he said, sharply. "This is not my private chamber of horrors. It is an entertaining and educational presentation that, I repeat, is presented totally FREE to the community. I also believe that parents can make the best decision as to whether their children should attend or not. If they want to come, they are most welcome. We haven't had any complaints in all these years. And, I might add, if you look down the waiting line, I don't think you will see anyone dragging bodies along and pushing them in the door. Do you?"

"No," she replied.

"Besides," Dire continued, "I firmly believe a good dose of horror is important to one's healthy psychological development. My bedtime stories were filled with threats of Patty Cannon crawling through my bedroom window to rip out my liver. And my mother told me if I didn't clean my room Bigg Lizz was going to take out her tobacco knife, chop off my head and I'd have to carry it under my arm when I went to school. I trust you can tell by looking at me that I haven't suffered any ill effects from being scared out of my wits at a tender young age."

Everyone but Diane Kramer laughed. She forced a smile and felt a definite chill as she stared at Craig Dire's cold, dark eyes.

"Now," he said, turning to his media guests, "let's get you inside Halloween House."

The Original

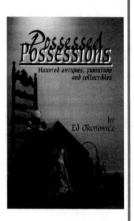

"If you're looking for an unusual gift for a collector of antiques, or enjoy haunting tales, this one's for you."
—COLLECTOR EDITIONS

" . . . a book that will be a favorite among collectors, dealers, and fans of the supernatural alike."
—THE MIDATLANTIC ANTIQUES

". . . an intriguing read."
—MAINE ANTIQUE DIGEST

" . . . a good way to relax following a long day walking an antique show or waiting at an auction. The book is certainly entertaining, and it's even a bit disturbing.
—ANTIQUEWEEK

112 pages
5 1/2 x 8 1/2 inches
softcover
ISBN 0-9643244-5-8

$9.95

A bump. A thud. Mysterious movement. Unexplained happenings. Caused by what? Venture beyond the Delmarva Peninsula and discover the answer. Experience 20 eerie, true tales, plus one horrifying fictional story, about items from across the country that, apparently, have taken on an independent **spirit** of their own–for they refuse to give up the ghost.

From Maine to Florida, from Pennsylvania to Wisconsin . . . haunted heirlooms exist among us . . . everywhere.

Read about them in **Possessed Possessions**, *the book some antique dealers definitely do not want you to buy.*

"If this collection doesn't give you a chill,
check your pulse, you might be dead."
—Leslie R. McNair
The Review, University of Delaware

" 'Scary' Ed Okonowicz . . . the master of written fear— at least
on the Delmarva Peninsula . . . has done it again."
—Wilmington News Journal

"This expert storyteller can even make a vanishing hitchhiker
story fresh and startling. Highly Recommended!"
—Chris Woodyard
Invisible Ink: Books on Ghosts & Hauntings

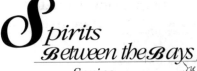

*S*pirits
Between the Bays
Series

True
Ghost Stories
from the
master storyteller
Ed Okonowicz

Volume by volume our haunted house grows. Enter at your own risk!

Open the door and wander through these books of true ghost stories of the Mid-Atlantic region.

Creep deeper and deeper into terror, until you run Down the Stairs and Out the Door in the last of our 13 volumes.

See order form on page 313 for prices.

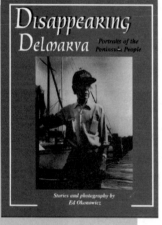

These people never made the news; they made America.

THE BUTLER, THE BAKER, THE FISHNET MAKER . . . ONCE FLOURISHING OCCUPATIONS ON THE DELMARVA PENINSULA, ARE A SAMPLING OF THE MANY SKILLS THAT ARE FALLING VICTIM TO TIME.

"For most of us, Disappearing Delmarva *is as close as we'll ever get to rubbing elbows with real treasure."*
—Brandywine Valley Weekly

(This) book will elicit feelings of nostalgia in many, but more importantly, it provides a permanent record of work and traditions that stand on the verge of extinction."
—Carol E. Hoffecker
Richards Professor of History, University of Delaware

This book is about people who have hung on over a lifetime to a cherished way of life while change boiled around them. It tells us to take stock today of what we cherish and not let change destroy it. . .
—Russell W. Peterson
former Delaware Governor

Disappearing
Delmarva
Portraits of the Peninsula People

Photography and Stories

by Ed Okonowicz

Disappearing Delmarva introduces you to more than 70 people on the peninsula whose professions are endangered. Their work, words and wisdom are captured in the 208 pages of this hardbound volume, which features more than 60 photographs.

Along the back roads and back creeks of Delaware, Maryland and Virginia—in such hamlets as Felton and Blackbird in Delaware, Taylors Island and North East in Maryland, and Chincoteague and Sanford in Virginia—these colorful residents still work at the trades that have been passed down to them by grandparents and elders.

208 pp   8 1/2" x 11"   Hardcover
ISBN 1-890690-00-7 $38.00

*S*tairway
over the
Brandywine

Two people meet during World War II, fall in love, and make a pledge on a stairway overlooking the Brandywine River. Can their love survive the war?

Meet Bill, an Army Air Corps pilot, and Jean, a small town girl, who meet in the early days of World War II. Like scenes from a 1940s movie, they fall in love, make a commitment and are separated by the war. Here is a good, old-fashioned, sentimental love story that is ideal for the young-at-heart of any generation.

24 pp
5 1/2" x 8 1/2"
ISBN 0-9643244-2-3

Softcover
$5.00

About the Author

Ed Okonowicz, a Delaware native and freelance writer, is an editor and writer at the University of Delaware, where he earned a bachelor's degree in music education and a master's degree in communication.

Also a professional storyteller, Ed is a member of the National Storytelling Association. He presents programs at country inns, retirement homes, schools, libraries, private gatherings, public events, elderhostels and theaters in the Mid-Atlantic region.

He specializes in local legends and folklore of the Delaware and Chesapeake Bays, as well as topics related to the Eastern Shore of Maryland. He also writes and tells city stories, many based on his youth growing up in his family's beer garden–Adolph's Cafe–in the Browntown section of Wilmington.

Ed presents storytelling courses and writing workshops based on his book *How to Conduct an Interview and Write an Original Story*. With his wife, Kathleen, they present a popular workshop entitled, Self Publishing: All You Need to Know about Getting—or Not Getting—into the Business.

Through Myst and Lace Publishers Inc., he releases up to three books each year. Most—including his novels—are set on the Delmarva Peninsula and in the Mid-Atlantic region.

Myst and Lace Publishers books are excellent for sales promotions, premiums, fund raising or educational use. Special discounts are available for quantity purchases.

For information, contact:

Myst and Lace Publishers, Inc.
1386 Fair Hill Lane
Elkton, MD 21921

410-398-5013